MADAME FIOCCA

A WW 2 NOVEL

SUZY HENDERSON

AVIS PRESS

Life is short.
–Euripides, 480-406 BC.

I hated the brutality, the sadism, and the insanity of Nazism. I just couldn't stand by and see people destroyed. I did what I could, what I had to do, what my conscience told me I must do. That's all there is to it. Really, nothing more.
–Oskar Schindler.

Nancy

There were three things I longed to do with my life. I wished to visit New York, London, and Paris. Well, I went to New York, and I loved it. I went to London and was uncertain at first, but I grew to love the city. Later, I travelled to Paris on a long weekend, and fell in love with the City of Light. Paris became the base from which I worked as a reporter for the Hearst Newspaper Group. Nancy Wake, a New Zealander who grew up in Australia, reporting the latest world news from France. To me, it was an exciting new life and a welcome change from the one I'd escaped.

1930s Paris was a city for women, both beautiful and chic. The ladies wore gorgeous dresses, all the latest designs, along with gloves and hats too. Theirs was a fashion set apart from the rest of the world. The city of romance overflowed with gallant men, champagne, fine dining, and flowers. What girl could ask for more? And my dates always picked me up and took me home.

I was a flirt, and I loved good-looking men. In truth, I was a dizzy young thing, but I never went searching for love. Love seized me quite unexpectedly at a time when everything was changing, soon after Hitler swept into power in 1933, unleashing his Nazi ideology onto Europe. So much political unrest, so much evil and inhumanity, and then the Spanish Civil War, the prelude to another world war. Not everyone saw it that way, but I did.

Then came the fateful day in 1940, when the German army marched into Paris, shrouding France with swastika flags, an enemy the sight of which reduced Parisians to tears, France defeated. And the flame of resistance ignited, slowly at first, and then gradually gathered momentum as more and more of us answered the call from General de Gaulle. It was the chance I'd longed for, to do something about the evil unleashed by Hitler and his Nazi Party, and I played my part. The French called me 'L'Australienne de Marseille', the girl who always laughed, and my war was filled with much laughter.

I've often been asked whether I'd have done anything differently. And always, after deep thought, I reply, 'If I had my time again, I'd do it all over, despite everything.' I live with the consequences, bear the guilt and the grief. Ghosts of my past fill the silence, their presence a faint kiss of breeze, their voices a whisper of memories; memories that live on until I breathe my last.

Marseille
AUGUST 1944

The wolves have fled. The ground grumbles beneath my boots; tremors snake up my legs to my hips and tingles ricochet along my spine. In the distance, a low growl grows into a roaring convoy of military trucks, the Allies, a sound as sweet and welcome as bird song on any other day, but not this day. Marseille is free at last. How I longed to share this day with you, Henri, my love. Our home, our perfect home. I bite my lower lip, blink away tears. The concierge, Monsieur Dufort, looked so shocked when I turned up earlier today. And, quite out of character, he embraced me, his thread-veined cheeks wet with tears. I didn't mind. We were all out of character.

'Madame Fiocca. I can hardly believe it is you,' he said, wiping his eyes. 'We all thought you were dead!'

I wasn't surprised, and I forced a smile. 'So many are dead or missing.' What I so desperately wished to say was that I'm dead inside, but I gritted my teeth, and said, 'I'm so glad to see you.'

'The Gestapo gave your apartment to female German officers,' he said, holding up his hands. 'There was nothing I could do.'

Well, that explains everything. The Boche did a great number on the place. Broken ornaments and rubbish laid strewn across the floors amidst overturned furniture. They took most of our possessions except for your armchair, which lay on its side by the fireplace.

3

As I dragged it upright, I pictured you sat there, nursing a crystal glass of brandy. You ran a hand through your black wavy hair, ruffling it so as you relaxed after a day's work. Madame Dumont was in the kitchen preparing dinner, and the delicious scent of saffron drifted out into the dining room. I closed my eyes and felt the warmth of your hand on mine, drawing me close. Oh, the sweet, delicate taste of liquor on your lips, your breath warm in my mouth, the velvet caress of your hand on my cheek. And as I opened my eyes to stark emptiness, a tightness gripped my chest and I couldn't think anymore.

I gaze at the tattered green book on my lap as I sit on a wooden crate in the cellar. *Anne of Green Gables*. My one surviving possession. Nothing left except a couple of armchairs and an old childhood novel. The walls hold our memories, exhaling the words we once spoke as whispers into the air. Earlier, as I stood in the bedroom overlooking the devastated harbour, I was sure I heard you call my name, '*Nannie*'. I close my misty eyes and suck in a deep breath, unable to stem the tide of tears. A salty tang lies thick in my mouth, wet on my lips. The musty air is stifling, and I recall the dream I had almost a year ago which had seemed so real.

'Come on, Duckie. Let's get you a nice cuppa.'

Den breaks my reverie. He means well and is a tower of strength, considering he's grieving the loss of his lover. Gulping down the lump in my throat, I wipe my eyes on the back of my khaki shirt sleeve. 'I need a proper drink, Den.' He crouches in front of me, his eyes full and concerned. 'They took everything. Trashed the rest. Everything of beauty, of worth, all that represented the life we'd built together, all gone.'

He places his hand on my shoulder, the light warmth a slight comfort. 'It could have been so different. Why did I get involved?' I was defiant, indulgent, and Henri indulged me. He never said, 'No!' I squeeze my eyes tight as I did as a small child. Back then, I thought it would chase away demons and bad things; only now, I know better. Now, I must deal with it and move on, but then my beloved Henri whispers in my ear, 'Nannie, you are impossible. Of all the women I could have married, how did I choose you?' Biting my lower lip, I wish he'd never chosen me at all.

'Nancy, you can't think like that or you'll go mad. Things happen, luvvie.' Den reaches into his grease-stained shirt pocket and drags out a packet of Players, hangs one in my mouth, and strikes a match. I suck in a breath as nicotine surges into my lungs. The cigarette butt glows scarlet, a single jewel of light in the darkness. 'You did what you had to do, what you thought best. And you've done some bloody amazing things. If not for you, there would be hundreds, maybe thousands more dead by now.' He flashes that warm smile of his, soft blue eyes crinkling at the corners.

He always makes sense, but I know he's making light of things for my sake, and yes, he's right. Together, we made a difference, but at what cost? I sigh, exhaling all my options into this cellar of decay, out of time, out of luck. I hear my mother's words pound my ears, her tongue acid, a brown leather-bound bible clutched in her hand. 'You'll come to no good, my girl, you'll see.' Words rasped with anger. 'She was right,' I say. She was right all along. I hunch over, trace a fingertip around the border of my tattered book. The young girl with the red hair on the cover stares back. Anne of Green Gables, the heroine of the story who faced hardships, overcame hurdles and made her way in the world. 'Her story ends well,' I mumble.

'What's that, Duckie?' Den casts me a puzzled look.

'It doesn't matter.' I hadn't understood Mum's anger when I was a child, nor really as an adult, but I came to realise the reasons behind it in time. Now it dawns on me we share a bond. All those years we fought, and all the bitterness cocooned in my chest. Maybe she had loved me. She couldn't help how she was. She was hurting. I bury my head in my hands. A cry escapes my lips, tears swim in my eyes, chest tight, aching, then I sit up ramrod straight, tilt my head back, and heave in a breath.

Den pulls me to my feet. This old book is all I have left of my childhood, my homeland, and memories of my father and his storytelling. Now the memories wrap around me like an old friend and I'm glad. I run a hand through my matted hair, strands coated in road dust. Time to leave. I blow out a breath as a hurricane of thoughts hurls through my mind. A sinking feeling stirs my stomach; my legs tremble. How I long to stay, to dream that everything will be how it was and should be, but mum was right. 'You silly girl,' she used to say. I've been here before, on the cusp of leaving, forced into a corner, luck swiftly diminishing. And I recall the words I'd muttered then as I'd walked away, head held high. 'Just one foot in front of the other, Nancy. One step at a time.' My eyes are awash with tears as I slip sunglasses on, gritting my teeth as we stride out into the glare of a stern sun, the faint breeze a furnace. The whiff of fish hangs in the air like death and nausea stirs in my gut.

I turn to glance up at our living room window and recall how I once stood there gazing out across the harbour, drunk on love and life. A piece of me has died, a piece I will never bury, and in my heart, Marseille will always be my home. Dear God, forgive me.

Chapter 1
FEBRUARY 1933

The RMS *Aorangi II* steamed steadily on as I gazed forlornly at the fading shores of New York and the diminishing lady in copper, the Statue of Liberty. I tried to imagine how people fleeing persecution felt, glimpsing her for the first time from the icy waters of the Atlantic, relief swelling their hearts. Faces relaxing as smiles erased frowns and worry lines, butterflies flitting in their tummies as they stared in awe, visualising freedom, safety, and hope.

I had fled my home at the tender age of sixteen. Life turned upside down the day Dad left. I loved my dad, adored the bones of him. He always found time for me, scooping me up in his arms at the end of a day's work, reading stories, making me giggle, singing 'Waltzing Matilda', and dancing. Every morning he went off to work, except for weekends, of course, and every evening I'd wait by the garden gate. And then one evening he didn't return home. And as I swung on the gate, Mum hollered at me to come inside for the twentieth time, and my older sister, Gladys, marched outside, a scowl glued to her face as she dragged me indoors by the hand.

'Dad's gone to America,' Mum said, muttering something about him making a film of the Maoris. I didn't understand back then. 'When will he be back?' But she'd already wandered away. I found her sitting

7

at the kitchen table, the *bible* in front of her, a frown masking her face. 'He'll be back home in a few months,' she snapped, before lowering her bulging eyes to the scriptures. Her coldness stung, and I missed Dad's strong, warm arms around me even more. I used to lie awake at night, listening to the creak and groan of the staircase, my heart leaping as I wondered if Dad had come home. My elder brother, Stanley, said all houses squawked in the night as they cooled down. It seemed to me that our home was miserable too.

We lived in a lovely spacious house in Sydney, having moved from our native New Zealand when I was two. I had five older siblings, two brothers, three sisters. They were wrapped up in their own lives, except for Stanley. He always found time for me, but he served in the navy and wasn't home much. One day, I noticed that the gilt-framed picture of Mum and Dad on their wedding day had vanished from its place on the oak dresser. No one said a word, and Mum became more distant, retreating to her bible reading. Right then, I realised Dad was never coming home again. A hole opened up inside me, a hollow that ached, and I cried myself to sleep at night. And for a time, I would swing on the garden gate in the evening, looking out down the street, waiting, hoping for a glimpse of my dad. The Galah birds screeched as they settled for the night, roosting in the Jacaranda trees, and I never saw him again. One day, while I played in the garden, Stanley called me over.

'We have to move, Nancy,' he said. 'To a new house, not far from here.'

'But I don't want to leave this one,' I said. Besides, if Dad came home, how would he find us?

'It'll be okay, I promise.' Stanley hugged me tight, swiped the tears from my eyes. 'Be a brave girl. Help me get your things packed up.'

It wasn't okay. Life with mum became unbearable, so I ran away at sixteen, became a nurse and worked in a mental asylum. At eighteen, I returned to Sydney, found a job and a place to live, which enabled me to get by, but I still dreamed of seeing the world. Then, a letter from Aunt Hinemoa arrived out of the blue. 'Thinking of you,' she wrote, with a cheque enclosed for a whole two hundred pounds! A lifeline.

Mum never approved of her sister, who had run away with the captain of a whaling ship. Hinemoa was the black sheep of our family, like me, I suppose. So, like her, I decided to leave Australia and sail around the world. Canada, New York, and England beckoned.

New York was everything I thought it would be and more! Talk about exciting. The big apple bustled with nightclubs and alcohol flowed, despite the Prohibition laws. I hadn't drunk so much in my life, and the funny thing was, I barely got drunk. And I'd never walked through snowdrifts before. Once the snow fell, it went on and on, icy flakes landing on my lashes, the taste of snow on my lips, and frozen toes. I was sad to leave, but I was looking forward to my next adventure. England beckoned, and a new life in London studying journalism.

Life onboard was pure opulence like a stately home, with grand lounges, sumptuous chairs, furnishings and real open fires! It was heaven to be waited on, a far cry from my real life, which had been less than perfect. I never felt settled in Australia. Maybe travelling was in my genes. I was New Zealand-born, with Maoris and Huguenots on Mum's side, British on Dad's. There was such a mix in me. Was it any wonder I didn't know who I was?

WE DOCKED in Liverpool on a grey, foggy day; the weather echoed the dreary mood that hung over us as we sailed along the Mersey. The mist slipped overhead, mingled with chimney smoke and draped over rows of dowdy buildings and homes, casting a frown over Liverpool. As we neared the dock, the fog lifted, revealing a splendid building with a clock tower and there, further along, was a majestic statue of King Edward VII on horseback. The port bustled with people. There were carts stacked with towers of wooden crates, while men hauled trolleys laden with sacks by ropes. The whinny of horses screamed into the manure filled air while the clickety-clack of trains rattled along the overhead railway.

A man strolled by with a little girl, hand in hand as they dashed to board a tram, jolting my memory, and I was back at the family home in Sydney, swinging on the garden gate. I swallowed the tender lump in my throat, turning away. Mum was so hard on me after Dad abandoned us. Later, I learned that the reason we'd had to move was because Dad had sold the house from under us. Even though I still adored him, that didn't excuse his behaviour. He was a bastard.

The porter loaded my luggage onto the train while I settled myself into the first empty carriage. The platform bristled with activity, and people soon filed in behind me. An elderly gentleman and a lady sat opposite while a tall, thin woman darted in like a minnow with a little girl in tow. I didn't feel the least bit afraid of journeying alone. Home life had been lonely, and I'd forged my own way for so long that I was happy with my own company. In solitude, I discovered peace and strength. The small girl suddenly cried out in her sleep, and her mother instinctively stroked the child's face, kissing her tenderly on the brow, and my chest pinched. My mother had never shown me much affection, and her growing obsession with bible studies had transformed her into a captive to the scriptures. Her idea of comforting words was recitals of biblical verses, usually damning me in the process. She often said I'd go to hell for this and that and I'd believed her. But the more I thought of it, the more I realised religion had become her refuge, a place of comfort after the breakdown of her marriage. Life had not been easy for any of us.

I turned my gaze to the window and the flashing English countryside, willing myself to dwell only on the future. The past could not be undone and was best left behind. Resting my head back against the seat, I closed my eyes.

When the train drew into Kings Cross, I waited for the others to leave the carriage as I gazed out across the platform. London! Well-dressed ladies strutted across the platform, and people bustled and jostled their way through the swarm. A group of soldiers stood around a mound of kit bags, dressed in their finest military khaki. As I stepped off the train, the atmosphere washed over me like a wave. I'd booked for two nights at the Strand Hotel, so I hailed a cab. I was looking forward to my time in London and had enrolled at the School of Journalism. Nancy Wake, reporter to be. It was exciting, and I had to work, so it had seemed like a good career choice. Besides, world travel was still in my blood and I was determined to see Paris.

Chapter 2
MARSEILLE. 9 OCTOBER 1934

The crowd heaved as people lined the streets, waiting for the King of Yugoslavia's arrival. I was ready, camera in hand, notebook and pen in my bag. I'd barely had time to settle into my Parisian apartment when I was told to cover this assignment. Marseille was beautiful, the French Riviera. It was so different from Paris, the polar opposite in many ways, yet I was quite at home. Paris had a unique rhythm punctuated with café culture, art, and fashion. The ladies there were frequent visitors of Chanel and other prestigious fashion houses, and it seemed as if all the women of France ought to be seen out wearing the latest designs. There was certainly a feeling of expectation to conform. But here, life was far more relaxed. Here, the old ways prevailed, traditional cultures and trades such as fishing and basket weaving. Marseille was a gemstone in the Mediterranean.

'Nancy, the king's here. His boat just docked.' Marie squeezed in beside me, her face glistening, rosy cheeks, and blue eyes sparkling. The crowd cheered, and in the distance, I glimpsed two figures by the harbour slipping into a black state car: King Alexander and the French Foreign Minister, Louis Barthou. I had the ideal spot on La Canebière, a clear view to the port. The state car crawled along to roars of appreciation and welcome from the throng. The king waved regally to the people on either side as his chauffeur-driven car sailed past us and then he was gone, swallowed up by the throng. 'Long live the king,' a man yelled from the masses. Seconds later, the crack of gunshots filled the air and screams erupted all around, followed by chaos as hordes of people turned and fled, dragging me in their wake.

'Ils ont fusillé le Roi,' a man said next to me.

'Oh, crikey! They've shot the king.' My heart drummed as I fought to catch my breath while running as fast as I could to keep up with the rush of people as well as to flee the madman with the gun. I did not know whether Marie was still with me. When I reached the end of the road, I turned the corner, and slipped into a bistro for refuge, slumping into the nearest seat at a table away from the window. Barely drawing breath, I pulled out my notepad and pen and jotted down the events. The story was going to be big. What a scoop! My heart drummed along to the beat of my pen, and I dispelled the wave of nausea that flipped in my tummy. My writing was a scrawl of ink as I rushed to recall the sordid, tragic events. Scouring the bar, I spotted a phone and hurried over to call the press office in Paris. Once through, I read out my account of the day's event, breathless.

'Marseille, The King of Yugoslavia, was shot today. It is unknown how serious his injuries are....'

Afterwards, I sank onto a barstool. 'Waiter, double brandy please.' I pulled my purse from my bag, but I was all fingers and thumbs, and I dropped a few coins on the bar, my hands visibly shaking. The waiter placed the brandy down, and I downed it in one as I glanced out the window. A crowd was gathering on the quayside, so I made my way across to the open door. A local gendarme was speaking from the heart of the gathering, but the people were chattering away, voices roaring in my ears.

'Quinze personnes blessés,' the woman muttered behind me. I turned around. My grasp of the French language was improving, but I had a long way to go. 'What are they saying?'

She looked up at me, her face pale, her brown eyes dull. 'The king is dead. Louis Barthou is badly wounded along with several others. They have taken him to the hospital.' She shook her head and walked away, muttering in her native tongue.

13

I returned to the bar. 'Another brandy, Monsieur.' For courage, I told myself as I glanced around the room. There were a growing number of people, either silent or chatting in hushed tones. The door swung open, and Marie drifted in on the briny breeze.

'What happened to you?' I hugged her, relieved she was safe.

'Oh, talk about exciting! I tried to keep up with you, but I got caught up in the crowd.' She sank onto a stool, placing her navy purse on the polished mahogany bar. 'You've made yourself at home.' She nodded at the drink in my hand.

'To calm the nerves,' I said, downing the last drop, glad of the warm spice glowing in my throat. 'So, what's the news?'

'The gunman went on a bit of a spree, firing into the crowd. I'm not sure if anyone else is dead, but fifteen people are injured.'

'Did they catch him?' The scene replayed over and over in my head, the crack of gunfire ricocheting around and around.

'Not sure. Have you called it in?'

'Yes, just.'

Marie blew out a breath and dabbed at her rosy cheeks with the palms of her hands before smoothing back her sleek black hair, which was pinned into a stylish chignon. She was resourceful and strong-willed. I needn't have worried, but the fact was we were all lucky to escape with our lives. Strewth! Talk about a close shave. That was my first real experience with danger, and it was a thrill being in the midst of the action. It was afterwards, when you learned what had happened, that it hit you. To realise that you're the lucky ones, alive to tell the tale. People with worn, pale, shocked faces surrounded us, all consoling one another. As for the king, well. The poor bloke had only come here to strengthen the alliance with France and raise support against the actions of Mussolini and his support of an anti-monarchist. We were both reporting the news as if it was fun. Marie said as much. In reality, the incident was shocking and tragic, but it was world news and the world needed to know.

Later, we heard that the assassin had been cut down by the sword of a mounted French policeman, only for the angry crowd to set on him. He was dead, of course, a life for a life. When I got back to the hotel, I left Marie and returned to my room. A long soak in the tub was much needed, along with another drink. I threw open the windows in my bathroom and lay soaking in sumptuous suds looking out across the harbour, the late afternoon sky milky-blue, flecked with white gulls crying into the air. It was peaceful, heaven, sad, so many things, yet I was in France and had never felt so alive. Luck was definitely on my side, having landed the job as a reporter for the Hearst Newspaper Group.

The interviewer had said, 'The downside is we need you in Paris.' Downside? Who was he kidding? Upside, more like. I soon discovered I had a talent for reporting, well, given I was such a chatterbox. It was amazing what you could do when you put your mind to it. Necessity was the mother of invention, as the old proverb went. And Mum would be surprised. 'You'll never amount to anything,' she often said. 'You're such an ugly girl, but perhaps that's God's way of punishing you.' I became almost immune to her acid tongue, having grown a tough hide over the years, yelling back at her as I grew older. I couldn't understand why she used religion against me. Her warnings didn't scare me. They created a gulf between us, and I distanced myself from God because if he was so cruel, then I wanted no part of that.

I sipped brandy as the memories softened to a hazy fog, and I wondered about the recent political grumblings. The world had its eye on Germany right now, on one man, Herr Hitler. Times were changing, and there was growing unrest in Europe. Germany had new laws and seemed intent on alienating the Jewish community. Now that Hitler was president, a new era had begun, and I couldn't help but wonder about the Fuhrer's intentions. Having left the League of Nations last year in a dispute over military parity with Western powers, they had affectively asserted their intentions to rearm. And no one could stop that, I doubted.

~

THE HOTEL WAS QUIET. Dinner was over, and I retreated to the hotel lounge with my colleagues for drinks. I'd admonished my male colleague for leaving both Marie and me in the lurch, and it was all he could do to rally round, keeping us plied with drinks. An icy breeze drifted over me as the door opened and a couple waltzed in from the street. They strode over to the bar, where another couple greeted them. The man turned and met my gaze while chatting away in French. His striking hazel eyes were sultry, enigmatic; his black hair slicked back. The blonde clinging to his arm wore a black evening gown, very Chanel-like. She followed his gaze and stopped at me, a stony expression drifting over her face as she linked her arm in his. He paused for a few seconds; the corners of his mouth twitched to form a faint smile before he tore his gaze away. It was only then I realised how fast my heart was beating. I turned away and took a drag on my cigarette. I was used to men staring, but there was staring and then staring.

'He gave you the look,' Marie whispered, nudging my arm.

'Yes, well, he can look all he wants.' He epitomised the typical wealthy Frenchman, a playboy, and I could do without the bother. I heaved in a breath.

'Enjoy life, Nancy, that's what I say. Take what you can.' Marie laughed.

'Damn right,' Richard said, draining the last drop of brandy. He ran a hand through his sandy hair, a wide grin lighting up his chiselled face. He hailed from America, and both he and Marie had taken me under their wings. They were the best of fun.

I puffed my Gitanes, the smoke burning the back of my throat. The man smiled and nodded after I caught him watching me. I froze for a moment, aware of that invisible force that draws your soul to another.

'His name is Henri Fiocca,' Marie said. 'I asked a waiter.' She lit a cigarette and exhaled a swirl of smoke. 'Very wealthy, apparently.' She hitched an eyebrow and winked.

I wasn't interested in finding a man and falling in love. I was already in love—with Paris.

'I have a friend, a news correspondent in Berlin.' Richard cut in, stubbed out his cigarette in the ashtray. 'She says it's absolute hell in

Germany right now. The Nazi Party is ruthless. Hitler's SA patrols the streets searching for Jews. If they find any, they beat them up in broad daylight. With everyone watching.'

'Oh, Lord. And no one does anything to help?' Marie's voice sailed up a pitch.

He shook his head. 'Come on, what are they going to do? They'd get arrested for trying. Yeah, as sickening as it is, they beat them with steel rods, break their arms, force them to scrub the cobbled streets, urinate on them, anything at all to hurt, injure and humiliate.'

'It's no way to treat an animal,' Marie said with a shake of her head. 'Surely they don't mistreat everyone. Not the elderly?'

'They don't give a damn: young, old, even the sick. Hitler and his cronies think their lives are worthless. A lot is happening in Berlin right now.' Richard looked away as he puffed his cigarette.

As I listened, I felt irritated and sickened that anyone could treat another human being like that. And I realised that if such acts were happening already, there was probably far worse happening behind closed doors, and far worse to come. I disliked the Nazi Party, which seemed to me to be rotten from the inside, evil, and it was time for the world to wake up and make a stand. People dressed in their finery surrounded us, dining extravagantly, oblivious to the suffering across the border, and I wondered if they realised how fortunate they were.

I was fortunate. The girl from Oz who had left on a whim courtesy of an old aunt I barely knew—dear Aunt Hinemoa. Her story had sounded so exciting and romantic to the much younger, naive girl I once was. She must have known how rotten life had been for me. Now her legacy had brought me to faraway shores to begin a new life.

I believed in destiny or leaving it all to the gods, as some say, and this reminded me of the story Mum told me of my birth. I was born in New Zealand, delivered by a Maori midwife who told Mum I was born with a veil over my face. According to the midwife, it was a sign of good luck to be born in the caul, and she'd said, 'Wherever your daughter goes, whatever she does, the gods shall bless her and take care of her, always.'

I'd never paid much attention to the story before, but I realised I was blessed with good fortune. I sensed a certain awareness within me; a gentle voice that whispered soothing words during the worst of times, a voice of reason and guidance. I'd finally landed on my feet, and I was determined to make the most of every day.

I'd found myself a cosy studio apartment in rue Sainte-Anne, just along the road from the Place de l'Opéra. As soon as the concierge discovered I was Australian, she told me the apartment was mine. She'd fallen in love with an Australian soldier in the Great War and adored my fellow countrymen. My new home was small, but all mine. As soon as I stepped through the door from the main street into the heart of the building, I knew I was home. A quaint cobbled walkway led into the main atrium, while ancient oak beams clad the upper walls. A sweeping stone staircase wound all the way to the top floor.

My apartment was light with period features. Large windows framed the room, beyond which lay a narrow balcony. I loved throwing open the windows whenever I was home and gazing out at the flow of people below as they strolled along, shopping, or enjoying the many cafés. I had a bed, a cupboard for clothes, two armchairs, a small table upon which my typewriter sat, and a radio. There was parquet flooring throughout, and an open fire, with a beautiful old grey marble surround. Plane trees lined many of the streets, their leaves bristling in the gentle warm breeze. The city was so feminine, beautiful, exotic. Even the cathedral, Notre Dame, means 'Our Lady.'

In Paris, women were free to go out alone and enjoy a drink in a bar, whereas in Sydney only a certain type of woman would dare do that. France had her own set of rules, so cosmopolitan. The language was still a barrier but a combination of my old French phrase book and new friends soon helped me to improve. I loved the way the locals said my name—'Nonceee,' often inviting me to join them at cafés. Tomorrow we were returning to Paris. The thought of getting back to my little flat raised a warm glow in my chest. Who knew what tomorrow would bring, or the day after that?

Chapter 3
PARIS. 1935

As I strolled along the banks of the Seine, the early morning rich scent of coffee and croissants drifted through the air. Picon, my wire-haired terrier, strutted along by my side. It was love at first sight when I spotted him in the pet shop window one day. His large brown eyes locked onto mine through the glass, and some invisible force lured me inside. The little chap was a bundle of energy, licking my hand and face, his tail wagging so fast. He'd already convinced me, and I couldn't help but laugh. 'You're too adorable,' I said, knowing I was smitten. I emerged a short time later, carrying my pup in my arms, a huge smile on my face as the two of us made our way home. Paris had never looked more beautiful, and from that day on, we were virtually inseparable. Two weeks later, having bumped into an American clergyman in a bistro, Picon was baptised before friends and strangers alike as I promised to raise him as a Christian. Everyone laughed, but he was my boy, and I loved him.

We trotted through the Jardin des Tuileries, passing beneath the shaded boughs of elms, past mulberries, and made our way to Rue Daunou, slipping into Harry's Bar. All literary and artistic types hung out there alongside those of us in the news business. I sipped pastis, savouring flavours of liquorice and aniseed while I listened to the words of the young man who sat at our table. Marie, astute as ever, scribbled down notes as he spoke, completely engrossed in his story. I picked up my cigarette holder and inhaled deeply. His name was Samuel Goldberg. He was nineteen years old and had recently fled Germany along with his parents and younger brother.

'I knew Hitler would be the leader as soon as Hindenburg died. Everyone did. But everything he and that Nazi Party of his stands for is evil. So many people are fleeing now, and not only Jews.' He gulped down the brandy Richard had bought him. 'There are those who don't agree with the new laws. They sense what's coming and they're getting out while they can.'

He said he'd arrived in Paris with his family two months ago, but he intended to apply for a visa to go to Canada. We'd all seen the refugees filing into Paris, flowing through France, many of them travelling on to England or further still, escaping overseas to get as far away as possible. The Nazi Party was intent on rearming Germany, building her defences, making new laws. The Nuremberg Laws were now in place. Hitler was on the march and had been for a while. The news was grim. A plebiscite last year revealed that ninety percent of the people approved of his powers.

'There are signs everywhere—"Juden Verboten"—Jews Forbidden in shops throughout Germany. We have no rights. We are powerless, and I fear he cannot be stopped.' Samuel pursed his lips and gazed out into the street, a lost look in his eyes. 'The Enabling Act means Hitler can make his own laws without the need for the Reichstag's approval. He can do whatever he chooses. Germany is no longer safe for Jews. If only they realised.'

The Aryan race was high on Hitler's priority list. Pureblood. The Nazis perceived Jews and other ethnic minorities as undesirables. I'd heard shocking reports. A breeding programme to purify the German race, for Christ's sake. Enforced sterilisation of women, taking the sick and disabled away. What happened to them? Other parties had been banned, meaning the Nazi Party was the only political party. Hitler had complete control over Germany and her people. The café was filling up, and the noise of multiple conversations bubbled all around. I overheard a group of Parisians at a nearby table complaining about the increasing number of refugees. Anti-Semitism had petered out in the twenties, following the number of Jewish men who had fought for France in the Great War, but it was resurfacing again. I was not political, but it was impossible not to engage with the times, especially for a reporter. Still, there was much I didn't agree with or fully understand. Overall, as far as I was concerned, humanity had to prevail, and Hitler's vision for Germany was anything but humane. And God help the rest of us.

'It is not simply the repression we have to face, but physical violence. The storm troopers are a law to themselves, so aggressive, so angry. They think nothing of lashing out as they walk past the Jews. So much evil, ransacking businesses and homes, terrorising Jewish people and humiliating them in public. Thousands are fleeing, not only to France but to Belgium, Denmark, Switzerland, wherever they can think of to go. And yet so many choose to stay. They do not see that it is no longer safe.' He adjusted his spectacles. 'They sit and hope for the best, praying for peace, refusing to believe that any harm will come.'

Hitler was on many minds. Just who was this man who had risen meteorically from nowhere to the ultimate power of Germany as its ruler? After Samuel left, we sat a while longer, chatting. Often, I liked to people watch, listening in on conversations. It wasn't rude exactly, more of a necessity in times such as these. That's how I saw it. You never knew what you might discover. Many people came here, natives and foreigners, prominent artists, writers, poets, actors.

'Hitler sounds like the devil.' I sucked on my cigarette.

'He survived the Great War,' Richard said.

And so many good men didn't, I thought.

'An interesting fact about Germany. Most people believe Paris has the greatest number of intellectuals, but it's not true, you see. They all flock to Berlin, which is the true capital of Europe. And all the railroad tracks that zig-zag through Europe end up in Berlin.' He smirked; his ice-blue eyes danced as he lit another cigarette.

Interesting indeed, but equally meaningless. I deduced that being the greatest writer or artist of all time did not guarantee safety, not in a country whose government had ordered the mass burning of books, unless pure Aryan blood flowed through their veins.

'Did you know the Pope made an agreement with Hitler which allows him greater power in Germany with no opposition from the Catholic Church, as long as he leaves the Church alone?' Richard dragged a hand through his hair, took a drag of his cigarette and exhaled smoke rings.

'Really?' Why was I even shocked? Religion had always been an overbearing presence in wars over the centuries. Politics, religion and money, all tightly interwoven. And the Pope wished to save his Catholic Church, and his priests and cardinals. It was contemptible to turn a blind eye. To me, we were all equal, each life as precious as the next, despite the divisions created by religion and now the Nazis. Yes, things were changing radically, and it was unnerving.

Since my arrival in France, all I'd heard about was the magnificent fortifications that formed the Maginot Line. Built following the Great War, designed to keep out 'the beast that sleeps on the other side of the Rhine,' as the French referred to Germany. However, it didn't extend up to the Belgian border in Northern France where the Ardennes lay, a fortification of natural means. The French remained convinced it was impenetrable by any army. Perhaps, but Hitler and his generals bore devious, unscrupulous traits.

Chapter 4
MARSEILLE. MAY 1936

It was wonderful to be back in Marseille again. It was only a weekend break at L' Hôtel Louvre et Paix with friends, but it was needed. Everyone had been working so hard lately. Life had slipped into a dreamy haze of cosmopolitan café culture, chasing news stories and living out of a suitcase. It wasn't particularly glamorous, but that didn't bother me a jot. Having dreamed of seeing the world for so long, I spent hours on trains zigzagging across France. That said, I always yearned for Picon and my small Parisian apartment, always glad to return home for a rest. Marseille, however, was different. There was something about this Mediterranean jewel that dazzled beneath the sun by day and rallied to pearlescent moonlight by night. Either way, I was going to enjoy my weekend away, shut out the rest of the world for forty-eight hours and forget all about the news.

'Nancy, come and dance,' Richard asked, holding out his hand, breaking my reverie. The melodic notes of 'Une Chanson d'amour' sailed high above the tobacco haze and swayed along with the sweet fog of champagne that settled in my head. I reached for his proffered hand. Richard was tall, good-looking, and a superb dancer to boot. He was slightly younger than me, not that it mattered. We were only friends. Can't a woman keep male friends without question? We took to the floor and swayed along to the music, Richard's hair slicked back with Brylcreem, the usual thin strand that refused to be tamed, flopping onto his forehead. I loved to dance. It was freedom, close to floating on air. The hairs bristled at the back of my neck, and as we sailed across the floor, I glimpsed a man in black sat at a table in the furthest corner hidden from the glare of the chandeliers, his gaze on me. Eyes locked, I suddenly and uncharacteristically glanced down, my cheeks burning. The music ended, and Richard led me to the bar.

'Another brandy, Nance?'

'You twisted my arm.' I raised an eyebrow, smirking. 'I won't be able to walk home at this rate.' Still a little self-conscious, I turned to where the mystery man had been sitting, the table now vacant. It wasn't the first time I'd caught men looking, and I usually paid no attention, but his eyes, his presence, well, it was as if we'd met before.

'You can drink anyone under the table.' Richard laughed.

'And I never slur my words.' He was kind; they all were, and helpful. Some of the more experienced journalists had already taught me so much, and it was thanks to them I'd passed my initial trial and now had a permanent job. The humid evening air sailed through the open windows and doors, moist, fresh, infused with spicy saffron, a familiar aroma in Marseille when the bistros and restaurants prepared bouillabaisse.

'Hey, Nancy. What is it the locals call you?' Marie grinned.

For a minute, she caught me off guard, and then I realised what she meant. 'La demoiselle avec la bagne.' I lit up a cigarette, inhaled, and blew out a swirl of smoke. 'When I first moved into my apartment, I asked for permission to have a bath installed. It caused great amusement, still does.'

Marie laughed. 'That's right, the girl with the bath.' She turned to the others. 'Permission to have a bloody bath installed. They still laugh when they see her coming.' She sipped her wine. 'Only the best for our girl here.'

So true. Whenever the locals saw me coming, one or two would call out, 'Noncee, come and have a drink.' And, unless I was dashing off on an assignment, I usually would. I was polite, and I enjoyed the company.

A dark silhouette caught the corner of my eye, and I turned to see my secret admirer leaving with his companion, saying his goodbyes to people he knew. Then, just when I thought he'd gone, he turned and headed directly for our table, and I found myself gazing into the eyes of Henri Fiocca.

Goosebumps prickled my arms, and I drew my scarlet wrap around my shoulders. Men rarely ruffled my feathers, but something about him had captured my attention.

'Bonjour, Mademoiselle. Henri Fiocca. Such a pleasure to meet you.' He fixed his gaze solely on me.

'Bonjour. Nancy Wake,' I said, holding out my hand. 'Delighted.'

'Ah, the pleasure is all mine.' He kissed the back of my hand before reaching into his breast pocket and producing a white business card. 'Please, next time you are in town, call me.' He placed the card on the table next to my drink and smiled. The blonde behind him huffed out a sigh. Her pouty ruby lips and scowl spoke volumes. The chatter at our table tailed off, and I was aware of the pause as my friends waited, eager for my response. I puffed on my cigarette, blew out a cloud of vapour and looked up into his soft, hazel eyes. 'I'm afraid I never call men, Monsieur. *They* call me.' I noted the flicker of disappointment in his eyes, promptly replaced by amusement as he smirked, drawing himself up to his full height. 'Another time, Mademoiselle. I wish you and your friends a pleasant evening. Bonsoir.' As he sauntered away, the blonde cast me a stony glance as she trailed after him like a puppy dog.

Marie nudged me. 'He likes you. You should call him next time you're in town.'

'You must be joking. I never call men. Cheeky devil! If he wants to see me that badly, he can bloody well call *me*.' I grasped my brandy glass and downed the shot in one, determined to push Henri Fiocca out of my mind. I was no man's pet, nor a diamond to adorn a man as he graced the town in the evenings. That old ache resurfaced in my chest, but I swallowed, banishing it to the darkness. No, I definitely wouldn't call him, but I wondered if he would call me. For whatever reason, Monsieur Fiocca had caused a ripple in my world. Well, fate, destiny, if it was meant to be, then it would be. Simple as that. I sighed, flicked a wistful glance at the door where seconds earlier he'd breezed out into the night.

Chapter 5
JUAN LES PINS. AUGUST 1936

Between Cannes and Nice, in the south-eastern corner, lay the popular holiday resort of Juan les Pins. Chaplin and Coco Chanel often holidayed there, although I'd yet to spot anyone famous. Monet and Picasso too, and they'd painted the resort. It was a haven of beauty, a slow pace of life by day, slipping into a vibrant, gay tempo as night took hold. Even Churchill and Hemingway had been spotted drinking gin in the bar of my hotel, Le Provençal. It was a stunning piece of architecture in the Art déco style, overlooking the Mediterranean. The sandy white beaches stretched out for miles, dipping into the crystal turquoise waters of the ocean. Such a tranquil scene and to think that over the border in Spain, civil war raged. Nationalists versus Republicans. The latest news reports cited much unrest with fighting in the streets. A Spanish police officer, José Castillo, was shot and killed on the street in Madrid in July. The day after, José Calvo Sotelo, a forty-three-year-old Spanish politician, was murdered. War broke out a few days later. People answered the call to arms from far and wide, including America and Britain.

The rebels had taken control in Morocco, the Canary Islands, and the Balearics. Initially, France supported the Republicans, but after weighing up the situation, now considered signing a non-intervention agreement with Britain, Russia, Germany, and Italy. Hitler and his troops had recently taken back control of the Rhineland in March, a direct contravention of the Treaty of Versailles. Neither Britain nor France wished to rock the boat. Everyone, it seemed, had no stomach to stand in Hitler's way. Of course, following the bloodshed of the Great War, who could blame them? War was a sleeping beast tucked in at our heels, dormant, waiting. And now Hitler could show Germany's military strength, having pledged his support to General Franco in the Spanish uprising.

Even on holiday, it was impossible to shut out the world. Locals spoke of young men kissing their mother's goodbye as they left France to join the Spanish Republicans and fight. Newspapers delivered daily reports while wireless sets blared out news bulletins at set times each day. People tuned in, conversations hushed, drinks set down, eyes fixed to the radio, ears glued to the speaker's voice over the airwaves. The Spanish conflict gripped us all.

Picon raised his head, his nose twitching as he sniffed. I crouched down, ran my hand along his back, the hair wiry like a coconut skin, then unclipped his tan leather leash. The morning air, salty, fresh, blew in from the ocean, lifted my hair. Picon trotted by my side as we made our way across the beach, then I watched him gallop down to the water's edge. The tide sailed out, then shushed back in, slipping over his white paws, and Picon yapped as he ran away from its hold, back to me. I giggled. Grainy sand clung to my toes, burning my soles, and I wandered to the water's edge. The next wave washed over my feet, lukewarm. I glanced down as the mushy sand shifted beneath my weight and a wave rolled in my head as I wavered.

After our walk, I found a table on the hotel terrace. In the distance, I glimpsed Marie in her ivory bathing suit as she waded into the ocean while Richard waved from waist-high depths, white-crested waves crashing around them. As I waited for the waiter to bring my coffee and croissants, I noticed Henri Fiocca seated at a nearby table with a female companion. What a coincidence, or a sign, perhaps. He never called, although I had been away many times on assignments. He was a womaniser, a playboy. Some men simply weren't the settling down types.

Henri was tall, medium build with sultry hazel eyes. He oozed a certain charm, with suave and sophistication, and rarely ventured out without a glamorous woman on his arm. I did not know his age, but I guessed he was older than me, more likely closer to my elder brother Stanley's age. He glanced over and smiled. I reciprocated the gesture and turned away. Goodness knows how he had a steady stream of girl-friends. Of course, I'd had my share of dates, but nothing serious. But as much as I hated to admit it, Henri Fiocca was an enigma, and the first man to rouse my curiosity.

WE DINED OUTSIDE on the terrace at eight while the sun slipped from her celestial pedestal. Marie sat behind a hand-held oriental fan in shades of blue and pink, her face flushed, smothered in a sheen of perspiration. The day had been long and hot, but the evening dragged a refreshing, delicious breeze from the ocean to fan my brow and cheeks. Dusk settled by the time we'd finished, and waiters stepped from table to table lighting tealight candles. The sapphire sky glittered with stars; a purple-pink band stretched tight across the horizon. Two violinists serenaded the diners. Sweet, melodic notes swayed and scythed into the night, lulling me into a relaxed, almost sleepy state. Marie wore an elegant salmon pink silk dress with lemon flowers embroidered on the chest, her mahogany cigarette holder precisely poised within the fingers of her right hand. Her bright eyes serene, sharp, taking everything and everyone in, forever the huntress. Focussed and determined, ruthlessly uncovering stories and reporting the news, generally without emotional involvement, and sometimes I wished I was more like her. I couldn't detach myself from suffering or injustice. Perhaps I should have considered a career in politics. At least then one could make a difference.

'You look tired, Nancy,' Richard said, a broad grin crinkling his eyes at the corners.

'Tired? She has enough stamina for the three of us.' Marie laughed. 'Let's go to the casino tonight.'

We'd spent the last two nights at the casino, which was probably the reason for my fatigue. Poor Picon was exhausted, and tonight I'd left him to sleep in my room.

'Let's dance.' Richard took my hand and pulled me to my feet.

As he led me in a gentle waltz to the rhythm of violin music, a fizz of energy gushed through my veins, and I smiled as we took centre stage, dancing before the ocean, beneath the diamante twilight. Couples dined around us, their indistinct murmur of chat a mere vibration. After the present tune ended, a new one began. The Tango. The dance of love. And I loved it. Richard was only slightly taller than me, the perfect partner, height-wise. As we sailed across the terrace, the hairs prickled at the nape of my neck, and then I saw him. Henri Fiocca, sat with his blonde companion from earlier, enjoying an apéritif, his gaze firmly fixed on us. I'm not sure why he caused me to feel so unsettled, but everything I did from then on made far more difference. My appearance, behaviour, everything mattered, and over the following week, I realised I spent more time in front of the mirror, perfecting my hair, touching up my lipstick, deliberating over what to wear as a fluttering grew in my tummy like a kaleidoscope of butterflies.

Over the next few days, I swam, enjoyed meals with friends, and spent my evenings at the casino, occasionally bumping into Henri, watching in awe as he appeared with a different girl each time. And then one evening, as I strode into the hotel lounge looking for my friends, I found him alone at the bar nursing a brandy, looking vulnerable and brooding. He spun around and flashed that playful grin of his as soon as he saw me and, like a magnet, drew me in, my heart drumming the Marseillaise, beating my ribcage beneath my black silk evening dress. I smiled as we greeted one another in the French way, exotic spices and cedarwood wafting in the air; divine.

'Bonjour, Noncee,' he said, his voice like velvet. He put his glass down on the bar and took my hand. 'It is a pleasure to meet you again.'

I gazed into his eyes, dumbstruck for a split second, as my heart thumped against bone. 'Bonjour.' He hung onto my hand as if waiting for something. I swallowed. *Come on, Nance, get a hold of yourself.* 'It's lovely to see you too, Henri.'

'Nancy, such a beautiful name. So, is it business or pleasure that brings you here?'

'Pleasure. I'm on holiday with a few friends.'

'Ah, I see, but your friends have left you all alone. No matter. Perhaps I can interest you in a bottle of red wine?'

Before I could answer, he snapped his fingers, caught the barman's eye and requested a bottle that sounded rather expensive. I gazed around, hoping for a glimpse of Marie at least, but to no avail. Henri was rather good-looking, with soft eyes framed with long, thick black lashes. His wavy hair, black as ebony, swept back from his forehead, a sheen of reflected light upon his face. I found myself drawn to him. We sat together on barstools, his knee softly brushing my thigh, a warm flush flaring in my cheeks.

He leaned in close. Tobacco and cologne toyed with my senses as I breathed in notes of pine and citrus. 'So, Nancy, what is it you do?' His breath was warm on my neck, earlobe. Scents of red berries and oak drifted from his mouth.

'I'm a journalist for the Hearst Group, based in Paris.'

Henri sipped a mouthful of wine before dragging a silver cigarette case from his jacket pocket. 'Ah, the city of love.'

I plucked a cigarette and leaned in for a light, meeting his gaze. I took a drag and exhaled slowly, deliberately, while he gazed on. 'So, Henri, what is that you do?'

'I run the family business in Marseille. Shipping.'

Strewth, that sounded important. 'Impressive.' I smiled, watching him, the master of disguise, trying desperately to work him out. 'How do you do it?'

He took a drag on his cigarette and exhaled a cloud of vapour, a puzzled look sailing across his face. 'Do what?'

'Every time I see you, you're with a different girl.' His little black book must be bulging with names and telephone numbers. I smirked. 'How do you go out with so many beautiful girls?'

He fixed his gaze on me, his eyes catching the light, twinkling like copper pennies, boring into my soul, intense, assured, sexy. I sat up tall, steeling myself to retain an air of coolness. The waiter brought a bottle of wine and two glasses and placed them on the table, and Henri reached into his pocket for money and gave the young man a tip. He then poured the wine, leaned back in his chair, and raised his glass. 'Santé.' He smiled, his mouth curving widely. 'In answer to your question, I do nothing. They all ring me.'

'Santé,' I replied. I sipped the wine, savouring the medium oak flavour while I considered his reply. The man was a magnet for women and while it sounded preposterous to me, I realised he was quite the eligible bachelor. 'They call you?'

'Oui. Everyone calls me, except for the one woman I wish to call me.' He fixed his intense gaze on me, his eyebrows raised in a questioning manner.

My face glowed with heat, the air stifling, but the windows and doors were open and now and then a refreshing sea breeze washed over me, dampening the furnace that raged in my cheeks. I took a drag of my cigarette and exhaled smoke rings as I stared into Henri's eyes. 'As I said before, I never call men. They call me.'

Henri grinned. 'Shall we dance?' He stood up and held out his hand. How could I refuse? The pianist played a slow, melancholic piece as I took his hand. I felt at ease, comfortable with this Frenchman beside me. A stranger and yet somehow, I felt as if I'd known him forever. And then he drew me towards him, his arm around my waist, cologne with notes of cedar and pine drifting into my face, filling my lungs, delicious. His skin, clean-shaven, bronzed, a descendent of the foundling Greeks perhaps, I mused, my imagination sailing away with every step we took. And then the music changed.

'Ah, a Tango. And now it is my turn to share the dance of love with you, Nancy.'

I almost burst out laughing, but his eyes flared with such intensity as he held me close and so I bit my lip, not wishing to kill the mood. My favourite dance. Suddenly, all my cares and demons rose in a flurry, as if to confront me. I'd worn their chains far too long, and now I could release them and relax in the safe arms of this Frenchman who guided me so graciously, so proficiently across the floor, teasing smiles from my lips. Our combined passion simmered to boiling point as we commanded the dancefloor, delighting in every step, our hands damp, his body a furnace next to mine. I extended my leg out in front of me, to Henri's delight. The Tango was dramatic, emotive, and a chance to show off. The other couples gave us a wide berth. It seemed we were the centre of attention. Well, I suppose we were putting on quite a display. We were one with the dance, our bodies harmonious in symmetry. Perfect alignment, a sign perhaps?

In Henri's arms, I discovered a haven, a sense of belonging, something I'd not experienced before. This man affected me in more ways than one, but despite the whispers of my heart, I remembered a tumultuous past. His world was a playing field, and I was not an object to own or abuse, and so I reluctantly reclaimed my feelings.

During the last few days of my holiday, Henri rang me at the start of each day to wish me 'good morning', and we met for dinner each night, and I couldn't help but wonder what he saw in me. After all, this bon viveur dined with a different woman each night. Why did he desire my company? I didn't complain. He was a charming gentleman, interesting and funny. But as much as I enjoyed spending time with him, I had no wish to fall.

On my last night, we said our goodbyes, and he assured me he'd call soon, mentioning something about visiting Paris for business. Well, I took that with a pinch of salt. For the time being, it was back to the real world, news assignments, and Parisian life—bliss.

Chapter 6

MAY 1937

Henri Fiocca had surprised me one evening, a month after my trip to Juan les Pins, as the summer heat cooled before slipping into autumn, and telephoned. We'd met up that weekend and had dinner together before he dashed back to Marseille. At first, I told myself not to get too excited, quelling the murmuration that rose and dipped in my stomach. But as the months passed, he continued to call every time he was passing on business. And I grew accustomed to his company, looking forward to our meetings. Henri was attentive, considerate, and romantic. He brought roses, champagne, and treated me to the finest dinners. Before I realised, I had become quite attached. I volunteered for news assignments in southern France whenever possible, so we could meet. Recently, he took me to Cannes for the weekend, introducing me to his good friends, Emma Digard, her partner, Emmanuel Martinez, and their lovely fourteen-year-old daughter, Micheline. We clicked instantly and had a wonderful time.

Meanwhile, the Spanish Civil War continued to rage, dominating every newspaper. Both Hitler and Mussolini continued to support Franco and his Nationalist forces. Hitler sent Panzer tanks, aircraft, and troops. The fighting on the ground was bloody, and now both the German and Italian air force attacked from the air, and bombs rained down on villages and towns. Reports came in of bloody battles, reprisals, and executions. Men, women, and children slaughtered. Towns destroyed. For Franco, it was a battle he had to win, to snatch power and control over Spain. For Hitler, I believed it was more personal. He seemed determined to get what he desired by any means possible, and the Spanish conflict gave him the perfect opportunity to test Germany's military strengths.

Recently I'd read an interview with General Franco by the American journalist, Jay Allen, who'd been in the right place at the right time and got permission to talk with the commander, who said, 'There can be no compromise, no truce. I shall advance. I shall take the capital. I will save Spain from Marxism at whatever cost.' When Allen replied, 'That means you will have to shoot half of Spain?' Franco reportedly shook his head, smiled, and replied, 'I said whatever the cost.'

And now news had reached us of aerial bombings in Guernica, which took place on 26 April, one week ago. The town, which was not of any military importance, was bombed and razored to the ground. The news report stated fires raged for three days, and around sixteen hundred men, women, and children were ruthlessly killed or injured.

France was concerned about a third fascist power on its borders. The people and government officials boasted of the Maginot Line, proud of the fortifications they had built that stretched from Switzerland to the Belgian border near Montmédy. Whispers of another war had already begun, drifting like autumn leaves on the wind, blowing this way and that. But you see, no one knew for certain. The older generation remembered the past and seemed more concerned, while the younger generation dismissed such talk. Meanwhile, my soul whispered a caution, and it filled me with unease.

Autumn in Paris yielded a vivid contrast of beauty. A certain crispness drifted into the air: fresh, delicious. The trees shook off leaves of amber, scarlet, and gold as they prepared to embrace winter. The aromatic scents of fresh coffee mingled with the drifting aroma of hot, freshly baked bread and pastries from the local bistros and boulangerie.

I hated to think of the possibility of another war; anguished at the thought of my brother Stanley, who still served with the navy. 'Do you think another war will happen?' I asked Henri one evening.

He pursed his lips, considering my question carefully as he poured himself another brandy. 'Non, mon amour. It will never happen.'

His answer surprised me because all the signs indicated otherwise. 'Really? But look at Hitler. The man's completely mad and so unpredictable.'

'Yes, Nannie,' Henri mused, using the pet name he'd recently given me. 'I have also heard of many things happening in Germany. I know about the persecution of the Jews and others. But war? Non.' He poured another brandy, this time for me.

I gazed into his eyes, unconvinced by his opinion, only to find an unsettled look, and I wondered if he was attempting to console me. Most of France was divided in their opinions on this subject, but one thing was certain. The people had every right to be concerned.

Henri slouched in a tan leather armchair by the fire. I usually only lit the fire if it was cold enough. Coal and wood ate into my budget, but as he'd visited this weekend, I'd set the fire especially. I loved seeing him settled there. The logs were well alight and warmed my small studio apartment easily. It was good for him to see where and how I lived. I had no airs or graces. He understood why I had to work. He also knew I wasn't the type of woman who was looking for a wealthy man to take care of her. Recently, out of the blue, he'd asked me to leave my job and move to Marseille. I just laughed. Although he seemed a little miffed, I told him how ridiculous it was. A girl can't give up all she's worked for on a whim, for goodness' sake. It's madness! Oh no, I had no intentions of doing that. I loved my life, and things were going well. But how he grumbled.

'I have missed you terribly, Nannie. Without you, I am lost.'

'Rubbish.' I laughed, enjoying the cheeky smile that played on his lips. 'You're full of it, Henri. We both know you can't be lonely.' His smile slipped, and he tore his gaze from me, peering into the bottom of his whisky glass as if considering what to say next. Well, he had no shortage of companions. When I called him last week, he was out as usual, and Henri never dined alone. A good friend told me she'd spotted him with a tall, leggy brunette at Chez Michel. Typical!

'You know, Nannie. I have never met anyone quite like you. You are a remarkable woman.' He flicked on the radio and fiddled with the dial until he found a station with which he was happy. Then he took my hand and drew me close. I nuzzled his neck, drank in his scent as we swayed to the music. 'You are most stubborn,' he mused.

I had to agree.

'Come and live in Marseille. Then we can be together more often.'

'Henri, I can't work from Marseille.' His hands slipped from my waist to rest on my bottom, and his mouth found mine before I could utter another word. His kiss was soft at first, then firm, searching, greedily snatching my breath away. Then, he took my face in his hands. 'Nannie, I'm in love with you, and I promise to take care of you, always. Come to Marseille.'

His deep hazel eyes emitted a promise of sorts, and for whatever reason, I believed him to be sincere, but there were no guarantees of security, something that left a nagging doubt. Thoughts of his other dinner dates pricked at my consciousness. I pursed my lips, pushed those thoughts aside as an ache throbbed in my throat. 'I'll think about it, I promise.'

He cupped my cheeks in his hands and kissed my lips with such passion. 'It is late.'

I stood up, smoothed down my dress. 'I'll get your jacket.'

'Non, mon amour.' He pulled me towards him, planted his mouth on mine. 'Must I leave?' His intentions were clear, and for a moment, I hesitated, surprised. 'Nannie, be with me tonight.' Henri leaned in, smothering my neck in soft kisses, his warm breath sending a cascade of tingles down my spine. I nodded, and, still with his hand in mine, led him to the bedroom and closed the door.

~

THE NEXT DAY, Henri left early. I hated seeing him go and a curious spring feeling blossomed within me, pleasant, exciting, leaving me perplexed as I realised I was in love. I spent the morning at our regular café. The banter was much the same, with the latest reports on the bloody battle for the control of Spain, and the growing number of casualties. Marie sat nervously biting her fingernails, a faraway look in her eyes as she listened to gruesome reports. War was ruthless, inhumane, abhorrent.

'Have you seen the painting by Picasso?' Marie said.

'No, but I heard about it. The Spanish Republicans commissioned him.'

'Well, it's doing the rounds. They took it to the Paris World Fair at the Spanish Pavilion and now there's an international tour to drum up support. They want to raise awareness of the war and raise funds for the Spanish refugees.'

'I can't imagine being bombed. To lose your home, your loved ones.' I flicked a gaze at Marie, who nodded in agreement; lips pursed. 'Well, what's this painting like?'

She frowned and huffed out a breath, as if trying to sum up her thoughts. 'It's a typical Picasso style, and, as they say, sums up his response to the news of Guernica. They say he was outraged. It's one hell of a way to make a statement.'

The world needed to know what was happening. The war was headline news, with Ernest Hemingway reporting from the front lines, and other well-known people, such as the French writer Antoine de Saint-Exupéry and George Orwell becoming involved. Even the poet W. H. Auden had spent several weeks in Spain with the International Brigade at the beginning of the year. His experiences inspired his poem, *Spain,* the proceeds of which he said he'd donate to the Spanish Medical Aid Committee. My heart ached for the Spanish civilians caught up in this hell. Politics was a dirty business. Why did nations have to be so complex, so divided? Could man not live in harmony with his fellow man? Why was there so much hate, greed, and disagreement in the world?

Chapter 7
SPRING 1938

The Hautes-Alpes in south-eastern France loomed up ahead, magnificent rocky peaks reaching into a milky-blue sky. Fir trees with snow-covered branches lined the narrow, desolate road that seemed to wind endlessly up through the rugged mountains. The recent snow had melted in the valleys but clung to the hills; the highest peaks shrouded deep in white. I couldn't believe my luck when Henri invited me along. 'Come away with me, Nancy,' he'd asked only last month, having borrowed his friend's chalet for five days. A cabin in the Alps, the great outdoors. I supposed there was a first time for everything. 'What will we do?'

'It is the Alps, ma chérie. We go walking.'

'Oh, well, I don't mind walking. And in the evenings, we can dine out.'

Henri laughed. 'There is nowhere to dine unless you do not mind a long car journey. We cook for ourselves. Think, Nannie. Good food, candlelight, log fires, and you lying in my arms.'

Well, I hoped he didn't expect gourmet cooking from me. My culinary repertoire was dreadfully limited. Marie had laughed when I told her. 'You'll be driven mad with boredom, Nancy. No nightlife.' Her words made me smile even now. 'I suspect Henri has some other plan for you,' she'd mused.

I glanced over at him. He seemed happy, free of work issues. I didn't mind what we did. I was happy to spend time with him. Marie's parting words, 'What girl doesn't want to be taken care of? You're so lucky, Nancy.' I gazed around at the large, imposing fortress of mountains. So many fell into the trap, gave their hearts away too readily, put all their faith in one person only to be let down. What followed was a trail of hurt, grief, and broken pieces. I'd grown up with broken pieces and was still trying to fit them all together. 'You're just an old sceptic,' Marie had said. I disagreed. Women oughtn't to rush into things. No matter how many times Henri asked me to move to Marseille, my answer would always be no. Why change something that worked?

Val Des Pres was a tiny village with a quaint church, nestled in the heart of the Hautes-Alpes, close to the Italian border. Several houses of various designs sat proudly lining the narrow road. White sheets flapped in the gentle breeze on a washing line in someone's front yard. An older man wearing a black beret nodded a greeting as he squeezed past us on his ox-driven cart. Picon sprang onto my lap and yapped, his nose pressed against the window, little tail wagging. He'd never seen such beasts. Henri had been here before, although he was careful not to disclose who with. There were so many of them, his 'friends'.

'Nous voilà.' He pulled into a long, winding drive and just beyond a sharp turn lay the timber cabin with green painted window shutters. A climbing rose chased the doorframe up and over, a thatch of intertwined green, gnarled stems, blistered with fresh buds. The breeze stung my face, the air icy.

'Come on in and see. You will love it. I shall fetch the bags in a moment,' Henri said in a bubbly voice. He almost skipped to the door, fumbled in his jacket pocket for the keys. Inside, a spacious hallway ran the depth of the house, and a rustic wooden staircase wound up to an upper landing with more doors. The kitchen had a large cooking range and pans of various sizes hung from the pot rack above, with bundles of lavender nestled among them, purple blooms emanating a sweet floral scent. A scrubbed pine farmhouse table sat in the middle of the room, with an ornate silver candelabra at its centre. A bottle of red wine and a basket of fresh fruit sat at the end. 'There should be some food.' He opened a few cupboards. 'Pierre is so generous. We have fresh bread, cheese, cuts of meat, and wine.' He slipped his coat off, draped it over an oak chair. 'It is a little cold, perhaps. I will light a fire.'

Goosebumps prickled my arms, and I kept my coat on as I followed Henri into the living room and watched as he crouched down at the hearth and dipped into the log basket for firewood. Red velour chairs and a sofa sat around an oak coffee table, facing the fireplace, plump ivory cushions on the seats. Not a speck of dust lay on any surface.

I tip-tapped across the parquet floor to the large window, smoothed a hand over peach chintz curtains while I gazed at the front gardens. The rugged snow-covered mountains stretched into the clouds, cocooned the valley. Henri sneaked up and wrapped his arms around me, nuzzling my neck with butterfly kisses.

'Well, what do you think?'

'It's beautiful.'

'Not as beautiful as you.' He turned me round to face him, cupping my chin with his hand. 'I am so happy to be here with you, Nannie. We will spend a wonderful week together.' He kissed me on the mouth, a kiss that made me feel wanted, safe. How was that possible?

After dinner, we sat together in front of the fire, staring into the flames while nursing glasses of cognac in our hands. I swirled the amber liquid around to warm it before savouring a mouthful, notes of vanilla, dark chocolate, and hazelnuts tantalising my taste buds. A dog woofed outside, an owl screeched, and the fire crackled and spat sparks as logs shifted in the grate. Henri was warm against me, his arm around my shoulders, strong and safe, drawing me close. At that moment, I felt as if I was having an out-of-body experience, looking inward. We had become an aged sepia photograph, a snapshot of life as a couple, together. It was heaven, and for a moment I dared to dream. Henri reached out, took the glass from my hand, set it down on the table with a clunk.

'It is late.' He stood up and pulled me to my feet, kissed the tip of my nose before leading me up the wooden stairs to the main bedroom.

The double room had a brass bedstead with a satin floral bedspread. Henri went over to the window and drew the curtains. I stood by the bed, waiting as he moved towards me.

'You are so beautiful,' he said, his hand sweeping a loose curl away from my face. 'I will remember this always.'

'Remember what?'

'This perfect moment. You make me so happy, Nancy.'

I wrapped my arms around him, buried my face in his neck, the squeeze of his arms around me.

'Je t'aime.'

'I love you.'

GOLDEN LIGHT STREAMED in through the thin bedroom curtains. I lay in bed, still in half slumber, squinting. Henri was not beside me. The house was silent. Memories of last night abounded, and my heart skipped to the beat of them all. Henri loved me. Lying in his arms, his smooth skin on mine, his weight pressing down, warm. I blushed, a mix of thoughts sparring inside my head as joy jostled with unease. Life was so unexpected. Just take one moment at a time, I told myself. Outside, the incessant chatter of birds as chirps and tweets scythed through the quiet. I dragged myself up, slipped on my pink silk robe and padded downstairs, my bare feet icy upon the cold wooden floor. The scent of coffee greeted me halfway down. Henri sat at the kitchen table, a faraway look in his eyes. 'There you are.' I swept over to plant a kiss on his mouth.

'Good morning, sleepyhead.' He grinned. 'You looked so peaceful. I could not wake you.' He slipped an arm around my waist and gently pulled me onto his lap. He poured the coffee. 'We have croissants for breakfast with a choice of strawberry or blackcurrant jam.'

Picon leapt from his basket and trotted over to sit at my feet, his brown, puppy-dog eyes communicating his needs. I tore off a small piece of croissant and offered it to him, much to his delight, his tail beating my thigh. I sighed with contentment. It gave me a flavour of life with Henri, and I mused how it might be if we were married, my mind slipping back to childhood games playing grown-ups. We sipped our coffee, not saying a word, just content to be with one another. But it couldn't last. We would return to work in a few days. Henri in Marseille and me in Paris and beyond, chasing stories. Wasn't life simply one long story where we all played our parts? Such an odd way to look at it, I supposed. The thing was to enjoy the present. That was the only way to live, appreciating each moment because none of us knew what would come next.

~

THAT SUMMER, Henri took me away to Cannes for a week. While we were there, we spent time with our friends, Emma Digard and Emmanuel, the owner of the Hotel Martinez.

'Henri thinks the world of you, Nancy,' Emma said one day while we were having dinner together.

My heart jumped, a warm, fuzzy glow spreading inside my chest as I thought of him,

'I have never seen him this way before,' she added, smiling, hitching an eyebrow as she tucked a stray auburn curl behind her ear.

'Well, we get on so well, but I don't think he feels it's serious.'

'Really? That is not how it seems to us. He will make the perfect husband.'

She was venturing somewhere private far too soon. I didn't doubt her words, but Henri wasn't looking to settle down with me. While he'd asked me to move to Marseille, he hadn't once talked of marriage. Fortunately, her daughter, Micheline, sprinted over and dragged me away just in time. I glanced at Henri, who was enjoying a drink and a conversation with Emmanuel. Emma's words echoed through my mind. The perfect husband. I wasn't sure Henri was ready for marriage, nor I for that matter. There was so much I wanted to do, and next month I was taking a short trip to Germany and Austria to see for myself what was happening across the border. Life was perfect as it was, and I had no wish to ruin everything.

Cannes sweltered in the midday sun, and palm trees shimmered along the promenade, before the turquoise waters of the Mediterranean. Such a fashionable destination, lively nightlife, and quite the place to be. Long, lazy days in the sun, and long balmy evenings dining on the terrace before slipping into the casino, brushing shoulders with the rich and famous. I didn't mind the casino, but it wasn't my idea of fun, and soon I found I had no desire to place bets using the chips Henri gave me. I opted to spend evenings at the Palm Beach Hotel whiling away the hours over drinks while chatting to Miracca, the manager. He was a remarkable man with so many entertaining stories about rich and famous people he'd encountered during his career. It certainly beat playing poker, and besides, it was fodder for my greedy, journalistic mind.

I'd slipped into life with Henri as smooth as silk. Sometimes, during the night, he groaned and thrashed around in his sleep, radiating heat like a furnace. Last night I laid my hand on his chest while he muttered away, 'Non, non. Fire!' When I asked him about it, he dismissed it as nothing more than a dream. A bad dream indeed, but of what? I knew Henri had served in the Great War, although he never spoke of it. It seemed I had much to learn.

September 1938

Nuremberg breathed beneath an oppressive sail of swastikas, masking the beauty of this ancient old town. Cobbled streets, half-timber houses and stunning architecture. Richard hailed a cab and helped the driver load our luggage. Marie climbed in next to me and as we drove through the busy streets, I thought about how normal everything seemed, aside from the heavy military presence.

That evening in our hotel, we enjoyed a pleasant meal surrounded by German officers before retiring to the cocktail lounge.

'Careful what you say. We're surrounded,' Richard whispered, nudging my arm.

'I have eyes.' I smiled back at him, taking his arm in mine as we found seats in a discreet corner. The lounge was brimming with a party of SS officers, all excited chatter and raucous laughter. More officers arrived, glancing at us as they trotted past to a nearby table. One looked straight into my eyes. He was tall with white-blond hair and striking blue-grey eyes, piercing yet warm. A gentle grin tugged at his mouth, and I swallowed, flashed a half-smile out of politeness.

'Would you look at that?' Marie said. 'Everywhere we go, you attract admirers.' She laughed as she stubbed out her cigarette in the crystal ashtray. I placed a cigarette in my holder, lit up and took a drag, all the while feeling a little vexed by Marie's flippant comment. It wasn't anything to make light of and besides, she ought to realise that the last thing I wanted was the amorous attentions of a Nazi. I exhaled a cloud of smoke, glancing over at the German soldiers. The blond stared back, an intense look in his eyes as he tried and failed to hold my gaze.

'Your dress is gorgeous,' Marie said.

'Thanks. I saw it in Georges. A little pricey. Of course, I shouldn't have bought it, but I couldn't resist. Now I'm just about broke.' I placed my hand on my knee, caressing the midnight-blue silk evening dress. Richard ordered drinks all round. Whisky to begin. The officers at the table behind us burst out laughing. I reached for my whisky and drank it in one fiery gulp.

The resident pianist, splendid in black tails, played 'Raindrops' by Chopin. I'd heard it before and liked it, and somehow, being played here, it seemed rather fitting. It was eloquent, haunting, and sad, and I settled back in my chair, cigarette holder in my white-gloved hand. The German officer continued to stare. My cheeks tingled and my skin crawled like that day years ago when a boy hurled maggots at me for a prank. It was rude to stare; it was annoying, and then my heart sank as he rose from his seat and strode towards me.

'Good evening, Fraulein. I am Obersturmfuhrer Erich Hartmann. May I have this dance?' He held out his hand, a smile playing on his lips.

I was well and truly on the spot, and the old fight and flight mechanism kicked in as my heart raced. After a moment's hesitation, I put down my cigarette and smiled politely. 'Of course.' I took his proffered hand as he led me to the dance floor. To have refused would have offended and drawn attention to myself, something I did not wish. Besides, perhaps I could extract useful information from him, somehow. His hand was light around mine, and he slipped his arm around my waist, drawing me close. I gritted my teeth. I told myself it was role-playing, a means to an end. As we moved around the floor, I caught Richard's eye, who watched us closely. Why couldn't he have asked me to dance?

'Are you in Germany on business, Fraulein?'

'Yes, my friends and I are news correspondents with the Hearst Group in Paris.'

'Ah, my favourite city after Berlin. I have been many times.' He flashed a warm, genuine smile.

He was a handsome man with a gentle voice and kind eyes, but then I remembered the ruthless laws aimed at alienating an entire population. I recalled the inhumanity, haunting images of the Spanish conflict, images I would never forget as long as I lived. Irrespective of how charming he was, he was the enemy, and I couldn't forget that. Once the music ended, his hand slipped from my waist. 'Thank you.' I smiled.

'The pleasure is all mine, Fraulein. I hope to see you again soon.' He bowed, then kissed the back of my hand.

I returned to my seat and swiftly downed the brandy waiting for me. I couldn't help but feel that the wolf was breathing down our necks here, a breath that would huff its way through Europe and further afield as it hunted men, women, and children like prey. But then surely, no one would be that evil, would they?

That evening, after everyone had retired to their rooms, there was a knock at my door.

'Richard. What are you doing still up? Fancy a nightcap?'

'You know me too well.' He breezed in and closed the door.

I opened a bottle of brandy, poured a measure into two glasses. 'Bottoms up.'

He grinned. 'That SS officer had his eye on you all evening. I think he's smitten.'

'Well, the feeling's not mutual.'

He downed the brandy in one and placed the glass down. 'I have it on good authority that there's quite a lot going on behind the scenes here.'

'What do you mean?'

'Well, for starters, the Nazis opened a prison camp at Dachau, and my source says it's for political prisoners. All those the Nazis want out of the way, those unfit for the new Germany. And it's a harsh life once they're in there. I have it on good authority that someone was beaten to death. There was a court case, but Hitler intervened. Regular laws obviously don't apply to concentration camps.'

I thought of Samuel, the Jewish man we'd met in Paris. Thank goodness he got out.

'The Nazis have been boycotting Jewish shops and businesses, expecting all decent Aryan citizens to do the same. They split the population, singled out the Jews and others.'

'What others?'

'The sick, disabled, Romani people, all those who they consider being a drain on society.' He looked down at his feet. 'Anyone who isn't of pure Aryan blood. People vanish, Nance, and no one ever knows where.'

An icy shiver slithered down my spine. Hitler had fought his way into the Reichstag, into power. The Nazi Party had grown and evolved during this time, and for what? Did he want to rule the world?

'Hitler is a gifted orator. He's got the people in the palm of his hand, and he's convinced them that the Jews are responsible for Germany's misfortunes.' Richard poured another brandy. 'You know he wrote a book, right?'

'I think I heard something about it.'

'Well, I haven't read it, but I know a guy who has. It's all in there, what's happening now, and what's coming. Everything Hitler thinks, everything he wants, whether for himself or Germany.'

I had no desire to read such a book. It sounded awful.

'Germany isn't safe anymore. Even American's have been attacked or arrested. The ones I know of were released, but not before being beaten, and then forced to spend the night naked in a cold cell.'

Suddenly I was homesick, and I couldn't wait to return to Paris and Henri.

'Many see his rise as an outstanding achievement, but the thing is, Nance, he's not finished, not by a long shot. I'd guess his plans are far bigger than anyone realises.'

Germany wasn't safe. Thoughts of a life with Henri had germinated, and images bloomed sweet as roses. I'd dared to dream, and at least France was free.

THE NUREMBERG RALLY WAS IMPRESSIVE, with Germany's military in their finest attire, with goose-step marches, torchlight processions, bonfires, and fireworks. This year's affair was called the "Rally of Greater Germany", to reflect the Anschluss. It was unsettling to see the thousands of Germans who had swarmed there to see their Fuhrer. Der Fuhrer had a show to put on, and he did it well. The people waved Nazi flags while larger flags bearing swastikas hung from buildings, tugged by the wind. The German army marched along proudly to the beat of drums as the crowd sang. Overhead, rows of bunting lined the route of the procession. We'd waited for Hitler to arrive for ages and my feet ached and then suddenly the crowd cheered, and a thunderous roar erupted as the people raised their right arms to chant, 'Sieg Heil!'

Hitler made his way up to the stage, a short distance from where I stood. I couldn't understand one word of his speech, but I gazed around at the crowd, noting their glazed eyes. It was as if they were in a trance, completely under his spell. As the speech went on, Hitler became more animated, more emotive, words etched with anger, and at one point, his fist punched the air, and the crowd loved him. I knew no German, nor did my friends. To us, it was simply noise. Men, women, and children, their faces illuminated with a mix of emotion, eyes wide, flushed cheeks from their chants and the cooler autumnal air, arms extended in a Nazi salute to their Fuhrer. An icy flow slipped through me, chilling me down to my bones. They were all possessed, completely taken in, demonised. How could they believe in this cruel tyrant? A chill gripped my shoulders, and I shivered.

When the speech finally ended, the crowd went wild, shrieking 'Sieg Heil' over and over, while performing the Nazi salute. It was unsettling to see the effect this small man had on the people. I supposed they thought Hitler was their saviour, there to raise Germany to the glorious heights of greatness. It was a relief to return to our hotel, away from the masses, and the chanting, and a power-crazed fanatic who seemed intent on creating waves wherever he went. I couldn't stop thinking about what we'd witnessed. It had been a monumental showcase of Germany's military might and the power of National Socialism, and I hoped that the rest of the world was listening, as I feared for our immediate future.

VIENNA SHONE beneath the morning sun, her cobbled streets collecting a few fallen leaves of scarlet and gold. From our hotel, we walked to the Cafe Louvre on the corner of Wipplingerstraße and Renngasse, an infamous haunt for the world's media. Swastika flags flanked official buildings, hotels, and cafes, while posters of Hitler flanked walls, trams, and buses. German soldiers marched everywhere, with some posted at the entrance of official buildings. The Fuhrer would surely be delighted to have conquered the country of his birth.

With the Nuremberg Laws in force, all Jews had been removed from public service, their homes and businesses raided by the SA. Forced to wear the Star of David on their clothing, we heard they were regularly subjected to humiliating acts by the SA or the SS, while the Nazis deported thousands of people to camps.

The cafe brimmed with people sat at marble-topped tables, many tucked behind a copy of the daily newspaper.

'It's the place to be,' Richard said as he dragged out a violin-backed chair for me. 'All journalists flock here.'

As I glanced around, I spotted a table along one wall filled with snacks and pastries. The aroma of coffee wafted in the air. We'd arrived yesterday for a brief stay, curious for a glimpse of Vienna following the Anschluss. 'Most of the foreign correspondents have fled,' Richard said. 'And a number of Austrian reporters who worked for British and American press were thrown into jail.'

The crackle of newspaper pages being turned and the clatter of cups from the kitchen echoed all around. The air roasted with caution amidst hushed conversations and furtive glances, and as I glanced around the room, I wondered who among them might be a spy.

'The head waiter, Gustav rustles up a fabulous schnitzel for only two marks,' Richard said.

'No thanks. Too early for me. Coffee will do nicely.' I had no stomach for food as I soaked up the oppressive air, wondering about the torrent of fascism sweeping through Europe, hoping to God it would never infiltrate France. After breakfast, we ventured outside to see the sights. We took the tram to Belvedere Palace and strolled through the beautiful gardens and woodland. I stood beneath the boughs of an enormous elm, basking in the tranquillity, glittering sunlight filtering through the leaves. Rhododendrons bore ruby-red blooms bordering well-manicured lawns, and a large pond brimmed with water lilies. I walked arm-in-arm with Richard and Marie.

'Thousands of Jews have fled already,' Richard said. 'Of course, the Germans were happy to let them go in exchange for their property and cash.'

'Why is no one willing to oppose Hitler? It's unbelievable how governments step aside when the German troops roll in,' Marie said.

Two SS officers strolled by. 'Good morning, Fräulein,' they said.

Marie smiled and nodded. I drank in fresh air, scents of cut grass, damp, dewy earth, revelling in the Indian summer, autumn nipping at her veil.

Back in town, we strolled through the city streets, slowly making our way to the station. Members of the Sturmabteilung, or SA, dressed in their regimental brown shirts, khaki trousers, and black leather boots stomped everywhere. They had helped Hitler in his rise to power, disrupting the meetings of the opposition and presiding over halls with their ominous presence whenever Hitler gave a speech. There was no escaping the ominous military presence, nor the shouts of 'Sieg Heil!'

A storm trooper on the other side of the road bellowed at a middle-aged man who cowered outside a bookshop. Then, with his whip, he lashed out, and the man doubled over, wincing in pain before scuttling away into the store. Another storm trooper, armed with a pot of paint and a brush, daubed *Juden* in large red letters across the windows of certain stores. Several SA emerged from various shops carrying piles of goods which they dropped into the middle of the street. Richard and I froze. I think we both realised what was happening, so it was no surprise when one brute poured kerosene over the haul and lit a match. Fire erupted, the dancing flames drawing people from nearby. Some laughed, but others shrunk away, their faces grim. In any other country, this would be illegal. The Nazi ideology was moulding a state and its people to a new existence. The adrenaline surged through me, leaving my heart racing and my mouth dry. I wanted to yell out, to cry, to grab the oppressors by the throat and throttle them. But here, we were all oppressed and powerless—for now.

As we headed to the train station, we rounded a corner and came face-to-face with a jeering crowd that stopped us in our tracks. In the road stood several SA next to a large wooden wheel. I looked twice, as I could hardly believe the scene before us. The SA had three men tied to the wheel.

'Juda,' a man yelled out from the crowd. The SA then pushed the wheel forward, with each man going round and round, crying out as they rolled over the cobbles. That must have been excruciating, partially crushing them. 'Christ. What the hell are they doing?'

Richard looked at me, his face creasing into a frown. 'What they're paid to do. To bully, intimidate, and torture.'

I'd never witnessed such cruelty and brutality. Then the storm troopers whipped and lashed each man in turn. My heart pounded, and the breath caught in my throat. 'You wouldn't treat a cat like that!' I glanced around, staring at the onlookers, balling my hands into fists. Some of them gawped, stony-faced, while others laughed and cheered. 'Why doesn't someone do something?' I stepped forward, but Richard grabbed my arm.

'Don't, Nancy.' He gave me a hard stare as he held me back. 'What are you going to do? They'll jump on you next, and the last thing you need is to be hauled off into some cell.'

I turned away and looked on as a storm trooper whipped one of the Jewish men across his back. The whip cracked, and the man winced, pain creasing his face, his eyes. The tormentors had created a spectacle of sick entertainment. A rage roared inside me and my eyes misted over. I bit my lip. 'Strewth, it's positively medieval.'

'Looks like all the stories are true,' Marie said as she clung to Richard's arm.

'Come on.' Richard turned away, dragging me with him.

A fire raged in my belly, and I made myself a pact. If ever the opportunity arose, I would do whatever I could to fight for the rights of innocent people and to fight the Nazis. The winds were changing while whispers of war rolled like wildfire. I hoped it wouldn't come, but if it did, I swore never to bow down to the Nazis. I would fight until my last breath if it came down to it.

At the station, we encountered a jostling crowd of people at the checkpoint.

'Camera please.' The young man spoke in a moderate tone, his face set, eyes narrow.

I exchanged glances with Richard, but the impatient youth grabbed the camera from my hands, opened the shutter door and yanked out the film. I looked on as the storm troopers grabbed one camera after another from fellow journalists. The Nazis were intent on keeping secrets from the world. Well, camera or no camera, I wouldn't be silenced. I'd lost my pictures, but I knew what I would write the minute I left. Hitler had unleashed his poison in Vienna, a slow, agonising poison that dripped into every citizen. How many of them could resist? The world needed to know what was happening, how the

Third Reich had grown, infiltrated neighbouring states, gathered support, spread terror while inflicting brutality. It was inhumane, bloody monstrous, and if I could do anything at all to stop it, then I would. For now, my voice could tell the story and create news for all to see, but deep down, a greater need rooted within me, a need to do more, a desire to act, only I had no idea what I could do. No one knew what lay ahead, but it was clear the dormant beast of Germany was wide awake and ready to roar.

THE NEXT FEW months slipped by. I was spending more time on assignments in southern France, volunteering to cover various stories so I could see Henri. We got along so well and enjoyed our time together. We grew closer, and even Picon approved, often preferring to curl up alongside Henri or between us. Marseille felt right. I loved it there, and Henri's home was very comfortable, but that razor-sharp memory of mine held me back, pricking my conscience when I became too cosy. It didn't help that Henri continued his attempts to persuade me to move to Marseille. He had no idea how hard it was for me to rebuff him each time, but I couldn't risk losing everything I'd worked so hard for, not until I was completely certain.

Chapter 8

SPRING 1939

'Are you going to call a waiter over, or do I need to do it?' I heard myself, bossy, impatient, irritated. Henri seemed on edge. I plucked a cigarette from the open case on the table and tucked it into my cigarette holder.

Henri reached for his gold lighter. 'I will summon the waiter, but first, there is something I wish to ask.'

I placed the menu back on the table, and, without raising my head, opened my eyes wide to gaze up at him, noticing how his left hand delved into his jacket pocket, lingering for several seconds. This suave, confident, sophisticated millionaire suddenly appeared nervous and out of sorts.

'What?' I pursed my lips and readied myself for his usual plea to move to Marseille again. 'I'm starving, Henri.'

'Nancy, you are the most infuriating woman in the world.' His eyes flared with a mix of annoyance and amusement as they bored into mine. 'You are also the most beautiful, elegant creature to walk the earth and I, for some mystical reason, am utterly lost without you.' His hand emerged from his suit pocket, clutching a small, black velvet box, which he gently set on the table. 'Nancy, I love you. Will you do me the honour of becoming my wife?'

I was in the middle of savouring a mouthful of red wine, and a

little slipped down the wrong way, forcing me to cough. A whirl-
wind of thoughts hurtled through my mind while my heart
drummed in my ears as he opened the lid. There sat the plumpest
diamond ring which he plucked from its velour bed and gestured for
my hand.

Aware of my gaping mouth, I blew out a breath, took a drag on my
cigarette, forcing as much vapour into my lungs, hungry for advice. I
longed to say yes. We had common interests and got on so well. We
were a perfect match, but as for marriage. My mind trailed back to my
parents. Their union didn't last, and I'd suffered the fallout—we had
all suffered. Could Henri be faithful? To marry and discover infidelity
was too wounding a prospect.

'Well, what do you think? Marry me, Nancy.' His words snapped
me back to the present moment, and I searched his eyes, that swam
with warmth and soul. He loved me, but marriage? His parents didn't
approve of me and probably assumed I was a gold digger. A warm
glow spread from my neck to my cheeks, and I blew out a breath,
desperate for fresh air. I shuffled in my chair. The hard wooden back
bulged and pummelled my spine. 'I'm not sure, Henri.' The smile fell
from his lips. I glanced around the room, caught sight of the waiter at
another table, and raised my hand. He acknowledged with a nod,
making haste to our table. 'Brandy, please, a double.' Henri's sharp
intake of breath, a hint of irritation.

The waiter returned, and I plucked the glass from the silver tray
before the young man set it down on the table. The brandy slid down
in one fiery mouthful. 'Are you actually serious? You keep a different
girl for each day of the week, sometimes two or three. You've never
talked about marriage before.'

'Nancy, I have given up other women. There is only room for you
in my life.'

Was there indeed? I knew for a fact he was spotted dining out with
a female companion only last week. 'You say that, but what about next
week when I can't go out to dinner because I'm away on an assignment? Then who will you call? You hate dining alone.' His brow
furrowed, a downcast expression settling on his face. I wanted to

believe him, truly. Then I assumed Mum believed in Dad all those years ago only to have her 'happy ever after' stolen.

'A leopard can't change its spots.'

Henri leaned back in his seat and, with a shake of his head, snatched a cigarette from his case and lit up, inhaling deeply before blowing out a string of smoke rings. 'All right, Nancy. I can see that you are not yet ready, and I am a little impetuous. But I will show you, you will see.' His mouth twitched to form that familiar, confident smile of his. Something was different about him, but how sincere was he? As soon as I returned to Paris, he would call one of his regular 'girl-friends' and ask her out to dinner.

He reached across the table and took my hand in his. A soothing warmth enveloped my skin and flowed like silk over my wrist and forearm. My pulse raced. I sighed. I was in love and wanted no one but Henri, yet the doubts flowed and ebbed in an uncertain sea, my past never far from the shore. He was offering me a life with him, and love, but how could I be sure it was real? My heart whispered to accept, but the voice in my head said I should wait. Marriage was too huge a commitment to make a mistake.

May 1939

Two weeks had dragged by, and we hadn't spoken. Not a word, until yesterday. It was a silence that communicated Henri's disappointment. Then the rain came, moody clouds washing the sky grey. Darkness blighted my days, growing darker still when night fell with an absent moon. And I despised the ache in my chest, wondering how he was, and, more importantly, who he was with, the stream of thoughts plaguing me night and day. Why did life have to be so damn compli-cated? Marriage? Talk about a surprise! From Paris, I'd carved out a new life, and it was exciting, and I was free, captain of my destiny. I worked hard, and I played hard, although not as hard as Henri. He was such a catch as my friends kept telling me, but I wasn't interested in his fortune. How could Henri ever promise to be faithful? He said he wished to take care of me, but I'd managed perfectly well by myself since leaving home. Marriage would lead to a different life. Was I ready to relinquish old for new? If things didn't work out, I'd have to start again from scratch, the thought of which filled me with dread. I reached for my glass and downed the last drop of brandy, but nothing would relieve the burning ache in my throat, the tightness in my stomach. When Henri finally telephoned, he asked me once more to marry him. 'I need more time, Henri,' I said. Afterwards, his voice grew downcast, and I sensed his patience was waning. I was scared and there were no guarantees in love. He invited me to dinner, and I realised he would expect an answer soon. It was time to make a choice.

~

VERDUN'S BUSTLED WITH DINERS, and a mix of perfume and sweat mingled with the humid evening air. I wore a loose-fitting navy dress along with red wedge-heeled espadrilles. Henri was at the bar downing brandy by the look of it, and then another.

'Bonjour,' I said as I placed my purse on the bar. 'Sorry I'm late.' His eyes twinkled rich hazel flecked with emerald and gold.

'Bonjour, Nancy. It is fashionable for a lady to be late, is it not?' He smiled, brushed my hand with his lips. 'Come, the table awaits.' Henri placed his hand on the small of my back as he guided me to the furthest corner of the restaurant, pulling out my chair. 'Nancy, do you remember some weeks ago when I turned up in Paris?'

'Yes, I wasn't expecting you then, but it was a lovely surprise all the same.'

'Well, I found you surrounded by men. Barely a woman in sight except for you, of course.' He leaned back in his chair and sighed. 'Nancy, I worry about you. I don't like to think of you all alone in Paris, living in such a cramped apartment.'

'I'm not alone. Work and friends keep me busy. Besides, I love my home.'

He shook his head. 'That's what I'm getting at. Your friends. Your male friends in particular.'

His brow furrowed and he pursed his lips. Oh! Of all the people,

I'd never have guessed he would succumb to the green-eyed monster. 'Henri, you're jealous.' I fought the smile that tugged at my mouth, but it was futile.

'Nancy, please don't mock me.' A crestfallen look crept over his face. 'And that American fellow. You are always dancing with him. Do you prefer him over me? Is it because he is younger? Perhaps I am too old for you.' He shook his head and huffed out a sigh.

I hadn't seen this side of him before. He looked quite wounded. His stern eyes, unblinking, with a hardness that paled away to a softer hue, his vulnerability revealed. 'Henri, my friends are simply friends. I'm not attracted to Richard or anyone else. We're colleagues.'

'It is not right for you to surround yourself with these men. Think of your reputation.'

A fire flared within me. 'Bugger my reputation.' I gritted my teeth and leaned back in my chair. 'You don't seem to realise that I'm doing nothing wrong. Those men are my friends. Besides, is it right for you to run around with a different woman every night?' I wondered how many marriage proposals he'd issued so far. I wasn't stupid. My mother's words drifted back. 'You'll never amount to anything, my girl.' My heart lurched; a lump tightened in my throat as tears pricked my eyes. I was approaching twenty-seven, and all too soon I'd be thirty. Then what? All the doubts and fears joined forces. Would I allow them to win? Did they make sense? If I rejected him again, it would be the finish, and I'd be alone. The thought of a life without Henri scared me. I'd given him my heart, my soul, and we were bound by an invisible, sacred bond. Life with him smelled of roses and champagne, of cedarwood cologne, and his warmth against me as I laid in his arms was all I needed to know how safe and loved I was.

'Nancy, I love you. What more can I say to convince you?' Henri exhaled a long breath and slouched down in his seat, a look of dejection shadowing his face. 'There has never been anyone like you. You are so special to me. I do not want anyone else.'

'I don't want to be a kept woman, Henri. Besides, I have my work, and I rather like it. And I'm not a fool either.'

'Nannie, I love you. Marry me. Let me look after you, although as much as I hate to admit it, you are probably the only woman I have ever known who could take on the entire world and win.' He reached across the table and took my hand in his, running his thumb over my wrist. 'You do not need to be looked after, but, if you will allow it, I would like to be at your side, always. Marry me, Nancy.' He took the ring box from his jacket pocket, opened the lid and set it on the table.

The same ring, but what a beaut! As I gazed at the plump sparkling diamond, my heart drummed, and the breath caught in my throat. 'Tell me you're sure, Henri. That I'm enough for you.'

'Nannie.' He reached across and took my hands in his. 'I am sure. Nannie, I will never hurt you and wish only to love you if you will allow it.'

The blood surged through my veins as I gazed into his eyes. I loved him, body and soul, and my heart whispered his words were true. All this time, I'd been under the illusion that I was simply another of his companions, a mere trophy. I gazed into his eyes. 'Oui.' The words slipped out, and Henri beamed as he slipped the ring on my finger.

Chapter 9
JUNE 1939

'The Jews have nowhere to run, and yet still they come in their droves.' Marie puffed on the cigarette, her cheeks sucking in, chiselling hollows as she momentarily closed her eyes.

'They'll come here too, before long.' I noticed the dart of fear in her eyes, which she quickly blinked away. 'Remember Vienna and Nuremberg? The people at the rally were all possessed. It was creepy.' I finished the last of my croissant and sipped my coffee as I thought about their plight. I could only imagine being in their shoes, torn between fleeing into the unknown or staying in your home, hoping that all would be well. Suffering such mistreatment, denied your existence. People, stripped of their rights, their lives peeled away one layer at a time. The world had tilted on its axis.

The café seemed quiet that morning. I'd only recently returned from my holiday with Henri and was seeing to my affairs here. So much was changing. After our engagement, Henri asked me to live with him. I'd given in my notice at work, given up my apartment, packed my belongings, and would be on route to Marseille shortly. Soon I'd be the wife of a wealthy industrialist, joining one of the more prominent families in Marseille. But while my life seemed settled, world affairs were not.

～

THE WAR in Spain ended in April, with around a million people killed, and General Franco seized power. It now seemed inevitable that war would come. The people of France and Paris, in particular, put on a front. Many hoped it would not transpire, while a growing number believed it was simply a matter of time. The German army advanced through Europe, and nothing and no one seemed willing or able to stop it. Would France be any different? As Men received their call-up, the French Government proclaimed the army would protect us. Talk of evacuation had already begun, but the women of Paris were resolute. 'It will not come to that,' one young woman said to me the other day, but older women, those who'd lived through the Great War, thought differently. They had lost sons and husbands. They remembered the worst. Yes, we'd won that war, but things were different now. Germany had been building its defences for some while now. Some said it was too little too late for France.

'So, how are the wedding plans going?' Marie broke my reverie.

'Well, we're thinking of setting a date for next spring.'

'Get a move on. Spring 1940 might be a little too late, don't you think?'

Her words exploded in my head like a rocket. Henri was still young enough to serve, just. Dread sank into me, cold and weighted. Paris hummed beyond my windows, her natural rhythm sailing across the warm, humid August breeze. The last vestiges of sunlight mixed with an azure sky, creating a rich palette of colour; pink, lilac, orange, and red seeped into the sky, deepening as the sun dipped further on the horizon. 'Perhaps you're right. I'm looking forward to my mini spa break at Champneys.' I wasn't sure why, but I'd suddenly had an over-whelming urge to visit London one last time, so when I heard about Champneys last month, it seemed the perfect opportunity.

'Ooh, what luxury.' Marie sighed.

'Come with me. It'll be fun.' Champneys ran a three-week slim-ming course at Tring, which was all the rage in France. Life had grown too comfortable. I glanced down at my stomach, aware of the snug fit of my skirt as it contended with more than several unwelcome pounds.

'I'd love nothing more, but work beckons. You know how it is, Nancy.' She shot me a wistful look. 'And Henri doesn't mind?'

'He's been so lovely, although he doesn't want me to go—says he'll miss me too much.' I took a drag of my cigarette. 'There's so much unrest at the moment, but he assured me it's safe to travel.' As I listened to my own words, I couldn't help but feel a little unnerved, especially as Belgium and the Netherlands were now mobilising their troops. The threat of war had hung in the air for a while, and everyone simply carried on. What else could we do?

AT FIRST, life in Marseille felt more like a holiday. Staff managed Henri's household. Imagine. I didn't have to lift a finger. It was all shopping, fine dining, and after-dinner drinks or time spent at the casino, one of Henri's favourite places. My new life was one of great privilege and took no time at all in getting used to, but I knew I'd never forget my roots. Then, all too soon, news of our engagement reached Henri's family. They were polite, but there was an underlying tension that simmered beneath the surface every time we met. Fortunately, that wasn't very often. Henri then asked me to find a suitable apartment for our first home together. 'Choose the best in Marseille,' he said. And so, I set myself a new mission and arranged a tonne of viewings while Henri worked. His father had recently bought a battleship to sell as scrap iron, but then the market crashed, and the business suffered serious financial losses. Henri now worked long hours to help repair the damage, determined to reduce losses.

From the moment I glanced at the details of the large apartment at the top of La Canebière, I felt a warm rush through my soul. Situated on a hill, on the top floor of a luxury block of apartments, it commanded the finest views over Marseille. On one side lay the harbour, and on the other, the zoological gardens, filled with rare and exotic animals.

As I wandered through the empty home, my heels clattering across parquet floors, I imagined the luxurious feel of Persian rugs beneath my feet while I placed chairs, tables, and lamps. I imagined sitting opposite Henri as we dined, candles flickering in the gentle evening breeze, and afterwards, drinks in the living room, gramophone music playing in the background. Perhaps we might dance, or I would sit curled up by his feet, in front of a cosy fire on a chilly night—just the two of us, together, always. I smiled to myself, aware that the estate agent was talking away to me, doing his utmost to sell the apartment, while I daydreamed.

I pushed open the door to the bathroom and glanced around. It was a substantial size, a little bland, with fresh white paint on the walls, but I could make improvements. The large window gave a delightful vista of the Vieux Port. Boats of various shapes and sizes filled the harbour, bobbing up and down with the beating heart of the ocean. I turned on my heel and flicked a glance at the grand white enamel bathtub which presided in the middle of the floor, perched on gold claw feet. It was the perfect place to bathe while admiring the view outside. From the main bedroom, there was a view that stretched towards the hillier side of Marseille, looking out over the garden of Palais Longchamp and the zoo, with mountain ranges rising in the distance, framing the skyline.

The next day, Henri met me during his lunch hour for a second viewing. I watched as he strolled through every room, resolute, calm, standing at all the windows, taking in the views. The neutral expression on his face perplexed me, as I couldn't decide whether he was pleased or disappointed. Finally, he turned to me and smiled. 'C'est parfait.'

'Phew! You had me worried. I thought you didn't like it.'

'Tell them we will take it right away.' Henri slipped his arms around my waist and leaned in for a kiss before lifting and twirling me round in his arms, his smile widening as he laughed.

'Tomorrow, we will go shopping for furniture, ma chérie. We have much to do.'

July 1939

My feet throbbed from hours of shopping and finally Henri and I agreed on a fine, large, oak dining table with matching chairs, and an exquisite monogrammed Sevres fine china dinner set along with the finest crystal glasses. 'We want the best for our dinner parties, Nannie,' Henri said.

I'd never hosted formal dinner parties in my life, and my mouth ran dry; I swallowed. The last thing I wanted was to let Henri down. My face must have conveyed my concerns as he pulled me to him and kissed my forehead.

'Do not worry. We will have a cook and other help. I do not expect you to do everything. You will find your way, just as you always do.'

THE BLAZING sun poured in greedily through the windows. The new drapes I'd chosen just moments earlier would look beautiful. Madame Cheval had just left, taking her sample of fabrics with her. Two hours of pouring over them, but I wanted the finest for impact. After all, this was our first home together. We'd recently hired help, a housekeeper for cooking and a young girl who already had some experience in service. She was very sweet and capable, or so it seemed. Either way, I was happy, and Henri was pleased, as we looked forward to moving in together.

Many British bombers had flown over Marseille yesterday, before returning to England. The news hailed it as a demonstration of Britain's air power. It seemed tensions were increasing. Japan was causing trouble in China, and Britain had recently conducted an air raid test. But what surprised me more than the ongoing political affairs was the opinions of our friends and neighbours. They made comments such as, 'Oh, France will not be caught up in any war,' citing the Maginot Line. Here, the French just got on with life without a care, but in Paris one publication cited the atmosphere there as 'panicky'. The government had requisitioned many private cars, forcing people to rely on public transport or bicycles. Perhaps it was the journalist in me, but I couldn't let go of the feeling of unease that swelled by the day. I didn't know what was around the corner, but I'd always sensed that Hitler would cause trouble for France. All anyone could hope was that France was prepared to deal with the Fuhrer. In the meantime, I took a leaf out of their book and got on with life, making a home with Henri, making wedding plans. La joie de vivre.

1 September 1939

 Germans Invade and Bomb Poland. Britain Mobilises.

I took the night ferry—a boat train—from the Gare du Nord in Paris and travelled to London, arriving 2 September. While France buried her head against the imminent threat of war, there was no mistaking the volatile air in London. After checking in at the Strand Palace Hotel, I telephoned Champneys resort at Tring, only to discover they had made an error with my booking and made it for October. Initially disappointed, I decided to make the most of my trip and indulge in some shopping.

THE NEXT DAY, I disembarked from my train at Waterloo to a sea of khaki. The platform bristled with soldiers waiting, kitbags at their feet, saying their farewells to loved ones. 'What's going on?' I asked a guard.

'War, miss. We're going to war. Again! Bleeding Hitler.' He shuffled off, shaking his head, muttering beneath his breath.

It was 3 September. As I glanced around, I spotted a newspaper boy with a pile of papers in his arms, crying out, 'Read all about it!' I glimpsed the headline: *Britain At War with Germany*. My heart sank. Oh, Henri. What about France? I had to return, and fast. Chamberlain's words rang in my ears, 'Peace in our time.' Even France's premier,

Edouard Daladier, had agreed with Chamberlain and agreed to Hitler's demands at the time in Munich 1938 to achieve this peace. What piffle and utter madness. The Fuhrer wouldn't stop until he had conquered the world.

THE NEXT DAY, I received two telegrams. The first from Henri, urging me to return home, and the second from our friend, Emma, begging me to bring her daughter, Micheline, home from a boarding school in Surrey. My first thought was that the girl might be safer here in England, but then I recalled how Micheline had complained of convent life and of how miserable she was at school. As I weighed up the situation, I felt obliged to return her safely home. On my way out that morning, the hotel receptionist called me over and handed me a compact cardboard box.

'It is a gas mask,' she said. 'They have issued everyone with one, madam.'

The moment I held it, a chill zipped through me and I hoped I would never have to use it.

MY MISSION TO collect Micheline did not go as smoothly as I'd expected. The Mother Superior insisted on permission from the girl's mother, which took a further three days while I sent a telegram and waited for the reply. Then, back in London, we queued every day for four days at the French consulate for travel permits. Meanwhile, a blackout was already in force, and nights in the city reminded me of the countryside: no street lights, not a chink of light peeping from windows. Even car headlights wore covers to dim them. People carried gas masks everywhere, fearful of gas attacks, while vast walls of sandbags guarded the entrances of many prominent buildings and hotels. It was a relief when we finally reached the ferry port.

'Are you certain you want to travel to France, miss?' The middle-aged customs officer seemed perplexed.

'Absolutely. It's my home.' I stared into his eyes, touched by the flash of concern there.

'I must tell you that if you sail today, you will not be coming back. You understand that, don't you?'

I sighed. 'Yes, that's okay.'

'But you're not French, and we're at war now, and if you don't mind me saying, you're going to be a bit too close for comfort to Jerry, if you ask me.' He raised his eyebrows and sighed, his ruddy cheeks turning a deeper shade of scarlet as he rubbed his smooth chin.

'I understand perfectly. I will be fine, I assure you.' He must have served in the Great War, given his age. My mind suddenly flashed to my brother, Stanley, serving with the navy. He'd seen the back of one war only to be hurled into another. An icy shiver ricocheted down my spine.

'Well then, I wish you the very best of luck, miss.'

I took our papers from him, grasped Micheline's hand and strolled onto the ferry. She was an absolute gem, no trouble at all, and so polite.

'Nancy, that man at the port did not wish us to travel.' Micheline gazed at me; her blue eyes wide, fearful.

I heaved in a breath of briny air, waves slapping against the boat. 'It's all right. We'll soon be home.'

Micheline gazed towards the diminishing mainland. 'We will be safe in France, won't we?'

Safe. Visions of the Nazis in Berlin sailed into my mind. I squeezed her hand. 'Yes, of course we shall. The war is a long way from us. It will all be fine, you'll see.' I had a bad feeling, so I turned my thoughts to Henri, waiting for me at home.

Night had snuffed out the setting sun, and the captain ordered all lights to be extinguished. Even smoking was banned in case the Germans spotted the glow of a cigarette butt at sea. The last thing we needed was to be torpedoed.

'I hate the dark,' Micheline said, stifling a yawn.

'France will be a beacon of light, you'll see.' I slipped my arm around the girl's shoulders as we stood on the deck, watching the last piece of England slip into the night behind us, a sickle moon eclipsed by wispy cloud. Micheline shivered against my side, probably more of fear than of cold, for it was still fairly mild. The waves roared, spraying the deck, and we wandered away to find a seat inside. Soon, Micheline was leaning heavily against me, her weight warm at my side, eyes closed. Eventually, land loomed ahead, tiny lights blinking in the darkness and a beam of white light from the lighthouse, guiding us into port. Boulogne-sur-Mer. As we docked, I looked on as cars drove along the main street, lights blazing, and music drifted towards us carried on the breeze. I turned to Micheline and flashed a smile, which gave way to laughter, more so with relief than anything else.

'Voila, La France,' Micheline said, a warm smile washing the tension from her pretty face as she gazed all around.

I drank in the scene. Even by night, France was illuminating in her beauty and peace slipped over me for the first time since setting sail. Home. Micheline threw her arms around me, hugging me tight, and we both carried on laughing, tears soaking my cheeks. The train station heaved with troops, and we pushed past bulky kit bags and hordes of men. We boarded a train for the Riviera. I would see that Micheline got to Cannes before I returned to Marseille. Thoughts rushed through my mind; my stomach churned. What if Henri was called up? Both Britain and France were readying for war, and with Germany's forces, it was certain to be a bloody battle. It was best to put all such thoughts aside. Besides, I had a wedding to plan and a rosy future to look forward to as Henri's wife. I smiled; despite the dire situation we were all caught within.

My body felt like lead as I walked the short distance home from the station, the sun a golden fiery globe rising from her aura of salmon pink and orange above the mountains in the east. The gulls welcomed me, their ravenous, wistful cry scything through the sleepy, humid air. Henri rushed towards me as I pushed open the door, engulfing me in his arms, squeezing me so tight I could barely breathe. His face was scratchy on mine, a shadow of whiskers evidence of a rough night.

His face fell as I told him about our journey home, especially the sea voyage. 'Nannie, I will never let you go again,' he said. 'I could have lost you.' Wrapping his arms around me, he held me tight.

I felt like I was going to throw up, drained, yet inside I bubbled like a bottle of champagne. Even so, I couldn't help feeling a little flippant about my overseas adventure. Once again, luck had prevailed. Our housekeeper, Madame Dumont, flitted around the kitchen, making fresh coffee and warming croissants for breakfast. Her rosy cheeks grew rosier as she worked, and a strand of grey hair worked loose from its pins to fall down over her left ear.

'Please don't bother for me,' I said, stifling a yawn.

'Nannie, you must eat.' Henri pulled out a chair at the table.

'Oh, Madame Fiocca. Such a terrible ordeal you have had. You need food. We don't want you falling ill.' Madame Dumont set a cup of coffee on the table, then smoothed her white apron, her hand resting on her rotund stomach.

I was so worn out and a little nauseous, with no energy to protest further, so I sipped the coffee and bit off a mouthful of warm croissant, sweet, flaky pastry with a rich buttery flavour teasing my taste buds, gradually quelling the sickness.

'We must marry as soon as possible,' Henri said, pressing his forehead to mine. 'I do not know how much time I have before...' His words trailed off.

I knew what he meant. The worst was happening, and people could no longer close their eyes or ears to the will of the German war machine. 'Yes,' I agreed. 'We must all be ready.'

Chapter 10
MARSEILLE. 1939

On the day Russia attacked Finland, Henri and I married. It was a glorious Thursday as we said, 'I do,' and the Red Army marched across the Soviet-Finnish border. The Soviets bombed Helsinki, lives were lost or changed irrevocably, and the stain of war seeped further into Europe. Since war began, Germany had beaten Poland into capitulation, Japan was still at war with China, and French forces had invaded Saarland in Germany. U-boats preyed on Allied ships, sinking the first British destroyer, HMS Royal Oak, in Scapa Flow just a couple of weeks ago. Meanwhile, the Luftwaffe had launched its first airstrike on Britain on 16 October, targeting ships in the Firth of Forth.

We had a simple ceremony at the Town Hall at three o'clock. I was twenty-seven, and Henri was thirteen years older, but I didn't care. My wedding dress of black silk was exquisite, embroidered with pink orchids. My heart drummed so violently in my chest I was sure everyone could see, but when Henri took my hand, I calmed a little, and as he slipped the gold band on my finger, my vision swam, a thread of tears slipping down one cheek. At the end of the ceremony, I grasped Henri's hand as we smiled for our guests and photographs, before taking a chauffeur-driven limousine to the reception at L' Hôtel Louvre et Paix. Henri had even taken it upon himself to invite some of my friends from Paris, which was the most wonderful surprise, and I was so pleased that Marie was there. I'd missed her. Emma and Emmanuel were also there, along with Micheline.

The wedding had almost killed Henri's father, the strain on his face visible on our big day. Still, I brushed it off, determined it wouldn't bother me. Henri was as prepared as ever for dealing with his family and had instructed the barmen and waiters to spike their drinks and spread a little joy. By the middle of the wedding reception, my in-laws were looking quite merry and heartily engaging in the big event, chatting, laughing, and dancing along with everyone else. The food was incredible. Marius, a well-appointed chef and his team, received much applause from our guests with every course they served. No expense was spared, with ingredients sourced from all over France, and such thought and detail had gone into the presentation of the food.

The latest news found its way into the dinner chat, with guest's adamant that the Maginot Line would save France. There simply was no getting away from it. After eating, Micheline and I vanished for a few moments as we grabbed the gas masks we had brought back from England. I'd had quite a lot to drink already, and the sight of Micheline wearing the hideous thing set me off with a fit of the giggles. I laughed so much she had to help pull mine on, taking care not to snag my hair. Our guests took one look at us and fell about laughing.

'Let me try,' Emma said, springing up from her seat. After that, our guests passed the gas masks around the room, with the photographer happily snapping pictures of the spectacle.

WE HONEYMOONED IN CANNES, having booked in at the Martinez. Our room was beautiful, a corner suite that looked out across the sea and the port on one side and the mountains on the other. The weather was perfect: dry, sunny, not too warm with a refreshing cool breeze. Henri certainly immersed me in the good life, and it was such a blessing and a contrast to being as poor as a church mouse. My old life was well and truly behind me. All the doubts I'd harboured vanished as Henri lavished me with love and care.

'We will have such a good life, Nannie,' he said as he slipped his arm around me.

The sand was cool and grainy-soft beneath my feet as we sat on the beach to watch the sunrise. 'If only it could always be like this,' I said. The war was a wolf, snapping at our heels.

'But of course.' Henri kissed the tip of my nose. 'Why would it not, ma chérie? Tout ira bien.'

Everything will be fine. I sat up and studied his face. Tanned olive skin, warm eyes, wise, with a shy spark of mischief. Henri was a good man, and I leaned in and kissed him. The sun climbed higher, dyeing wispy cirrus clouds pink, orange, and gold, and I wondered just how long Henri's version of 'fine' would last.

BACK IN MARSEILLE, I settled into married life, determined to do all I could for Henri while he showered me with gifts, affection, and anything my heart desired, no expense spared. It would soon be Christmas, and we were determined to have a wonderful end to the year and worry about what might come later. Friends had received their papers, and I sensed it was only a matter of time for Henri. There were no bombing raids, no invading Germans. They called this 'le drole de guerre'—the phoney war.

I concentrated on improving my culinary skills to distract myself from all the uncertainty. Not that I was clueless, but my range was basic, and I wished to broaden my repertoire, stretch my culinary muscles and venture into French cuisine with all of my heart. The infamous Provençale dish bouillabaisse continued to elude me, despite a couple of efforts to make it. Our housekeeper had cooked it just the other evening as it was Henri's favourite dish, and I wished to master it. Fortunately, with Henri's connections, help was close at hand. Pepe Caillat, the master of all the great chefs of Marseille, had agreed to take me under his wing and show me the ropes that very day and, by hell's teeth, I was determined to make Henri proud.

As I observed Pepe at work in his kitchen, Henri's stories drifted in my head. 'It is said that bouillabaisse was first made by the ancient Greeks, who founded Marseille around 600 BC. And it is also said that Venus fed this dish to Vulcan, her husband.' I smiled, and my pulse raced as I recalled how Henri had then scooped me up in his arms and kissed me with such passion in the Vieux Port beneath a twilight sky, the ocean slapping the harbour wall behind us.

Pepe's voice broke my reverie. 'The secret to a wonderful bouillabaisse, my dear, is more than just ingredients. The secret lies in the herbs and spices and in the cooking.' Pepe prepared the fish—a variety of seafood, including scorpionfish, shellfish, sea urchins, mussels, spider crab, and lobster.

A variety of vegetables lay spread out on the scrubbed pine bench as I peeled potatoes, leeks, onions, tomatoes, celery, garlic, not to mention herbs. Once I had completed the spuds, I moved on to the rest, rinsing leeks in running water, dried earth running brown into the white ceramic sink. Next, I peeled and sliced the onions, tears falling down my cheeks. Bouillabaisse, I learned, was a simple, filling dish, often cooked by local fishermen in the port of Marseille. Simple? There was so much preparation, so many ingredients, and it was time-consuming. I reached for the herbs, chopped a bulb of fennel, a rich bouquet of aniseed filling my lungs, sweet, reminiscent of liquorice. Next, scarlet threads of saffron, their sweet fragrance of flowers and honey evoking my senses. 'The Romans bathed in saffron-infused baths in Imperial Rome,' Henri had told me, as he'd sprinkled a little into my bathwater one evening. A smile toyed with my mouth, so I pressed my lips together, aware of the scrutiny of my teacher.

'One of the key ingredients,' Pepe stressed, 'is rascasse—the scorpionfish. They live in the coral reefs close to the shore.' He grasped a bunch of thyme in his fist, lifted it to his nose, and inhaled deeply. 'And herbs, spices.' He held his hand under my nose, the lemony scent intoxicating. 'The lemon is intense. It is not enough to add the basic ingredients. Cooking is a fine art. Does an artist paint with only three or four basic colours separately? Non! He mixes the colours; he creates his palette. Now you must create yours.' Pepe smiled, as if to reassure me. 'Be bold, Madame Fiocca, be daring. It is all within you.'

He nodded approvingly. Pepe made it sound so simple and made perfect sense, but I realised it was going to take practice. The first time I'd served the stew to Henri, his nose had wrinkled up, his face twisting somewhat and then, after swallowing the first mouthful, he'd reached for his wine and drank the entire glass. At least I didn't mind rolling up my sleeves. Hard work wasn't a chore, and if perseverance was the key, then I had a bucketful.

'Add the fish one at a time,' Pepe instructed, 'then bring to the boil.'

And this wasn't just any fish stew. Oh no. And that's down to the serving, as I soon learned. You see, in Marseille, they serve the broth first on a soup plate with sliced bread and rouille, then you serve the fish separately on a large platter. A glance at the clock told me it was four in the afternoon. Henri would be home soon, and I couldn't wait to tell him about my day.

My cooking lessons paid off when, just a short time later, my father-in-law asked me to prepare bouillabaisse for a luncheon party to which the famous actor and singer, Maurice Chevalier, was to attend along with many prominent guests. He was a charming, kind man, and I listened as he spoke with Henri about the Great War. Maurice, wounded in battle, was captured by the Germans and spent two years in a camp where fellow British prisoners taught him English. The event was a complete success, and Maurice couldn't believe that an Australian had cooked the main course. That was praise enough, although I was happy to see my father-in-law singing my praises, something I thought I'd never see.

January 1940

The Soviets, pushed back by the Finnish, retaliated with fierce air attacks. It was one of the coldest winters on record, with temperatures plunging all across Europe. I was glad of the warmer climate of southern France as I strolled through the Vieux Port, past lovers arm in arm, past bars and cafes which bristled with locals and tourists alike drinking at tables out in the sun. Local fisherman lined the harbour, with crates of the freshest catch at their side, calling out to people as they passed. Christmas had been wonderful. We'd spent the holidays at our cabin in the Alps, with a couple of friends. Henri had received his call-up papers days before, and we were determined not to let that cloud our celebrations. The drive home, however, had been a little gloomy, knowing what we were returning to, wondering how much time we had left. Whenever Henri went away on business, I became desolate. It was as if I needed to spend every second with him as the clock was ticking. As well as worrying about the war and his call-up, I'd realised that married life, and life as the wife of a wealthy man, was one of indulgence and luxury, a far cry from my childhood, and, as a pampered socialite I was sure I ought to have felt settled.

Well, I was happy, but now it was as if my only purpose was to be there for my husband. I'd given up work at Henri's request, and I was a good wife and dinner party host. I did as other French wives did, indulged in the finest couture, daily rounds of manicures, visits to beauty salons, hair salons, dress salons, restaurants, and the cinema. Mornings were lazy. Claire, my maid, would bring me breakfast in bed, and I'd lie reading the daily newspaper with Picon beside me, feeding him a little croissant, which he adored. Then, around ten, I'd take a bath, with a glass of champagne as I read a book, occasionally glancing up to admire the view of the harbour. Sometimes the days were long, passing slowly, and sometimes, when Henri was home, they flew. Madame Dumont was a marvellous cook, and she kept Claire in check. The girl was only nineteen and unmarried, but as Madame Dumont said, 'she was a good Catholic girl who lived at home with her parents.' Claire's gentle nature appealed to me and, like our housekeeper, she didn't indulge in gossip.

Henri and I attended many farewell parties every other night as more men prepared to leave for the Front. 'Soon, it will be my turn,' he said.

I tried to be stoic for his sake. 'We'll worry about it when the time comes,' I said. But all too soon, on a cool morning in March, the time came, and my heart dived. He was to report for service in two weeks. It was Henri who was now stoic and brave, gently reminding me of his service in the Great War. 'Do not worry, Nannie. We beat them the first time, and we will do it again.'

'Of course you will,' I said, trying desperately to believe him, a burgeoning ache in my heart. I swallowed, gazing out across the harbour, watching the gulls as they swooped and soared, listening to their cry, which mimicked the anguish I carried inside. The cry I bound tightly within, the cry I'd shield from Henri, who all too soon would leave. I couldn't sit at home, wondering where he was, if he was warm at night, if he was hungry or alive. I clenched my fists. Our perfect life was to be torn apart after such a short time. I gritted my teeth. I knew what I had to do, and it didn't involve waiting at home for news from the Front like other wives.

HENRI SAT in his leather armchair by the roaring fire, sipping his brandy while I curled up on the hearthrug at his feet, gazing at forked flames, feeling the warmth colour my cheeks. 'I've been thinking about what I should do when you leave for the Front.'

'What do you mean? You will be here, safe.'

I bit my lip. 'I want to go to the Front.'

'What? Do not be ridiculous.' Henri threw his hands up in the air, gesticulating, his eyes wide.

'I thought I could be an ambulance driver and with my nurse training, I'll be useful.' And needed, I thought.

'It is out of the question. You are my wife and a battlefield is no place for a woman.' He drained the last of the brandy in one gulp, setting the crystal glass down on the mahogany table. 'Anyway, you know as well as I that France barely has enough ambulances. They are requisitioning buses now. God help us.' He shook his head, running a hand through his hair.

'Henri, we are at war with Germany. Look at the Luftwaffe and the damage they did in Spain. That's coming here.' He sprang up and strode across to the drinks cabinet for another brandy. 'Give me one of the company's trucks and kit it out as an ambulance.' I waited with bated breath, irritated by his comment about women and war.

'But you are not thinking, Nannie. You do not drive.'

'Then teach me. You know I'm a quick learner, and adaptable.' I knew nursing wasn't right for me, but I had got on with it, and later, I learned the tricks of the newspaper trade. As Shakespeare once said, 'All the world's a stage, and all the men and women merely players', and I could act. We all had our roles to play, and it was amazing what one could do when faced with adversity.

Henri poured another large brandy. 'How many times have I told you about the last war and how I won it for France?'

I sucked my lower lip, suppressing a laugh. Indeed, so many times, his own story told as if he'd won the war single-handed, but I'd always known he meant the entire French army and the Allies. He was still my hero.

'Now I will win it again.'

'Not if I win it first.' Adrenaline flooded my veins as a fire burned in my belly. All that I'd seen, all that I knew, collided like a myriad of stars at that moment. I believed in the cause, and I believed in myself. Me. Nancy Wake Fiocca was going to make a stand for Henri, France, and all humanity. This, I felt strongly, was my purpose. France needed more than soldiers, and it was my chance to be useful.

Henri's eyes widened, and we stared at one another before a grin tugged at his mouth, and we both burst into laughter, tears filling my eyes, streaking down my cheeks.

'I give up, Nannie, you win.' Henri sighed, lifting a hand to his forehead. 'I can see you have decided, so I will teach you to drive.'

With a shriek of joy, I flung my arms about his neck and planted a kiss on his mouth. 'Thank you.' I never thought I'd ever learn to drive.

'I do not understand why you wish to be in the midst of battle. It is so dangerous, and I will worry about you.'

'I know, but you don't have to, truly. I can take care of myself. Besides, I'm not like other women, Henri. I can't wave goodbye and sit at home knitting balaclavas and socks.'

He stared at me for a few seconds before bursting into laughter once more. He laughed so hard tears slipped down his cheeks. 'Now that would be a sight. Old woman Fiocca with her knitting needles.'

'Cheek.' I applied my best frown, but even that made him laugh.

'Stop it, Nannie. You are more formidable than the entire German army. I can hardly breathe.'

He sank back into his armchair, and I curled up at his feet like a cat, while Picon slumped down next to me on the rug, yawning, wondering what all the fuss was about. Henri stroked the top of my head, his hand slipping to my neck, fingertips gliding over my skin. 'Stop, it tickles.' I laughed, basking in the beauty of the moment, all too aware it was soon to end. 'Promise that whatever happens, you'll find a way back to me.'

'You know I will, mon amour.' He bent down to plant a kiss on my lips, a kiss as soft as snowflakes.

Chapter 11
THE FRONT. MAY 1940

I rammed the gear stick into first, and with a loud crunch, the old truck lurched forward and rolled off down the bank, jolting me around in my seat as I drove over the rough, hole-ridden track. My mind flicked to Henri. His last letter had sounded grim, not so much with the update on the war, but I'd sensed it in his tone, an underlying current. I sighed. Glancing down, I caught sight of the bloodstain on my trouser leg and gritted my teeth. The last casualty. His bloodied hand had brushed my thigh. His last breath as I'd cradled him in my arms at the roadside. The road ahead swam again, and I rubbed my eyes, muttering curses beneath my breath. 'Just a child. Damn the Boches.' An innocent child, who moments before had been walking alongside his mother, his small hand in hers, as they fled their home, joining the hoards that traipsed the road like a great army of ants. In a moment, a wailing from the sky like a screaming bird of prey, then a flash of a yellow-tipped nose, a black swastika on its belly as the enemy roared overhead, firing at everyone on the road. His mother had dragged him into the ditch, but it was futile. I squeezed my eyes shut for a moment, then gazed at my hands, knuckles white from gripping the wheel, sweat forming on my palms, skin tinged reddish-brown, nails caked in dried blood. A fleeting thought of a manicure; if I should make it back in one piece. A swell of nausea.

'We're only supposed to be delivering supplies today,' Louise Beaumont said in a flat voice, frowning at me from the passenger seat.

'I know, but we can't ignore the poor souls if they're hurt.' Louise was rather squeamish and so delivering supplies, clothing, and blankets suited her perfectly. Stopping to help the injured was not on her to-do-list.

'It is all right for you, Nancy. You were a nurse.' She sighed, crossing her arms as we rolled along the bumpy, hole-ridden track, swerving here and there to avoid the debris from the latest air raid.

A film of dust from the road covered the windscreen, like the smog that clouded my mind. I'd been determined to do my bit, but Henri had known what I would likely face, and he was right. As for my nursing training, even with it, I felt ill-prepared. If anything, my journalism career had prepared me more for what to expect. The enemy was merciless, fighting dirty, and seemed hell-bent on an agenda of complete annihilation.

'Welcome to hell,' Louise said in a sing-song voice as we hit another pothole, the truck lurching us both forward. 'Please, God, let this be the last trip today.' She raised her chin, fixed her gaze on the burning blue. Her blonde hair, still immaculate, curled and pinned at the nape of her neck, tucked neatly beneath her tin hat. I think she'd thought that the Red Cross sounded glamorous, and she'd spend her days pouring tea and coffee for injured soldiers, looking pretty in her clean, starched uniform. Huge mistake! At least she had some paint on her face. Mine hadn't seen colour in weeks, not even a hint of ruby on my lips. I grew more tired with every passing day.

As the road levelled out, I passed several people wandering towards the next town. Squeezing the brake pedal with my foot I drove slowly around the bodies that lay in the road, picking my way through the debris of scattered belongings, swerving around one man and then around an elderly woman, grey hair poking out from beneath a black hat, stray strands tugged by the breeze. I saw no blood on her, but I knew she was dead, laid prone, legs bent at abnormal angles, motionless, blank eyes staring into the burning blue. I stamped on the brake, pulled on the handbrake, and jumped out.

'No, not again, Nancy. Mon Dieu! You are determined to get us both killed.' Louise's face paled, and she held her head in her hands.

She could be so dramatic! 'Just a minute,' I snapped. 'We have to check. Come on.' It was the Stukas that terrified her. They were hunters, like screaming birds of prey. The late afternoon sun beat down on my neck, my head roasting beneath my tin hat as I wandered along the road, checking for anyone who might still be alive. I stumbled over the stony track. A faint sound. I stopped and listened, holding my breath. The wind puffed at my ear while my heart galloped. Maybe that's what it had been, a shriek of wind. I plodded on. There it was again, almost a cry. My heart pounded my ears more loudly than before. Someone was alive. I scanned the edge of the road on both sides. Someone must have missed a casualty. I stooped over the bodies, one by one, checking for signs of life as I picked my way among them. A woman about my age, no wedding ring. A middle-aged man and an elderly lady. Anger rose within me like a blazing fire. What had they done? They didn't deserve this. 'Bastards!' I clenched my jaw. The cry rang out again, this time carried on the wind, louder. I was close. I flicked a gaze across the road. A violet-coloured scarf lifted and fluttered in the breeze. I darted across the road and looked into the shallow ditch. A woman lay with a woollen bundle on her chest. A baby!

'Please, help.' She winced, her face deathly pale.

'Over here, Louise.' I fell on my knees beside her and took the baby. I unwrapped the blankets and slipped my hand beneath the child's clothing. The chest was warm. A steady beat drummed beneath my palm. No sign of a bullet hole or blood. Thank God. I blew out a breath, wrapped the baby up and settled him or her by the roadside. I cast my eye over the mother. Young, in her twenties, probably. I grabbed her wrist. Weak pulse, but fairly steady. A crimson stain glistened on her thigh, another on her left shoulder.

'We need the stretcher.' I scrambled up and dashed back for the stretcher. Louise helped me to carry the woman to the ambulance. While Louise went for the baby, I grabbed my medical supplies. I needed a tourniquet. 'May I?' I grasped the scarf and gently pulled it from her neck, and before she could object, tied it tight around her thigh to slow the blood loss. Next, I dressed both wounds as best I could. Louise tucked the baby next to its mother, and we set off to the field hospital, passing crumpled corpses, abandoned prams, cars and carts, and I clenched my jaw, feeling its hardness of bone like steel as an iron fist closed around my heart. I would never forgive the Germans. They'd gone too far with depravity and senseless killings, and I was going to do whatever it took to bring them down.

BY THE TIME I returned to my lodgings, exhaustion had taken over, eliminating hunger and thirst, and I slumped on my bed. It was dark and cold, and I dragged the blankets over me. I'd joined a voluntary ambulance unit in the north of France, at Saint-Jean-de-Basel, which had a mobile hospital unit. Louise and I were drivers, primarily tasked with collecting and delivering supplies to clearance stations and field hospitals. I offered refugees lifts out of kindness and often ferried locals into town for their shopping. The government had commandeered most of the buses for ambulances, so getting about was difficult. We all worked like mules, and any time off was short and used for sleep. My clothes hung off me, my eyes dark, skin pale. The grub was dreadful, much of it tinned. Bully beef and biscuits were a frequent offering.

The phoney war was over. The German army had attacked Luxembourg, the Netherlands, and Belgium on 10 May. For the following two weeks, we had seen minimal military activity, but now the Germans were growing closer. The Dutch surrendered on 14 May. We heard that the first Germans had emerged from the Ardennes the day before and had crossed the River Meuse. They had done what the French thought was impossible. And many of the Allies were caught up fighting in Belgium. France was in jeopardy, our forces retreating. On a better note, Britain had suffered a political shake-up as Chamberlain had resigned and Churchill had stepped into the breach, a military man through and through. The speech he gave in Parliament was so inspiring and had given me hope. His opening words, 'I have nothing to offer but blood, toil, tears, and sweat.' He said, 'You ask what is our policy? It is to wage war by sea, land, and air. You ask, what is our aim? I can answer in one word: It is victory, victory at all costs. . . for without victory, there is no survival.'

On 28 May, Belgium capitulated, and the Allies withdrew, retreating at speed towards Dunkirk, with the German army and their mighty Panzers nipping at their heels. The British sent ships to evacuate their troops, but the Germans continued to bombard them with artillery and bombs as they waited. They say carnage reigned in Dunkirk. Raging fires painted the night sky crimson, as houses burned, and people fled. And lines of troops stretched out into the sea, waiting to board boats, not knowing if they would live or die as the Stukas screamed overhead, firing mercilessly, bombs falling. Abandoned vehicles smoked into the summer haze while horses and troops lay dead among the dunes. Paris bore the brunt, their hospitals overflowing with injured soldiers and civilians. Panic had gripped the people who dared not go anywhere without their gas masks. And I prayed for Henri because, for once, prayer was all I had to comfort me as I dug for hope. And I thought of Mum, at home with her bible, my memories softening, an ache in my heart. Please, God, keep Stanley safe too.

Chapter 12
INVASION. JUNE 1940

News of the advancing Germans was terrifying, especially to many of the local people. The British were still evacuating according to the latest news reports. Their ships arrived over a week ago, and now many small boats had risked the Channel crossing to take the troops home. Meanwhile, the Luftwaffe continued to dive-bomb the troops on the beaches and the hospital ships. The Luftwaffe sank a ship loaded with casualties as it left port. Everywhere I've been the people wear the same look; Dark eyes, frown lines, thin-lipped, some with vacant stares, shocked by the swift hand of defeat. Those who recalled the last war gave warnings, making others even more fearful of the enemy. The people had lost all hope, and many were angry by the Allied retreat and felt betrayed. It was as if Britain had deserted us in our hour of need. I hoped to God they'd return. They'd had little choice. Yesterday's bombing raid in Paris killed hundreds. Men, women, children, the sick.

I'd found myself caught in another air raid and had to dash into a shelter. It was so humid, people from all walks of life crammed into every inch of space. The wealthier ladies stood prominently dressed in their Parisian best, smoky eyes darting this way and that. They sat together, with over-stuffed handbags probably hiding their jewels and money. One cast me a fleeting, snooty glance. I looked a sight.

Exhausted, my khaki shirt and trousers dusty and grimy from work, my hair dull, lank and flattened thanks to my tin hat. A vein throbbed in my temple and I shot a stern glance at the woman as I folded my arms. Vexed with society, expectations, and greed, I was risking everything for France, for *her*.

The rest of the people huddled together near me, a mix of anguish and disbelief on their faces. 'This cannot be happening,' one woman said. Another woman muttered under her breath, clinging to her crucifix. I thought of Henri. The Germans were taking prisoners. Was he among them? Was he making his way home as he'd promised? He had to be alive, as I would surely feel if he were dead. My eyes swam, and the people around me merged into one dark swirly mass. I swiped tears away with the back of my hand. It did no good to fear the worst. I had to hold on to hope, as it was all I had. Small children and babies huddled into their mothers while men looked on, helpless. An eerie shriek outside. I held my breath and braced, waiting for the explosion, not knowing whether we would live or die. A crump in the distance. The ground shook beneath my feet, vibration in my legs. A sprinkle of dust overhead. Couples held one another tight, the rest of us sat frozen. At that moment, my life hurtled at speed through my mind. I thought of Mum, Dad, my brothers and sisters. Stanley at war, somewhere at sea. Henri, somewhere in France. Everything I longed to do, things I've already done, places I've seen. I longed to be free, to live a good life with Henri, safe and loved. The Boches would soon take Paris. How long before they reached Britain? It was unthinkable. The air was foul, thick with sweat and something putrid I couldn't place, and my head felt fuzzy.

An old woman tapped my arm. 'Hitler did not want to destroy Paris. Do you think he has changed his mind?'

Her wide eyes were watery, yet I sensed she was not afraid. No, she saw out the first war. Its horrors lined her face. 'I don't know.' What could I say? 'I don't think they'll destroy Paris.' She nodded, leant back on the bench and rested her head against the cool, rough stone while I wondered if German bombs rained down on England. So many people displaced, and what of us? What would happen to those of us who were not French citizens? British, American, Australian. Henri would know what to do. A prayer slipped from my mouth, simple words I mumbled in desperation more than anything. 'Please, God, keep Henri safe, and let us get out of here alive.'

Hours ticked by and when the all-clear siren finally wailed, we filed outside, welcomed by the drift of fresh air. A silvery blue light slipped over the cobblestone road. I raised my chin, watched tones of pink, purple, and blood orange wash into the sky. A new day. My heart soared.

THE LAST OF the Allied ships had set sail from Dunkirk. Some troops stayed behind and were fighting to the last, the Germans taking prisoners along the way. The enemy was reportedly fifty miles from Paris, and the French Government had retreated south. My unit was instructed to head south to Nimes. It appeared retreat was the only option. It suited me well enough, as the journey would take me close to home. I packed my things and stowed them in my truck. Louise came with me to Nimes. Her home was in the north, but she had family in the south, she'd said. The roads were worse than ever. Straggly lines of cars crammed with people and belongings, with towers of suitcases and mattresses strapped to their roofs. Marching columns of people, young, old and the infirm. I pulled in at the roadside and stuck my head out the window. 'If anyone wants a lift, hop in,' I said. I opened the rear doors, and people streamed towards us, clambering inside, packed tight like sardines. I hoped the journey might at least avoid the attention of the Luftwaffe, but after a short time, a familiar droning sliced through the summer haze, growing into a scream, and I stamped on the brake. 'Everyone out! Take cover.' We all jumped into the roadside ditch, and I glimpsed the grey underbelly of a Stuka as it zipped overhead, spitting out a hail of shells. One of our passengers cried out. Others covered their ears and heads while ducking down low. Dust billowed all around, scratched at my eyes. 'Bastards,' I muttered, rubbing my face, tasting dried earth. We waited for a minute to make sure the pilot didn't return and then continued. That episode set the course of our journey, and every twenty minutes or so we would repeat the drill as another Stuka screamed overhead. Once we were far enough away from central France, they finally left us alone.

A woman shrieked out in the corridor. I yawned, rubbed the sleep from my eyes as I lay, listening—loud banging on doors, more voices. I stretched out, then swung my legs out of bed. 'What's all the fuss about?' I padded across the wooden parquet floor to the window, opened the shutters, and gazed out into the streets of Nimes below. There was a loud knock on my door.

'Come in.'

The maid stood in the doorway, her face pale, tears glistening in her red eyes. 'What's happened?'

'Madame Fiocca, the news is terrible. Paris has fallen. The Germans are coming.' She turned and fled down the corridor, leaving my door to swing shut. It was June 13th. The last week had been the worst. Norway had succumbed to the occupation too, with their king and his family fleeing into exile in London. France's day had finally arrived. A painful lump swelled in my throat as I choked back tears, to no avail. My vision swam as a huge sob escaped my lungs. The enemy was at the gate, and I was, like many, an illegal alien. I returned to my bed, curled up, and cried. Where was Henri? I hadn't heard from him in weeks. Surely, if he could, he'd make his way home to Marseille. And I would be waiting. I jumped up and pulled on a pair of brown trousers and a cream blouse. Next, I scooped up my belongings, hastily stuffing clothes, shoes, and cosmetics into my bag. I had to get home. A German welcome party was a sobering thought, and I had no intentions of being arrested. My unit had disbanded, with the French returning home, and the British headed to the coast where a ship was waiting to take them to England.

The sun beat mercilessly down, a heat haze flickering over the road and in the air, while rich pollen-filled my nose, sweet, stuffy. The road to Marseille endured a steady stream of refugees travelling on cycles, in cars and on foot. I threw my bags into the truck and climbed in. The heat was stifling; hot metal tainted with the sickly stink of oil and fuel. Hungry, I dug into my holdall and found a small bar of chocolate I'd saved. I took a bite, savouring the rich cocoa as it melted in my mouth. It suddenly struck me how peaceful it was. No guns or aircraft, only birdsong, the rumble of wheels, and the thrumming engine. Of course, it would surely be peaceful in Paris, as the conquerors were upon them and I supposed there was no longer a need to fight. With the government fleeing south, I learned Paris had been declared a free city. At least they spared her.

After a couple of hours, with Marseille almost within reach, the truck lurched and jolted, and black smoke belched out from beneath the bonnet. 'What now?' I pulled over at the roadside, popped the bonnet and lifted the hood. There was a smell of burning and a hiss of steam. I realised it was hopeless, so I grabbed my bags and resigned myself to walking the final twenty kilometres home, the sun burning. I checked my watch. Four o'clock. Soon, a rumble behind. I put out my hand and luckily, the driver of the car slowed to a halt and agreed to give me a lift.

I arrived home on a gentle breeze, humid yet cool for June, with faint scents of coffee and pastries from a nearby café. Marseille seemed still, her pulse slow. As in Paris, the news had been a shock. I wondered then if the might of the German Army was unstoppable. As I turned the key in the door of our apartment, I sensed the emptiness. Madame Dumont had cleaned recently, as there were no traces of dust on the furniture, and the rooms smelt fresh. My plants thrived in moist soil. The cushions were plump on the sofas; Henri's whisky decanter remained half full as we'd left it. His brown leather armchair with the seat cushion worn from his use stood proudly by the marble fireplace. I trailed a hand over it as I strode across to the windows, sucking in a deep breath. Traces of sandalwood lingered in the air.

I went into the bathroom, checked my face in the mirror. Smudges of grime streaked my forehead, cheeks and chin, fingernails worn, grubby. Fresh lines furrowed my brow and framed my eyes. I no longer recognised the woman who stared back. A shadow had descended and who knew how long it would remain? I washed and changed, then headed to my father-in-law's home to ask if he'd received news of Henri. He did not receive me with welcome arms, but he was polite, and no, he hadn't heard from Henri. His worn face told me he, too, was desperately worried.

'We are bound to hear soon,' he said. 'I will telephone when we do.'

I could tell he wished me to leave. 'Yes,' I said, forcing a smile, aware of my shaky voice as I caught sight of a photograph of Henri smiling and my heart pinched yet I felt numb and angry. Before the war, I hadn't thought it possible to hate anyone, but the last two months had shown me otherwise, and hate burned inside me, a dark spot like rot in an apple, the worm burrowing deeper, forcing my hand.

When I returned home, I poured a double whisky before going to bed. I missed Picon, but I'd telephone Madame Dumont the next day and let her know she could bring him home. The photograph of Henri stared up at me from my bedside table as I breezed into our bedroom. I sank onto the bed and stared at him until my vision swam, then swiped tears from my eyes. As I smoothed my hand over the gold satin bedspread, his voice whispered in my ear. 'You are the home-maker, Nannie. I do not care what is on my bed. I only care that you are lying beside me.' Our home had been our haven, a place of love and safety, but without him it was a shell and that old familiar friend, desolation, slithered in all the way from my childhood in Sydney. And in a heartbeat, I was back there swinging on the garden gate, waiting. But unlike Dad, Henri would return. He had to.

18 June 1940

 'I, General de Gaulle, currently in London, invite the officers and the French soldiers who are located in British territory, with their weapons or without their weapons, I invite the engineers and the specialised workers of the armament industries... to put themselves in contact with me. Whatever happens, the flame of the French Resistance must not be extin-

guished and will not be extinguished.' Charles de Gaulle, 1940.

ITALY DECLARED war with France on 10 June, and yesterday, Italian aircraft bombed Marseille. Ironically, they hit the Italian quarter, missing the main street and our home. Over one hundred people died with many more injured. There has been no armistice and so the war persisted. On 21 June, I was sitting at the bar in Basso's when a droning noise filtered in, grew to a crescendo, followed by several mighty crumps. I leapt from the stool and dashed to the windows that looked out to sea. The glinting bodies of grey aircraft filled the sky. Smoke rose in the distance from one part of the town. Aircraft roared overhead as people fled from the building, running to the shelters amidst raining bombs. I had no desire to run and so I returned to my seat and drink at the bar. 'I think you should join me, Albert,' I said to the barman, who nodded and poured himself a large brandy.

THE NEXT WEEK went by in a blur with no news of Henri. Still, the war had brought chaos, dissolving all organisation. Refugees still clogged the roads, heading to goodness knows where. Picon jumped onto my lap. He'd missed me terribly, but our friends had looked after him so well. He was happy to be home and followed me everywhere. I sensed he was afraid I might leave him again. 'Come, Picon. Let's listen to the news.' I flicked on the radio just in time for the latest bulletin. France had formally surrendered to Hitler. To add insult to injury, Hitler had insisted on rubbing salt into the wound and had used the exact railway carriage that was used in 1918 when Germany surrendered. It was the ultimate humiliation as Hitler brought France to heel. As I listened, I clenched my hands tight, nails digging into my palms. My heart ached for France, a country I loved and cherished more than my own. Tears pricked my eyes, but I sucked in a sharp breath and gently exhaled, holding them at bay. I opened the French doors and stepped out onto the small balcony. Looking out over the Vieux Port, people filled the cafes, sitting out in the morning sun. Below, many more filled the streets, going about their business. Just as thousands had fled Paris and the advancing German army, many refugees now poured into Marseille. French people from the Occupied Zone, British soldiers, Belgians, Czechs, Poles, anti-fascist Italians, anti-Nazi Germans, Spaniards fleeing Franco. So many people uprooted, displaced, many of them intellectuals, artists, and Jews. The hotels were brimming with them.

What did the future hold? I needed Henri. I closed my eyes as an old, buried memory resurfaced with a sharp jab in the chest. Dad. I'd often wondered why he'd left. Was it me? What had I done that was so terrible? I never saw him again, and I doubt I'd want to. Of course, I'd learned the truth later, the truth of his affair and how he'd gone to live in New Zealand with his new love. He'd sold our house to pay for a new life and a new family. My chin trembled, and a tear snaked its way down my left cheek, cool, irritating. I swiped it away and sniffed as I recalled the radio broadcast given by Charles de Gaulle a few days ago. Broadcast over Radio-Londres, he'd given a rousing speech, having fled France himself ahead of the invasion. He'd insisted France was not beaten. There was hope, hope and fight that lay in its people. He said that this was a world war, and that France was not alone. Right then, it seemed as if we were completely alone. But his speech, his words echoed his heart, strength, and determination, and every Frenchman listening to the wireless that evening must have surely felt it.

Picon raised his head and stared at me. 'Don't worry,' I said as I tickled him under his chin. 'Daddy will be home soon.' I truly hoped so. The Germans had divided France into two. The Occupied Zone, with their HQ in Paris, and the Free Zone in the south. This divide was called the Demarcation Line, the route of which roughly followed the path of the Loire. It was heavily patrolled, and while it was a blessing not to have German soldiers stationed in the south, friends whispered of German spies. That was wholly plausible. Most towns had seen a major influx of new people, and it was impossible to know who they were or what their purpose was.

July 1940

I poured brandy from the crystal decanter, took a sip, and savoured the fiery tang on my tongue. I strode across to the window and looked out across the town. The night was closing in, and the waxing crescent moon glowed brightly, surrounded by a myriad of shimmering stars scattered across a sapphire sky. A commotion suddenly erupted out in the hallway, Picon's yappy bark causing such a furore, followed by the shrieking voice of our housekeeper. Just what was going on? As I dashed into the hall, the breath caught in my throat. 'Henri!' He was kneeling on the ground, stroking and hugging Picon as best he could while the little scamp jumped all over him, wagging his tail with such fervour.

'Thank God,' I whispered as I ran to him and fell to my knees, into his arms, holding him tight. He kissed me, whiskers scratching my face, but I didn't care. He was home. 'Let me see you,' I said, drawing back to gaze at him. His pale face bore sharper features than I remembered. 'You're so thin.'

'I have not eaten properly in weeks,' he said.

His eyes were dull and heavy, eyes that had seen so much. His clothes were grubby and smelled of earth, tobacco, and sweat.

'Nannie, I have missed you.' He lifted my chin with his hand and gazed at me for a moment before placing his mouth on mine. He was safe, and I held him tight, not daring or wishing to let go.

'How did you avoid the Boches?'

'It was such chaos, people fleeing, clogging up the roads. I slipped away. An old woman gave me these clothes. She told me they had belonged to her son once, long ago. He was killed in the last war.' Henri sank into a chair, lowered his head. 'After that, it was easy. I blended in with the crowd on the roads. I kept my promise.'

I didn't care how he'd made it. He was home, and it was heaven.

~

August 1940

'Au revoir. Je t'aime.' I smiled as Henri stooped to pick up his tan briefcase and left for work. The door closed behind him, and Madame Dumont mumbled something about going to the market for supplies, stomping out into the kitchen, and I found myself alone once more. I stood by the window in the living room, enjoying the view out across the town, the blue of the ocean in the distance shimmering beneath summer's caress. Henri was getting back to normal, eating well, his face gradually regaining its fullness.

I took a stroll into town after my bath. Besides, there were essential supplies to source from other avenues, ones that Madame Dumont stayed away from for fear of any reprisals. We were better off than most, being able to pay extra for certain products. Henri's wealth maintained us, and I could still buy almost anything I desired, but more importantly, what was needed. I indulged, but it was never solely for us. I bought as much as I could, from food to other essential items such as soap, which was becoming increasingly scarce, but of course, the black marketeers had plenty. Having bought the soap, I then spent hours melting it all down, adding a little of my favourite perfume before pouring it into moulds to set. In doing so, I'd changed the product, just in case any officials were to turn up and check. We had a well-stocked larder, and I could give food parcels away to friends who needed them. The Ficetoles were a family in need, and I regularly visited, leaving food with them. In return, if ever I needed someone to watch over Picon, I knew they would step in. Monsieur Ficetole had also served in the war, and now he was home, Henri had helped him with a little venture as he'd started up a transport business and needed a horse and cart.

The occupation was always there, from the moment you woke to the moment you fell asleep at night—if you fell asleep. Like a shroud, it hung over every citizen, and secrets became a way of life. After all, you never knew who you could trust—even friends and family. I trusted no one aside from Henri. The British had sunk the French fleet at Mers-el-Kébir on 3 July, and many of the French were angry and uncertain whether to trust the British. Britain, our ally, had committed a violent act, with the loss of hundreds of lives, and I too was horrified by the tragedy.

'They did not trust the Germans and the Vichy government's agreement over the fleet,' Henri said.

I nodded. Hitler was not one to be trusted, and if the Germans had commandeered the French fleet, Petain wouldn't have stopped them. It was blatantly obvious that Petain and his government were puppets, bowing down to the German occupiers, willing to do the enemy's bidding.

The Luftwaffe were bombing British towns and cities and had recently bombed London. Of course, Britain had immediately issued a stern response and sent dozens of aircraft to bomb Berlin the following night. That must have surprised the Fuhrer! And best of all, the RAF was fighting back, night after night, downing bombers and a number of the Luftwaffe's fighter aircraft. There were reports of dog fights over London and out across the Channel.

I often wondered about Henri's experiences in this war. He hadn't spoken of it, but I could sense it troubled him. He must have witnessed such horrific sights, but whenever I asked, he would say, 'There was not much fighting where we were.' However, he was drinking heavily at night, and I was worried.

ONE EVENING, not long after the Armistice, Henri and I were enjoying a quiet drink in the cocktail lounge of L' Hôtel Louvre et Paix, when a Frenchman came over and introduced himself. He said his name was Commander Busch, and he was polite, charming even. He and Henri got on like a house on fire, and the commander showed great interest in Henri's war efforts. Busch was an army officer staying at the hotel.

He had intended to go to England with General de Gaulle; however, as he explained, 'my colleagues begged me to remain in France where I may be more useful.' I remembered de Gaulle's speech immediately, and the 'flame of Resistance' of which he'd spoken, and my heart quickened.

'So, what is it you do?' I looked around. We were quite alone, aside from Antoine, the bar manager.

'I run a small organisation, Madame. We print leaflets, propaganda and more besides. France is on her knees, and there is much to be done.'

An insurmountable task, I thought. Britain was fighting back, while some of our French soldiers were still hiding, having escaped the Germans at Dunkirk. The Germans were storming through multiple countries, rounding up groups of people they objected to, such as Jews, Romanies. They wouldn't take too kindly to anyone they found opposing them, either. Resistance was dangerous, but I felt strongly about doing what you could for your country, and I thought that if I could help just one person, then it would be worthwhile.

'We are always looking for good people to help us.' Commander Busch looked directly at me.

I wasn't sure how to respond. I wished to volunteer, of course, but something held me back. Dark thoughts. How could we be certain this man was who he said he was? I glanced at Henri.

'Anything we can do to help, please, ask.' With that, Henri reached into his breast pocket and took out a business card, placing it on the table. 'But not next weekend as we shall be in Cannes.'

Busch downed the last of his whisky, looked around as if to check no one could hear, before saying, 'It just happens that I have something to deliver in Cannes. Would you be willing to take it?'

'Oui,' Henri said, without hesitation.

~

WHEN WE RETURNED HOME, Henri poured himself a generous brandy and sat in his armchair.

'I presume you trust this Busch fellow.' I sank to the floor at his feet, resting my head on his knee.

'Of course. Nancy, we talked at length about the war and our regiments. Besides, I know of his organisation already. One of the workers at the factory brought in a stack of leaflets.'

Many people wandered round in a haze of disbelief following France's defeat. Some flippantly dismissed the problem of the German occupation, saying 'it is a problem for the north of France.' Foolish words. I wondered how long it would be before the Germans occupied the south. For now, we had some breathing space and how joyous that some of our citizens had heeded de Gaulle's speech, igniting the flame of Resistance. All I hoped was that we could trust Busch. Times were changing quickly, and people, well, people had a natural survival instinct and would do whatever they felt they must.

Chapter 13
OCTOBER 1940

As we walked around to the rear entrance of L' Hôtel Louvre et Paix, I sensed Henri's irritation.

'Why can't we use the main entrance like everyone else?' Henri threw his cigarette to the ground, crushing it beneath his shoe.

'You know why. It's always filled with Germans, and they make my skin crawl. You've seen the way they eye up women.' I blew out a breath. I preferred to slip into the hotel without drawing attention to myself, slipping into the small bar behind the foyer, well out of the way of the enemy. They frequently used the hotel, and although they were in mufti, we all knew they were Germans. I could endure their loud voices and roaring laughter once the drinks flowed, knowing I didn't have to look at them. As I stepped inside, the warmer air swaddled me like a shawl.

'Are you sure you won't join me in the casino, my darling?' Henri slipped his arm around my waist, drew me close to kiss my cheek.

'No, you go on. I'll be perfectly fine here at the bar. Besides, Antoine here is excellent company.'

I watched as Henri flicked a gaze at the barman. 'Very well. Enjoy your evening, mon amour. I will be back soon.' He kissed me once more before striding away.

The lure of the tables was too strong for Henri, but he was usually sensible, and I never worried. I perched myself on a barstool and rested my navy silk purse on the polished mahogany bar. 'Antoine, how are you this evening?'

'I am very well, Madame Fiocca. Thank you. Your usual?' He nodded.

'Thanks.' I gazed around the small bar, which this evening appeared rather quiet with only one other gentleman sat at a table, reading a book. Unusual. I'd never seen him before. Perhaps he was travelling. The book looked familiar too. *Tender Is the Night* by F. Scott Fitzgerald.

Antoine placed the brandy on the bar. I grasped the crystal glass and took a sip. 'Antoine, that man behind me, have you seen him before?'

'Never.'

'Have you seen what he's reading? An English book, with the Germans just through there.' I traced a fingertip around the rim of my glass. Intriguing. Rumours were rife of spies, and of neighbours spying on one another, some eager to denounce those they suspected of resisting, even family.

Just then, a gentle voice whispered in my ear, warm breath caressing my skin as a mist of brandy floated in the air. 'Henri. That was quick.'

'I decided I am not in the mood for cards this evening.'

I smiled before drawing him close. 'You see that man behind us? Antoine and I think he may be a spy.'

Henri turned to stare. 'Don't make it so obvious,' I hissed.

'Tell me, why do you think this?'

'He's reading an English book for a start.'

Henri leaned on the bar, his hand rubbing his chin. 'Ah, I see.' He smiled. 'Do not worry. I know exactly what to do.'

'What's that?'

'I shall ask him.' He strode away, leaving me at the bar, my mouth gaping. What if the man was a spy?

All I could do was sit and watch as the pair chatted in hushed tones, which was incredibly frustrating as I could barely hear a word. Henri then shook the man's hand and reported back to me.

'No need to worry. He is an English officer and a prisoner of war, held at Fort St Jean. He is one of many. Talk to him.'

I was so excited at the prospect of meeting a fellow British person and I slipped off my stool and went across to introduce myself, with Henri in tow. His name was Captain Leslie Wilkins.

'What exactly are you doing here?' I was almost certain he was British, but of course, there was always that nagging doubt at the back of your mind. Nothing was certain anymore, nothing assured, and trust was the most fragile of silken threads, easily broken.

'After Dunkirk, hundreds of us remained. The French military has around two hundred of us here at Fort St. Jean. We're on parole, you could say. They allow us to venture out during the day, as long as we're back by curfew each night.'

'I see.' His skin was pale, his cheekbones prominent, more so than would be usual for a man of his build, I thought. 'How are the conditions there?'

He smiled, dull eyes lighting up for the first time. 'Poor. The grub's terrible, and there's not much of it. It's also pretty cold, and especially now winter is setting in. The men are gasping for cigarettes.' He laughed, a half-hearted laugh.

I turned to Henri, who gave me one of his looks, the type he offered when he knew what I was cooking up in my mind. 'Sounds rough,' I said. 'Why don't you meet me at Basso's tomorrow at midday? We can chat about the *conditions* over coffee.'

'Well, yes, if you're sure it's no trouble, Madame Fiocca. I'll look forward to it.'

'No trouble at all, and please, call me Nancy. Everyone does.' What else could I do after hearing his plight? He was desperate, as anyone would be in those circumstances.

That night at home, I tossed and turned in bed, unable to sleep, drifting off only to re-awaken as my thoughts refused to quieten. What if he was a German spy? He was so convincing. I detested this way of existence. Bloody war! None of us were safe now, nor would we be until France was liberated. I decided all I could do was trust my instinct, and my heart said this Englishman was genuine. He needed help, so there was nothing more to consider.

I STROLLED along the Vieux-Port and slipped into Bassos. I made my way over to the barman. 'Albert, I have a meeting here. Can you take these for me and hide them behind the bar? If anything should happen, I wouldn't like them to fall into the wrong hands.' I handed him a bundle of cigarettes.

'Very well, Madame Fiocca.' He glanced around before taking the package.

I found a table with a clear view of the street. Before long, I saw Captain Wilkins making his way along the road, chatting amiably to the other men. For a split second, my heart drummed, but then I noticed one man wore the most ridiculous, large, bushy moustache, and I relaxed. Only an Englishman would tolerate such a thing, and no German could replicate that. I turned around. 'Albert, it's okay. You can give me the package.'

THAT EVENING, back at the apartment, I instructed the housekeeper that there were three guests expected for dinner. Unfortunately, I hadn't had time to inform Henri, who was now running late as usual. The business was struggling. All of France was struggling, but Henri shouldered the responsibility, doing his utmost to keep things afloat. It was fine, so he said whenever I asked him. I strode into the living room and poured myself a brandy, and then I stood at the window, gazing out across the harbour. The sun shimmered across the water, a fiery globe dipping down, skimming the skin of the ocean, and in the distance, a ship loomed, the red flag prominent with a central swastika. I gulped the brandy, fire flaring in my throat, radiating down, flaming in my heart. I reached for the letter that had arrived that morning from Marie. Both she and Richard were returning to England. I read her words once more, her gentle voice echoing in my mind, a pang striking my heart. It was for the best.

~

AS HENRI STEPPED through the door to their apartment, laughter peeled out to greet him, but it was not only Nancy's sweet laugh. There was someone with her. He set his brown leather briefcase down on the hall table and removed his jacket.

'Bonsoir, Monsieur Fiocca,' Claire, their maid, beamed from the kitchen doorway. 'Madame wished to let you know that you have dinner guests.'

'Bonsoir, Claire.' So that explained the male voices. He raised his eyebrows, sighed, and rubbed the back of his neck. Nancy was indefatigable. 'Who?'

'I do not know, Monsieur.'

Henri nodded before going into the bathroom and closing the door. All day his thoughts had been of a quiet evening alone with his beautiful wife. He stood at the sink, stared at his reflection in the mirror above before splashing his face with cold water. His eyes were bloodshot. He squeezed them shut as a memory resurfaced. That day at the Front. The Germans opened fire on their position. Men fell like flies, crying out, dying in the mud. An officer yelling at them, 'Hold your position', 'Do not break rank.' But it was futile; so hopeless and he'd known then all was lost; France was lost. The tanks had overwhelmed them. It was chaos, bloody, brutal chaos, and his friend Charles, always at his side until that day. How it had wrenched his heart to leave Charles behind, his blue eyes wide, staring blankly one last time into gentle sunlight. Henri's heart raced, and he gasped, fighting for breath like he always did when he looked back. Never look back, only forward. He stared hard at himself, saw panic skim his face, lift and twist every line, every crease, tug at his eyes, his mouth as his skin drained dusky, sallow grey. 'Charles,' he muttered, his knuckles white where he gripped the basin.

A knock at the door made him jump. 'Henri, are you in there?'

He took a deep breath in and puffed it out slowly. 'Oui.'

The door opened, and he gazed at her reflection in the mirror.

'Are you all right, darling? Did Claire tell you we have guests?'

'She did. I just wanted to clean up first.' He turned to face her, and her smile slipped.

'Henri, you're not all right at all.' She moved towards him and threw her arms around his neck, pressing her face against his chest. 'I wish you'd tell me what's going on in that head of yours.'

He held her tight, sighing, nuzzling her silken hair, drinking in soft undertones of lavender. He would not be a burden. Besides, she had enough to contend with, especially now she seemed so intent on helping captured Allied soldiers. An uneasy feeling had already settled over him, and it was growing by the day. 'All is well, my love. Do not worry.' He gave her a light squeeze and brushed the top of her head with his lips. 'Now, time for dinner. Our guests will wonder where their beautiful hostess has gone.'

Chapter 14
DANGEROUS LIAISONS. JANUARY 1941

Henri arrived at work and sank down in his chair at the desk. The door to his office opened as his secretary brought in a steaming cup of ersatz coffee.

'Merci,' he said.

'Monsieur Fiocca, your father is coming in shortly. He rang earlier.' She pursed her lips and clasped her hands tightly together.

'Thank you, Anne.' Henri sighed. What did he want to discuss now? He shook his head, picked up the cup and took a sip, wincing at the bitter acorn taste. He'd never get used to this rubbish. Thank heavens Nannie had fresh ground coffee at home. He glanced out the window: blue skies, barely a wisp of white. His thoughts turned to dinner last night. Nannie had been in her element, the grand hostess doing what she always did so eloquently. Entertaining with such an infectious laugh, much to the delight of their guests. She glowed brighter than all the stars. She was his star, the light of his life. But he had seen the fire in her eyes. Already she had offered to feed men from the fort every night—four, maybe five, she had said without even a glance at him for confirmation. No, because she knew he would agree, as always. He gave her everything she asked for and more. Was he a fool? She deserved it, and he knew she loved him deeply, but yes, maybe he was foolish. She was playing a dangerous game, and they must all be extremely vigilant from now on. One of the men from the Fort was a Scottish chap, the name of Ian Garrow. He spoke of an escape line, and of helping the Allies slip through France, and escape via a southern port or across the Pyrenees. This intrigued Nannie. Garrow had watched her closely, flicking a gaze at me as he spoke of acquiring funds.

Nancy was a British subject living in Nazi-occupied France. If she came to the attention of the Gestapo, it would not look very favourable if they suspected her of helping the Allies. The consequences would be harsh. He swallowed, gritted his teeth. There were whispers of horrific stories. The Gestapo would stop at nothing to unearth traitors. No, he would not let anything happen to his wife. Henri sipped the coffee and grimaced. Nancy was not a bird to be kept in a gilded cage. He ran his hand through his hair. No, he had to let her fly. But if the Germans did ever suspect her, the consequences would be far-reaching. The brutes would ransack their home, his father's home, perhaps. There would be arrests and consequences for the entire Fiocca family. He would have to make sure he was aware of everything Nannie was doing, and if he felt it necessary, stop her at any point.

~

HENRI STOOD IN THE DOORWAY, watching as Nancy applied ruby lipstick. He loved the way she puckered her lips, often catching his gaze in the mirror and smiling, just as she did now.

'Darling, I didn't hear you come in.' She dashed towards him and leaned in to kiss his cheek.

'I finished on time, as you asked me to.'

She studied him for a moment. 'Hmm, for once.' She breezed back over to her dressing table, picked up the bottle of Chanel perfume, and applied a dab to each wrist and a little behind her ears. 'It's just Ian and Bruce coming tonight.'

Only two, Henri thought. 'A quiet evening for once.' The men from the fort dominated their lives. A room full of guests most nights. Could he not have Nancy to himself for one night? That was selfish, perhaps, but he was in love. He sighed as he loosened his tie and unbuttoned his shirt collar. 'I take it they are arriving at the usual time?'

'Yes, now hurry, and I'll fix you a drink before they get here.' She kissed him on the lips as she breezed past him, a veil of jasmine and rose scent enveloping him like soft music. Henri sank onto the bed for a moment. Things had changed since Captain Garrow had turned up. He was astute and cunning and had recognised the merits in Nancy immediately. She was incredibly resourceful, useful to have for his operation, but she was also desperate for money. Nancy had been eager to help, perhaps too eager. They were already assisting Commander Busch. It did not help matters that their neighbour across the landing was a Vichy Commissaire. If the escape line was discovered, he did not want Nancy to be caught up in the middle of it. He rose and discarded his shirt, reaching into the wardrobe for a fresh one. Right now, it seemed Garrow was turning their flat into his headquarters for his escape network. They came most nights, discussed plans to move more men, most of whom were soldiers interned at the fort. Bruce was a good sort, an Australian, and got on with Nancy very well. The sudden interjection of male voices alerted him to the arrival of their guests. 'Here we go again,' he muttered as he fastened the last button on the shirt. Not that he disliked them. On the contrary, he empathised with their plight, but it was Nancy who concerned him. She had a zest for adventure and was daring—too daring—and this burden preyed heavily on him. Her safety was his priority.

As he strode into the living room, he heard the assured, yet soft Scottish voice of Garrow.

'I sent someone to Le Petit Poucet bar to check for evaders.' Garrow took a drag on his cigarette, exhaling slowly. 'Picked up another two chaps.'

All the airmen knew that if they went there, they would be picked up. Funny how word spread. 'Good evening, everyone.' Henri grinned as he glanced around. Garrow and Bruce flocked around Nancy, who was sitting on the sofa, drink in hand. Bees buzzing around a scarlet rose. He poured himself a generous measure of brandy.

'Henri, there you are. Dinner's ready. We were waiting for you, my darling.' Nancy rose, and the others stood up. 'So where are the airmen now?'

'At the mission for the time being, but we'll be moving them on as soon as possible.' Garrow stubbed out his cigarette in an ashtray. 'Thank you for the food parcels you sent. Lord knows we need as much help as possible.'

Henri sighed. Money, food, clothing. Where would it all end? These Allies loved Nancy, but then again, both he and Nancy had just what Garrow needed, and Henri wondered if they were simply convenient. His stomach churned. He downed the brandy in one fiery gulp, recalling the recent words of his doctor, a good friend. 'You must moderate your drinking. More rest and less liquor.' Henri huffed out a breath, watching their guests who hung on Nancy's every word.

The men talked of evaders and safe houses as if it were office business and nothing more. How odd such danger could be simplified, eased into one's way of life. Garrow had sucked them into this world of evasion and espionage piece by piece. How much would be left to salvage?

LATER THAT NIGHT, as they lay in bed, unease gnawed away at Henri like a rat and refused to subside, while a dull ache pummelled his right side. 'Nancy, I think you are doing a little too much for the British.'

'What do you mean? We give them food and a little money to help. How is that too much?'

'You know what I mean. Just think about what you are doing, my love. France has eyes and ears. You do not know who to trust. We live opposite the Vichy Commissaire, for goodness' sake.' Henri puffed out a breath.

'I know you're worried about me, but I can't back out. Those men need our help.'

They were in too deep. The trouble was, he did not wish her to go any further. She was infuriating at times, stubborn, and so determined to save the world. How was he going to keep her safe? 'Be careful tomorrow, Nannie.'

'I will. I'm only delivering a food parcel to the mission.' She rolled towards him and into his arms as he drew her head to his chest, nuzzling her hair. 'Besides, Bruce will be there, too. I'm taking him out to lunch afterwards.' The Seaman's Mission was busier than ever, with a steady stream of evaders. Reverend Caskie took a tremendous risk in doing such work. He was Scottish, in his late thirties, and had been the minister of the Scots Kirk in Paris, but the church was closed following the German occupation. He'd then moved to Marseille and held services at the mission, but had also become involved with the Resistance.

The Seaman's Mission was a major safe house and now the hub of the escape line. It was from there that a courier led evaders south on their journey to cross the Pyrenees and reach neutral Spain. People usually left food parcels in the mission's doorway at night, but Nancy preferred to deliver in person and as yet had never been stopped or followed. If anything should happen to her, he'd never forgive Garrow.

Marseille was changing, and Henri recalled the rumours of the growing number of German and Italian spies. Meanwhile, the French police were loyal to the Vichy government. The pain in his side intensified, fleeting, sharp and caught his breath. He gritted his teeth, not wishing to alarm Nancy, then steadied his breathing, feeling nauseous.

THE JOURNEY to Lyon had been uneventful and quiet. Today was the first time I'd used my new identity papers, procured for me by a doctor friend of Henri's. We'd decided I needed to change one thing — omit my British citizenship. I was still Madame Fiocca of Marseille, but as far as the Vichy gendarmes or any Germans were concerned, I was French. Christmas had been wonderful, and Henri and I had celebrated the day along with friends and several officers from the fort. Bruce had recently joined the Garrow Line, and we'd fallen in together like brother and sister. We were a similar age too, both in our late twenties. It was wonderful to meet a fellow Aussie, and Henri had taken us all to dinner to celebrate. Now it was a new year, still marred by war, and I wondered how much longer it would last. Rationing was biting hard, winter harsh. Supplies of coal and food had dwindled, but I was glad to share what we had with friends who needed help.

An icy chill surrounded me in the small waiting room. Heating was a luxury even a doctor couldn't afford. The surgery door swung open, and Dr Jean Fellot stood there, beckoning me inside. 'Madame Fiocca. It is lovely to see you.'

I followed him inside and waited until he closed the door. Despite the empty waiting room, I kept my voice low. 'Bonjour.' I handed over the brown suitcase. I knew what was inside. A radio. Jean was my Lyon contact and trustworthy. He'd assisted many people already, evaders and civilians, and at this moment was sheltering a Jewish family in the cellars below. He opened the suitcase.

'Merci, Madame. I wish you a safe journey home.'

It didn't do to stay long. Prying eyes were everywhere, and I wished to return home. I took a slip of paper from my coat pocket and handed it to Jean. 'That's the address of our chalet in Névache. If ever you need it, please use it. The key is under the doormat.' Safe houses were always needed and where better to hide than the Alps?

AS THE WEEKS FLEW BY, I made more trips two or three times each week, to Lyon, Cannes, and Toulon mostly, working for both the Garrow Line and Commander Busch. Small packages secreted into the bottom of my handbag or sewn into the lining of my coat became a regular occurrence. I relished the thrill of it all and the feeling of doing something of great purpose. I escorted evaders to the Spanish borders, taking the train to Toulouse or Perpignan. Sometimes, Bruce came too, not that we sat together. It was reassuring to have someone watching out for me.

The business took much of Henri's time and he worked long hours.

He was tired and frequently concerned about my activities, but I assured him I was aware of the dangers, and I was doing everything possible to avoid detection. During the day, I stuck to my routine of shopping in the mornings, meeting up with friends for lunch, and spending the odd afternoon at the beauty salon, being pampered and preened. In between times, I'd slip away to run my extra errands, taking 'parcels' to their destination, and often the 'parcel' was a person, usually more than one. I became used to taking evaders by train to the foot of the Pyrenees, via Perpignan which lay about twenty miles from the Spanish border, and trekking uphill, to the meeting point with the *passeurs*—guides who would take over and lead them the rest of the way across the perilous peaks of the Pyrenees to Spain. Since my work began, the number of people moving along the escape line had grown. More Allied soldiers, downed airmen, and citizens fleeing persecution, mainly Jews. With not enough safe houses, we became desperate, and I'd occasionally hidden people at Henri's factory, in a basement there. It wasn't ideal, and we couldn't let the workers know about our clandestine operations, either. Henri complained to the hills about it. 'You'll have the entire Marseille Gendarmerie at our door, Nannie,' he said, throwing his hands up in the air. 'One night, that is all we can risk.'

He was as desperate to help those in need as I was, and I couldn't blame him for being concerned. 'They would never think to suspect you, Henri.' No, of that I was fairly certain.

Chapter 15
JULY 1941

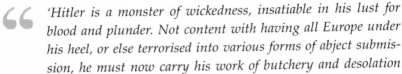 *'Hitler is a monster of wickedness, insatiable in his lust for blood and plunder. Not content with having all Europe under his heel, or else terrorised into various forms of abject submission, he must now carry his work of butchery and desolation among the vast multitudes of Russia and of Asia… Let us redouble our exertions, and strike with united strength while life and power remain.'* Winston Churchill. 22 June 1941.

Henri had never felt so ill. The diagnosis meant no more drinking. Well, the doctors had warned him before and advised him to cut down. Now they were telling him to give up alcohol completely. What did they know? 'You must tell your wife,' the doctor said. That was the last thing he was going to do. Nancy had a lot to think about, and he had no wish to worry her further. But later, when Nancy visited, her face fell.

'Henri, you're so pale. You look worn out.'

He could not hide how he looked, but he was determined to put on a front and convince her it was simply a minor virus. But she was right. Worn out, exhausted, he'd never felt this frail. His sun-kissed skin masked a slight jaundice. And now she had to suffer seeing him propped up on pillows in a hospital bed, fragile and sick. 'I will be all right, Nannie. Please, do not worry.'

Nancy bent over to kiss his cheek before pulling up a chair and sitting beside him, taking his hand in hers. 'The doctor wouldn't tell me anything. He said I was to ask you.'

Bless her, awash with concern and confusion. 'I have a virus, that is all.' She cocked her head to the side, a puzzled look on her face. 'A week in hospital, with treatment and I should be well again.'

The truth, however, was not so straightforward. 'Your kidneys are struggling, Henri,' the doctor had said. 'Which is why you must stop drinking alcohol. Light exercise only, and you must take better care of yourself.' All of it was too awful, giving up all that he loved. 'What is my prognosis?'

'Well, if you follow all the medical advice, you will live for some years yet.' The doctor pursed his lips, then with a heavy sigh, placed an information sheet on the bedside table — light reading. Henri didn't bother asking what would happen if he didn't do as he was told.

Nancy's voice fractured his reverie. 'I'm supposed to be going to Toulouse tomorrow.'

'Well, you must go, but be careful.'

'How can I leave you?'

'Am I not in the best place?' He reached for her hand. 'You go. And in a few days, I will be home again.'

I STOOD ON THE PLATFORM, but my heart was not on this mission at all. It was with Henri, and I wished I was with him by his side. I'd never seen him looking so ill. Something didn't feel right, but my train was due at any moment, and I had to concentrate. People milled around, and two small boys raced up and down the platform in a figure of eight, giggling, their laughter shrill, fracturing my thoughts.

The newsstand bulged with daily papers, all reporting on the German invasion of Russia. This had amazed the French, who recalled the history of Napoleon's defeat. He had tried to take Moscow over one hundred years ago and failed. Hitler had taken his war onto Soviet soil, and in the first week alone, there were reports of around one hundred and fifty thousand Soviet soldiers either killed or wounded.

The Jewish family I was taking to Toulouse stood a little distance away, just as I'd instructed them to do. They wore clean clothes and carried forged papers. As the train pulled in, I took a deep breath. I'd made this journey several times now, usually with servicemen, and I was confident all would be well.

The guard opened the carriage doors, and we boarded. I found a seat for myself and waited as my special cargo filed in and sat opposite.

I glanced at the boy. Joseph was fifteen, but already a fiercely independent young man. His mother was very thin and pale, and I wondered if she'd be up to the perilous crossing of the Pyrenees. It was a long journey, steep, climbing part of the way where the air thinned. I recalled stories of those who had become too weak to go any further, only to collapse in the snow and freeze to death. I clenched my jaw. Joseph's mother muttered under her breath, clasping her hands tight, perhaps in prayer. Her husband placed his hand on hers. He was tall, well-built, calm, and positive, and reminded me of Stanley.

Joseph's round hazel eyes were firm, filled with defiance and strength of spirit. His mother's, however, were wide, darting this way and that. The carriage door slid open, and the guard stepped in. 'Papers, please.' I reached into my bag and handed them to the aged man, who smiled back. His eyes flicked over them, and he peered back at me before glancing down again.

'Merci, Madame.' He thrust the papers into my hand and turned to the others. It was a simple formality, and all was well as the guard departed and closed the door. We all breathed a sigh of relief.

'How long will we be in Toulouse, Madame?' Joseph whispered.

How long's a piece of string? I mused to myself. 'A day or two perhaps, until it's safe to move on.' I flashed a reassuring smile. As a matter of course, I tried not to get involved with the people I helped along the escape line. Sometimes, with the Allied evaders, that was difficult. They were often British, and I loved them, and I couldn't help chatting, but with refugees, it was different. Some of them had fled appalling treatment at the hands of the Germans, escaping just in time while thousands more were trapped, rounded up, and sent to camps. But this family, for whatever reason, had become close to me. Joseph's mother had witnessed her parents' arrest. 'The Germans sent them to Drancy,' she said. Her eldest son was shot and killed just months earlier, for aiding the Resistance. It didn't do well to know too much, the less, the better for all concerned. But I couldn't help being touched by their plight. News of the arrests of Jewish men in Paris reached us back in May. Men between the ages of eighteen and forty had been told to present themselves to the police. Over five thousand Jews were arrested and sent to camps, sending shock waves throughout the city and beyond.

The train slowed as it eased into Toulouse, exhaled a breath of steam. I sat for a few moments as people disembarked before making a move. 'Follow on behind me, as before.' I nodded to them, smoothed down my navy skirt and jacket, and stepped off the train. I made my way to the Hôtel de Paris, passing my contact as I strode through the bar. 'Gin and tonic, please.' I turned and saw the family standing in the foyer, locked eyes with the contact, and nodded in their direction. He returned the gesture.

Please let them make it, I thought. Was there a God? Did heaven exist as my mother had so often proclaimed? All I knew was I had to return home and avoid awkward questions about my reason for travelling by any police and that I would remember Joseph, his family, their faces and voices for the rest of my life.

∼

I RETURNED HOME from shopping one morning, eager to kick off my red espadrilles and enjoy a lunchtime drink. I unclipped Picon's lead and watched as he trotted off to the kitchen. Claire stood in the doorway, a pensive look on her sweet, youthful face. 'Madame, Captain Garrow is waiting in the drawing-room. He is not alone.'

'Thank you, Claire.' I put my bag on the hall table, pausing briefly at the mirror on the wall to check my hair. Garrow sat at our desk in the corner of the room, writing. He stood up to greet me. The other man did not stand but continued to sit in Picon's favourite leather chair, which immediately raised my hackles and was extremely rude, I thought. As I caught his eye, a bad feeling stirred, like darkness descending, and I wasn't sure what to make of that, except he made me feel so uncomfortable.

'Garrow, lovely to see you.'

'Nancy, please forgive the intrusion. Meet Harold Cole. He's joined our operation, so you might run into each other from time to time.'

The man, Cole, managed a begrudging smile without meeting my gaze and muttered, 'Hello,' almost as if it was a bloody inconvenience.

I noted the crystal glass in his hand and the copper liquid within. A bottle of whisky stood open on the bar. Henri had been saving that for the day victory came, and this impertinent man had opened it, this man who didn't have the manners to greet a lady properly. His shifty shark-like eyes, dark, cold, gave me the shivers, and I hoped never to run into him again. Something inside me suddenly snapped. 'I would prefer it if you left, please,' I said as coolly as I could manage, looking at Cole. He glanced at Garrow, then back at me, before snorting, his face crinkling into a sneer. Slowly, he rose, downed the last of the whisky, and slammed the glass down on the mahogany table by the chair.

Garrow shot me a puzzled glance. 'I'll catch up with you.'

Cole left without another word. 'I don't care who he is or where he's from. I don't trust him, and you shouldn't either.'

'Nancy, I can assure you he's absolutely trustworthy. Cole's been assisting Allied evaders in Northern France. A contact recommended him and so far he's proved very worthy.' He folded the letter he'd written and slipped it inside his jacket pocket.

'Well, I don't like him. There's something about him, that's all. I hope you're right.' I poured myself a brandy. 'Anyway,' I smiled at him and sat on the sofa. 'What was it you wanted?'

'We need more money, I'm afraid. We have a batch of papers to pay for and safe houses. Well, you know how it goes. The money from England has run out. We're waiting for a drop, but meanwhile, we're rather stuck.'

My heart sank. Poor Henri was always being asked for something. 'How much do you need?'

With an apologetic expression, he said, 'Twenty-thousand francs.'

'I'll ask Henri later and sort something out.' Garrow didn't seem his usual self. My little performance had rocked the boat, but Cole had made me feel more uneasy than I had ever done facing any German soldier, so that was a definite red flag in my book.

We saw less of Garrow after that. He got his money, of course, and Henri and I came to the same conclusion. They only visited when they needed something. Well, it was nothing personal. It was war and survival. I suddenly realised how tired and anxious Henri had become. He was more relieved by the snub, whereas I was a little hurt. We'd risked so much, and I'd felt good about myself, fantastic. The work had given me a purpose; still, it was just as well not to have Resistance workers or Allied evaders at our home every other day. A few days later, the police raided one of Garrow's regular meeting places, Noailles Hotel, making several arrests. I heard through the network that they were looking for Garrow. I guessed he'd go into hiding, but I couldn't help wondering if there was a mole in the organisation, one by the name of Cole, perhaps.

September 1941

 Reds Battle Nazis In Leningrad Streets.

Névache was beautiful in autumn. I loved gazing at the majestic views of the rugged mountains from our chalet. Henri whistled. He looked so relaxed here. It was strange waking up to silence, occasionally to the faint sounds of chopping wood or a barking dog. Birdsong carried on the mountain breeze, raw, pure as nature itself. Sometimes at night, the faint drone of aircraft drifted over us. Whether it was the enemy or Allied forces, we couldn't see, but we hoped it was the Allies, perhaps on their way to give Mussolini hell.

'I wonder how Churchill's getting on with his meeting with President Roosevelt.' I glanced at Henri, who was sitting in front of the log fire, brandy in one hand, a smouldering cigar in the other. He shook his head.

'I cannot see the Americans joining. They recall the first war.' Henri downed the brandy, then reached down and threw another log on the fire. 'Look at the war in Russia. American mothers want to keep their sons safe, and who can blame them?'

He had a point. The Germans were determined to take Russia, but the siege in Leningrad was a bloody, brutal battle. The city lay in ruins, heavily bombed. News reports claimed the Russians had beaten the Germans back from the Front, while another claimed there had been about three million German lives lost. Even though the British had help from the commonwealth, such as the Aussies, Canadians, and South Africans, to name a few, it seemed to me that a larger force such as America would help tip the balance more in favour of an Allied victory. I went to the gramophone. One of Henri's favourite records was still on there—'L'Accordéoniste' by Edith Piaf. I wound up the gramophone, then placed the needle on the record. The sweet melody drifted out, sweet tones skipping into the air, filling our hearts. Henri looked at me, his face creasing into a warm smile, Picon asleep on the sofa next to him, and in that moment, I wished I could freeze time. Nothing was certain, but the present moment was perfect.

~

IN OCTOBER, we heard the shocking news of Garrow's arrest. They sentenced him to ten years in Meauzac Concentration Camp, but first, he was to spend three months in solitary confinement at Fort Saint-

Nicolas in Marseille. It was a dreadful blow. A Belgian called Pat O'Leary was now in charge.

'It is time for you to step back, Nannie.' Henri shot me a beseeching glance. 'Just for a short time, as a precaution.'

O'Leary came to see us one day soon after the arrest. He was tall, perhaps about thirty, with blue eyes and thinning blond hair. I liked him and immediately felt he was trustworthy.

'We need money,' he said, with a fleeting apologetic smile.

Henri passed him a glass of brandy, and we sat at the dining table, where we had a commanding view of the harbour. As O'Leary spoke of re-grouping and changing safe houses, my instincts grew into a frenzy as Cole preyed on my mind. I had to say something. I'd been right about him, I was certain. 'One person in particular is right under your nose. I'd stake my life on it.'

O'Leary shot me a knowing glance. 'Cole?'

He'd said that without hesitation, a clear indicator that he too was suspicious. 'Yes.'

He sighed, drank his brandy. 'I don't know. I haven't had much to do with him, but there are things that need checking.' He rubbed his chin, deep in thought.

After O'Leary left, Henri hugged me tight. 'Stay away Nannie. It is becoming too dangerous.'

I knew he was right. Henri always was, so I did as he asked, for now.

December 1941

O'Leary visited to request further funds. That awful man, Paul Cole, was, as I had suspected, not one to be trusted. He'd been stealing funds from the escape network and O'Leary, along with Bruce and a few others, had questioned him a few weeks ago. 'I said we should shoot him,' Bruce had told me later. 'But the others locked him in the bathroom while they decided, then the bugger escaped.' Word was the Germans had him. For the time being, this compromised the line. Bruce and O'Leary had travelled to Lille to warn as many others as possible, but the Gestapo made many arrests. We lost couriers, organisers, and safe-house keepers. My mouth ran dry at the news, bile surged in my throat. We'd have to lie low and re-group.

There was the question of two downed airmen who needed to cross the Pyrenees. It was becoming more and more clear to me that having such activities going on at my home was not good, so I asked Henri one evening about the possibility of renting another flat. 'It will be safer,' I said, 'and it means that O'Leary can use it as needed.'

Henri sighed. 'Yes, I think you are right. Leave it to me. We will find somewhere on the other side of town.'

A few days later, O'Leary told us the Gestapo had caught Bruce, and I felt the life drain from my body. Sinking into a chair, I sucked in a deep breath.

'They are holding him at St Omer in Lille.'

'But they'll interrogate him.' A stupid thing to say. It was obvious, but I couldn't bear to think of it. 'He won't talk.' I knew him too well. 'Bloody Cole,' I spat, clenching my fists. Garrow should have listened to me. 'You should have shot the bastard when you had him.' Bruce had wanted to. Too much bloody deliberation and the worm had wriggled away. One man had sealed the fate of so many. Henri passed me a glass of brandy, and I took a sip, got up, and went to the window. The streets below bustled with black Citroens and locals on foot, women with baskets of shopping. I opened the window, icy air washing over me, stinging my damp eyes. I downed the brandy, fire in my throat flaring in my belly. Trust no one. Take nothing for granted. I clenched my jaw, swiped tears from my eyes, an ache growing in my throat. 'Perhaps we can get him out, somehow.'

O'Leary shot me a blank look. 'I have men in Lille. There should be news soon.'

~

 The Japanese aerial strike force attacked the US Pacific Fleet on 7 December 1941 at Pearl Harbour.

THOUSANDS OF CASUALTIES and deaths were reported, and now, finally, Britain had the ally she'd been seeking, and suddenly it seemed as if the tide might turn. The new year began as it ended with war, fuel and food shortages. The people were cold, unable to heat their homes for long or at all. They were hungry, with reports of children growing sick with malnutrition, prey to diseases, even adults too. All I knew was our clothes were a little looser, but I had no complaints. Our cellar was well stocked. I continued providing food parcels for the Ficetoles, whom I knew to be struggling, along with other friends in need.

HENRI SAT SLUMPED in his armchair by the roaring fire one evening, shivering, having caught an awful cold. He didn't feel well, and he was uncharacteristically quiet and withdrawn. I'd exhausted all avenues of conversation and failed miserably at cheering him up. I switched the radio on, keeping the volume low while waiting for the BBC London broadcast. 'You'll soon talk if the Gestapo catch us,' I said.

Henri fixed his gaze on me as a frown flitted across his face. 'I suppose I will.'

I'd meant it as a joke, but it was a sobering thought, and Cole's menacing face flashed in my mind, unleashing a heavy feeling of foreboding. I swallowed and stared into the flames, tongues of amber leaping up the chimney.

Chapter 16

THE BREAKOUT

 Darwin Heavily Bombed in Two Raids

The Japanese launched an aerial attack on Darwin on 19 February 1942. Ninety-three aircraft in total. Reports stated that the damage was considerable. Waves of nausea rushed through me when I heard, and I immediately thought of my family in Sydney. Thank goodness they were safe, but for how long? It was all too awful. I opened the morning mail. There was a letter from Garrow. Henri had already left for work, so I poured myself some coffee and read my friend's news.

Picon trotted into the room and sat by my feet. I put the letter down on my desk as Garrow's words whirled round in my head. He was sick and starving in Fort Saint-Nicolas, and he'd asked me for food. His solitary confinement had ended, and he was waiting to be sent to Meauzac. When Henri returned home for lunch, he asked me about the letter. 'How did you know?'

'I saw it in the mail-box this morning.' He poured himself a small brandy. 'I recognised his hand-writing.'

I began telling him what Garrow had said.

'I forbid you to visit him, Nannie. It is too dangerous.' He wrapped his arms around me and held me close. 'I could not bear it if anything happened to you.'

I knew he was right, but my conscience gnawed away at me, digging deep, tugging at my heart, and I knew I'd never forgive myself if the worst happened to Garrow. 'Henri, he's ill, and he needs help. There's no one else. Why do you think he wrote to us?'

Henri huffed out a sigh, then kissed the top of my head. 'I do not approve, but if you must do something, then send a food parcel.'

I replied to Garrow, and knowing the mail to be censored, I pretended to be his cousin. O'Leary wasn't pleased and felt it was too dangerous, but he had no alternative plan. Soon, I received a visitation order.

I STROLLED THROUGH THE VIEUX-PORT, looking across to Fort Saint-Nicolas which stood on a hill above the harbour, grey, cold-looking. I'd packed a basket of goodies for Garrow—soap, toothpaste and brush, and food. When I saw him, I caught my breath. He was a tall chap, and his clothes hung from his emaciated frame, his face pale, sunken cheekbones, dark circles around his eyes.

'Thank you for coming,' he said in a quiet Scottish voice. As he opened the food parcel, his face lit up a little, a weak smile stretching his mouth.

The prison official said I could visit three times a week, so I decided to do that as Garrow desperately needed building up. We didn't speak of the escape network, but he asked after Henri. The conditions inside were as he'd described to me in his letter, and when it was time to leave, I assured him I'd return soon.

O'Leary was keeping his distance for now because of my actions. While disapproving of my work for Busch, he considered my visits to Garrow an immense risk. On the days I didn't visit, I wrote letters to Garrow, something that annoyed Henri.

'Why do you busy yourself so writing letters to him? Is it not enough that you see him three times every week? Anyone would think you were in love with him?'

'Oh, Henri, don't be silly. He's all alone. Having a letter to read every other day means the world to him, I'm sure because I know it would to me if I were in his place. I'm his friend, that's all.'

Henri sighed. 'A wonderful friend,' he said, flashing an apologetic smile.

~

SOON AFTER MY FIRST VISIT, a Frenchman and resistance worker called Frank Arnal came to see me. He'd been imprisoned at the fort, in the next cell to Garrow, and had just been released, having won an appeal. He urged me to help Garrow appeal his sentence but also informed me about a guard at the Meauzac Camp where Garrow was to be sent, who was most receptive to bribes. Apparently, more than one successful escape had resulted from that, so I asked O'Leary to see what could be done.

The next time I visited Garrow, I discovered he was gravely ill at the Michel-Levy hospital, having contracted jaundice. When I visited him, I whispered news of our plan to try to cheer him up, and it was a relief to see a glimmer of a smile on his sallow face. At least he was receiving proper treatment. When I returned home, I told Henri. 'We have to get him out, somehow.'

Henri stared at me blankly for a few seconds. 'You are doing all you can, at great risk.'

I knew Henri wasn't sleeping well. There had been many restless nights recently. 'I promise I'll be careful. No heroics.'

An appeal was Garrow's best chance, and I hoped O'Leary could arrange it. In the meantime, I continued to visit Garrow, taking food parcels with an added bottle of scotch whisky, disguised with hair tonic or cough mixture labels. After a month, Garrow was discharged and returned to his prison cell at the fort to await his appeal.

~

THAT SUMMER we heard the most awful news. Gendarmes had arrested thousands of Jews in Paris and herded them into the Vélodrome d'Hiver before transporting them away in railway cattle trucks. I could only imagine the scenes there, and at the height of summer too. Rumour had it there were no proper facilities, no food or water. Those poor souls. As I ranted about the injustice of it all, Henri's eyes glazed over, but you see it was hopeless. What could we have done? I wept for the children, babies, all so innocent. Apparently, some adults grabbed their children's hands and jumped to their deaths. Can you imagine feeling so afraid, so desperate, that you would do such a thing? Damn the Nazis, damn Hitler. It was all about resettlement, so we were told. Well, I didn't believe that for a minute as I recalled what I'd learned prior to the war.

I continued my double life, collecting evaders from safe houses and escorting them to the foot of the Pyrenees, where the passeurs would guide them over the crossing to Spain. My latest identity papers named me as Lucienne Carlier, a secretary to a doctor. It was a useful cover.

One day, a Gendarme questioned me at the Gare du Toulouse-Matabiau. 'How is it, Madame, that you can travel so widely, given that you are a mere secretary?'

Travelling came at an expense, and I always dressed for the occasion. 'Well, you see,' I fluttered my eyelashes and dipped my chin. 'I am a special secretary, Monsieur.' I raised my eyebrows, noted the twinkle in his eye. His face broke into a craggy smile, and he waved me through. It was my good fortune that some Frenchmen indulged in such guilty pleasures.

Battles raged on multiple continents: Africa, Europe, the Soviet Union, and out in the Pacific. And Pierre Laval, head of government, recently announced his hopes for a German victory. It's one thing to survive under the occupying rule, and quite another to sacrifice your honour, France's honour, to appease the enemy. Collaboration was an ogre, an ugliness bursting forward with willing violence, and I wondered how such people might live with themselves once the war ended.

November 1942

In the early hours of 8 November, one hundred thousand Allied troops landed in Vichy-held North Africa, at Algiers. Their commander was the American lieutenant-general, Dwight Eisenhower. Of course, the news was exciting and hopeful. The downside to this was soon revealed when the Germans marched across the Line of Demarcation two days later, unleashing an occupying force across southern France and now my beloved Marseille languished beneath vile swastika flags. They established their headquarters at Vichy, cloaking all public buildings with those vile flags; as instructed, we wound clocks forward one hour to German time, and they imposed a curfew. German soldiers mingled in the streets, cafes, and hotels. They flirted with French women, pretended they wished to be friends, but none were worthy of trust.

It had been a busy few months. Garrow's appeal had failed. In reality, his legal team had let him down, and I'd made certain to let O'Leary know just how angry I was. They sent Garrow to Meauzac, and I tried to visit weekly. It was quite a journey by train each Saturday, taking me beyond Toulouse, returning Sunday. I realised the Germans would introduce tighter regulations with more identity checks when travelling, and the risks would be considerably greater. The sooner Garrow was free, the better. I'd told O'Leary about the guard who took bribes and of my thoughts on breaking Garrow out. 'If I make the arrangements, will you arrange for someone to get him away from Meauzac and out of France?'

O'Leary blew out a breath, then nodded. 'Yes.'

Each week I visited Garrow, taking food parcels, hoping to identify the guard, but failing. Eventually, I thought he might contact me, especially as it seemed he was accustomed to making extra money on the side. The prison was a foreboding sight. Top security with searchlights, guard towers, and enclosed with three rows of barbed wire. I needed to discover the guard who might help us, as I feared time was running out.

One day, after I'd made many visits over many weeks, I was sitting in a bistro in Meauzac when a man approached me and sat down at my table.

'Madame, I have seen you before. You visit Captain Garrow?'

'Oui. He is my cousin.'

He glanced around before leaning in and whispering, 'Five hundred thousand francs and a policeman's uniform.'

Well, that was that. I agreed in a heartbeat. When I returned home, I would let O'Leary know, and then we'd have to arrange the payment and make the arrangements.

～

BEFORE THE MONTH WAS OUT, German forces surrounded Toulon. Their target was the French fleet, but the navy scuttled the battleships before the enemy could seize them. At least the Admiralty had no intentions of collaborating. There were, of course, repercussions. Travel regulations were tightened again, and diligence was vital. Our world was on fire, yet we carried on. We resisted and fanned German flames with a soupçon of French courage.

8 December 1942

I hoped Garrow was ready. Our plans to break him out of Meauzac were all in place. The guard had been found, bribed appropriately, and was now two hundred and sixteen thousand francs richer, thanks to the joint efforts of Henri and O'Leary's organisation. Fortunately, the guard was anti-Petain and anti-German. Dawn's honeyed light glowed hungrily beyond the curtains. I glanced at the clock—half-past five. Garrow would have slipped into the lavatory to pull on the police uniform, procured by O'Leary and smuggled in by the guard. A car was ready and waiting near the camp. At six forty-five in the morning, with the changeover of guards, Captain Ian Garrow walked directly past the sentry at the main gate and out of Meauzac Camp, striding down the road to the nearby woods and the car that would take him to Toulouse. O'Leary was close by, hidden in the undergrowth, along with another two men, just in case.

I'd barely slept, lying awake listening to Henri's occasional rhythmical snores while dreading today's great escape. Garrow had to make it. Only a few weeks ago, he'd sent a message to O'Leary as he'd heard from a guard that he was to be transferred to Germany. The escape had come just in time, with O'Leary getting the go-ahead from England. All I could do now was wait for news and get on with my life. I needed to be seen out in public as Madame Fiocca, shopping, lunching, doing my usual routine things. I had to play the part of the dutiful French wife, at least for a short while, to avert any unwelcome attention.

AFTER A WEEK, news came that the escape had gone well. Garrow was in hiding and would soon be on his way to Spain. Within a few weeks, all being well, he'd reach England. The relief I felt was immense. He had a greater chance of survival now, thank God. Ian was a good man, and I wished him well.

Since the occupation of the southern zone, O'Leary had moved his headquarters to Toulouse, which pleased Henri since it kept him further away from us. Of course, I was still actively involved with courier work, and the small flat Henri had rented for me was a little hub of activity as people came and went.

The other day when I called around, the lady in the flat below caught up with me. 'Madame, you poor woman,' she said, much to my surprise. 'Your cistern went at least twenty times last night, and I was so worried about you. The colic must be awful.'

I gritted my teeth. How many times had I told the evaders to only flush when necessary? 'I'm much better now. Thank you.' As soon as I went into the flat, I reprimanded the four men there. The last thing we needed was to stir suspicions and attract accusations. There were too many people just looking for an excuse to denounce someone. It was something that the Germans actively encouraged and rewarded. Families denounced family members, old feuds serving as catalysts to settle scores, and the financial reward was a great motivator. No one could afford to take any chances.

Chapter 17

JANUARY 1943

As I strolled along the Vieux Port with Picon, harsh shouts cut through the chilled January air. People in front of me stood gazing into the streets on my right, sullen faces. I squeezed the leash as I stopped to look. German soldiers had sealed off the Vieux Port. It was a warren of streets, with ancient buildings filled with rooms and apartments where a multitude of people lived, the poor, Jews, and black marketeers. To the Germans, it was the undesirable quarter, a hub of criminal activity, drugs and prostitution. 'What are they doing?' I asked a fisherman.

'Evicting everyone, and rooting out Jews,' he said before shuffling back to his stall of fresh catch.

I watched for a few minutes more. A surge of people emerged from buildings, tramped into the cobbled road, dragged on winter coats, children by their sides, bewildered looks etched on their chubby rosy faces, some crying amidst the yelling Germans. The air nipped ever icier at my cheeks, nose, and neck. I pulled up my collar. 'Come along, Picon.' I strode further along the quayside, gazed out to sea. White yachts moored in the harbour danced around on the current. Gulls screeched as they soared over masts, and German troops shouted as they trawled through the streets. It was ruthless. Where would all those people go? Why were they being evicted?

They weren't all Jews either, but what would be the fate of the Jewish?

That evening, when Henri returned home, I asked him if he knew anything.

'They are going to destroy the Vieux Port. That is why they have evicted everyone.'

'What will happen to them?'

'I do not know, but they will deport the Jews.'

I knew what that meant. Numbness blanketed my thoughts, my feelings, and I poured double brandies for both of us.

IT TOOK a few days for the authorities to clear the Vieux Port. They checked tens of thousands of identities. Most people could then go on their way, but they detained a smaller number and bundled them into trucks. It was a chaotic place to be, brimming with people, most refugees, with belongings crammed onto carts, people laden with huge bundles on their backs, others lugged bags, tatty suitcases and all they could carry.

We later heard they had deported the Jews to camps in northern France, crammed into cattle wagons, with barely any room to breathe. It is all one can do to pray for them, especially the children. Whatever was their crime?

I STOOD AT THE WINDOW, looking out towards the Vieux Port, my maid and housekeeper alongside me. The dust had shrouded the buildings and risen to greet the grey sky. Now, it had dissipated, exposing mounds of rubble, and devastated shells of homes ripped apart, inner rooms exposed, where furniture, people, and lives had been just days earlier. I lit a cigarette and filled my lungs, then passed it to Claire. She took a drag, then handed it to Madame Dumont. There were no words. Images flashed through my mind. A frail, elderly woman dressed in black hunched over. Distraught children among the crowd of people detained on cold, damp streets under the close armed guard of German troops before being taken away. My eyes misted over. I sniffed, ground my teeth as I wrestled with a demon of hopelessness.

~

I PICKED UP THE TELEPHONE. 'Bonjour, Henri.' I listened to his complaints about something his father had done at work, and suddenly a series of clicks snapped in my ear. The breath caught in my throat, and I froze for a moment. Was someone listening in? Maybe I'd imagined it, but then I heard it again. I had to get off the phone. 'Henri, I'm so sorry, my darling, but Picon is desperate for his walk. I'll see you this evening. Au revoir.' I replaced the receiver and puffed out a breath as icy prickles scratched my spine. I shivered, crossed the room and stood to one side of the window, peering out into the street below. The people of Marseille strolled along, stopping off at shops and cafes. Bicycles and black cars chugged along the road. I realised I'd have to be extra vigilant from then on and careful about what I said, especially over the telephone.

The following day, when I collected my mail, I noticed that all three envelopes looked as if someone had opened them before clumsily resealing them. Was someone intercepting my mail? Thoughts of Paul Cole returned, and I remained convinced he was working for the Germans. After Garrow, the Germans arrested several more main organisers. It was too coincidental. And Cole knew where I lived. Suddenly I felt sick, breaking out in a clammy sweat. Luckily, there was nothing incriminating in the post. Then I recalled something Claire had said about a man acting suspiciously in the lobby of our apartment building. She had spotted him loitering by the mailboxes just a few days ago. Were we under suspicion? If so, how long had the Germans been monitoring us? I tried to recall if I'd heard anything suspicious over the telephone before, but a rush of thoughts, fear, and fog clouded my mind.

Later, after taking Picon for his daily walk, I called in at the local bistro on my way home. It was eerily quiet. Since the Occupation, the locals loathed spending time brushing shoulders with German soldiers. We passed them in the street, faced them at checkpoints and train stations. Why would we drink with them? The manager stood behind the mahogany counter polishing glasses. 'Bonjour, Francois.'

'Ah, Madame Fiocca.' He smiled. 'What can I do for you today?'

I often bought provisions there and knew Francois very well. He'd been a soldier of the Great War, like Henri, and now helped with the local Resistance. He glanced nervously towards the door and out into the street.

'How are things?'

'Ah, busy, as always, Madame.' He glanced at the door again before ushering me closer.

He leaned over the counter and whispered, 'This morning, when you left home, a man followed you down the street.'

I swallowed. 'Are you sure?'

'Yes. I am convinced he was German. He wore a long black trench coat.' Francois placed his hand on top of mine. 'Please, Madame Fiocca. Be careful.'

I stepped out into the street, slipped on my gloves while casually glancing around. I blew out a breath, silver vapour curling in crisp winter's air. 'Come, Picon. Everything will be fine,' I muttered, waiting for the black Citroen to pass before I crossed the road, fingers of ice tapping my shoulders.

At midday, when Henri returned, I told him what had happened. The colour drained from his face as he sank into his chair. 'I have dreaded this moment, Nannie. We have to get you out of France.'

'What?' He wasn't serious, surely. 'I can't just leave.'

'Nannie, we have no choice. You must go.' Henri suddenly looked ten years older. 'You are on the cusp of being caught. The Gestapo could be on their way here any minute. Look at what happened to Monsieur Reynard. Vanished, never seen again. I will not let that happen to you.'

'I can't go without you. I won't.' My vision swam, tears wet my face as I threw my arms around his neck, clinging to him, drinking in his scent, filling my head with the memory long enough for it to take root.

'It is too difficult. I will tell everyone you are taking a break at the chalet, should they ask.' Henri held me tight, smoothing my hair, his touch soft, warm, comforting.

I glanced at him, aware of irritating droplets hovering on my eyelashes. 'I don't think I can do it.' My throat tightened with fear, not for myself, or of being caught, but of leaving all that I held dear behind. What if I couldn't return, ever? What if I never saw Henri again? My heart hammered against my ribs, my mouth dry, throat aching.

Henri smiled. 'Nannie, you are the strongest person I know.' He cupped my chin. 'You can do this.' He dismissed the shake of my head. 'You can do this for me. Oui?'

I swallowed, sniffed, and swiped the tears from both eyes. 'Only if you promise you'll be right behind me.'

'I promise, just as soon as I have secured things here, I will find you in London.' He drew in a breath. 'Come, we need to make arrangements.'

I couldn't believe this was happening. The wolf was almost at our door, and there was no time to waste. Whatever you knew, the Gestapo always knew more.

'But surely there's time. I don't have to leave today.'

'The enemy does not wait. We must act now.'

The Germans preferred to surprise their prey.

'Nannie, I love you, body and soul. I hoped this day would never come, but our luck has run out, and I have to save you. Quickly, you must pack.'

I wandered to our bedroom and dragged the enormous trunk into the middle of the dressing room. I opened the wardrobe and stared at my clothes, dresses, skirts, jackets hanging neatly. What should I take? I realised I'd have to leave some things behind, so it looked as though I would return. Henri came in shortly afterwards to find me sitting on the floor, folding garments. He dropped a stack of French notes onto the floor beside me.

'Fifty thousand francs,' he said, sinking onto his knees beside me, grabbing my hand. 'It should be enough to get you to England and find us somewhere to live. Take the jewellery too. You can always sell it if you need to raise extra money. I will send the trunk on ahead.'

I nodded, feeling dazed and numb. I took a fresh change of clothes and two silk nightdresses and placed them in an overnight bag, along with my jewellery and the money. All the while, thoughts hurled through my mind. We were both involved, and while Henri didn't know many details, he knew the names of some of the people involved, and he'd financed the Resistance. If the Gestapo called, they would surely question him. It was a terrifying thought. Bile swilled into my throat and I swallowed, gritting my teeth. Twenty minutes later, the trunk brimmed with clothes, yet still I hesitated over what else to take.

'Nannie, whatever you find missing when you reach London, you can replace,' Henri said, his voice becoming more urgent. 'I will get a message to O'Leary. We need help to get you safe passage to England.'

Fresh tears spilt down my cheeks. After the last few years and all the people I'd assisted along the escape line, I was now the evader. 'I'll find us somewhere to live when I reach London, and wait for you.' Gathering the money, I stuffed notes into my brassiere, as much as I could house without my cleavage looking too conspicuous. Next, I slipped my three-carat diamond engagement ring on my finger and stuffed the rest of my jewellery into a small velvet bag and tucked it safely into my handbag, along with the rest of the money. My hazy mind was a hurricane of thoughts so thick I couldn't grasp a single one. What was happening? Gripped by dizziness, I swallowed, placed a hand on the bedpost to steady myself. Until that moment I'd been strong, confident, capable of anything, but now I was a trembling, needy slip of my former self and it terrified me as I stared into Henri's eyes and glimpsed a flash of fear.

'Nannie, you are the strongest person I know.' Henri smiled, pressed his forehead to mine. 'I'll have the trunk sent on to Spain, care of Thomas Cook, Madrid. You can collect it there.' He kissed me hard, but there was no passion, more a desperation, as I felt it too.

I was packed and ready to leave within the hour. I slipped my coat on in the hall, Picon strutting around me, his feet tap-tapping on the tiled floor, his tail wagging. He thought I was taking him for a walk, except I was leaving him behind. My heart ached; a sob slipped from my mouth.

Henri drew me to him, his lips finding mine. A lingering kiss. 'I love you, Nannie. Be safe. Reach London.'

'I love you too.'

'And remember, you still have the safe deposit box at the bank. We have around sixty-thousand pounds in there, in money, bonds, and a little gold.'

Why was he telling me this? That was his savings, money he'd collect later. Doubts clouded my mind, but there was no time for questions.

'Nannie, remember that when you leave, you are going shopping, and will be back later, just in case anyone hears.'

Picon yapped, something he rarely did, and I knew he sensed I was leaving. I bent down. He jumped onto my knee and nuzzled my face and neck. 'Picon, I'll see you soon, my angel,' I said as I hugged him and stroked his chest. 'Take care of him, Henri.'

As I looked into Henri's sorrowful, tear-filled eyes, I thought my heart might break. 'This isn't goodbye. We'll see each other soon, won't we?'

Henri nodded, his mouth forming a faint smile. 'We will, Nannie. I will make sure of it.'

He walked me to the door, his hand on the handle. I swallowed, his other hand still in mine, soft, warm skin, his hold firm, confident, safe. What would I be without him? For the first time, I realised I needed him. I squeezed my eyes shut for a moment and sucked in a deep breath.

'It is time, mon amour. Be brave, Nannie.' Henri folded me in his arms one last time, nuzzled my hair, kissed my ear, the tip of my nose and my lips. He tasted of brandy. I pressed my face into his neck, inhaling the scent of him, greedily drinking him in, filling my lungs with shaving soap and undertones of cedarwood. The air smelled of saffron, the faint cooking smells of earlier ingrained into the fabrics.

I had to go now, and Henri could see how difficult it was for me, so he led the way, opening the front door wide. Picon yapped again. I picked up my bag, checked my hat was straight in the mirror and kissed Henri on the cheek, as I always did when I left the house. Out in the corridor, I turned, my heart jumping so violently in my chest, taking my breath away. I was adrift as my legs carried me to the stairs, fear and adrenaline coursing through my veins. What was I doing? I swallowed, raised my chin. 'Au revoir, Henri. See you shortly,' I said, hearing the quiver in my faint voice, a sinking feeling in my gut. The corridor screamed with silence as I strode away and headed down-stairs, my shoes tip-tapping on the stone steps. My voice screamed to Henri in my head. Please don't close the door. Come after me, my love. Please. Behind me, the distinct clunk of a door, muffling Picon's voice. No! My heart clenched as I stifled a sob, forcing myself to take deep breaths as my stormy mind raced and my heart pounded in my ears. A little voice in me begged for Henri to call me back for one last look, one final kiss, but he didn't, and I stepped across the marble floor of the entrance hall, the click-clack of my heels louder than usual, surreal, echoing. My legs felt like dough, muscles juddered and moving was like wading through treacle. Out in the street, a black car sailed past with a German officer sitting in the back. My heart lurched, but I held my head up high and carried on walking towards the station.

At Gare de Marseille-Saint-Charles, I boarded a train for Toulouse, conscious that any of the passengers might be Gestapo. Wracked by nausea, chest tight, I blew out a long breath. As the carriage filled, my heart drummed, my mouth ran dry, my palms soaked. Henri always mused over how nothing phased me. I'd embraced the Resistance work and never once felt afraid. It was thrilling and rewarding in so many ways, but now, here. I sucked in a breath and turned to gaze out of the window. A whistle cried out and then we were moving. I'd trav-elled this route numerous times—if only it was one of *those* times and I was returning home. Now, I too was a refugee, with nowhere to go.

The carriage door slid open, and I glanced up to see a familiar face. O'Leary. My heart lifted, and I smiled hesitantly, not wanting to draw the attention of the other passengers. He must have boarded the train somewhere along the line. He sat down opposite without speaking, and I turned to stare out the window, watching flashes of trees and green fields as the train raced through the countryside.

When we reached Toulouse, I followed O'Leary out of the station. Hopefully, he'd been able to plan my escape to England. O'Leary glanced around in the street. 'Come on. We'll get something to eat first.'

My body was heavy like lead, my eyes watery. It was surreal to be on the other side, to be the hunted. The Hôtel de Paris was well known to evaders and the Resistance. Inside brought welcomed warmth and no sign of any Germans. O'Leary picked a table away from the window and pulled out the chair for me. 'Thanks.' My stomach grumbled amidst a wave of nausea. I didn't feel like eating. My mind wandered as he glanced at the menu, and I was vaguely aware of him speaking as my thoughts returned to Henri and home. Home—where I longed to be. Why did I ever get involved? I'd been such a fool. Images of evenings snuggled up to Henri by the fire, drinking brandy, Picon resting at my feet, flashed before me. My chest ached, and tears misted my eyes.

'Nancy?'

His voice fractured the memory, and the image vanished. 'Sorry, miles away.' A single tear rolled down my left cheek, and I swiped it away, my finger wet with sadness.

O'Leary reached for my hand, stared into my eyes, his mouth forming a consolatory smile. 'I know it's hard, but it will work out.' He nodded. 'We do what we must to survive,' he whispered. 'Now, eat.' He handed me the menu.

He had arranged for me to stay there at the hotel. The proprietors, Monsieur and Madame Montgelard also worked with the Resistance and took great delight in housing some of the German soldiers there while sheltering evaders at the same time. I shook my head as I looked down into the street below, watching a pair of German soldiers strolling along the street, rifles over their shoulders. Adrenaline rushed through me like the tide, and I felt lost, alone, and broken. How had it come to this? I sucked in a breath and drew the drapes, taking a last look at the stars that gleamed so brightly against the midnight sky. Was Henri thinking of me right now? I glanced at my watch. Eleven-thirty. I clambered into bed, the chill of the sheets causing me to shiver through my silk nightdress, so I dragged on a cardigan and lay staring at the ceiling. Doors out in the corridor slammed shut, floorboards creaked and groaned as the old building breathed and sighed throughout the night. Sleep would not come easy, if at all. Each time I heard a noise, I caught my breath, waiting for footsteps and a knock at the door.

What was I going to do? Hopelessness engulfed me, tears washed my eyes, and my mind raced with a torrent of thoughts. Soon I would head for the hills and climb the Pyrenees to freedom. O'Leary was making plans. Henri would follow behind soon, and we'd be together once more, together forever. I would keep that image in my head. My brother's words echoed in my ears. 'It'll be okay, I promise. Be a brave girl.'

Chapter 18
ESCAPE

I gazed at the flashing countryside as the train raced to Toulouse from Perpignan. Three times I'd tried to escape across the Pyrenees, only to be turned back because of the weather. Only a fool would risk such a crossing. I sighed. I knew the route so well and needed no courier to deliver me to the guides. O'Leary had made the arrangements, but once again, I was returning, disappointed, frustrated, cross. The station lay up ahead, yet the train was slowing down, and halted short of it amidst the shouts of men. Milice. The carriage door slid open and armed Milice stormed in and commanded everyone to get off. I followed the line of passengers. Outside, a fleet of trucks and more armed Milice gestured to us to climb in. From the crowd of passengers, I saw my chance and made a run for it, headed for a side street. Unfortunately, I ran into a crowd of demonstrators who stopped me dead. 'Blast!'

'Halt!' a man yelled.

I turned. Several Milice raced towards me. I pushed on, shoving people out of the way. I had to get through, had to flee, but as I heaved and jostled at the dense mass, there was little give in their ranks, and I realised the jig was up. A heavy hand on my shoulder lashed my spine with chills, and I froze, turning to face my captors, who led me away to the trucks. Wild thoughts filled my head. Were they looking for me?

I felt as if I was going to throw up, my skin cool, clammy. I swallowed and sucked in a breath.

~

THE CELL WAS DARK, damp, and empty, the stench of piss and fear lining my nose. I glanced at my grazed knees, stockings shredded from when the guard had roughly shoved me inside, and I'd fallen to the rough stone floor. Reluctantly, I sat on icy flagstones in a corner, legs outstretched. The metallic tang of blood filled my mouth, my bottom lip full and stinging like hell. The blow had been a shock. Pathetic really, as I ought to have expected it. How was I going to escape? I suddenly thought of the Maori midwife who delivered me into the world. 'The spirits will take care of her,' she'd told my mother. 'Well, if you're listening, help me, please.' My side nagged and ached. It was one thing to slap a woman in the face, but quite another to punch her in the gut. The Milice enjoyed being able to rough people up, especially women. Blasted brutes. My mouth was dry, so dry, and there had been no offer of water or food, not that I was hungry. A sliver of honeyed light slipped in through the barred window above, stretching out a golden finger across the cell floor. Dawn. Soon, my captors would return.

I huddled tight in the corner, faced the wall where vivid green moss sprang like a sponge in clumps between the joints in the stone, the damp, mouldy odour filling my nose. I closed my eyes and thought of kinder times, of happier days with Henri. Our strolls through the Vieux Port of Marseille. Parties, my work friends, and finally, family. Dear Stan, still serving with the navy. How was he? Please, God, let him be safe. I thought of my sisters, Ruby and Gladys, and of the siblings I'd lost, Hazel and Charles. And Mum. I sucked in a deep breath, exhaling slowly. I screwed my eyes tight shut as I summoned their faces, and Henri's. Beloved Henri. My vision swam as I tried to stifle the sob, my chest aching. Those bastards would not see me fall apart.

Somewhere above a door slammed, the noise crashed into the

bowels of the building. The echo of footsteps. Milice HQ was awake, preparing to commit more inhumane acts.

Footsteps fell on the stairs leading down to my cell, a jangle of keys and a whiff of ersatz coffee. A young milicien grasping an enamel mug and a small plate with a thin piece of bread and jam.

'Good morning, Madame.' He crouched down to open the small flap in the door of my cell and set the mug and plate on the stone floor. He shot me a glance, his mouth forming a weak smile. 'Hurry, Madame, before they come for you.' He stood up tall, stepped back, and glanced nervously up the stairs.

He'd taken a risk for me. There was still some humanity. Well, I didn't need prompting. I couldn't remember how long it had been since I'd drank or ate. The bread was verging on stale, but the delicious strawberry jam made up for that, and while the ersatz had always been repulsive, right now it was heavenly. 'Merci.' Touched by his kindness, I passed the plate and cup through the flap.

The guard smiled, nodded briskly before heading up the stairs.

Within five minutes, two more guards appeared, grabbed me roughly by the arms and dragged me upstairs to the grand office of the Vichy Commissioner. A plump man, probably in his fifties, sat slouched behind a grand, mahogany desk. He glanced up from a stack of papers and rested his cigarette on the side of a crystal ashtray. 'Bonjour, Madame. Please, sit.'

The guard, who had a vice-like grip on my left arm, shoved me into a chair.

'It would seem you've had a rough night, Madame.' The officer stood up and walked towards the window.

A flash of red and black caught my eye at the window as the wind grabbed at the Nazi flags that shrouded the building, tugging them in anger. I'd already decided, just like yesterday, that I wouldn't talk. I'd withstood the first beating and could do so again.

'Ah, it looks to be a stormy day once more. The mist is rolling in from the mountains. The peaks will be treacherous.' He turned and smiled, a leering smile. 'And so, Madame. You refused to talk yesterday. It is pointless to resist. We will find out what we need to know. I seriously ask you to cooperate, and then we may conclude this matter.'

He sat down, his rotund belly like a barrel before him. Lord knew how he squeezed into the uniform. I was suddenly struck with the giggles and tried desperately to suppress any laughter but couldn't prevent the smirk from forming, and so I dipped my head and bit my bruised, swollen lip. The intense flash of pain did the trick and strangled all frivolity.

'So, what is your name?'

I gritted my teeth. 'Madame Fiocca. My husband is Henri Fiocca, a businessman in Marseille.'

'Yes, yes, you said all this yesterday.' He slammed his chubby fist on the desk, and I jumped. 'We know you are lying. We have made enquiries in Marseille, and there is no trace of you, nor of a man of the name Fiocca. You are wasting my time, Madame. Now I will ask you again. What is your name?'

'Madame Nancy Fiocca.' I stared into his dark eyes and saw him glance at the guard and give a signal with a nod of his head. I steeled myself, ready, but the blow to my stomach forced the air out in a wild rush as I doubled over, unable to breathe. Then, the guard grabbed my hair and yanked my head back, dragging me upright. Nausea surged in violent waves as I coughed, tasting blood and bile.

'We know you are a prostitute from Lourdes. There was an incident, an explosion at the cinema in Toulouse the night before your arrest. People saw you at the scene. It is no use denying it as we have several eye-witnesses who will swear to this.'

A prostitute? I could hardly believe what I was hearing. I was fleeing the Germans. Weren't they looking for Madame Fiocca of Marseille? I'd got it all wrong. But they were talking nonsense, and I realised I was a scapegoat. Regardless of any pleas, I would be found guilty and imprisoned, or worse. After several hours of interrogation, the beast finally allowed me to go to the toilet. I peered at my reflection in the mirror above the sink and my heart sank. My hair, matted with blood and my face, black and blue, red-brown blood ingrained into the slight lines around the mouth, and the pores in my chin, smears streaked across my cheeks. I turned on the tap and held my shaking hands in the flowing icy water. I splashed a little on my face and gently washed away the dried blood, skin stinging, throbbing. My left cheek ballooned, while bruising blossomed around my left eye. 'What a shiner. Bastards,' I muttered, gripping both sides of the sink. I took a few deep breaths, tucked the hair behind my ears. 'Well, Nance, this is one fine mess you're in. How the hell do you get out of this?'

As I lay in my cell, every inch of my body ached or throbbed. Four days passed, each one brought another round of beatings and questions. After a while, one became accustomed to pain, and I surprised myself with my resilience. They could charge me, for I wouldn't break. A familiar voice from above called out, 'Nancy,' and I looked up. Footsteps on the stairs, growing louder. The guard appeared first, followed by a man in a suit. O'Leary. Jesus. They'd arrested him too. He cast me a smile as he spoke with the guard. I couldn't hear what was being said. What was he doing? He'd blow my cover. My heart hammered faster than ever, and my mouth ran dry. The chink of metal keys in the lock and O'Leary was by my side, crouching down, kissing me on both cheeks.

'What are you doing?' I whispered.

'Play along,' he said quietly, and then in a loud voice, 'Ma chérie, come. I am taking you home.' He helped me to my feet and took me in his arms.

I was confused. What plan had he concocted? We followed the guard up the stairs and along the corridor, which I knew so well, to the commissioner's office.

'Ah, Madame, sit down.' The commissioner smiled, although his expression remained stony.

O'Leary placed his protective arm around my shoulders.

'Monsieur Dupont has told us everything. Madame, I knew you were lying from the start. If only you had told us the truth, then you could have avoided all of this unpleasantness.'

I sat and listened as he prattled on, occasionally gazing at O'Leary, longing to know what cock and bull story he'd told them. Look at him, larger than life, grinning back at me, playing the part. My God, he had some guts. Before I knew it, the commissioner discharged us both. A guard returned my handbag and coat, and O'Leary took my arm as we walked into freedom. I stood in the street and gazed around for a moment. How surreal that life rolled along in Toulouse; people chatted as they went about their day, shopping, working, unaware of the brutality that took place in the building behind us, delivered most efficiently by fellow Frenchmen. They'd have their day of reckoning soon enough. I devoured fresh air in huge gulps while smiling at the ocean of sky, the winter sun stroking my face. For a fleeting moment, the pain of leaving Henri behind vanished, supplanted by the pure relief of freedom. But it could not last.

'Come on.' O'Leary said.

'What the bloody hell did you tell them?'

'That I was a member of the Milice, and you are my mistress.' He smirked. 'I said that your husband works in Marseille and we had been away together. I suppose you could say I appealed to him as one Frenchman to another.' He hitched an eyebrow.

I laughed for the first time in days. O'Leary was a great actor.

'When you did not return, we knew something had happened. We knew the weather had turned, so I made enquiries which led us here. I obtained false papers that identified me as Milice, and I told the commissioner I was a very good friend of Pierre Laval, who, incidentally, is conveniently in Berlin. So, when the commissioner wished to verify things and telephone Laval's office, I told him that Laval would be most annoyed if they inconvenienced Madame Fiocca any further.'

I shook my head, grinning, despite the throbbing pain in my mouth and face. 'You've got some nerve, that's for sure.' I suddenly remembered the money and my jewels and delved into my bag, felt the rough pile of notes, the cool metal of gold chains. 'Phew!' Now that was lucky.

~

FRANCOISE WAS a lovely lady about sixty years old. She welcomed me into her home and wasted no time in cursing the enemy. 'The Boches captured my nephew near Dunkirk. They sent him to one of their camps in Germany.' She wiped her hands on her apron, her grey hair bound into two plaits over her head. Adjusting her black spectacles, she said, 'I despise the Germans.' Her blue eyes narrowed.

We shared a bond. It was such a relief to have somewhere to hide at first, but as the days dragged on, I became more restless. Four more failed attempts to cross the Pyrenees took their toll, my brave face waning. Each one coincided with the Germans making many arrests, forcing our contacts and guides underground. Finally, my temper boiled over. 'There's a mole in the network, Pat. There has to be!' While I left him to make fresh plans, I had to remain where I was. I spent my days cleaning, cooking, anything to take my mind off my own problems, desperate to banish the pain that gnawed away in my gut and chest. Why hadn't Henri followed on as he'd promised? Too much care for his work, the family, no doubt. But what about me? He was my husband. Tears pricked my eyes, my cheeks burned as I clenched my fists. 'What have I done?' I muttered. Henri would have done what he felt was right, and I knew he would have tried. Perhaps he had fled, perhaps, but my actions had placed him in peril. I thumped my fist on the table, the bang jostled and chinked cups on saucers, pain throbbed through the side of my hand.

The Germans held all the power now, and had taken everything from me, and for the first time in my life, I had to accept my situation. It was hopeless, and I had to wait. And I had to quell the screaming urge to contact Henri and ask him what the devil was happening. Had to resist. It was all I could do to keep him safe.

I wasn't the only person on the run. Francoise was also hiding ten evaders at her flat. By day, I washed laundry, and by night, we played cards. Francoise, with her bamboo cigarette holder resting between her teeth on one side, permanently smoking, while sipping coffee from the other side of her mouth. 'The Milice and the Germans are swarming everywhere now, with more patrols at the Spanish border,' she said. O'Leary was organising a new escape party, and I hoped and prayed that it would be successful.

∾

WE SPLIT INTO TWO GROUPS. I travelled with O'Leary, a French Resistance Radio Operator called Philippe, a French policeman known as Guy and a New Zealand airman. The train to Perpignan was crammed, but there were no signs of German soldiers. It was a pleasant day, with a light breeze and a clear sky. I had a good feeling about this journey. The door to our compartment slid open, and the guard stood there, breathless, his face flushed. 'The Germans are searching the train. Get your papers ready, please.' He turned and headed further along the train.

The train was slowing, and we were nowhere near a station. O'Leary glanced at me, his eyes darting all around. 'Jump,' he said in a low voice, his eyes urgent. 'I will see you at the top of that hill. There is a vineyard. Go, quickly.'

Without even thinking, I dragged the window down, reached for my bag, looked at the ground below as I clambered up onto the seat, then hurled myself out the window, hoping for the best. I hit the hard ground with a thud, rolled over a few times before coming to a stop. My entire body ached, while stone chips had ripped my stockings, stinging my knees. A screech of brakes as the train slowed to a halt, and the accented voices of German soldiers, followed by machine-gun fire. There was no time to lose. I looked around and glimpsed one of the others sprinting towards the trees at the foot of the hill and followed, not daring to look back as bullets zipped over my head. Within a minute, the voices had trailed off, but I ran like a deer, through the vineyard and beyond, until I reached the top of the hill. Beneath the wide, low boughs of an oak tree, I sank to the ground, breathing hard, sweat trickling down my back, drenching my chest and brow, my lungs beating like bellows. Overgrown grasses shushed and rattled in the breeze. As I took in the surroundings, keeping an eye out for the enemy, my heart sank. In the heat of the moment, I must have dropped my bag. My jewellery and the cash. My rings. No! Why did I take them off? My beautiful engagement ring and a diamond eternity ring now lost. Stupid, so bloody stupid. Then there was the diamond-encrusted watch, brooches, and bracelets, all gifts from Henri. I exhaled, my eyes misting with tears. Where was O'Leary? Guy arrived, breathless, rosy-cheeked, surprise drifting over his face. I sniffed and blinked the tears away, resting my hand on my chest. It was a little padded, and something rustled. The money! I'd taken some of the money and stuffed it in my brassiere. At least I had some cash.

'Have you seen O'Leary?' I glanced all around, looking for signs of the others. The second party had also been on the train.

'Non. No sign.' He sat down, opened his coat, and sucked in a deep breath.

After a few more minutes, O'Leary arrived. 'I went back to see if the others made it off the train, but I didn't see anyone.'

Guy stood up. 'I'll go back and see what has happened.'

'Be careful. The train is still there, so the soldiers will be searching.'

I glimpsed the other two men as they made their way uphill towards them. 'You made it. Any sign of the others?'

They both shook their heads. 'Nothing. Didn't see or hear a thing except for Nazis on my tail.' The New Zealander sat beside me.

'Well, we can't stay here,' O'Leary said. 'Come on.'

THE WIND HOWLED AS it nipped at the sides of the stone barn. Inside was freezing, riddled with draughts and I thought to myself it would be just as warm sleeping outside. At least it had a roof. We lay huddled together for warmth. I sat snuggled between O'Leary and the New Zealander. It was times such as these when morals and modesty had to take a back seat. Survival was key, but it didn't stop me from wondering what Henri would think if he saw me now. Under any other circumstance I would have laughed, but here, trapped in such a predicament, I felt like crying. Life seemed to be at its bleakest, darkest ebb. The French Resistance fellow was on watch duty, although it looked more like he was asleep as he'd been sitting on the floor in the same position by the door for an hour. Either that or he'd frozen to death. It was our second night in the barn. I desperately needed a bath and a fresh change of clothes, if only to feel human again. My eyes grew lead-heavy, fluttered, and I gave up fighting the darkness, the darkness from which the Germans and the Milice had an annoying habit of waking and pulling you from in the middle of the night. Did anyone ever sleep properly anymore?

THE TREK back to Francoise in Toulouse was tiring. We left at sunset on the third day after our escape from the train. My stomach gurgled, protesting as we trudged along rural lanes, dust and dirt lining our clothes and bodies. If the police spotted us, they'd arrest us in a heartbeat, so we stuck to the minor routes to avoid them and any German patrols. As we passed a field, I spotted crops and couldn't resist jumping the ragged stone wall to see what I could scavenge. For the fruits of my labour, I sourced a lettuce, tugging it from the earth, brushing off clumps of moist soil and a cluster of tiny black bugs that clung on for dear life. Re-joining my party, I offered the food around, but the men declined, pulling ridiculous squeamish faces. The lettuce was fresh, healthy, and better than nothing, I thought as I ripped off leaves and ate them.

After five days, we finally reached the safe house, hungry, dehydrated, exhausted. We'd slept and rested by day, sheltering in barns, sheep pens, any old farm structure we found along the route, and as a result, we had a rash and itched from head to toe. It transpired we all had scabies and had to be scrubbed down with disinfectant. Francoise was a welcome sight, and we embraced like old friends. Inside, the waft of cooking drifted to greet us as she ushered us to the kitchen. She poured coffee while we sat around the wooden table with O'Leary and began making new plans to escape.

As I listened, my thoughts turned once more to the possibility of a spy in our organisation. I knew in my heart that something was amiss. Meanwhile, my clothes were filthy, and Francoise kindly took them to the launderette.

O'Leary turned to me. 'I have a meeting tomorrow with a recruit who has joined our group in Paris.' He lit up a cigarette and inhaled a lungful. 'It is funny, but he claims he has heard of you, Nancy.' He raised an eyebrow. 'Said he wishes to meet the amusing girl from Marseille.'

'Does he indeed.' I swallowed, a bad feeling drifting over me.

'Do not worry. I have no intentions of bringing him anywhere near you; besides, I have not met him yet.' O'Leary looked into the distance for a moment. 'Yes, he was quite insistent.'

Something wasn't right. I could smell it. 'Be careful tomorrow, Pat.' I longed to tell him not to go, but it wasn't my place. We took risks, that's just how it was.

2 March 1943

The following day, I was busy sorting my clothes in the kitchen with Francoise when a young Frenchman burst in, wide-eyed, breathing hard.

'The Germans have O'Leary.'

I felt queasy, my heart and head raced. The new agent, the man who'd wanted to meet me, must have been a double agent.

'We have to get everybody out.' Francoise dropped her wooden spoon onto the table and moved the pan off the stove. With her hand on my arm, she said, 'Hurry. Get ready to leave while I round the others up.'

I dashed to my room and grabbed my brown leather shoes from beneath the bed, cleaned and recently resoled after dear Francoise had taken them to the cobblers. I slipped on my camel coat, then snapped the gold clasp on my black handbag shut, my hands shaking. My heart drummed in my ears, and my head swam. Please, God, keep O'Leary safe. Wild images flashed before my eyes. He had to be all right. At worst, they'd send him to one of their camps, and he would survive because he was a fighter. He was clever, resourceful, diplomatic. I knew that someone in the network, someone close had betrayed us. An informer. The net was drawing in tight. When I emerged from my room, a friendly face from the network stood in the kitchen.

'Bernard.' I smiled, aware of Francoise busying around, grabbing her coat, keys and bag as she called to the other evaders she was hiding.

'I see you've heard about O'Leary. Francoise says you cannot go with the others. I have somewhere for you to stay tonight.'

'Merci, Bernard.' He was a saviour.

He nodded. 'I will take the others to their safe house, then we will travel back to Marseille before we do anything else. We must warn everyone.'

Once again, I was reliant upon the kindness of others for my safety. My mouth was dry, tightness spreading across my chest, and I paced the floor as I thought of O'Leary. He'd risked everything to get me out of prison, and I felt I ought to help him, but Francoise warned me off. 'It is madness. You will get arrested, and it will be a far worse situation for both of you.' She hugged me tight, then kissed my cheeks several times, the stale odour of cigarette smoke on her skin and hair. Tears trickled down my face, partly because of her kindness, partly because I was leaving again.

'Merci, Francoise. I will never forget what you've done for me. Bless you.' I squeezed her hand, not wishing to run again, yet I had no choice. The tide had turned, and I was the prey. But Marseille. Henri. My heart leapt with joy and sadness. I'd be so close and yet so far, unable to stop by or telephone.

~

AS THE TRAIN drew into the station at Marseille, the breath caught in my throat. There, standing on the platform, was a policeman I recognised from my arrest. 'Bernard,' I whispered. 'That policeman knows me. He saw me at Milice HQ.'

He glanced around. 'Follow my lead.'

As we stepped off the train, Bernard took me gently in his arms and kissed me. With my sunglasses on, I hoped the man would not recognise me. The kiss was warm and sloppy, but I didn't care just as long as it did the trick. Bernard broke away, and with a quick glimpse at the man, slipped his arm around my shoulders as we turned away. Thank God no one challenged us, although I expected it, my heart in my mouth. As we descended the stone steps from Saint-Charles station, Marseille called to me with whispers as delicate as the light sea breeze, urging me home into Henri's arms. My eyes filled with tears, a familiar ache tightening in my throat. A voice in my head urged me to run home. It would be fine. No one would see or know, but I clenched my jaw and fought hard to push the thought away.

'This way,' Bernard said, taking my arm in his.

He was keeping to the side streets, but all I could think of was strolling down Boulevard d'Athenes to La Canebière, turning right, as my heart drew me to Henri. At that moment, I longed for the safety of home, to close the door behind me and hide from the war and an oppressive enemy, wishing it would all vanish as quickly as the mist that rolls in from the sea. But wishes weren't ours to command, and I followed Bernard like a forlorn puppy, fighting with every step to suppress the scream inside.

The briny air sailed overhead, and I inhaled deeply, savouring the tang in my nose and mouth, momentarily closing my eyes, reminiscing by-gone days. When I opened them, people hurried by in the road, the stress of the Occupation etched on their faces. What if Henri had left? He'd promised to follow on, but then O'Leary would have known, and he would have told me. Bernard called at two houses to warn the occupants of the latest news, only to learn that word had already spread. Apparently, there were evaders at my little flat, the one Henri had rented.

'We'll go to the flat first before we go on to Nice,' Bernard said.

THE TRAIN PUFFED out of Marseille and Bernard rested his head back as he blew out a breath. Henri's money was scratchy against my chest, and my soul ached and sobbed for all I was leaving behind. We had collected a package from my flat—two Allied airmen. At least they had a chance with us. I was also conscious of not having an identity card, well aware of the repercussions of being caught without one, but luck was on our side, as our journey to Nice was uneventful. We headed to Madame Sainson, to her little flat in Rue Barralis, one of the safest safe houses there was. She was a lovely, remarkable lady, about ten years older than me, married with children. Both she and her husband were involved with the network. They could house up to seven or eight evaders at a time, their home a hive of activity. I'd often made the trip from Marseille to Nice with a few evaders in tow to deliver to her or to collect them, and we'd become firm friends over the past two years. She was such fun, although a security nightmare, posing for photographs with evaders in tow alongside Italian soldiers! The entire population of Nice knew to send her any waifs and strays. She made me smile and laugh though, which during dark times was a blessing indeed, and I needed to see a friendly face.

Chapter 19
MADAME SAINSON

We climbed the stairs to Madame Sainson's modest apartment. The doormat was straight today—one of only three security measures. The second was a crooked mat which signified danger, and the third was a hand grenade kept inside by the door, intended to be thrown at the unwelcome visitor. I knocked, and Madame Sainson opened the door, a huge grin breaking out on her face. 'Bonjour, mon ami.'

'Nancy! How are you?' She ushered us all inside, locking the door behind us before greeting me with a firm hug, kissing me several times on both cheeks. 'You are safe. I have been so worried.'

'I'm so happy to see you.' I gazed around. The apartment looked the same as always, cosy. The delicious aroma emanating from the kitchen sent my senses reeling, and my stomach grumbled out loud.

'Nancy, look at you. You are so pale and thin!' Madame Sainson frowned, her large hazel eyes twinkling. 'Come, sit down and I will bring you some food.'

'Merci.' I followed her to the kitchen, where the smell of coffee drifted under my nose. Rather than coming here to collect a 'package', I was the package, and the realisation hit me, sapping the wind from my lungs. A young man with sandy-coloured hair poked his head around the doorjamb. 'Any chance of coffee, Madame Sainson?'

'Oui.' She smiled and cast me a glance, rolling her eyes. 'There are five of them now, and last week there were eight!' She shook her head. 'It is incredible. They swarm like ants across France, filling safe houses, and just as they go, more arrive. Non-stop.'

I smiled, thinking of how alike we were, aside from the security issue. She was a jolly soul, but her eyes were dark and freshly lined since I'd last saw her. It was a strain, clandestine work. A constant threat hung over you, and you were always waiting for the knock on your day, especially at night. But like me, she was upbeat and refused to let anything get her down. She had the heart of a lion.

'Everything is being arranged,' Madame Sainson said. 'I will have your new papers ready in two days. You will have three Allied airmen with you too, and I will arrange fresh clothes.' She smiled, her full brown eyes kind and warm, as any mother's, and I loved her for her friendship.

THREE WEEKS PASSED, three weeks of daily life, trips to the cinema with the Sainson children, and shopping. Armed with fresh identity papers, I felt confident enough to venture out. News of O'Leary had reached us, and it wasn't good. The agent who had betrayed us all was known as "Roger Le Legionnaire". He had been looking for me, and once again, O'Leary had saved me. Now he was on his way to Dachau. I prayed for his good health and survival, and I wished with all my heart for the tide to turn soon.

We'd recently discovered that the guides had resurfaced and were once more escorting evaders across the Pyrenees. Bernard made preparations, and soon I was getting ready to leave again.

'I am going to England with you,' Bernard said. 'I have friends there.'

The only problem we had was in finding the man who arranged the *passeurs*. No one knew how to contact him. I thought of my trips in the past. One time, O'Leary left me on a street corner in Perpignan while he called at a house to arrange a guide. I told Bernard. 'When we reach Perpignan, I'll go to his house. I remember where it is.'

'But we do not have the password. He will not listen to you.'

'He bloody well will. I'll make sure of it.' I'd not gone through hell for weeks to be turned away. As I gazed out of the window across the city, a sense of finality consumed me, and I felt I wouldn't be returning.

Chapter 20
THE PYRENEES. MAY 1943

I stumbled as I traipsed up the hill. My thighs and calves ached while my tummy grumbled under protest. One minute my heart leapt with joy as the prospect of safety loomed, and the next it lurched and ached for all I'd left behind. After so many failed attempts and so many months, England drew nearer with each step I took. The old man in front of me tripped and fell onto the grass, puffing and panting. 'Come on, up you get.' I took hold of his arm and hauled him to his feet. I wasn't about to be held up, not after waiting this long. He staggered, so I placed my hand on his back and gave him a light shove to propel him up the hill. 'I'll push you all the way if I have to.' I was aware of the harshness in my voice, but we had to carry on. If any of them fell behind now, it wouldn't end well. Cruel to be kind. The moon vanished behind a dense cover of cloud and the night grew dark. The man in front stumbled again. 'Come on, not much longer now, and you can have a rest when the truck comes.'

After half an hour, the guide leading our party stopped up ahead. 'We rest here until dawn,' he said.

'Thank goodness for that,' I mumbled, glancing at my watch as I sank where the ground dipped on the hillside. It was just gone three. The chilled night air nipped at my skin, and I pulled my coat tighter and wrapped my arms around myself. I half-smiled as I thought of my bolshiness when I'd tracked down the man who arranged the passeurs. When he'd answered his door in Perpignan, I'd said in one breath, 'I'm Nancy Wake. We both work for O'Leary, and I need to get to Spain. I've had one hell of a journey getting here, so don't give me any crap.' Luckily, he laughed and invited me inside. Job done. I lay, listening to the sounds of the night, rustles from the men sprawled out on the surrounding ground, the screech of an owl, the whispering pines that stood around our little band. All too soon, the guides were shaking us awake. I squinted in the early morning sunflower light, a mist hugging the ground, rising to shroud the mountain peaks. We tramped up a track through woods and emerged onto a road, my heart soaring as I spotted the awaiting coal truck. The driver, dressed in a black coat and beret, puffing on a cigarette, glanced at us briefly and turned away.

'Come,' the guide ushered us into the back of the truck. 'Lie on the coal.'

He dragged hessian covers over us and the cargo. Coal dust lined my nose, and I made the mistake of licking my lips, the tangy dust making me wince. The truck lurched forward and trundled along windy roads, climbing steadily, braking harshly on sharp hairpin bends. We were in the military zone. No one was allowed there unless they lived there, of course, and they had to have a residential permit. I lay frozen among the coal, heart drumming. Lumpy nuggets of rock jabbed my head, prodded my back. We passed through several German checkpoints, and each time soldiers searched the truck, but not the cargo. And each time we lurched away, I heaved out a breath of relief despite punches from the coal beneath my body. It was excruciating as everything ached and throbbed. My backside was numb, and I thought if the Boches found us now, at least it would be a relief to climb off this damn coal heap.

Finally, the truck stopped, and the driver hauled off the covers, momentarily dazzling me with honeyed light. 'We have crossed the military zone,' he said, his voice gruff. He gestured for us to go into the woods. 'Wait in there for the passeur.' He nodded, and as he climbed into the lorry and drove away, I prayed our guide would be along soon.

I dusted myself off, aware of thick smears of black on my trousers, shoes, coat, skin. Coal wasn't just dusty; it was damp too. I shivered as icy tingles prickled my back. No doubt my face was as sooty as a chimney sweep's, but we were safe, and that was all that mattered. I had a small amount of food, like everyone else, and had to make it last, so I nibbled on half a slice of bread and reached for my bottle of water. 'I could murder a real drink.'

'Here.' The New Zealander offered his silver hip flask. 'Brandy.'

I smiled, savoured a mouthful of fiery liquor. 'Thanks.'

At sunset, the *passeurs* arrived: a Spaniard called Jean, and a younger girl called Pilar, accompanied by her terrier. My heart leapt at the sight of the little dog, who greeted me with a wagging tail. Thoughts of Picon howling for me and of Henri flashed through my mind with such force that tugged at my soul, and I gritted my teeth, determined to remain focussed.

'Now, everyone must do as we say. These routes are notorious, and people have died. Change your shoes and put on the espadrilles. They make no sound. The Germans patrol the mountains with dogs, but they dislike the higher peaks. That is where we will be. The tracks are uneven, very rocky and you must watch your step.' Jean wore a good few days' worth of stubble, his voice gravelly. I'd heard stories of the guides—*passeurs*—smugglers and black marketeers, rough men, but they knew the terrain and were indispensable.

The Canigou Massif began with lower slopes of scenic forests, rising steadily into higher peaks of rock, scree and cliff, where the air grew thin at around nine thousand feet. The rope-soled espadrilles gave some grip, but one still had to tread with care.

'From here, the crossing will take us maybe forty-eight hours. We walk for two hours and then rest for ten minutes. We walk by night, rest by day. When we rest, change your socks if they are wet. There is snow higher up. When we move, put the wet socks back on, or you will get frostbite.'

One of the American airmen grumbled about what lay ahead.

Jean flashed a stern look, aware of voices competing with his own, and he raised his more. 'There is no talking, coughing, or smoking allowed. If you have to cough, do whatever it takes to muffle it. Use your coat or your fist. You must not make any noise. Up here, sound travels, and we must not alert any patrols.'

Jean went on ahead, while Pilar formed the rear. We set off as the last vestiges of sun slipped from view, leaving a strawberry candy wash beneath clouds of slate grey. Some tracks coiled up tight around the highest peaks, forcing us to scramble on hands and knees as we hauled ourselves up. Climbing was the hardest part and the grumbling American only made matters worse as he kept breaking Jean's no talking rule, complaining about the cold, the wet, and his aching feet. As we climbed, snow fell, and all too soon we were walking in it, six-inches deep, my legs and feet throbbing, eyes growing heavy, gasping for breath as the air thinned.

Behind me, someone complained they were starving. We were all hungry, thirsty, tired, but I ignored my rumbling stomach and grabbed handfuls of snow, stuffing it in my mouth as I climbed, quenching the thirst a little despite the icy pain zipping through my teeth. Well, it was better than nothing. As dawn washed into the sky, we stopped to rest at a wooden hut. It was a relief to get into the dry and to collapse on the floor. I took out my food and ate some bread and jam, my stomach gurgling as I chewed. Outside, pine trees flecked the valley below and above, with the highest snowy peaks poking into the heavens. Now that we'd stopped, my body felt so heavy, my legs like jelly. As I chewed, my eyelids grew heavier, and I closed my eyes, laid my head on my bag, and allowed sleep to take me away.

Twelve hours later, after nightfall, we staggered into a raging blizzard. The snow swirled around us in a frenzy, whipping my face, cheeks and ears stinging. Jean, who was by then barely visible, showed no sign of slowing and we pressed on. The American grumbled louder and sank to the ground in front of me.

'Get up. If you stay there, you'll die.' We were all drenched.

'I can't go on. This is crazy. I say we go back.'

He can't be serious. We've come so far. 'Get up, or we'll leave you behind to the Germans, and you know what they'll do to you.' I tugged at his arm and half-dragged him to his feet. 'Come on, or I'll push you into a gorge!' With a grip on his arm, I dragged him along amidst a torrent of swearing and protests.

He walked just ahead of me, slowing my pace, so I pushed him along, aware of his grumbling as he plodded and stumbled through the snow, his words eaten by the biting blizzard. Jean had certainly chosen the rockiest route. There was no way the Germans would venture up here with their dogs. Only a bloody fool would dare attempt this crossing. We clambered up slopes of varying gradients, slipping, clawing our way up in places, clinging to rocks as we climbed. My hands stung. They were so frozen, fingers almost numb, gloves soaked through. Jean had stopped and waited up ahead.

'How much further?' My lungs felt as if they might burst as icy snowflakes nipped my lips and nose.

'One more mountain. You are all doing well,' he said, his Catalan accent thick. 'We rest here for ten minutes. Change your socks.' Snow frosted his eyebrows.

Never had I felt so bad. Well, maybe when I was locked in that cell, but this was still preferable to that. At least I was free, I thought, as I perched on a low rock, grabbing my dry woollen socks from my bag. One by one I peeled off the wet socks, my feet pale with red blotches, toes numb, blanched white. I pulled on the dry ones and rubbed my feet to restore the feeling. They tingled and throbbed as I longed for warmth and I thought of all the people who had traipsed this path over the years as they fled civil war in Spain and, more recently, the Germans. So much fighting and suffering and still it persisted.

All too soon, Jean was on his feet. 'Time to go.'

I groaned, wincing as I dragged on the wet socks. 'Come on, Nancy, you can do this,' I muttered, determined not to freeze to death on a mountain peak. On we tramped and climbed and plodded and stumbled, as we followed in Jean's tracks. The climb grew steeper, and I clawed at freezing, jagged rocks, hauled myself up, feet slipping in snow. Eventually, we reached a plateau where the ground levelled out, and Jean was waiting. Puffing and panting, I snatched at the air, admiring the view. There were no more peaks, and my heart lifted.

'It is all downhill from now.' Jean flashed a brief smile.

I felt as if I was at the top of the world. Thousands of feet below, in one direction, lay Spain, her arms wide open, waiting, and behind us, France, hidden by a sea of wavy mountain peaks, a once beautiful tapestry now ruined by a jackboot army and a tyrant Fuhrer. The sky, lighter with the approach of dawn, was thick with grey cloud, while the snow had eased to a flutter. 'Hard to believe we've crossed over that lot and here we are, the last leg.'

'Si. Come, we must carry on. It is a steep descent, so watch your footing.' Jean strode on ahead.

I glanced towards France one last time, glimpsed her through misty eyes, wondering how long it would be before I could return. Pain clenched my throat and my stomach churned as I prayed Henri had left Marseille.

The descent was steep at first and a little treacherous, and we all slipped and slid at certain points, but the further down we came, the weather cleared, and soon we trod on drier, snow-free ground, trekking through a dense forest, pine trees stretching skyward. A small building lay below us. As we grew nearer, I saw it was a small, wooden hut and Jean was waiting by the door.

'Rest here a while,' he said gruffly, gesturing us inside where it was warm and dry. 'I will light a small fire, and you can dry your clothes. The river is further down, and once we cross it, we will be in Spain, free of the military zone.'

I warmed my hands by the fire, rubbing them together as my fingers tingled and throbbed from the severe cold. The others were slipping off their wet things, and the grumbling American removed his trousers and now sat on an upturned wooden box by the fire, holding his pants, as he called them, up in front of him as he tried to dry them off. I wasn't one to be prudish, but there were limits, and so I removed my overcoat, if only to feel the benefit of its warmth when we ventured outside later. My trousers were damp, the bottoms drenched, so I sat with my dry socks on, legs outstretched by the fire, staring into the flames, savouring peace as fatigue weighed heavy. The fire crackled and spat ruby sparks into the air, the tranquillity of the moment prodding me while adrenaline ebbed away, leaving me flat, morose, desperately missing my two loves, Henri and Picon.

All too soon, we were moving again. The river was shallow, not fast flowing, and I caught my breath as I waded in, icy water soaking through my espadrilles, my feet and ankles freezing. I glimpsed a bed of smooth grey and salmon pebbles in the crystal-clear water.

Jean reached the riverbank first and stepped out. 'Welcome to Spain,' he said, his bearded face breaking into a wide smile, blue eyes twinkling in the sunlight.

'We made it. Thank you, Jean.' I looked him in the eye. He merely nodded as my thoughts turned to Henri. 'I hope your journey is as straightforward and blessed as mine has been. Be safe, mon amour,' I muttered into the faint breeze huffing at my back.

Jean strode off ahead. Pilar gestured to us and led the way through a wooded area. 'This way, please,' she said.

Before long, we emerged from the forest where the land stretched out before us, fields and rolling hills with a speckle of whitewashed farmhouses. Pilar led us to a farm and ushered us into a barn. 'We stay here tonight and tomorrow, too. The people here are expecting us. They will bring food and drink.' I sank onto a hay bale, my feet throbbing. Pilar disappeared for a short while, returning with the owners of the farm, bearing trays of food and jugs of water and wine. The farmer's wife, a woman in her fifties, stretched a linen tablecloth over two hay bales and laid out the food. My stomach grumbled non-stop, and I suddenly realised how hungry I was.

Later that evening, I bedded down in the hay, alongside the others. Jean had gone on ahead to Barcelona to inform the British Consulate. In the meantime, we had to wait for a car to be sent to collect us. As I settled down, the hay scratchy beneath my legs, the sweet smell in my nose, a rush of thoughts streaked through my mind in a river of adrenaline. We'd made it. I swallowed, tears pricking my eyes. Henri. Please, God, keep him safe. My heavy eyes closed, and I allowed myself to drift.

A door slammed. Voices. I opened my eyes to golden sunlight streaming in through the cracks in the barn door. I held my breath, listening to men's voices—rough Spanish tones. 'Come out,' a man shouted. 'You are surrounded. It is the police.'

The others stirred. From the corner of my eye, I saw a flash of clothing leap up—Pilar. The young girl peered out of the window at the back of the barn and then, obviously satisfied that the coast was clear, took her leave, throwing herself out. Damn. I huffed out a breath. 'Wake up,' I said to the Americans lying either side of me. There was nowhere to run. Besides, I'd heard about the Spanish police. They'd take us away for questioning, lock us in a cell, perhaps, until the British Consulate sent an official. My body was lead-heavy, limbs and muscles ached and throbbed. The thought of shelter, any shelter, with food and drink was tempting, even if it was in captivity. It was, at least, not German captivity.

Chapter 21
FULL STEAM AHEAD

I stood on the deck of SS *Lutitia*, straining to pick out the rest of the convoy: seventy ships, dark, grainy forms in the distance on all sides. A huge plume of spray burst into the air up ahead with a whoosh. The destroyers were dropping depth chargers as they swept for German U-boats. We sailed from Gibraltar at dusk, blackout regulations in force. The lights of Spain winked as we slipped by. It was a curious thing spending the night at sea, I thought, especially with no light at all, because you couldn't tell where the ocean ended, and the sky began. Everything merged into one inky blot. I was lucky to be on this ship as there were so many Allied refugees waiting in line, including the Maltese wives of British officers, all desperate to sail to Britain.

The Spanish authorities had released me and my fellow evaders from the jail in Besalu after a few days. Satisfied with their enquiries, they provided me with a lovely hotel room after charging me with illegally entering Spain and fining me one thousand British pounds. Let's say I raised an eyebrow at that point. Having contacted the British Consul, they took care of things from then.

Reaching Gibraltar was like a momentous exhale, elation promptly smothered by emptiness. I could scarcely believe I'd soon be in England, safe, yet the thought of life without Henri was too painful, and in the confines of my hotel room, I wept until my chest ached and my voice grew hoarse. Outside, I clenched my jaw and forced a smile. I was lucky to be alive and had no right to be miserable. The only choice was to go on. So, while I waited for news of my passage to England, I spent my days at the Rock Hotel, reading the daily newspapers and getting pissed. What else was there to do?

The RAF had launched a daring raid on German dams, using bouncing bombs. How amazing! Meanwhile, the Allies were driving Rommel and his troops back in Africa. From my seat on the terrace, I'd squinted at the hazy African coastline far across the sea, trying to picture the raging battles.

I'd sent a coded message to Henri via a friend, telling him I was on my way to England. I closed my eyes for a moment, raised my chin while savouring the damp, cool sea air, a refreshing breeze. As I stood, the ship bumped along, riding over waves in a turbulent ocean, and I realised I was alone. How long had it been since I'd kissed Henri good-bye? Questions like that raised their sorry flags in my mind as I clawed desperately for the answers as if it was vital to remember. And it was vital and dear to me while I summoned his image, my eyes misting over, a growing sinking feeling inside. My throat constricted, chest tight. Please, Lord, let Henri be on his way. It wasn't safe to stay. How long before the Germans arrested him? I bit my lip, ground my nails into the palms of my hands.

For three years I'd been a part of something important, helping the war effort, and now I questioned what had been the point? My life lay in tatters, finished, and somehow, I had to pick up the pieces. For the first time in a while, I felt wretched, and in danger of breaking down as anger, fear, and self-pity rolled and crashed into one. The life I'd built was over. Faces flashed in my mind, and one stood out from the rest. Captain Garrow. I'd contact him when I reached England. I blew out a breath. One step at a time, Nancy.

Chapter 22
LONDON, JUNE 1943

L ondon was not the same as I remembered. The Luftwaffe had ravaged her soul, endless bombing raids reducing buildings and houses to mounds of rubble. Some homes stood defiant, like giant dolls' houses, their entire front walls ripped away, beds, wardrobes and personal effects visible, sheets flapping in the breeze.

Piccadilly suited me, at least for the time being. I'd found a modest flat to rent and spent the first few weeks cleaning, decorating and shopping for furnishings. I had the parquet floor professionally sanded and polished, as I wanted everything to be perfect for when Henri arrived. Through Garrow, I was able to source some French champagne and the brandy Henri loved so much.

The capital brimmed with busy people, and it seemed everyone had a purpose, except me. I craved my old double life in France, the Resistance worker and wife, and as the days ticked by, I grew increasingly restless. My worries over Henri's whereabouts persisted, and I was desperate for another focus. Garrow had been a godsend, arranging my hotel accommodation initially and taking me out for dinner. Soon he re-introduced me to others I'd helped through the escape line in Marseille, men who introduced me to their wives and families. Afterwards, dinner invites flowed in abundance. The more affluent people invited me to restaurants and shows and before long, my evenings became busy. But the days dragged, feeding my anxiety, fuelling my sadness. Friends advised me to join the Red Cross or the Women's Institute. Charles de Gaulle had set up his HQ here and was the commander of the Free French. Perhaps I could return to France as a special agent. In the meantime, a fellow evader and lieutenant in the Seaforth Highlanders suggested I might volunteer to work at the canteen of the Combined Operations Headquarters in Whitehall. 'They're so short of hands,' he'd said, and so I agreed to work four hours a day. Meanwhile, my plans to return to France were a priority, and I was determined to make it happen.

THE FREE FRENCH didn't want me. The rejection hurt. After everything I'd done, I'd convinced myself that they'd jump on me without hesitation. I tried to explain my exploits in France, but to no avail. 'We are well aware of your efforts, Madame Fiocca,' the recruitment officer said, 'but I am afraid we do not have a position for you at this time.'

Talk about having the wind knocked out of you. They'd scuttled my hopes.

'Don't fret,' Garrow said. 'Let's just say there's a wee bit of friction between Churchill and General de Gaulle, so I doubt it's personal.'

It was personal to me as I clutched at straws, desperate to return to France.

'Have you heard of Buckmaster's group?'

I shook my head.

'He runs SOE. Special Operations Executive.' He lit up a Marlboro, inhaled deeply. 'They're always looking for people fluent in French, of a certain character. People like you.'

I considered Garrow's suggestion, and after hearing a little more about it, decided that it was my only option, aside from swimming the Channel, of course.

Chapter 23

RAF TANGMERE. 29 APRIL 1944

D ressed, ready for the off, I clambered into the car and sat wedged between Vera Atkins and Hubert. The drive to the airfield was quiet, sombre perhaps, although I was in high spirits as thoughts of France and Henri soared in my head. Four months of SOE training had sailed by. Yes, it had been tough, but equally great fun. I was ensign Nancy Wake, F.A.N.Y. having signed up using my maiden name. To London, I was Hélène, and to the French Resistance, I would be Madame Andrée.

At Tangmere, the security officer demanded to search us, dealing with Hubert first. Then he turned to me. 'You don't need to search me. Besides, I'm wearing too many layers. It'll take ages.' There was no way I was removing any clothing at this late stage. I glanced at Vera, who merely rolled her eyes, red lips twitching as she stifled a smirk.

Even when the man protested, Vera remained tight-lipped, glancing at papers on her clipboard. 'Look here. I'm not wearing anything I shouldn't. My money is French, and my false papers are in order. There's nothing British on me whatsoever.' Vera waved him away with a flick of her manicured hand, then took him aside and muttered something in his ear that appeared to appease him. Meanwhile, all sorts of minor thoughts raced through my mind and then I remembered I'd forgotten to arrange to have my rent paid on my little flat. Darn. I sat down at the small pine table, grabbed a pen and paper and hurriedly scribbled a note to my bank manager, asking if he would organise the monthly payments.

'What do you think you're doing?' The security officer peered over my shoulder, his eyes bulging, a scarlet wash rising from his neck to his forehead.

'Writing a note to the Germans to let them know I'm on my way.' I flashed a tight-lipped stare.

'You can't do that.' He turned to Vera. 'She can't do that.'

'Here.' I thrust the note into his chest. 'Post this when you get a moment.' He glared at me.

'Take a seat, Nancy,' Vera said, blowing out a breath. 'You need to have your ankles strapped for support.' She gestured to the security officer, who frowned, muttered something incomprehensible, and produced bandages for the job.

I swear he pulled those bandages as tight as possible. My legs felt as if they might balloon under protest, but I would not give him the satisfaction of seeing my discomfort.

At ten o'clock, we tramped across the grass to the waiting Liberator. I cast a glance at the full, gibbous moon, which hung large and low in the east. An aircraft droned at the far side of the field, and I watched as it lunged forward, hurtling along the runway, slipping by blazing orange lamp markers. The sweet smell of aviation fuel hung in the air and I blew out a breath, wispy silver vapour curling like a ribbon in the cool breeze. Vera embraced both of us in turn, casting me a Mona Lisa smile. She had been good to me, but I found her so hard to read.

The bulky parachute sat awkwardly on my back, slapping the backs of my legs with each step as I struggled to climb into the Liberator. Then, I felt a shove against my backside as someone thrust me inside and I landed on all fours, scrambling to get up onto the seat—not that there was much of a seat taking into consideration the damn chute—but I squeezed myself on somehow. Hubert clambered up and sank down beside me. The engines roared and thrummed, the thunderous noise drowning out all attempts of ordinary conversation.

The dispatcher, a young man who surely couldn't be any more than eighteen, climbed in and closed the door. 'We're about to take off now, so settle back and hang on. We have some calm weather on our side, so it ought to be a smooth flight.' He smiled reassuringly, leaning in towards me. 'Say, are you really Witch?'

He was so skinny, his Adam's apple bobbing up and down in his throat. 'Yes.' I raised an eyebrow, tickled by his intrigue. 'Rhymes with…' I grinned at the lad. It was only a code name after all, and you'd think he'd be used to that by now, flying agents out of England. His American accent was familiar, southern perhaps.

'Gee, we ain't never dropped a woman before. You sure you wanna go?' His eyebrows furrowed as he sucked on a pencil.

I smiled. The sweet boy looked so worried. 'Quite sure, thanks.' I couldn't wait to leave, to return and rid France of those bastards. I'd excelled at weapons training and was a damn good shot, and I could kill a man with my bare hands, not that I'd actually done that of course. Not yet.

His eyes searched mine and then, with a nod of his head, he shuffled to the back of the aircraft to check over the cargo.

France wasn't as bleak as they all thought, and I wasn't afraid of the Germans or the Milice. I reached into my pocket, my hand brushing against the cold, smooth silver compact given to me by Colonel Buckmaster. 'A going-away present,' he'd said before kissing me goodbye in the French fashion, a waft of sweet pipe tobacco drifting from his tunic jacket. His last words resonated in my ears. 'Merde!'

The engines growled to a thunderous roar, and the vibration thrummed through the entire aircraft, rumbling up through my feet to my head. My jaw quivered; my head filled with the growl of engines. Oil and rubber hung stagnant in the air, forcing me to swallow as waves of nausea rolled through me. I shivered. The fuselage was icy, and I was glad of my warm, camel-hair overcoat. Beneath that, I wore a smart French outfit, silk stockings and a pair of overalls on top for extra warmth. My ankles felt bulky and tight, and I couldn't wait to be in France, relieved of the cumbersome clobber. On the brighter side, I had applied make-up and my treasured red Chanel lipstick sat tucked away in my breast pocket. Stashed by my feet was a large bag which contained our plans and almost one million French francs in cash, along with a pair of three-quarter heeled shoes for me to slip on after the drop. A lady in France ought to be well dressed so as not to draw any unwanted attention or appear to be a wanted person—even though that was precisely what I was. Beneath my tin hat, I wore my hair neatly styled, and carried two revolvers, one in each trouser pocket. Best to be prepared. At least I thought so, but as I sat there, I wondered who I was. Was I Nancy Wake, SOE agent or Nancy Fiocca, French housewife? What about Nancy, the journalist? Or the girl from Oz? Was I frightened or a little nervous? I knew I was angry, so angry, and frustrated, desperate to get to France and do something, anything, because it was all I knew to combat this inner turmoil that burned inside. Henri hadn't turned up, and I hadn't heard from him either, but I clung to hope. As Garrow had said one day, 'No news is good news.'

The dispatcher settled himself down next to me and flashed a reassuring smile, leaning in closer. 'Are you all right, ma'am?'

I nodded. Secretly, however, the thought of parachuting out of an aircraft once more terrified me and this time there would be no round of drinks afterwards as there had been at training. I'd made some wonderful friends and gelled with a lovely girl, Violette. Well, we got up to all sorts of fun, playing pranks on the trainers. I was going to miss her, all of them. Now it was time to be serious, and there was nothing more serious than dropping into occupied France. A special agent. Not in uniform. If the Germans caught you, the outlook was bleak. Just what was I doing? My heart raced. I longed for France, for Henri, and for our home together. As I screwed my eyes shut for a few seconds, the image of Vienna flashed through my mind. I gritted my teeth.

The engines roared, and I lunged forward as the Liberator taxied to the end of the runway, turned and halted. The thunderous noise increased as the pilot ran up the engines to full capacity and then we were off, gathering speed along the concrete before soaring upwards into the night sky. It was my third flight, but a wave of nausea still surged through me. As we climbed steadily, I watched the ground diminish into the darkness from a small window. There were no further lights to see thanks to the blackout and all too soon the darkness swallowed buildings and land.

The dispatcher produced a flask of tea and enamel cups. 'It'll keep out the cold,' he said. Next, he picked up a brown paper bag. 'Spam sandwich?'

'Thanks.' I took one, despite feeling sick. It might be many hours before I could eat again. I glanced at Hubert. Even now, he was calm and collected. Nothing ever seemed to worry him. He was self-assured, slightly younger than me, twenty-five, tall, athletic, handsome with cropped sandy hair and blue eyes, and incredibly annoying at times.

'We're over the Channel now,' the dispatcher said, straining to be heard over the engines.

I wondered how long the crossing would take. Land was safer than the murky depths which waited below, should the unthinkable happen. I suddenly felt very sick and leaned back, taking deep breaths. Hubert finished his tea, settled back a little, and closed his eyes. Typical. My eyes were heavy, and I stifled a yawn with my hand, but I couldn't sleep while feeling as if I would throw up at any moment. Before long, Hubert slumped into me when the aircraft lurched, his head heavy against my shoulder, sleeping soundly.

'We're crossing the Loire,' the dispatcher's voice sang out. The aircraft bucked and shook. 'Flak. The weather ain't too good either.'

I cast a glance out the window and glimpsed a flash of orange as a shell exploded beneath the wings, rocking and shaking us around. Anti-aircraft guns. The Loire snaked through the valley below, a silver ribbon beneath the light of the moon, luring us deeper into France, and elation zipped through me, lifting my spirits as home whispered. What a long way I'd come from the immigrant who had arrived in Paris years ago, young, eager for excitement and a new life away from my mother. I'd forged a new path, found love, lived the dream before the enemy ripped it away. As I waited to touch down on French soil, I realised I'd gone full circle.

Suddenly, the aircraft climbed steeply, throwing Hubert to the floor.

He opened his eyes wide, a confused look on his face. My stomach lurched and tightened. 'Oh strewth, what's happening?'

The dispatcher glanced towards the cockpit, to the pilot. 'Don't worry. You're in safe hands,' he said as he staggered to the front. The aircraft turned sharply one way and then the other before diving steeply downwards, tipping me onto the floor, where I landed in a heap almost on top of Hubert. I blew out a breath as I flicked a gaze at him, his eyes wide, eyes which for once screamed in alarm. I sucked in deep, steady breaths, desperate to quell the swell of nausea. Finally, the aircraft levelled out.

'A German fighter,' the dispatcher said. 'But the captain knows his job. He's lost him.' He extended his arm and pulled me to my feet. 'There, don't look so worried, ma'am.' He patted my knee. 'This ship's brand new. The captain won't let anything or anyone take her down but him.'

I managed a faint smile, but I wouldn't be happy until we'd landed. I grabbed a paper bag and sat prepared. With the next lurch, it was no use. I wretched, depositing the tea and spam sandwich into the bag before leaning back against the fuselage. I caught the dispatcher's gaze.

'Say, if you don't wanna go, we can easily take you home.' He smiled; a smile filled with compassion.

'Just get me to the dropping point and shove me out. Give me a kick up the backside if you have to.' Hubert had closed his eyes again. 'Bloody typical,' I muttered. I spun around on the bench seat and gazed out the window. The night sky was clear, moonlight capturing the rooftops of buildings below. Almost three hours had passed.

The dispatcher shook Hubert awake. 'Time to get ready.' He tightened our parachute straps and hooked us up to the static line. I grabbed my bag, aware that the Liberator was slowing, tilting slightly. We were turning. The pilot would look for a sign below from the welcome party, a flicker of torchlight jumping out from the black. A red light flashed to life in the rear of the fuselage.

'Get into position.' The dispatcher gestured towards the hatch on the floor. 'Once you jump, your chutes will automatically open,' he shouted. He opened the hatch, and the ground flashed by as we flew at around four hundred feet. I sat down, my legs dangling through the Joe Hole. A rush of icy wind hit me hard, biting my face, suffocating, leaving me gasping for breath. I made out the silhouettes of trees, and a silvery patchwork of fields interspersed with winding roads. Lights loomed from a nearby village and then more trees, casting their dark shadows beneath the wings. My heart raced, and I suddenly thought of England, my cosy flat, the ride out to Tangmere squashed next to Vera in her powder-blue uniform. She'd been so kind. What if Henri was in London looking for me? My stomach sank, and I thought quickly. No, it had been too long. I was certain he was still in France.

'Sure you're okay? We can take you back if you like.' The dispatcher placed his hand on my shoulder.

'I'm not doing this again,' I snapped, taking a deep breath. 'Just let me out of this thing.' The plane banked, turning to make one last run. The wait was excruciating. Beneath us, bonfires blazed, torches blinked, and the faces of some of the welcome party were visible as they gazed up at the belly of the Liberator. I couldn't believe what I was seeing. They were bloody mad. No security measures.

The plane lurched as it slowed further, and the dispatcher slapped me on the back. The red light blinked green. 'Okay. JUMP!'

I felt sick, my mouth dry, heart beating against my ribcage. It was time, my least favourite part of the training, falling through the darkness, falling through uncertainty, except this was no dress rehearsal. Momentarily frozen, my mouth gaping wide, all I could think of was my fear of heights, of falling. Then Henri's face flashed in my mind, and my love for him burned fiercer than the bonfires below. The firm press of the dispatcher's hand on the small of my back thrusting me forward, and I slipped out into icy darkness, buffeted by the slipstream, panic rising in my chest as I plummeted. Only then did I realise I was screaming. An old joke from training resurfaced. They said if your chute didn't open the first time, go back, complain, and request a new one. I'd laughed when I first heard it, but now, somehow, it didn't have the same ring.

The words of my instructor came to mind. 'Elbows close to your sides. Remember what your mother told you? Legs and knees together.' I muttered this over and over, like a mantra, remembering how I'd roared with laughter during training. There was a hard jolt as the chute blossomed overhead, and the harness straps tightened, digging into my thighs and groin. I blew out a breath. The night air whistled as I descended at speed. Overhead, the Liberator droned her way back to England, the roar of the engines fading into the midnight sky and I wondered if this was the point where others regretted the fact they were dropping into occupied France. Well, not me. I couldn't wait to get on the ground.

I sucked in a breath. The sky was silent except for the whoosh of wind from my descent, and I marvelled at the sparkling galaxy I found myself closer to than ever before. Suddenly, the breath caught in my throat as I fell through a greyish white cloud that chilled my skin and trailed wet, icy breath over my head, face, and neck. My skin prickled all over, and I shivered and shook as I dangled in the night sky.

The chute billowed above like a white silk balloon and as the ground rushed to claim me and clouds smothered the moon, my view of what lay below slipped into darkness. I dropped through a thicket, crashing through branches, coming to an abrupt halt about eight feet above the ground. 'Jesus Christ.' I swallowed, dangling still for a moment, listening, aching. An owl screeched overhead. I tried several times to release my harness, but the darn thing wouldn't budge. 'Shit!' As I ceased wriggling, I looked all around, listening out for signs of Hubert. My heart pounded against my ribs, which throbbed and ached, along with my legs, forcing me to wince. An icy breeze blew, and leaves cackled and scuttled across the ground. A sharp, crisp snap of a twig from nearby and I caught my breath. A streak of movement caught my eye. The figure of a man striding towards me. He wore a black beret at a jaunty angle, and the glow of the moonlight illuminated his surprised face as he gazed up. I noted the rifle slung over his shoulder and the cheeky look that sprang across his chiselled face.

'Bonjour, Madame Andrée. I did not know that trees bore such lovely fruit at this time of year.' His mouth curved up into a playful smile, and he bowed.

Yup. Definitely Maquis. 'Don't give me any of your French shit! Help me down.' Cold and tired, all I wanted was a place to rest and a warm drink.

'Here.' He reached up and hit the harness release, and I dropped to the forest floor with a thud that knocked the wind from my lungs. 'I am Henri Tardivat.' He held out his hand and pulled me to my feet.

I looked around for my colleague, but we were alone. 'Where's Hubert?'

'Do not worry. He is with the others. We saw you drifting.' He scooped up my chute, folding yards of white silk into a tight bundle, tucking it beneath his arm. Was he keeping it?

'I have to bury that.'

'Non, it is silk. It is so useful.'

I shook my head. Security definitely was a major issue.

Within minutes, men's voices faded in and I froze. My training and the stories we'd heard resurfaced, tales of agents who had dropped into German camps, directly into enemy hands. A dark figure ran towards us, and I reached for one of my revolvers. Henri Tardivat placed his hand on my arm. 'It is okay. He is one of us.'

'Bonjour. I am Francois. Welcome to France,' the young man said in hushed tones, shaking my hand. Hubert traipsed behind.

'You landed all right?' Hubert glanced down at my bag.

'No. I got caught in the trees, but I'm in one piece. And don't worry, I've got the money and the plans, safe.'

'Hurry, please.' Tardivat led the way across a field, through the gate, and out onto a lane. A light breeze drove fresh scents of pine from the dense cluster of trees on the forest edge.

We turned down a narrow path. 'Where are we?' I glanced at Tardivat.

'Just outside Montluçon.' He grinned at me. 'There is a car waiting beyond the trees.'

I turned to Hubert, who returned my wide-eyed stare. We weren't supposed to ride in cars. 'Isn't that risky?'

'Non, Madame Andrée. It is a gazogene; besides, we stick to the minor routes and drive without lights. Then, if we see lights up ahead or behind, we know it is the enemy.'

When we reached the car, Tardivat introduced us to the driver and his wife, Monsieur and Madame Reynard. 'They will take you to a safe house,' he said.

'When will we meet with Hector?' Hubert said.

Tardivat looked blank. 'Who?'

Hubert cast me a glance, hitched an eyebrow. 'No matter.' He climbed into the back of the car and took my bag for me.

'I will see you tomorrow,' Tardivat said, casting me a reassuring glance.

'Merci.' I climbed into the car, and Tardivat closed the door. Monsieur Reynard drove away, while his wife talked almost non-stop about their lives, the occupation, and how overjoyed they were that we'd arrived. Apparently, they were expecting us, and our arrival had already caused a great source of excitement. It was for me too, and my heart quickened with a beat of joy, one I hadn't felt in a while. It reminded me of my first trip to Paris, that sense of elation that convinced me I could live there, and then as quickly as it had surfaced, sadness smothered it as swift as an axe blade on wood, because I knew I could not run back to Henri, nor even check to see if he was safe. The mission and many lives rested on me doing my duty. I was torn, caught in the middle, not sure whether to smile or cry while Madame Reynard chatted incessantly as we drove through the inky darkness.

Chapter 24

COSNE-D'ALLIER

everal hours later, I awoke to the smell of bacon. Daylight streamed in through gaps in the old wooden blue-painted shutters, slices of golden yellow casting strips of light across the wooden floorboards. I stretched out, looked around the room and realised I was alone. I hauled myself out of the old brass bed, dressing quickly. A glance in the dressing mirror, brushing my hair before slipping downstairs.

Madame Reynard was standing by the stove, watching over a large pan of sizzling bacon, fresh eggs in a bowl on the bench next to her. 'Good morning, Madame Andrée,' she said, 'have some coffee.'

'Thank you. Where's Hubert?' I sat down at the pine kitchen table. Madame Reynard brought fresh bread in a basket and raspberry jam.

'Ah, he is outside with my husband. Breakfast is almost ready.'

Our mission plans hurtled through my mind as I brooded over coffee, watching the fire crackle away in the grate. For every bright orange flame that stretched up towards the chimney, I had a wish or a prayer to send to my husband. The door creaked open, and Hubert appeared, dark circles around his bloodshot eyes. I poured him some coffee. Our hosts had a radio shop in the town, and we were staying in their little flat above. Unfortunately, we had to share a room with a double bed, so Hubert, being rather chivalrous, had spent a most uncomfortable night on the wooden floor.

'When do you think Den will get here?'

'Not sure.' Hubert sipped his coffee. 'They're flying him in by Lysander, so we must be patient.'

'Well, until he does, we're stuck with no radio. Can't do a bloody thing.' Poor old Den. 'Denden' I called him, and he called me 'Gertie'. I didn't mind. He was fun, gregarious, about ten years older than me, and mad as a hatter. We'd met during training. He was one of our instructors. We'd got on like a house on fire from the start. Den had already had a colourful war, arrested twice in France. He escaped the first time, but a brutal encounter with an interrogator left him nursing a crushed foot the second, so no parachute jumps. The irony, I mused, surrounded by darn radios and no operator. I drained my coffee cup, unfazed by the sour taste of ersatz, my gaze falling on the vase of daffodils next to the small window, golden in the morning light. And I thought of the bouquets of orange or yellow lilies I used to buy that sat in the crystal vase on the antique table in the hall. The sweet scent in my nose, orange or brown stamens spilling onto the table as the days sailed by. 'They symbolise passion and gaiety,' Henri had said before kissing the tip of my nose. 'And beauty, like you.' I felt the ache of our separation once again, and I nursed it while Hubert chewed the last mouthful of bacon.

After breakfast, we both returned to our room to go over our plans.

'The Reynards know too much. They know we're from England and why we're here.' Hubert sat on the edge of the bed. 'I went into the village earlier with Monsieur Reynard, who introduced me to some locals. They were very pleased to see me. Been expecting us, apparently.' He shook his head.

'Oh, Lord. The security's a joke. We'll need to make changes.' But I couldn't help smiling. The French were just so friendly and hospitable, welcoming us with open arms, something they did so naturally. Sadly, it had to stop.

~

THE NEXT MORNING, I was busy bathing my feet in a bowl of water in the bedroom, chatting to Hubert, my Colt revolver next to me on the bed, when there was a knock on the door. As it creaked open, a man stood in the doorway, a look of surprise on his face. Monsieur Reynard stood behind him. 'Your contact,' he said.

Hector. A short man in a brown pinstriped suit, a Fedora and a neatly trimmed moustache. I smiled, heat rising in my cheeks, amused as his face creased into a wide grin, and then he chuckled. 'Madame Andrée. I see you're making yourself at home.'

Hubert burst into laughter, and I joined him. Not that it was that funny for me. It was more a release of tension than anything, but either way, the tears ran down my cheeks, and even Hector swiped at his eyes.

What a time to make an entrance. Still, it was a great relief to meet him. Things could move forward now. Hector was *le patron* of the Stationer circuit and our direct route to Gaspard, the leader of the Maquis in the Auvergne, with whom we were to work. Unfortunately, he didn't have the information we needed to hand, such as the location of safe houses. Hubert shot me such a cheesed-off look. 'My courier will bring the names and addresses in two days,' Hector said before leaving.

'Is anything going to go right?' Hubert returned to the window and gazed up into the blue as if seeking divine intervention. He lit up a cigarette and stood there for a while. It was best to leave him to it, so I went downstairs for coffee and a natter with Madame Reynard.

THE NEXT DAY, having put up with Hubert's grim mood, thinking that things could be worse, Monsieur Reynard burst into our room, his ruddy cheeks glowing like hot coals as he stood in the doorway, breathing hard. 'The Gestapo arrested Hector yesterday.'

'No!' I glanced at Hubert, who blew out a breath and rolled his eyes.

'The Germans have made many arrests in Montluçon. And your radio operator has landed in their midst. He will never get through with the number of Gestapo in the area.'

At least Denden was in France. 'What do we do now?'

'I can take you to Laurent. He can find Gaspard,' Monsieur Reynard said. 'We will go now.'

Hubert and I piled into the car with Monsieur Reynard, who set off at quite a pace. He kept to the minor routes, narrow, twisty lanes that climbed steadily in places. My ears became muffled several times along the way as we drove higher. The Auvergne, known as the Fortress of France, was a mountainous region. Now I understood why the Maquis used cars. Bicycles were not much use in dense forests or when faced with mountains standing six thousand feet high.

Eventually, we found Laurent hiding out at an old chateau near Saint-Flour. 'He's in hiding,' Monsieur Reynard told us. 'He is wanted for the shooting of several Germans in Clermont-Ferrand.' I liked him already.

Laurent was a tall man, with short dark hair and steel-blue eyes, ruggedly handsome. He greeted us cautiously. A faint smirk flitted across his face as he stared at me, and I had the feeling the prospect of a female agent amused him. We explained our position, and he invited us to sit down and ordered one of his men to bring food and drinks.

'What is it you want from me?' Laurent asked.

'We need a meeting with Gaspard. He has thousands of men in the region, and we're here to train and arm the Maquis, as long as they're on board to help the Allies. We have money and can arrange arms drops,' Hubert said.

Laurent leaned back in his chair, eyeing us suspiciously as he scratched his bristly chin with his left hand. 'Where is this money?'

'Somewhere safe,' I said, 'until it's needed.' Well, it was safe, tucked into the money belt around my waist. Laurent stared me in the eye, and I could see he was trying to decide whether to trust us.

'I can find Gaspard. You can stay here while I'm gone.'

At least we had food and shelter while we waited. But how long was it going to take? The Allies were planning the big push, the invasion, and we were useless without Den, cut off from London. In the meantime, Hubert didn't look happy. We both had our roles to play. Hubert had to establish a network—Freelance, a task that would take him away frequently while I stayed behind, working alongside the Maquis. It was the waiting around that made everything so uncertain, and Hubert was growing more impatient by the day. Well, I empathised, but hopefully Den would find his way to us soon and we could begin.

We bid Monsieur Reynard farewell as he returned home to his wife. As I gazed around the grounds, I noticed several vehicles at Laurent's camp. 'How do you have all these cars?' I asked one young maquisard, called Achilles.

He flashed a sly, wide smile. 'Madame, we are the Maquis. We take what we need.'

Just as I'd thought, they were running around the French countryside like a band of thieves.

'Come, I'll show you where you can rest.' Achilles led us up the grand winding staircase and opened the first door we came to on the landing. 'Rest. I will come for you when it is time to eat. For now, stay here.' He glanced at me and his face softened. 'You will be safe, Madame.'

'Merci.' We put our bags down. Achilles closed the door, and I listened as his footsteps faded away. 'What do we do now?' I glanced at Hubert, then strode across to the window. Our room overlooked the front of the chateau, and I could see the traffic on the main road heading in and out of the village — a good vantage point.

'We have to wait. There's no other option. God knows when Den will turn up. Without him, and his wireless, we have nothing. No use at all. That's why Gaspard is keeping us hanging on. He knows we're useless.'

I noticed another door. Curious, I opened it. 'Oh, would you look at that?' I turned and grinned. 'An entire bathroom to ourselves. What luck.' A large crystal chandelier hung in the centre of the room in front of two large windows, so reminiscent of my home in Marseille. I looked out the window to the view of the hills and fields of green, my heart dipping in disappointment. No sea view, no harbour or bobbing sailboats. I gritted my teeth and blew out a breath. 'Not to worry,' I whispered to myself. I'd make the most of any luxuries. After all, this time next week I could be sleeping rough in the forest or kipping in a barn.

～

THREE DAYS LATER, Laurent sent word. 'Madame Andrée,' Achilles said. 'Gaspard will be here at the end of the week.'

I looked at Hubert and thought he'd explode. He'd spent the last few days moping around and was becoming more despondent by the hour. Why did we have to wait so long? This Gaspard was sending London a message. He was the chief and wouldn't take orders. We'd been told he had three to four thousand men hidden in various places throughout Allier, Puy-de-Dome, Haute Loire, and Cantal. Hubert and I had the arduous task of determining their use to the Allies on D-Day. If Gaspard would be loyal to our cause, then Colonel Buckmaster would provide arms and finances, while I dealt with training and supplying the groups.

Well, we'd meet Gaspard soon enough and, in the meantime, it was no good feeling frustrated. I left Hubert to mope while I took a stroll around the gardens. The chateau stood at the end of a winding, stony track. It was a large stone house with shutters on the windows, the once sky-blue paint now faded, patchy and flaking off. The grounds were vast, edged with tall pine trees and a variety of shrubs. I sat on a wooden bench beneath an oak tree and listened as the light breeze nibbled my ears, nesting birds chirped, and cattle lulled from a nearby field. While I yearned for Henri, and worried for his safety, I knew I must bury the thoughts and keep my mind on my work if I was to get through this mission. Just then, Hubert strolled out onto the terrace. And as the sun slipped further from her seat, she trapped him in a blaze of gold, his hair as yellow as straw, his honeyed face grinning toothily back at me. Just look at us, I thought. We had a job to do, and I vowed to overcome any obstacles and complete the task. He gestured to me, raised his hands, lifting a bottle in each. Marvellous. He'd found something decent to drink. Hubert and I would make this work. We were a team; besides, there was no going back.

Chapter 25
IN LIMBO

With the money belt around my waist, tucked beneath my clothes, I followed my nose to the kitchen, Hubert in tow. A long pine table stretched out before us, a cluster of maquisards at one end, some with grubby faces and curly, bushy hair. They looked up, two of them fixed their wide eyes firmly on me. They spoke in gruff voices, laughing, complaining as they discussed a raid they'd conducted recently, stealing supplies from a store in a nearby town.

Locking eyes with one sitting opposite, I saw suspicion, and I ate in silence, preferring to avoid a lynching, aware of Hubert wolfing his food down, clearly following my lead. The hairs on the back of my neck prickled. It was only after several mouthfuls that I realised we were eating rabbit stew. Please let Den arrive before Gaspard gets here, I thought, then at least we won't be so useless. Once back in our room, Hubert placed a chair up against the door, jamming the handle. Trust no one. The training at Beaulieu had been vigorous. And always have an escape route. I went to the window. We were one floor up, and I spotted a sturdy trellis to one side. If need be, we could easily slip down there.

'Cigarette?' Hubert offered his Gitanes.

'Thanks.' I filled my lungs with nicotine, savouring the stimulating vapour. 'What the hell are we going to do here for an entire week?' I opened the window, bathed in the fresh evening breeze as pine trees shushed the wind and birds chorused a mixed melody.

'Christ knows. This is the biggest crock of shit I've ever known. You'd think we were the bloody enemy the way they're behaving.' He took a drag. 'Let's hope Gaspard is reasonable when he turns up, if he turns up. Besides, without Denis, we're fucked.'

'I'm beginning to wonder what I'm doing here.' Outside, the sunset washed the sky pink, purple, and orange, while the moon waited in the wings for her time to shine.

'It's a little late for second thoughts. Mind you, I feel the same. Bad enough we're here at all, beneath the nose of the enemy, but this, well, it's a bloody mess.' He drew on his cigarette purposefully. It was about all he had to concentrate on for now—that and staying alive. Vera's unemotive voice whispered in my mind. 'You realise that the life expectancy of an agent in the field is around six weeks.' Words uttered to inform, and to separate the wheat from the chaff. She hadn't rattled me at all; besides, I'd already braved three years in Nazi-ruled France.

'I'm exhausted. I'm going to bed. See you in the morning.' I turned down the blankets and climbed into bed, fully clothed, in case I needed to jump up in a hurry. Hubert remained by the window, gazing out, probably thinking about his wife back in Surrey. He'd become a father for the first time a few months ago, and I thought he was quite mad for volunteering for SOE; still, we were here now. I dragged the blankets up over me. It might be warm by day, but it was still chilly at night. 'Do you mind if I turn out the lamp?'

'No, go ahead.'

Lying there in the dark, thoughts swam in my head. Henri. Marseille. Home. Perhaps the need would arise to travel there soon. Perhaps he'd spot me if I walked by our apartment, but I knew it was hopeless. I couldn't risk sending a message to the Resistance there. It was too dangerous. Henri's absence troubled me. Escaping France wasn't easy, but he'd promised to follow me. Something had gone wrong. Every day I ached for him, his soft voice, those hazel eyes gazing into mine, his touch, but the nights were the hardest. The memory of our last kiss, my parting words. Leaving with tears in my eyes. The Gestapo had been watching me. Strewth, it was a miracle I'd escaped at all. Time had transposed my memories into sepia fragments, snippets I craved, yet the more I grasped at them, the more faded they grew, and it was exhausting thinking of things you had no control over. I sighed, exhaling hurt, frustration, desperation into the darkness.

A shuffle of footsteps across the floorboards. I felt Hubert's form slip between the light of the moon and myself, then his weight beside me as he lay down on top of the bed, cigarette smoke sailing up my nose, dragged in deeper with every breath.

'Hubert?'

'Yes?'

'You remember what I told you, back at training?'

'How could I forget?'

I sighed, knowing it was wrong, reckless, mad even. 'Do you suppose I could slip away sometime soon?' I swallowed hard. Uttering the words out loud made it even more real. Tears pricked my eyes.

'I'm sure you could do anything you wished, but please don't. It's too dangerous. Besides, if I'm organising the circuit here, I need you. You'll be far too busy seeing to supplies, dealing with drops.' He sighed. 'You've had a rotten time of it, but I can't let you go. I'm sorry.'

'I know.' A glimpse of Henri was all I wished for, just one glimpse to know he was safe. I waited a moment, listening as Hubert sucked on his fag, the hiss of breath exhaled through teeth, a light cough. I rolled over and dragged the covers over my head to silence my thoughts. My mind was a cyclone, hurling memories of my past around and around and I yearned for sleep.

TWO DAYS LATER, Gaspard stormed in as we were having coffee with jam and bread for breakfast. He chatted and laughed with the men in the room, turned to glance at me while he sat down, puffing away on a cigarette, his dark brown eyes boring into me, cold, aggressive.

'Gaspard.' I stared him in the eye, but he said nothing. 'You know who we are, why we're here.'

He took a long drag, exhaled a cloud of smoke. 'Oui. You have come to save us.' He glanced around at his men, smirked, and they laughed. 'A mere woman will save us all from the Germans.' His voice roared theatrically.

What a brute! 'I can get everything you need, arms, ammunition, money if you agree to cooperate with the Allies.'

'But how? You have no radio. Your man is stranded behind enemy lines.' He narrowed his eyes.

'He'll be here any day now.'

Gaspard strode over to me. 'You are no use to me at all. We have managed so far without London.' He waved his hand in front of my face, every word uttered in contempt. 'I don't take orders from London, and I certainly don't take orders from a girl. We will beat the Germans without you and liberate France.' Gaspard strode off, his men in tow.

~

LATER THAT DAY, as I walked with Hubert outside through the grounds, I overheard one of Gaspard's men from an open window, and we ducked down closer to the house, eavesdropping.

'The woman has the money. I know it. I will talk to her later and try to seduce her. Then, when she falls asleep, I will kill her and take the money.'

Gaspard laughed. 'You? She'll fall asleep well before you can seduce her, Jean.' He roared with laughter.

Hubert looked at me, and we both grinned. 'This is the best thing I've heard since getting here,' I said. 'Let him try it. He won't get far, and he'll come off worse.'

~

AFTER DINNER THAT NIGHT, one of Gaspard's men approached us. I locked eyes with him as he sat down opposite.

'Madame Andrée. How are you this fine evening?' His voice confirmed my suspicions. Jean.

Honestly, if that was the best he could do, there was no hope, but I was game for playing along. 'Couldn't be better.'

'You are very beautiful. Will you have a drink with me?'

I pondered his offer. 'Why? You wouldn't be hoping to get me drunk, kill me, and steal my money, would you?'

'But Madame, why would you say such a thing?' He tried to feign a look of surprise, but he wasn't fooling me for a second.

'I heard you plotting earlier today. Well, think again, because I wouldn't sleep with you if you were the last man on earth.' I grabbed the collar of his dusty black jacket and pushed him away.

The other men overheard and laughed. Jean's face flushed scarlet as a scowl clung to it, fury etched in his eyes. He stormed out of the kitchen, leaving me to revel in a thin wisp of smugness. Talk about a war zone. The trouble was, these men hadn't decided whether they could trust us.

THE NEXT DAY, I wandered in on a small group of maquisards talking about a raid they had planned for that evening, after nightfall. A man called Rene was in charge.

I sat down. 'Can I come along?'

The rumble of voices cut out abruptly as René stared at me, clearly surprised. 'Why?'

'Why not? I'm going mad with nothing to do. Besides, I can handle a gun as well as any man.'

René paused, rubbed his bristled chin, then nodded. I dashed off to find Hubert, who was lying on his bed, looking a little pale.

'Don't think I'm going. You're mad. If anything goes wrong, you'll be arrested.'

'Well, if I can pull this off, the men might have some respect for us.'

Hubert shot me a troubled look, then carried on reading his book.

As darkness fell, I changed into black clothes and joined the men outside. René nodded to me as he handed me a rifle. It differed from the Browning assault weapon I'd used in training. He gave a short briefing and then we were ready to go. 'You shadow me, okay?'

I didn't need to shadow anyone, but first impressions counted. 'Of course.' I sat up front in the truck squashed between him and another man as we headed into St Flour, breaking the curfew. We drew up outside a sports store.

'The owner is a collaborator, so we are not harming innocent people.' René's eyes looked like glossy black beads there in the cover of darkness, and his tone was so blasé.

One of the men broke in through the main door and we rushed inside, searching for anything useful. I plucked blankets from shelves, tossed them into the trucks. The others lifted tents, boots, warm clothing, and anything else that might come in useful for outdoor living. Outside in the street, all was quiet. In less than five minutes, the trucks were brimming with loot, and we returned to the chateau.

'Well, Madame. Welcome to France,' René said. His lightly lined face made him look around thirty years of age, I thought. His mouth curved up into a wide smile, transforming him from a grumpy rogue to a rather pleasant chap.

'Thank you. It went like clockwork. You have a good haul out of it.' I'd made my point at least, proved I wasn't completely useless. I ran upstairs and found Hubert lying in bed, still reading.

'You're back then.' He cast me an uninterested glance over the top of his book, Orwell's *Homage to Catalonia*.

'Yes. I had a ball. No Germans. We nicked loads of stuff.' I drifted through to the bathroom and scrutinised my reflection in the mirror, noted the spark in my eyes, the flush of my cheeks, a radiance not seen for a long while. I turned on the taps in the basin, cupped my hands under the flow of water and splashed my face. 'Let's see what Gaspard has to say about this.'

Hubert sighed. 'It won't make any difference. We still don't have a radio. We're bloody useless.'

Strewth, he sounded so despondent. Come to think of it, Hubert didn't look well either. He was pale, and his eyes seemed dark. Perhaps he was coming down with something. And Gaspard. A brute of a man, so arrogant. Well, he needed London. Where else was he going to get enough ammunition and arms for his men? He needed London just as London needed him and he'd realise it soon enough. I decided Gaspard would not be armed first. We'd make him stew a while as we chose a more amenable group.

Chapter 26
ON THE MOVE

Chaudes-Aigues was a beautiful town, well known for its hot water springs. Gaspard had banished us there while we were non-operational. Still, I was relieved to be out of his way. I climbed out of the car. 'If Denis doesn't get a shift on, I'll find him myself.'

Hubert rolled his eyes. The whitewashed farmhouse sat on the outskirts of the town: another place, another Maquis. I took a deep breath in, savouring the fresh scent of pine from nearby trees that drifted on the breeze. The door of the house swung open, and a man stood there, tall, slim, around mid-forties. He ushered us inside, unsmiling, serious. He spoke to our driver, one of Gaspard's men, and while Hubert looked puzzled as he strained to hear, I knew what they were saying. 'Useless? I'll show you who's useless, mate in a minute.' I scowled at him. 'Yes, I understood every word, and if you want to be able to fight the Germans and win, you'll be wise to listen up even if your leader is a great bumbling ox.'

The driver stared at me, drawing himself up to his full height, straightening his shoulders. The buffoon didn't intimidate me. The other man rubbed his stubbly chin with his right hand, as if sizing us up, his face relaxing as his mouth curved upwards and his eyes creased.

'Forgive me, Madame. I am Fournier. Pay no attention to this man. He is an idiot.' He sent the driver back to Gaspard then called for his wife, requesting coffee and food. My stomach rumbled and groaned as he invited us to sit at the kitchen table. His wife set the coffee pot and cups down. As Fournier poured black coffee, his wife brought bread, ham and cheese. 'Please, help yourself. You must be hungry after travelling all this way.'

My mouth watered as I took some bread, ham and cheese and made a sandwich. The large kitchen was clean and bright. A row of copper pans hung on the wall near a black cooking range. Madame Fournier busied in the background, washing dishes and generally tidying things away. It was clear she preferred to stay in the background while her husband discussed Resistance matters.

Fournier lingered his gaze on me as an amused smile tugged at his mouth. 'I am surprised London sends a woman. Courier work is dangerous, Madame. Usually, they send men.'

I smiled. 'You'll see that I'm as good as any man. Now, can we discuss plans? We've been here for almost two weeks and achieved nothing. Gaspard has made it clear he has no wish to cooperate.'

'Hah! Gaspard would not know a gift horse if it sat on him and pinned him to French soil. The man's a pompous ass. I cannot stand him. Arrogant and a bully.'

Hubert laughed. 'If you agree to work with us, London will finance you and your men with money, arms and all the ammunition you need.'

Fournier drained the last of his coffee and set his cup down with a bang. 'What exactly is it that London wants?'

Madame Fournier had stopped what she was doing, a linen tea cloth in one hand, a cup of coffee in the other as she listened intently.

'Well, we have certain tasks to carry out, before the Allied invasion,' Hubert said.

'Ha! What did I tell you?' Fournier banged his fist on the table, a huge grin spread across his craggy face as he turned to look at his wife. 'The Allies are coming, and together, we will beat the Boche. His wife stared, a frown forming on her face. 'When is it, this invasion?' His eyes darted from me to Hubert like some wild animal.

'We can't tell you that. We don't know the exact date, only that it's soon. The bad news is we still don't have a radio. Our operator parachuted in a few days ago but he hasn't turned up. We think he's having problems getting past the German patrols.'

'Well, without a radio we cannot do business.' Fournier's smile faded as he thought. 'I will ask some of my men to search for this radio operator. In the meantime, there is a safe house in Lieutades, a sleepy town. You won't be bothered there. As soon as we find your man, we can begin. Now eat.' He reached for a hunk of bread and ham, shovelling the meat into his mouth all at once.

THE SMALL GUESTHOUSE in Lieutades suited me very well. The only Germans were ones passing through, thankfully. After a few days of kicking our heels, I took a stroll to the quaint church, cutting through the graveyard, glancing at the headstones and tombs while soaking up the stillness, the peace. No cars passed; no people were around, just the baa of sheep grazing in the surrounding fields. I heaved myself up to sit on the craggy stone wall, turned my face to the blazing sun. A droning sound filtered in from the west, and as I watched the flawless sky a myriad of dark shapes sailed into view in the distance, masses of them. Americans, a white star visible on the fuselage of their aircraft. They were headed east, wherever they were going. 'Good luck, boys,' I whispered into the breeze. Hubert had gone for a walk, preferring to be alone today. He was fed up with all the waiting. 'It's been a complete farce,' he'd said earlier, kicking his bag out of the way in his room.

I wondered what Henri was doing right now. So near and yet so far away. My heart stung. All men hurt you or let you down sooner or later, so I used to think. I closed my eyes, pictured Dad, his grainy image faded by time and absence. Henri had convinced me otherwise, offered love and commitment. Tears stung my eyes. 'I'll find you soon, my love, once this is over,' I whispered. Skylarks soared overhead, gliding through blue, their sweet call piercing the silence, breaking my reverie, serenading the dead.

In the distance, the faint rumble of a vehicle grew louder before a black car rounded the corner of the road and drew to a halt a few yards away. The driver's door swung open, and a familiar voice sailed out.

'Hello, Gertie. Have you picked your plot yet?'

'Denden!' I jumped down from the wall and rushed over to throw my arms around him as he emerged from the car. 'You made it.' The smell of cigarettes and sweat engulfed me in a cloud.

'Thank the Gods! It was touch and go for a while back there.' He grinned.

'We're staying at a quaint guesthouse up the road. I'll show you.' I stared at him for a moment. His blue eyes were dull, his face tanned but worn. He'd obviously had one heck of a journey. 'I'm so thrilled you're here. Now we can get down to work.'

'Oh, let's not be too hasty, luv. I'm worn out and starving.' He got back in the car. 'May as well drive, save me lugging the case around.' He patted the seat next to him, and I jumped in.

His jolly face cheered me right up. 'You're all dusty.' His blond hair was a little matted too.

'Yes, well, I've been lying low for days. The place was crawling with Germans, and you'll never guess, but I ran into an old friend.' His face broke into a broad smile.

An old friend, indeed. One of his conquests by the look of that grin. Typical Denden. 'Now I know the real reason you're so damned late. Honestly.'

LATER, when Hubert arrived back at the guesthouse, he found us tucking into a hearty meal, prepared by Madame Gilbert, our hostess. 'Denis, you're here. What the devil happened?' Hubert shook his hand.

'Well, let's see. I landed the wrong side of Montluçon to find the place swarming with Germans. Jackboots all around. Well, the Resistance sent me here, there, and everywhere. I've had the most wonderful tour of France, I must say. It was a little hair-raising at one point.' He swallowed a mouthful of stew and reached for his wine to wash it down. 'Lovely grub. Ooh, I think I've been missing out.' He shovelled another forkful into his mouth.

'You haven't missed much,' Hubert said.

Then we told him all about Hector's arrest, and our unfriendly meeting with Gaspard. 'Fournier and Tardivat are definitely with us. We're going to arm their groups first and leave Gaspard to stew a while. He'll soon come around.' He'd be mad as hell once he discovered the others with new weapons and cash in their pockets. Oh yes, he'd soon be with us.

THE SUN PEAKED over the horizon, sailing into an azure sky; the long grass whispered in the breath of wind as a faint haze clung to the hills. It was warm and muggy. Today was a new beginning. A feeling of joy mixed with excitement stirred in the pit of my stomach. I reached beneath my pillow and grabbed my revolver, tucking it into the pouch at the back of my trousers. Den drove us back to Fournier in Chaudes-Aigues.

'Ah, I see he turned up. Bonjour.' Fournier beckoned us into a barn. 'You can set up in here.' Den got to work, setting up the radio, aerial and flicking through his book of codes.

'What happens now?' Fournier said.

'We'll send a message to London and advise them of the drop site,' Hubert said. 'We've already spotted a few fields that will be suitable. Next, we ask London for arms and ammunition. We will supply your group first.'

'Merci. I will tell my men; they will spread the word. More will come to join us.'

'Well, we're still hopeful that Gaspard will see sense.' He had the largest group, three or four thousand-strong and he'd soon see he was missing out.

'Ha! That bumbling oaf has no sense. He thinks he knows everything, but he does not listen. He will soon realise when he sees our new weapons.' Fournier laughed, pulled a black Basque beret from his trouser pocket and set it on his head.

He wasn't wrong there. For our first haul, we were about to ask London for hundreds of Sten and Bren guns, grenades, and thousands of rounds of ammunition.

Denden checked his watch and glanced round at me. 'Almost time, luvvie,' he said in a sing-song voice, his code book in front of him. 'Right, here we go.' With his headset on he tapped out a message to London in Morse, while we all waited. I held my breath for a few seconds, aware of my heart pounding my ears. Fournier stared, eyes wide, a mix of intrigue and awe flashing there. Two minutes later Denis dragged off his headset. 'That's it, folks. We're on our way.' A broad grin danced on his lips.

I slapped him on the back. 'Let's hope so.' I loved Denden. His cheery manner lifted my spirits.

WE CHOSE the plateau above Chaudes-Aigues for the first drop. Fournier agreed it was ideal as the Germans weren't near. Now, all we had to do was spend hours listening to the radio for a message from the BBC to confirm the drop. I'd used the code name strawberry for the parachutage site, along with my personal code, 'the cow jumped over the moon.' While I waited around with Denden, Hubert made his excuses and left with Fournier as he attended to his tasks – organising the network. I strode outside and turned my face to the mid-afternoon sun, glancing further westward to the hills, where beyond lay home and my heart.

Chapter 27
IT BEGINS

The following morning brought the rain. The long, dry spell had finally yielded and the rain that fell hammered the earth's crust, ricocheting off the ground, the smell of wet earth drifting all around, rich and intoxicating. A mist hung over the plateau. Three white geese strutted through the farmyard, stepping around muddy puddles, honking in disgust as they waddled away to the confines of an open barn, picking their way through straw and muck. I finished dressing and went downstairs, the delicious smell of coffee wafting from the kitchen. Madame Fournier stood at the stove.

'Ah, Madame Andrée. Help yourself to coffee and food.'

'Merci.' I took a slice of white bread and a little strawberry jam.

A cat lay upon a threadbare green rug in front of the stone fireplace. It was a cool, damp May day. I pulled my emerald cardigan tighter around me and savoured a mouthful of ersatz hot coffee. The outside door swung open and in walked Fournier, rain dripping from his coat and the brim of his beret, forming pools on the grey flagstone floor. Madame Fournier admonished him immediately, a scowl on her round face, her cheeks reddening by the second. He returned the scowl and told her to be quiet. He removed his coat but retained the boots, trampling mud across to the table where he sat down. He ran a dirty hand through his dark, soaked hair.

'What did I tell you would happen as soon as word got out?' He stared at me, his eyes searching, an amused look on his face.

What was he blustering on about? I raised an eyebrow. 'Tell me.'

'I said they would come – the men, from the local villages. Word spreads fast here. Already we have another twenty men and more on the way.' He chuckled as he poured coffee into an empty cup. Without so much as a twitch, he downed the ersatz in one mouthful, wiping his mouth with the back of his hand. 'All we need now is for London to hurry and send us arms. Then we can begin.'

I nodded. 'Yes, I'll be listening in today for the signal.' That was the worst of it. Sitting around, waiting, glued to the radio along with Denden. Just as well, he was completely mad and hilarious. He was one of the best radio ops and knew everything about radios, inside and out.

Madame Fournier brought over eggs, bacon and sausage for two. She glanced at her husband. 'Any word from Alain?'

Fournier's face fell, and his eyes dulled. 'No. Not yet.'

She turned her gaze to the window, looking blankly out, a look of anguish etched upon her face.

'Merci, Madame.' I glanced at Fournier. 'Who's Alain?'

He sighed. 'Our son. He is twenty. He went on a raid with another group a week ago. They fled the Germans, went on the run. He will be lying low on the far side of Montluçon. His mother worries.'

I stabbed a sausage and took a bite. The succulent flavour of pork left me wanting more as my stomach gurgled.

'The war is hard on Alice. I was in the first one and waiting for news of her two brothers and me, was a huge strain. Her brothers never returned. It is a pity Herr Hitler survived when so many good men fell.' He shook his head, and hatred crept into his face, setting his mouth stern, squeezing his eyes. 'Back then, France felt Fritz's presence, but they only occupied a small area in the east. They did not have Paris. Now, they have all of it, squeezing us dry.' He slammed his fist on the table, making me jump.

It was the first time I'd heard him speak like that. And to hear his wife's name made her appear softer and more feminine than the sullen woman who kept to the shadows, snapping at her husband's heels incessantly. 'I'm sorry. I'm sure you're right. Alain will be back soon.' It was a pathetic attempt of reassurance that was not mine to give, nor appropriate but I was compelled to say something, anything, and Fournier smiled.

I gazed around the large farmhouse kitchen. The Fournier's didn't seem to want for food, but the house was shabby, as were their clothes. But as Fournier had said, he'd sunk most of his life savings into funding his small group of Maquis for the best part of one year. He already had hundreds of men of various ages, ranging from seventeen up to sixty. Many of them had fled their homes to avoid the *service du travail obligatoire* – conscription to work in Germany's industries, fuelling the Axis Forces. The sooner London came through, the better.

THE BARN WAS QUIET. Denden sat on an upturned wooden crate, his headset clamped to his ears, listening. I lay on a bed of sweet golden straw, gazing at the barn roof riddled with gaps and holes. 'The rain's stopped.' No response. He probably didn't hear. Fleeting shadows sailed by above as darker clouds gave way to the sun, and flecks of gold filled the gaps in the roof, fingers of gold sweeping the barn floor. Thousands of dust motes danced wildly in the golden hues. I sat up and took out a packet of cigarettes, offered it to Den, who plucked one, casting me a wink. Lighting up, I strolled around, stretched my legs, savouring a lungful of nicotine as my lower back ached. 'So, come on. Tell me what you've really been up to, Den.'

'Well, Duckie, as I said before, I was lying low for days. The place was swarming with Germans.'

'Lying low, eh? I bet you were. Who with, though, that's what I want to know?'

He threw his codebook at me, and it bounced off my thigh. Laughing, I hurled it right back. A stomp of footsteps out in the yard and I held my breath for a moment. The sound of men's voices drifted in through the closed barn doors, French. I crept over to the door and peeped out through a crack in the wood. Three tired-looking men, wearing a week's worth of stubble stood in the muddied yard talking to Fournier who slapped one of them on the back jovially and led them towards the house.

'Looks as if Fournier's little army is growing. Word is spreading.'

'Good. Well, nothing is happening here. Oh, Lord, I could murder a drink. Be a darling.' Den shot me a puppy-dog look.

'Fine. I'll go.'

'And if there's any grub going, luvvie.'

Madame Fournier was going to love me, asking for food in the middle of the afternoon. I sighed. Leaving my dirty boots by the farmhouse door, I stepped inside. The kitchen was empty, and there was no sign of the men who had just arrived. I stood and listened. Then I heard a man's laugh. They must be in one of the other rooms. The coffee pot was on the stove, still hot. I grabbed two enamel cups and poured. With sharp eyes, I scanned the kitchen for food – nothing in sight. Then I remembered the chocolate bar in my bag. One left. I ran upstairs and retrieved it. It would have to do. There was no way on earth I was taking food from Madame Fournier's larder and risking upsetting the formidable Frenchwoman. Besides, it was bad manners. Back in the barn, I dropped the chocolate in the straw by the radio.

'Oh, I am being spoiled. Thanks, Gertie.'

'I take it you've heard nothing?'

'Not a dickie bird, my luv. Not a darn thing.' He sat down and stretched out his legs, tearing open the chocolate wrapper, biting off a chunk. I sat next to him and sipped my coffee. The only sound was of Denis munching. I wasn't very good at waiting. Doing was more my thing, but right now we were slaves to this radio.

'You're quiet.'

'Just thinking, Den.'

'Hmm, well it's best not to dwell too much, whatever it is.'

'I wonder how Hubert's getting on.'

'Famously well, I'm sure.' He patted the back of my hand. 'We're all mad, doing this. Could have been safe and cosy back home.'

It was too late for that. Nowhere was safe. I'd never been afraid except once. The day I left Henri. Suddenly, it seemed as if I'd been running for some considerable time, but I wasn't running now.

He stared at me for a few seconds. 'Are you sure you're okay?'

I swallowed the lump in my throat. 'Yes, I'm fine.' I sprang up and wandered across to the barn door, opening it just far enough to glimpse the sunshine. The sky was clearing – milky-blue with hazy white clumps of cumulus hanging, patchy, drifting slowly east. I rubbed my arms to dispel the icy prickle that flowed over them. I'd never hated anyone in my life before, but I hated the Germans and Hitler. *By God, I'm going to thrash them if it's the last thing I do.*

'Psst.' Denden waved his arm, beckoning me over, his headset clamped firmly over his ears, listening intently to the small set, down in the straw. 'We're on for tonight.' He grinned.

Chapter 28

THE DROP

The moon was full and white, rising high in a cloudless sky. I stood at the edge of a field on the plateau above Chaudes-Aigues, the scent of pine drifting from the trees, trapped in the fresh evening breeze. I tucked my .45 revolver into the waistband of my trousers, aware of the metal blade of my knife that pressed flat against my leg, inside my boot. The drop could be anytime between ten-thirty and four in the morning. The men carried torches; their rifles slung over their shoulders. My breath, a silver ribbon danced on the air, and I was thankful for the woollen jumper and jacket I'd dragged on before leaving. I reached into my pocket and pulled out a black beret, slipped it on. The ground was drenched in dew and glistened beneath the moonlight. The sounds of the night filtered in, the echoing hoot of an owl, the rustle of swishing long grass, and the protest of crickets, their sweet rhythmic chirp a lullaby. My belly fluttered. Our first parachutage and Hubert would miss the fun. We'd manage. I'd planned it to perfection, and it would go like clockwork providing everyone pulled their weight.

'Madame?' Fournier waved a packet of Gitanes in front of me.

'Merci.' I plucked one and leaned in for a light, watching as he flicked a glance at the sky.

'Will they definitely come tonight?' He turned to me, his dark eyes like granite.

'Oui.' Unless something goes wrong. 'We just have to wait.' I drew on my cigarette and glanced around at the others. Always waiting! Fournier reached for his hip flask and took a swig, and then with a look of satisfaction offered it to me. I didn't wish to drink after him, but a refusal might offend, so I took a good mouthful, fiery warmth tingling on my tongue and in my throat. He looked surprised. I could hold my own where alcohol was concerned, and I thrust the hip flask into his hand. 'Merci.'

The faintest drone from the west cut through the low rumble of gruff voices. 'Shush.' I strained to listen. A twig snapped. One of the men coughed.

'What is it?' Fournier glanced up.

'Hear that?' The droning grew, and soon the thrum of many engines filled the air. Dark crosses silhouetted against the sky glided into view. The maquisards grinned and pointed at the aircraft. I counted fifteen Lancaster Bombers. Several aircraft dropped our containers on the first pass; dark bullets sailed down to earth beneath black parachutes. The formation of Lancaster's circled and came back for a second pass, releasing the remaining containers from their bellies. I raced to the nearest one, unclipped the chute and opened it. Bren guns. The others did the same, working quickly to remove the chutes, folding silk to re-use later. Containers were rounded up and carried to the edge of the field, beneath the cover of the trees, all one hundred and fifty of them.

'Jon-Luc bring the trucks,' Fournier instructed. 'Madame Andrée, we will load up the arms.'

The last container lay at my feet and was marked 'personal for Helénè'. I opened it and gasped, a smile tugging at the corners of my mouth. 'C'est beau!' Reaching in I pulled out Elizabeth Arden face cream, face powder, bars of chocolate, stockings, and a pair of black leather heeled shoes. I picked up the shoe and by the light of my torch checked the size – a six, exactly right. 'I can hardly believe it. Bless you, Vera.' A small cream manila envelope addressed to me sat tucked in between my goodies and I tucked it inside my jacket to read later. One of Fournier's men helped me carry my container to the gate where two trucks waited. 'Careful, these things are for me.' He nodded.

For a moment I stood looking out to the north-west, where across the cold waters of the Channel, England lay. A warm glow suffused me from the inside out. To know that people were thinking of us and had acquired these items solely for me, meant so much. My eyes misted over, and I sniffed. Smart shoes for non-field duty days, stockings, and cosmetics. What a treat. I smiled to myself as memories of the first time I met Vera resurfaced.

My interview at Orchard Court had been so strange. The doorman had led me to a bathroom to wait of all places, and I'd perched on the side of a jet-black bath. Several people came and went and then I was ushered into an office where I met the chief – Colonel Maurice Buckmaster. After an initial chat, I'd followed him to another office where he introduced me to a stern-looking woman, perhaps in her mid-thirties, with blue-grey penetrating eyes. 'Miss Atkins will look after you from now on,' he'd said, and how right he'd been. As Vera spoke, it became evident she knew so much about me already, and yet she had no file in front of her. She knew of my marriage to a French businessman and about our life together in France, as well as my involvement with the escape network. I'd already run rings around the Nazis and survived. But then Vera explained that I was on the Germans most wanted list. I was the 'White Mouse' of whom the Gestapo had printed leaflets and distributed in Marseille and throughout France. I'd been warned they were watching me at the time but hearing such news from Vera had filled me with terror for Henri. 'I'll understand if you wish to change your mind,' she'd said, softly.

'Do you want a lift back?' Fournier broke my reverie. His eyes sparkled in the moonlight, a pleasant, boyish tone in his voice. His haul – hundreds of guns, ammunition, and grenades, put a spring in his step.

'Yes, it's freezing.' The drive back to camp took around five minutes. The men offloaded the containers and hid them in a pit in the ground. My things were bundled into a spare box and driven back to the farm for my last night. Tomorrow I was to join the Maquis and Denden in the woods. It was safer that way. The next task was to train the men how to use their new weapons. How hard could that be? There were also orders from London to carry out. The truck lurched violently, Fournier cursed, and I lunged forward. What was I doing? It was madness. I'd had a life with Henri before all of this. I'd started everything. If it hadn't been for me, then Henri would probably never have become involved. Had I forced his hand? How he'd worried, for himself and for me. The dream I'd had in England, Henri, a firing squad, gunfire. A hard thwack, the truck lurched again almost jolting me out of the seat and Fournier ranted in French. The Gestapo had been searching for me, and there was no news of Henri. What if they'd arrested him?

We turned off the main road, and the truck rumbled across the rough stony track that led down to the farm, bile rising in my throat, a fluttering in my chest.

'Thank you, Madame Andrée, for arming us,' Fournier said. 'My men were very restless before you arrived. Now, we all have a purpose. We have money and weapons.'

'Yes, and your men need to learn to use them. All we need now is Gaspard.'

'Ah, he is bloody-minded. He will stick it out alone for as long as possible.' Fournier's eyes narrowed.

'Yes, but he has thousands of men, and we need them.' I'd rather hoped that Gaspard would have come looking for me by now. Word must have reached him.

Fournier muttered something under his breath as he pulled up at the house. I went to the back of the truck for my box of goodies. Just as I was about to reach in, Fournier's strong arms were there. 'Allow me, Madame.'

'Merci.' I smiled, looking him in the eye and saw his black glassy gaze give way to a softer stare.

'I am sure you will have Gaspard any day now.' He set my things upon the oak table.

Madame Fournier appeared. 'What is this?' She pointed to the box.

'None of your business, woman,' Fournier snapped as he went to the stove to see what was bubbling in the pot. He sniffed. 'Ah, rabbit stew. Let's eat.'

Madame Fournier seemed interested in the contents of my haul, so I opened it, reached inside, and grabbed the face cream. 'From London, just for me.'

She took the glass jar from my hands and gazed in awe. 'They dropped it from the sky?' Her hazel eyes grew wide with surprise.

'Yes, isn't that wonderful?' I pulled out the shoes to show her, watching as she held one, weathered fingers stroking leather, a huge smile tugging at her mouth. Shoes were impossible to buy in France. 'Go on, try the Lizzie Arden cream.' She shook her head, a shocked look on her face, so I dipped my finger in and dabbed a little on the back of her hand. She laughed, all the while Fournier's eyes darted from me to her while he shovelled stew into his mouth, slurping. Madame Fournier took the cream and dotted a little on her cheeks, rubbing it in softly, a wide smile tugging at her mouth. It's surprising how the little moments in life persist even in the darkest of times, lighting a spark of joy even if for only a few seconds. Smiles and laughter were so important, I felt.

Chapter 29
RETRIBUTION

Hubert was in Montluçon, making plans with another Maquis group. We had a list of targets we'd been instructed to take out once the Allied invasion was underway. Each group had their part to play. Den and I had been busy here, cleaning weapons, de-greasing them after the parachutage. Fournier was strutting around like a peacock, his men now equipped with new boots, and weapons. Each man was issued one pair of British army boots and two pairs of socks. Word of our activities was circulating, and in the last week alone, around four hundred men had arrived. My days were filled with weapons training, planning, and visiting other Maquis in the surrounding area of the Auvergne, assessing their needs. Den spent much of his time chained to the radio, listening to the broadcasts, waiting for messages as we'd organised another drop. Nights were spent upon the plateau, soaked to the bone amidst sheet rain, or freezing up on colder evenings while preparing drop zones, lugging containers from the parachutage before collapsing in a heap onto my forest bed, sleeping beneath fading stars. My body ached and grew heavier by the day, sleep a distant memory, a much-desired luxury.

As I sat on a log, drinking my morning coffee, a slice of bread and jam in my other hand, a car approached, grinding to a halt. A hubbub of gruff voices erupted, and then someone called my name. 'Madame Andrée.' A young man, tall, with short brown hair strode towards me. I nodded, drank the last of the coffee and took a bite of my bread, sweet strawberry coating my tongue.

'Bonjour, Madame Andrée. It is Gaspard who has sent me. We have captured a German spy.'

They had? I jumped to my feet. 'Come on.' I slapped him on the back, felt the back of my trousers, my hand brushing over the hard metal of my Colt.45. We drove to Gaspard's place in silence. As I hauled myself from the car, there was the most blood-chilling cry from the barn. 'What the hell are they doing?' I yanked open the barn door and, in a few seconds, scanned the scene, my eyes darting all around. The German stripped to the waist, tied face down over a bench, his defined muscled torso glistening beneath a sheen of sweat. Blood trickled down one side of his face from a head wound, white-blond hair coated reddish-brown. I spotted a bullet hole in his back. He was about to be branded by the look of things as one of Gaspard's men stood over him, brandishing a smouldering iron. Gaspard looked up. 'Madame, have you anything you wish to ask this dog?'

I walked across to the man who was lying on a bench, held down by two men. My eyes flicked over his body. Another bullet had pierced his thigh. The man's blue eyes danced wildly, and I knew enough to realise he wouldn't survive his wounds. 'I've never seen him before,' I said, glancing at Gaspard who seemed to enjoy showing off his spoils.

'He has denounced many good people. He says he is responsible for O'Leary's arrest last year. I have a signed confession.' Gaspard waved a piece of paper in front of my face, the confession signed by the prisoner.

The breath caught in my throat. O'Leary had saved my neck, and this was the bastard who'd brought him down. The one O'Leary had saved me from, the man who'd longed to meet me. I clenched my fists and my jaw, anger bubbling up inside me, but I wanted no part in his torture. 'Put the bastard out of his misery now, or I'll do it myself.' Gaspard stared at me through narrowed eyes, huffed out a breath. 'This isn't the way. I mean it.' I reached for my revolver.

Gaspard shook his head. 'Very well.'

I turned and left, glad of the fresh air as bile lurched up into my throat. Christ, I hated the Germans, but there was no need for torture. That was their game. A crack of gunshot cried out behind me and a flock of black crows scattered and cawed as they took to the trees. I closed my eyes and leant against the car, trying to suppress nausea, but it was too late, and I bent forward and vomited. After a few deep breaths, I climbed in, leaned forward, rested my head in my hands. The man's face, eyes as blue and deep as the ocean, searching, desperate. An icy tingle graced my spine. Well, he wouldn't spy any more. Footsteps crunching over stones. My driver. Without a word, he slipped behind the wheel and started the engine. I slammed the door and sat in silence as we drove back to the camp, wondering how long it would be before the Germans came looking for their man. A dark feeling of foreboding crept over me, and I shuddered. Reprisals were on the rise.

IT WAS four o'clock and the late afternoon sun beat down as I reached the drop site on the plateaux. I jumped out of the truck, wiped beads of sweat from my brow, embracing the light breeze. The men were already at work, preparing the ground, making sure the lights were in position. I went to the edge of the field, to where the trees gathered in a cluster. Behind them, in the thicket was a covered wooden hatch door in the undergrowth that hid a cavernous ditch beneath. I opened the hatch and dragged out one container, my biceps straining, heart thumping. Our latest recruits needed boots and socks. After checking that everything was going to be ready for nightfall, I drove back to camp.

THAT NIGHT the moon loomed large. Smoke vapour filled the air above the plateaux, silver ribbons swirling this way and that as the men smoked their Gauloises, talking in little more than low murmurs. The lights were in place. Den and I stood beneath the trees, waiting, Sten guns slung over our shoulders.

'It's bloody chilly tonight.' He reached into his jacket pocket and pulled out his woollen gloves.

'Here.' I offered him my hip flask.

'What's in it?'

'Wine.'

'Ooh, lovely.' His eyes lit up, and he swigged a generous mouthful.

'You know, Den. We need someone else to help us train the recruits. In fact, to help us lick the entire group into shape. For a start, they haven't got a clue about the new guns.'

'Yes, I know. I was told someone would be coming, but I don't know when. As ever it's a case of waiting, luv.'

The men were becoming restless. The smoking had ceased, and a hip flask was doing the rounds. The breeze puffed harder, chilly, nipping at my ears and neck. The cloudless sky revealed a myriad of silver sparkles. The grass, wet and dewy, forced us to remain standing. There was no place to rest, and I thought of my bed and my pillow. Sleep was the only respite in this damn war. Turning my face to the stars, I listened to the shush of the trees, a rhythmic song that rose and fell. Another sound filtered through, and the men dispersed, taking up their positions. They were more in tune this time. I smiled, pleasantly surprised by their organisation. The men stood in a line, equal distances apart, ready with the lights. The noise of engines grew until black silhouetted aircraft soared into view. The men switched on the lights. Aware of Den's body close to mine, he whispered in my ear, his breath warm.

'I wish I had a seat on that one, being ferried back to Blighty.'

It was no good wishing. A smattering of black bullets expelled from the bellies above, sailing down into the field, beneath blossoms of billowing silk. Engines roared overhead, the silhouettes of aircraft sailed over the land. Banking steeply, they turned to make one more pass, the last of the group releasing their cargo. I stared up, watching as the formation droned away westward with a waggle of wings, a final farewell. The thrum of engines faded into the night, and I glanced at Den, a wistful look set on his face. The maquisards moved stealthily through the field gathering up containers, hauling them to one side of the field to unpack. The guns needed to be de-greased and re-assembled, and we'd be working on through till late morning with the haul.

'Oh well, that's that,' Den said.

'Here.' I held out my hip flask and his face creased into a smile.

He took several mouthfuls, wiped his mouth on his sleeve then held out his arm. 'Thanks, Ducks. You're a lifesaver.'

We strolled back to the trucks, arm in arm. Den just needed a little cheering up, that was all. My thoughts turned to the Allied invasion. We were still waiting for the exact date, and then the fireworks could begin, and I couldn't wait.

Chapter 30
JUNE 1944

The car sped along the rough track, leaving a cherry dust cloud in our wake, hanging in the humid late afternoon air like smoke. 'Strewth, slow down, can't you or you'll have us both killed.' I glared at Jacques, my driver.

'It is not that fast. It just seems that way because the road is winding and narrow.' He laughed, dragging a hand through his dark hair, thin slivers of grey streaking across the top of his head.

Montluçon stretched out in the distance, sweating beneath a flawless azure sky. The drive from Chaudes-Aigues had taken almost four hours. I reached into the footwell for the canteen of water and took a swig. I hoped I had the right address. Since Hector's arrest, I'd had to do a little digging on contacts. 'Jacques, remember to stop outside the town. I'll have to cycle in.' A bicycle lay on the back seat. I wore flat shoes for the mission, and a pale blue printed dress with a white cardigan. 'Right, when I collect Anselm, we'll leave on bicycles and meet you back by the car. If anything happens and you have to leave, we'll cycle out on this road and catch you further on. Okay?'

'Oui.' He turned off the lane and pulled up by a small, wooded spot. He dragged the bicycle from the back seat and held it while I smoothed down my dress and checked my face in my compact. 'How do I look?'

Jacques shrugged his shoulders. 'Like every other woman in France.'

'Great What a compliment!' I frowned. 'You'll never get a girl if that's the best you can do.'

He laughed, taking out a cigarette and lighting up. 'Be careful. The place is swarming with Germans.'

'Thanks. Wish me luck.' I wasn't afraid of the Germans. And soon we'd have them on the run. I could feel it in my soul. I longed for the day, impatience simmering away.

'Merde!' Jacques called after me. Since arriving in France, I'd barely ridden a bicycle, and almost as soon as I sat on it, my backside protested. The saddle was more like a wooden pommel, and in a short time, my derrière throbbed. As I pedalled into town, I passed another cyclist and noted two German soldiers at a checkpoint who had stopped a citizen and were checking his papers. I cycled past, not daring to look, turning into Rue Saint-Jean, scanning every door for number 40. I sailed past 36 and on, slowing to a halt and dismounted, shocked by how badly my legs ached. Number 40 stood before me, a white painted house with a pale blue front door and shutters. I leaned my cycle against blue-painted railings, climbed the steps to the front door, and knocked. Within seconds I heard footsteps, and the door creaked open.

'Madame Renard?' The aroma of fresh baking drifted out into the street. I recalled the password. 'You have a cake for me.' The woman put a hand up to her white hair, stepped back, beckoning me inside.

'Bonjour. Through here, Madame.'

I followed her along a dark, narrow hallway to the kitchen at the rear of the house. She coughed. 'It is all right. You can come out now.'

I peered around and noticed a cupboard door opening and out stepped Anselm, brandishing a .45 revolver. I recognised him immediately – we'd met during SOE training. 'You're Anselm.' I hugged him tightly, kissing him on each cheek.

'Ah, Chérie. We meet again.'

'I had no idea it was going to be you. Well, you took your time in getting here. We could have done with you at least two weeks ago. Have you got a cycle?'

'Oui, outside.'

Madame Renard brought food and coffee and then served us her homemade Rum Baba, the aroma sending my tummy into a frenzy of gurgles. It was delicious.

'Well, we'd better get going. We'll cycle just outside the town. I've got a car waiting to take us back to Chaudes-Aigues.'

'A car?'

'Believe me; it's much safer and quicker than cycling everywhere. You'll not get far without one.' I stared at him briefly, happy to see another friend. 'Come on.'

'You've got papers, haven't you?' Now we were two, there was a greater chance of being stopped.

'Yes, I have everything.' He grinned, his brown eyes softening. He looked exactly as I remembered: slim, chiselled face, neat pencil moustache, and slicked-back dark brown hair. I rode ahead. At the end of the road, a black Citroen passed us, probably headed for German HQ which was only streets away. Up ahead, German soldiers stood in the road, so we turned off and made a detour. Fortunately, lady luck beamed, and we had a clear run out of town and back to Jacques.

'You made it in good time. I will put the cycle on the roof. There is not enough room for two,' Jacques said.

'Just take mine.' I jumped in the front.

Anselm threw his bicycle into the long grass and got in the car, holding his Colt .45 revolver. 'This isn't a gazogene. How do they get petrol?'

'They steal it from the plant.' I laughed. 'They'd steal anything if I let them.'

The drive back was long and humid. The only breeze was the rush of the slipstream through the open windows and even that was warm. 'Don't worry. If we get stopped by the Germans, I came prepared.' I picked up one of the Sten guns and a grenade from the stash of ammunition stowed in the footwell.

'I might have known.' His tanned face creased into a wide grin.

'You were probably the best shot in training. Hopeless at running, but you know your way around a gun.'

Cheek. I thumped him softly on the arm. We arrived back late evening. The men at the camp were drinking, heavily by the looks of them, and laughing. Den was there, his face rosy, glassy-eyed, a bottle of something in his hand. 'What's going on?' I grabbed the bottle from him and took a swig. Rum.

'It's happened, Gertie. It's finally happened.' He threw his arms around me and kissed my cheeks.

I stood open-mouthed. 'The invasion. The Allies are here.' I smiled, took another drink, then punched the air. A wave of relief washed through me, with a mix of disappointment, especially as Den then proceeded to tell me all about their exploits over the last twenty-four hours. Planting explosives like daisies, he said, blowing up targets as requested by London. And I'd missed it all. Oh well, never mind, I thought. 'Den, say hello to our old friend, Anselm.'

'Well, well, fancy seeing you here.' Den's face was a picture, and the two men shook hands. 'You made it just in time. Big job ahead of you.' He dragged a packet of fags from his shirt pocket. 'The BBC broadcast at nine-thirty this morning. They said, "Under the command of General Eisenhower, Allied naval forces, supported by strong air forces, began landing Allied armies this morning on the northern coast of France." Yes, I'll never forget that. So exciting.' Den sank down at the foot of a tree, slumped back against the trunk, and puffed on his cigarette.

They'd sabotaged railway lines, the underground telephone cables that the Germans used, bridges, a factory in Clermont-Ferrand, and a railway junction at Moulins. 'What about the petrol plant at St Hilaire?' That one had been an issue of debate as it was the source of our petrol.

'No, we left it, Duckie,' Den said. 'We'd be screwed otherwise.'

I slumped down next to him. There was so much to do. I had drops scheduled almost every night over the coming week, providing nothing went wrong. Then there were local Resistance groups to visit, and I'd have to introduce Anselm.

'Some of the men are at the drop site. Why don't you stay here for once? Have a rest.' Den poured me a glass of wine.

'I know you wanted to be here when the Allies landed, but I'm afraid they couldn't wait for you, Ducks.'

'No, suppose not.' I drained my glass.

'Steady on old girl. There's only so much of this.'

'What? I'm just warming up. Fill her up.' The Allies were on their way. The Germans would soon be retreating; a sight I couldn't wait to see. The tide was turning, and soon there would be a Nazi wave rolling back to Germany. 'Are you going up there tonight, Den?'

'Yes, my love, if it helps you.' He smiled. 'I meant what I said. You have a rest and an early night.'

'Thanks, you're a darling. Oh, will you check the containers for my things?'

'Oh, Lord, help us. The great cosmetic treasure hunt again. Yes, I'll save them from those hairy gorillas.'

'And hands off the silk stockings. I don't want any runs in 'em before I've had a chance to wear them.' I sipped my wine and looked up as Anselm joined us. 'Have a glass of red.'

'Thank you.' He grinned and sat down. 'I had not realised we would be living in such luxury.' He gazed around the camp.

'We do all right.' I'd become used to sleeping rough, my bed on top of a carpet of leaves and dust, rain or shine.

'I guess I'll make a start in the morning with the men.' He ran a hand through his hair. He looked tired.

'Well, a number of them think themselves experts, so best of luck.' I drained my glass. 'And some of them are still drunk the morning after, so watch out for that. Come on, keep up.'

'Oh, no. I'm not playing that game with you. You could drink anyone under the table and still walk away.'

'And shoot straight,' I added. He obviously remembered our heavy drinking sessions during training. It was so wonderful to be reunited with friends. The evening passed in a heartbeat and dusk drew the men away to the plateau. With a slightly fuzzy head, I took myself off to bed, settling down with my sleeping bag beneath an old oak tree, plumping up my red satin cushion. It would soon be morning, and it would all begin again.

~

I FOUND Den by his wireless, sitting on an upturned wooden crate. On the far side of our camp, I glimpsed Anselm through the trees, a Bren gun at his side. He'd made an early start.

'Morning, Gertie. Don't say I never get you anything.' Denis thrust a small box into my hands.

'My things.' I opened the lid and peered inside. 'Lizzie Arden. Silk stockings. What a beaut! And lipstick. How do they do it?'

'Beats me, love. And what do I get? Sweet bugger all.'

'Oh, don't be like that, Den. I'll share my face cream with you. You know how you like to take care of your skin.' I giggled, glad of the grin spreading across his face, but the sudden sound of an explosion in the distance shattered the silence. 'Strewth, what now?'

The men looked across to the hills behind us. Another explosion boomed, and a grey dust cloud billowed into the distant sky.

'It's coming from Mont Mouchet.' I called one of the men over and asked him to go and take a look. 'The Germans are attacking Gaspard.'

'There's nothing we can do.' Den lit up a cigarette. 'We told him not to keep his men all in one place. If only he'd listened to you. Let's hope they can get out of that.' He shook his head. 'What about the parachutage tonight?'

I huffed out a breath. Damn! 'You'd better radio London and tell them it's off.' We couldn't take the risk, not now. I went in search of coffee and food. Gaspard was a stubborn fool. The first rule of warfare – don't keep all your troops in one place. They'd made themselves easy pickings for Jerry. As I cut a thick slice of bread and spread on a layer of raspberry jam, a droning filtered in from above. Turning my face to the sky, I glimpsed the grey shape of an aircraft, sunlight glinting on the fuselage. The enemy had launched aerial attacks too. God help you, Gaspard. An icy shiver rippled over my shoulders, slipped down my back. Well, I had lists to trawl through and supplies to arrange, so I found myself a shaded spot beneath a pine tree, sat down with my mug of coffee, and began to work.

An hour later, the young Frenchman I'd sent out as a scout to check on Gaspard returned. 'Madame Andrée, the Germans have launched a huge attack on Gaspard's men. There are hundreds of them, probably fifteen hundred at least. The battle is raging across the plateau above us. They have tanks and aircraft.'

'Strewth. The man's a fool. How are they holding up?'

'They are heavily outnumbered. Some of the men are scattering, but the Germans have them virtually surrounded.'

'Damn it.' They had to come through. He had around three thousand men up there, and I needed them.

I got on with my work as best I could, my concentration interrupted by the boom of exploding grenades and tank cannon fire against a background noise of machine-gun fire in the distance. Reports filtered in throughout the afternoon and early evening and then Fournier turned up with the news that Gaspard's men had captured an armoured car and two cannons. They had sustained some injuries and deaths, but the losses on the German's side was far greater. 'This is payback for killing their man, Roger the spy.'

'Well, Gaspard's men are holding their own for now, but they will not last much longer.' Fournier stared at me, the frustration evident in his eyes, and I felt it too. Our fellow Frenchmen fighting a battle they would not win, and we couldn't help.

'We can't get involved. The men aren't ready, and besides, we can't risk losses on our side. Just pray that Gaspard and his men can get away.' And assuming they did, they'd be certain to join us, and fresh arms and ammunition would be needed more urgently than ever.

DURING THE NIGHT and the early morning, Gaspard's men arrived in waves, amidst explosions and gunfire. They brought with them weapons and ammunition they'd managed to salvage. At the same time, new recruits streamed in from all directions, young and old, desperate to escape the Germans, desperate to eradicate France of an occupying force. Amidst the chaos, Hubert turned up and found himself having to organise our growing band, while I armed the recruits and passed them over to Anselm for weapons training. It was as if the sound of the raging battle had lured them in, igniting the fire in their bellies. Before long, I realised our supplies were dwindling. We were almost out of boots and socks, and so I ventured up to the plateau and opened the remaining containers. I took a few of the men with me, and we quickly grabbed our supplies and returned to camp. The men were happy to receive the luxuries of good footwear and fresh socks, but all too soon, I was swamped with fresh recruits and out of supplies once more.

'Don't fret, Gertie,' Den said. 'The drop's on for tomorrow. One hundred and fifty aircraft dropping fifteen containers each.' He grinned.

'Can't come soon enough.' We were relying on a daylight parachutage for the first time. That would be more than two thousand containers with fresh supplies. It was an exciting prospect.

A day later, Gaspard arrived with the last of his men, waltzing into our camp with a smug and authoritative look etched upon his tanned face. 'Madame Andrée, I see you have been helping my men. We will not trouble you for long. I plan to camp out up on the plateau above here. The hills make a good sanctuary.'

'Gaspard, I'm glad to see you're alive. Your men fought well, but perhaps now you might consider splitting into smaller groups.'

He stared at me for what seemed like ages, his brown eyes hard, and then they softened as his face creased into a smile. 'The winds are changing, Madame, and so we will talk.' He sat down in the clearing at the edge of our camp, where a small fire burned, hot water boiling for coffee. 'My men fought well. We have lost about one hundred or so, but the Germans have lost far more.' He looked down at his muddy boots, a pensive look on his face.

I could see how it wounded him to have lost good men. 'Gaspard, your men are safe here, and you can re-group. Join us. Together we will achieve far more.'

Chapter 31
REPRISALS

The sunrise was a beaut, and I gazed in awe at the first glimpse of light as it flooded the land around us during the drive back to camp. The moody sky was awash with colour with a rich palette of pink, purple, and red. 'Red sky at night, shepherd's delight. Red sky in the morning, shepherd's warning,' I muttered. The driver, Jean, one of Gaspard's men, braked softly, his eyes fixed on the farm up ahead on the left, where thick, black smoke drifted from a barn. I flicked a gaze at him, a middle-aged man of maybe thirty-five, a perplexed look etched on his sun-bronzed face.

He squeezed the brake, and the car slowed to a halt. We clambered out, and I peered all around, pushed my sunglasses up onto my head, my hand poised on my revolver. There was no one about, no vehicles, but the flash of a blue sweater on the ground caught my eye. Cautiously, I picked my way through the yard, stepping around discarded pieces of furniture, broken china, and other ephemera, the buzzing of flies growing louder. Their tiny black bodies frantic, swarming over the blue sweater on the body of a little boy, the wind tugging at his brown, curly hair. A little girl lay curled at his side. A single bullet hole through their foreheads, the wound clean, scarlet. Nearby lay the bodies of a man and a woman, both dead. 'Do you know them?'

'Oui. Reprisals. They are happening more and more,' Jean spat in a gruff voice as he traipsed back to the car.

I shook my head. 'Bastards!' A little further along, we passed through a village, eerily silent. The Germans had been busy there too. The bodies of seven men swung to and fro from trees, and a little further along, the still form of a woman tied to a post, her pregnant belly slit open, her baby in a pool of blood, dead at her feet. I had to look twice before looking away, raising a hand to my mouth as my gut lurched violently. How could anyone do that to a woman? Jesus Christ! 'We should untie her, at least,' I said.

'Non. The Germans insist their victims remain there for a length of time. We cannot help her now. Why make things worse?' He swiped beads of sweat from his brow with his hand. The air was heavy, humid, fetid.

He was right. It would make it worse for the locals. The Germans were waging a separate war against the French, making the innocent pay for every German killed or for every attack the Resistance made. Did they have no humanity? How could they do that to innocent children? Rage pounded my ears, raced in my heart, and I clenched my jaw as I wrestled the images from my mind. 'They'll get what's coming to them.' The words slipped out; an affirmation tainted with bile. All I knew at that moment was that I hated the Nazis and the only good one, was a dead one.

THE AFTERNOON SUN WAS HOT, the air humid. The shade of the trees in our camp brought a mild respite, but my back itched as beads of sweat trickled down the bumps of my spine, my hair damp, clinging to my neck. I took a mouthful of water as I heard a rumble which growled into a black Citroen, pulling up in a cloud of dust. Instinct drew my eye to my Sten gun, which lay on the ground by my feet, but the rush of maquisards to greet the driver helped me relax.

Henri Tardivat sprung from the car, a wide grin upon his suntanned face, and my heart leapt. He was a wonderful man, so likeable and easy-going. Still unmarried, so a good catch for someone. I smiled to myself and was reminded of my Henri, the smile fading on my lips as the lump swelled in my throat. I swallowed.

'Bonjour, Tardi. Great to see you.' We embraced like two old friends. 'Come on. I'll get you some coffee before we start.'

'Is Gaspard still here?'

'Yes. His men have been trickling in for a couple of days now. Most of them have made it. Reckons he lost around one hundred and fifty.'

'I hear the Germans lost many more.'

'Well, with his men here, that means we now have around seven thousand maquisards.' What a number! 'Look, Tardi, we need to get it through that thick head of his that he can't keep all his men together. He's had a lucky escape this time, and that's only down to the terrain – it's tough out here even for the Germans, but that doesn't mean he'll get away next time.'

'I know. We will tell him, but we need to be clever about it.'

Clever indeed. Well, I could do clever. I could do cunning. I could do just about anything, and I would if it meant accomplishing this mission and finding my way back home. So, I drew myself up to my full five feet, five inches, took a deep breath, and assumed my warrior face as I turned and led the way to where Gaspard was camped out with his men. There were things to address, now that I had him here. After Tardi had finished greeting his comrades, and everyone had food and drink, I stood up. 'There are certain things we need to sort out before we go any further. As you know, London is prepared to meet all costs, for weapons, ammunition, food, and clothing, but you have to agree to follow orders otherwise there will only be chaos, and it jeopardises the other groups.' I glanced around at the men, their dark, hard eyes upon me, sizing me up. 'So, no more stealing from your fellow Frenchmen. It doesn't help our cause; it turns them against you. We want them on our side.'

'My men take from collaborators,' Gaspard said. 'They are not out patriots.'

'True, but even so, if we can avoid it, then we must. Take all you want from the Germans. We want them to see that we mean business. We must be organised, disciplined, pull together like an army. Trained, equipped, looking the part. Secondly, each group must have planned escape routes from now on. They make the difference between being able to withdraw and re-group elsewhere or being picked off one by one by the German's machine guns.'

Tardi nodded, Gaspard drew heavily on his cigarette, his eyes narrow as he stared at me, and I was convinced he was going to protest, create another uproar, but he remained tight-lipped. Perhaps the surprise attack and the loss of his men was still too raw. The Allied landings had been rough with many lives lost, but now the soldiers had a foothold and were fighting their way through France, inch by inch, and it was down to us to distract the Germans, cut off their supplies, and eradicate as many of them as possible. It was time, finally, to make a stand.

LONDON ANSWERED us once again as thirty Liberators flew overhead at half-past-eleven that night. Four hundred and fifty containers peppered the sapphire sky. After checking supplies, we took what we needed for the following day and stored the remaining containers in our hiding place. It was almost five o'clock when we reached camp. Coffee was ready and waiting, along with bacon and bread. A feast! We were all so tired, and there was still so much to do. The men unloaded the trucks and opened the containers one by one. Then, we began the arduous task of dismantling the Sten guns, de-greasing and re-assembling each one. I sipped my coffee beneath the pine trees as dawn's first light spread out overhead, a crimson and pink wash, and the trees swished and swayed in the breeze. My eyes lowered, and a shadow fell across me.

'Gertie, have a refill.' Den passed me a mug of coffee. 'Looks like you need it.'

'Thanks.'

He lifted the gun from my lap and finished the job, and I didn't say a word. My arm felt like lead as I held the cup to my lips. I sat back against a tree trunk, my eyelids lowered, and I didn't fight it. I breathed, the men's voices a low hubbub, the crackling fire close by, the first chorus of birdsong among the trees, Henri, a smile curving his mouth just for me. Mon amour.

Chapter 32
BATTLE

The days were relentless. We were dealing with the drops, visiting the various Maquis groups in the Auvergne region, assessing their needs, equipping the men. Sleep had become a luxury to be snatched wherever you were, whenever you could. The situation with the Germans and their attack on Gaspard still troubled me, and while the men considered they'd been victorious, I wondered how long before the enemy attacked again.

'The drop's on for tonight.' Den's sing-song voice. He poured some coffee.

I sighed; my body felt like lead, my head fuzzy. 'I'm knackered, Den.'

He smiled and kissed the top of my head as he sailed past. 'You have to be there. They're dropping a tonne of French francs.'

'Any signs of Jerry?'

'Spotted the other side of Chaudes-Aigues.'

Well, they had unfinished business, and that proved they weren't leaving any time soon. Gaspard's men had swelled their ranks enormously, and now, the seven thousand-strong groups of Resistance fighters were split into smaller, more manageable groups, each with their own leaders. As I'd told them, it made sense, and they would not be so vulnerable. They were spread out on the plateau above Chaudes-

Aigues, within sight of the single road that snaked through the valley and the hills. Men took it in turns on guard duty, patrolling the road, armed with Sten guns, and grenades.

That evening I took ten men, and we drove up to the plateau. Just after midnight, our parachutage arrived courtesy of an armada of fifty Liberator Bombers from the west. When I opened the container filled with money, Den piped up, 'Let me see.' His face was a picture. Tight rolls of French francs crammed inside the canister. 'Ooh, so that's fifteen million big ones. If only...'

'You and me both, mate,' I said. It was late by the time we got back, and I was too exhausted for the bath I'd promised myself. After a nightcap of brandy, I settled for a strip wash, discarded my dirty clothes, and slipped on my pink Parisian silk negligee, feeling more my old self even if it was for a mere few hours. It was four o'clock in the morning as I bedded down with my blanket and satin cushion beneath the pines, the breeze light, a faint rustle from the trees.

AN EXPLOSION in the distance dragged me from slumber with a start, just as dawn was breaking. The rat-a-tat-tat of machine-gun fire echoed through the forest chased by another explosion. I rubbed the sleep from my eyes, jumped up and pulled on socks, slacks, and a shirt, slipped my feet into boots, forgetting all about the negligee which I hastily tucked into my trousers. Those sleeping woke, jumped up from where they'd slumped, grabbed their weapons, ammunition, and gathered together.

I slipped my pistol into my holster, reached for my Sten and gathered up all the cash. We drove to the plateau, collecting Fournier from his house on the way. Two of our scouts said SS troops had almost encircled us. They had mobile guns, tanks, mortars, the Luftwaffe, and thousands of troops, according to one of the men. We headed to nearby Freydefont, to meet with Gaspard and Hubert. 'My men will fight to the death,' Gaspard said.

'They bloody won't,' I said, glaring at him. 'Den get a message to

London and cancel today's drop. Don't stop transmitting until you get a response.'

'Okay, Gertie.'

'And Den,' I leaned in close to whisper, 'Tell them what's happened and that we hope to escape tonight. Tell them to order Gaspard to leave, or the fool's going to get every one of those men killed.'

'Right, leave it to me.' Den raced back to the car to retrieve his wireless set and found a spot to begin transmitting. Machine-gun fire echoed all around, interrupted by intermittent explosions. The Germans were closing in, making their way towards the plateau. We all agreed that we'd escape that night when darkness fell, all of us, except Gaspard. He was adamant that he and his men would stay and fight.

After an hour or so, I checked in with Den, but he'd had no joy. 'London refuses to listen, Gertie. It's an unscheduled transmission.' He shrugged and carried on while mortar shells rained down, some falling onto a building nearby. There was an ear-deafening crash and debris flew through the air.

'Jesus, that was close.' Den froze. 'Keep going!' I yelled. 'I'm going for more supplies.' I left him to it and drove off alone to the field higher up, the site of our last parachutage. Supplies would be needed. I worked quickly, unpacked containers and loaded guns, ammunition, and mortars into the truck. Once I'd finished, I drove off towards the various fortified points of the Maquis, distributing weapons and ammunition where it was needed. All along the main road that led up to the plateau, shells rained down, heavier than before, and the low growl of an aircraft filtered in overhead. Squinting into the sun, I glimpsed sunlight glinting on metal as it circled above. The open road stretched before me, no woods for cover, so I continued driving, down the winding route to Freydefont. Den looked up when he saw me, his face scarlet, hair drenched in sweat.

'I've made contact with London. The drop's cancelled, but I'm still waiting on the message about Gaspard.'

'Bloody fool's digging in up there.' Why was he so stubborn? I thought he'd finally seen sense, but it seemed I was wrong.

ONE OF OUR lookouts told us that the entire area was swarming with Germans. London had to come through with that message. We had to be ready to withdraw by nightfall, and that included Gaspard. My body ached, muscles strained and trembled from lugging those containers around, and I longed to sleep. 'Den. I'll be at the farmhouse down the lane if you need me.' Fournier had commandeered it for our use. Den nodded and turned back to his radio. I'd no sooner shut my eyes when someone shook me by the shoulders. Fournier.

'Madame Andrée, you must not sleep here. It is too dangerous. Can you not hear the bombs?'

Bombs? I'd heard the odd explosion. I paused and listened. Gunfire rattled into the silence, the drone of aircraft overhead, followed by an ear-splitting crash, and tremors beneath me.

He pointed upward. 'The Luftwaffe. They might hit this house.'

I slumped back down on the bed. 'I'm so tired.' I didn't care anymore. I was knackered. For once I really couldn't go on any longer.

'Up you get.' He grabbed my arms, pulled me up to my feet and led me outside. The sun glared, I squinted, half-staggered over the road to where some old trees stood tall and proud. I sank down beneath them, in the shade. 'I'll be here if anyone needs me.' Fournier shook his head and went away muttering, and I closed my eyes, surrendering to myself.

'GERTIE, I'VE GOT IT,' Den's voice, thin, breathy, his cheeks scarlet from the run. 'The message. London has ordered Gaspard to withdraw.' He waved a slip of paper in front of my face while I struggled to focus. I rubbed my eyes and stood up, my legs shaky, nausea swirling in my gut. I swallowed. 'Good. Sign it, Den. From General Koenig.' Den looked at me, his eyes widening. 'Go on.' He pulled a pen from his shirt pocket and scrawled a signature on the slip. Koenig was de Gaulle's main man, commander of the FFI, so if Gaspard was ever going to listen to anyone, it would be him. 'Right then. Let's take it to him.' Den followed as we went to find a car and set off to give Gaspard the good news.

The road out of Freydefont was clear, but the crump of mortar shells grew louder. The Germans were closing in. As we neared Gaspard's position, four German Henschel's zipped overhead, spitting tracer fire over the Maquis. One of the aircraft broke away and headed straight for us. I ducked at the wheel. 'Get down!' I swerved, a clatter of bullets peppering the Citroen. 'Jesus Christ!' I carried on, my foot to the floor. The Henschel made a sharp turn and came back for a second pass lower than before. The pilot fired, and I speeded up and then slammed the brakes on, doing my best to avoid his aim. As he came around again, I stamped on the brake, we screeched to a halt and flung ourselves from the car, landing in a ditch by the side of the road. As soon as he roared overhead, we dashed back to the car. The bugger wasn't going to give up, though, and he banked steeply, heading back towards us. I rummaged in the back of the car and grabbed my face cream, a packet of tea and my scarlet silk cushion before running for the cover of the trees, a trail of bullets at our heels, peppering the ground, red dust billowing up all around. The roar of an explosion behind us. A brief glance back confirmed the car had exploded, flames leaping all around it, smoke billowing. The woods gave us cover, but still, the Luftwaffe pilot circled above, strafing our position, bullets ricocheting off rocks and tree trunks. Poor Den was worn ragged. We both were.

Puffing and panting, he did his best to keep up but lagged behind. We scaled a hill to reach the plateau above. 'Den. There he is. Waft that slip of paper under his nose.' Gaspard, tall, defiant, talking to one of his lieutenants as the men all around ducked and crouched while firing at the enemy, a hail of return bullets zipping through the trees. I took cover behind a large boulder, still clutching my things to my chest. Well, there was no way I was losing everything. The sun was low, washing the sky scarlet as she slipped away. As I looked around, I noted several bodies lying motionless on the ground. I glanced at Gaspard as he read the note, surprise flitting across his face, an exchange of words and then Den ran back to me. 'He's given the order to withdraw.'

I blew out a breath. 'Thank Christ.' The maquisards gathered whatever weapons they could carry and withdrew. Nightfall would grant us some time, the cover of darkness our camouflage. There was no choice but to leave the dead where they had fallen. Anselm appeared from within a group of men. I stood up, caught his eye. 'Boy, am I glad to see you.'

Anselm grinned, his eyes crinkled at the corners. 'Ah, we meet again, Chérie. I see you persuaded Gaspard to leave.'

'Well, in a way.' My eyes hovered over the khaki rucksack slung over his shoulder. 'Don't suppose I could put my stuff in your bag?'

He looked at my things, raised an eyebrow. 'By all means.'

The wounded were helped along as we made our escape via dirt tracks, scrambling down hillsides, clambering over rocks and streams. Fournier's men were just ahead of us, by the river – our escape route. The River Truyère was high, the water fast flowing. There was no bridge, but Fournier had devised a plan a few weeks back. His men had created a footpath from logs that lay just beneath the surface of the water, having driven them into the riverbed, one by one. The first man across knew his way. The next also knew the crossing and acted as a guide for the rest of us and one by one, we were led across the stretch of wooden stepping stones to safety. Anselm went ahead of me.

'Stay with me,' he said.

'Okay. If I fall in, you can fish me out.' I took my time, ice-cold water seeping into my boots as I picked my way across. By mid-way point, my feet were almost numb, and as I stepped onto the next log, I slipped and would have fallen in headfirst if not for Anselm's quick reactions as he reached out and grabbed me. I held onto him, following in his steps. When he reached the bank, he hauled me up alongside.

'Thanks. Just as well you like to fish.' I sat down on the bank; my heart still drumming. Anselm laughed.

'Come on. We have a way to go yet.'

Saint Santin was about one hundred kilometres away. My heart sank. We kept to the minor routes which kept us out of the German's way but made the journey longer. We ventured along rough tracks, climbed hills and hiked across the valley throughout the night and the next morning. Around mid-afternoon, we crossed paths with Gaspard and some of his men who had taken an alternative route.

'Ah, Madame Andrée. We meet again.' He smiled, took my arm in his. Anselm took my other arm, and the three of us strolled along with hundreds of maquisards, marching behind.

I turned to Gaspard. 'How many dead?'

'Less than one hundred, but the Germans lost more.' He wore a smug look, and I smiled to myself. If only he knew what we'd done. We'd saved his bacon, not that he'd have seen it that way. Still, all's fair in love and war.

Chapter 33

AN EPIC JOURNEY

After three days, we reached the outskirts of Saint Santin, a filthy, exhausted, rabble that we were. My feet ached and throbbed, my heels rubbed raw from the many kilometres we'd trekked. The small villages we'd passed along the way had welcomed us, with locals offering us shelter and food. The people were overjoyed, filled with hope, talking excitedly of the Allied landings, asking us about our battle with the Germans. They were desperate, impatience burning in their eyes, especially now they could taste victory.

Den was quiet, trudging along way behind. He seemed troubled, and just as we walked into the town, he sidled up to me.

'Nancy, there's something I need to tell you.'

'What?'

'I'm sorry, Ducks, but when we were fleeing, and the Germans were a bit too close for comfort, I destroyed the radio and burned my codebook. We can replace the set, but my codes, they've gone. I can't transmit.' His face crumpled into a frown.

No codes meant no supplies. Shit. 'Don't worry, Den. I'll think of something.' We needed to contact an operator from another group. Perhaps Tardi or Fournier would know of someone.

We set up camp at a farm a short distance from the village centre.

We were all bone-weary, and I sank heavily into an old brown leather armchair in the kitchen, my body burning, drenched in sweat, my mouth drier than any desert. Fournier, Tardi, Anselm, and Gaspard sat around the pine table. After a short rest, and refreshments, my mind was straight back to that radio. 'Den, can't you think of anyone? You've been here a while. There has to be someone.' We were back to where we'd started. No radio, no contact. Useless.

He shook his head. 'I can't think, Ducks, I can't. There are people, but I have no idea where the hell they are, especially right now.' He took out a cigarette, lit up, and took a drag while he paced the floor. After a few minutes, he screeched, and my heart flipped in my chest. 'I remember now. There is a chap, at Chateauroux. Why I didn't think of him before I don't know, probably too damn tired.'

'Chateauroux? Jesus, Den, that's bloody miles away!' How the hell do we get there? It was roughly a four-hundred-kilometre round trip, and the area was crawling with Germans. The checkpoints would have to be dealt with, although it might be possible to miss some of them out by sticking to minor routes. One of us had to do something. A car was out of the question. 'I'll need a bicycle.'

'Sorry, love, what?' Den looked confused.

'Keep up. A cycle – where can I get one?'

'Bloody hell, Nancy. You can't cycle to Chateauroux. It's too dangerous. You'll never make it.' His eyes were wide, his mouth open.

Fournier raised his head. 'What's this?'

'Madame here thinks she can cycle to Chateauroux to reach a radio op I know.'

'Impossible, you will never make it.' Fournier glanced at Gaspard who sat in silence, puffing a cigarette.

'Well, what do you suggest? I can't travel by car. The Germans have tightened up security at checkpoints and set up dozens of roadblocks on the main roads.' They were also going to be bloody furious at failing to exterminate us all on the plateau.

'It will take you days to get there and back,' Fournier snapped.

'I can do it.' They all looked at me as if I had two heads! 'For Christ's sake, one of us has to do something. There's no other option;

besides, a woman is less conspicuous than a man.' We were back at the beginning. No radio, no codes. At least we had the operator, but we'd lost London, our lifeline. 'I didn't sign up to fail, and I'm not going down without a fight.' Den and Fournier exchanged transient looks, a mix of worry and doubt. I could do this, and I knew I must. Memories of past 'trips' resurfaced, delivering messages, parcels, people. I gritted my teeth. Failure was not an option. 'Fournier, please find me a decent bicycle, and I'll do the rest. I'll go to Aurillac tomorrow morning and see if I can find something decent to wear.' I had to blend in with the locals, and I was less likely to be stopped and searched if I was a clean, well-dressed French woman.

Fournier shook his head, glancing nervously at Den. 'I do not like it, but you are probably right, so I will find you a bicycle.'

'And the tailors? Are they onside?'

'No need to worry about Monsieur Dupont. We can trust him.' Fournier nodded, fixing me with a troubled stare.

I sighed, shrugging off their tedious dubiousness. Henri never doubted me, although he'd always worried. An unsettled feeling struck swift as a sword. Had Henri believed in me? I'd always thought so, but now, with the passage of time and separation, I wondered. All those times the Allies used our flat for meetings and plotting escapes. His face flashed in my mind, and I remembered his furtive glances, the concern in his eyes, the odd time he expressed it in words. But I'd always insisted, headstrong as usual. I exhaled. Henri was always reliable, strong, and I believed in him. He ought to have made it to London. I stared out of the window at the blue wash of sky, watching swifts soar and dive, wild thoughts scrambling in my mind as I searched for an answer. My escape had been treacherous. Perhaps Henri was hiding somewhere. Perhaps he was at our chalet in Nevache. Of course. He would have gone away somewhere quiet. Friends would have helped him. But I knew better than to brood. I had a journey to plan, and that had to be my focus, and as hard as it was, I had to push thoughts of Henri away for now.

～

THE NEXT MORNING, I found a sturdy, decent looking bicycle leaning up against the stone wall of the house. 'My carriage awaits,' I mused, running my hand over the black seat.

Later that afternoon, I cycled into the town of Aurillac, taking a minor route to avoid any German patrols. I found the tailors easily, and as I stepped through the door, a man in his fifties looked up from behind the counter, a tape measure draped around his neck.

'Bonjour, Madame. Can I help you?' He pushed his black-rimmed spectacles up off his nose.

'Oui, Monsieur. I wish to buy something new, perhaps a navy skirt, a blouse, and a jacket? Oh, and I need it urgently, Monsieur. Tomorrow.'

A look of surprise flitted across his face like a shadow. 'Oh, Madame, that is impossible. It will take time to …'

'Please, it's most urgent and,' I leaned in towards him, 'you would be doing France a great service.' I stared into his eyes, noting the realisation that settled within.

'Oui, Madame. I will see to it. I need to take some measurements first, if I may please.'

'Of course.' The tailor worked quietly, catching my eye several times for a fleeting moment, muttering measurements beneath his breath, scribbling down numbers in pencil on a small note pad afterwards.

'Your outfit will be ready tomorrow, Madame, and I will have it brought out to you,' he said hurriedly, his voice low, strained. He rested his hand on my arm. 'Do not return. The Milice are next door.' He cast me a concerned look, his brow furrowed, his brown eyes wide.

'Merci, Monsieur.' I was almost out the door before I realised I hadn't given him my address. 'Monsieur, you don't know where to find me.'

'I think I do, Madame. Saint Santin.' He nodded.

I sensed he was genuine, although doubts always niggled at the back of your mind. When I returned to the farm, the leaders were waiting, along with Hubert. 'It's done. The tailor said he'd deliver my clothes, so I'm all set.'

'I will send word ahead. There will be places you can stop along the way for rest and food. And I will have lookouts, so you do not run into trouble,' Fournier said.

Everyone looked so worried, except Gaspard. I wasn't exactly sure what he thought, although he didn't seem doubtful, so I took that as a good sign. I intended to make the best of my last night, to eat as much as I liked, and have a bloody good drink.

~

THE FOLLOWING DAY, I woke to birdsong, in a comfy bed with real sheets and blankets. Luxury. I rolled over, hugging the pillow, thoughts drifting like smoke. Hens clucked around outside. This was someone's home, a family home, and I longed to be in my home with Henri. It was impossible to put into words how much I missed him. Can you imagine what it's like to have no communication at all? No letters, no telephone calls, or telegrams. Only distance, time, memories, and wishes. But the Allies were making headway, and we would play our part, keep the Germans occupied here to give the Allies a chance. It wouldn't be long now; I could feel it.

'Gertie!'

Den's voice. I dragged a brush through my hair, then slipped downstairs. He was waiting in the hall with a large, brown paper package in his arms.

'Parcel from the tailors.'

I took it from him, carefully removed the brown wrapping and lifted out the jacket first. 'Very elegant.' The thin ivory blouse with matching blue skirt was perfect. It was such a blessing to have new clothes, and I smiled.

'Lovely, Ducks,' Den said. 'A rather handsome young man delivered those. He was quite chatty.'

'Oh, I bet he was Den.'

'Well, you know me, Ducks. Sink or swim, my love, sink or swim.' Den chuckled as he walked away, leaving me alone in the hall, wrapped in happiness with my new outfit. I slipped into the kitchen and grabbed a hunk of bread and spread on a thin layer of strawberry jam before dashing upstairs to finish my hair. I slipped on my new outfit, checked my appearance in the mirror on the dressing table. They fit well, I mused – one last finishing touch as I dabbed on a little ruby lipstick.

Outside the sun hung in a flawless milky-blue sky. It was almost time to leave, and just for a moment, an uneasiness surfaced in the pit of my stomach. I wasn't frightened, I told myself, but even so, it refused to slip away. Turning to the chest of drawers in my room, I glanced at the bottle of brandy. One drink for Dutch courage. Returning to the window, glass in hand, I spotted Den checking my bicycle over, a warm glow spread in my chest. I downed the brandy, savouring the fiery heat in my mouth that radiated down into my stomach, snuffing out the unease.

I stuffed two carrots, a leek, and a handful of green beans into a string bag and dropped this into the basket on the front of the bicycle. The aim was to appear as a French woman out shopping, nothing more. The less conspicuous, the better. I'd decided against carrying a weapon. It was far safer to blag my way past any Germans, using my feminine charms as necessary.

'Be careful, Ducks.' Den smiled, but fear clouded his eyes. He kissed me on each cheek and handed me a bottle of water for the journey.

'It'll be fine, Denden. Don't worry.' I could tell he still felt bad by what had happened, but it was what it was, and I resigned myself to the journey ahead, a mix of emotions stirring inside. Was I afraid? My tummy murmured so, but a hurricane raged through my mind while a fire burned in my heart. People often said fear was a natural reaction, but I doubted that I'd ever been afraid. I'd worried about things or people. Of course, I had, but one had to get on with life. Besides, the stakes were too high to succumb to doubts or fear.

Pierre, a young maquisard, sat astride his bicycle, smoking. He wished to visit his heavily pregnant wife in Montluçon, so for the first part of my journey, I had an escort. I climbed on my bicycle, the thinly padded seat hard beneath me. Thank goodness I was fairly fit. For a fleeting moment, I thought of my mother, her bible in her hand. What would she think of me now? A different time, a different world, all so far away. I heaved out a breath.

'This is for you, Henri,' I muttered, 'and for France.'

Fournier waved us off. 'Merde,' he said, concern blazing in his eyes.

As we set off, Den's final goodbyes faded into the breeze, and I waved without turning around, my focus now solely on the journey ahead.

'We will use the minor roads,' Pierre said. 'That way we will avoid the Germans.'

The Germans rarely ventured off the main routes for fear of an ambush, as had happened before many times. I raised my chin, felt the sun's glow on my face. Sometimes, on such a beautiful day, it was almost inconceivable to think we were in the midst of a bloody war, but it was delicious to imagine, even if for just a few seconds.

A little later, when we came to the crossroads, Pierre said, 'We walk from here. This is one of the main roads to Montluçon. If we are on foot, we have a better chance of seeing German patrols headed our way. We can take cover in the ditch by the roadside.'

'Great.' I glanced across at the ditch as I dismounted and began to push my bicycle alongside Pierre. We hadn't spoken much before, but he talked as we strolled along. The Germans were ruthless, he said. Reprisals were on the rise. His own brother had been arrested and shot. It seemed everyone in France had lost someone or suffered in some way.

All too soon, my feet began to ache. The new shoes looked the part but now began to pinch and rub. No matter what it took, I had to do this, reach the destination and get that damn message sent. Were London and Buckmaster even concerned about our recent silence? No contact and after all that fighting. They might well have feared the worst.

The mid-afternoon sun beat down, and sweat trickled down my neck, sliding down my back, but then a fresh mountain breeze drenched us; invigorating. My stomach grumbled. It had been hours since I last ate.

Fortunately, there were no German patrols, and as we reached another crossroads, Pierre bid me farewell. We mounted our bicycles and headed off in different directions, Pierre to Montluçon, while I took the road to Saint-Amand. Fournier had given me information on several checkpoints which was useful. My thighs chaffed and ached while my backside throbbed from the saddle and I longed to stop. The sun hung low, the sky flooded with hues of pink and amber. I told myself that once I reached the small town, I could eat. My stomach grumbled once more at the thought of food. I was out of water. The long, snake of a road gradually unfurled before me, revealing lights in the distance. Lights blinked as I passed through a small village with welcoming scents of basil and garlic mingling in the air. Following my nose, I cycled to a small bistro and stopped for food. I ate a simple meal, washed down with a glass of red wine. A few people were dining, speaking in low tones, but I overheard there was little German activity, and all was quiet on the Western Front. Refreshed, I set off again, glimpsing the faint silhouette of the moon to the east.

It wasn't long before my legs began to ache and chafe. The trees cackled as I passed beneath, shaking their leaves, showering me with a cool breeze snatched from the nearby river, Le Cher. The terrain was hilly, unforgiving, and I was flagging, sore, and desperate for rest. As I approached an old stone barn, I hesitated. It looked empty, no one was around, and night was closing in. It was as good a place as any for a brief rest. Inside a generous scattering of straw lay across the floor. I undressed. My clothes had to be crease-free and clean. One thing I mustn't appear to be was someone taking a long journey. That was too suspicious. I lay down on the straw and covered myself with my jacket, Goosebumps prickling the flesh of my arms. Outside, an owl hooted a haunting cry that echoed all around.

There wasn't time to sleep, not really, but my entire body ached for slumber. And it was so peaceful, so inviting, and my eyes hovered and flickered as if weighed down by lead. Exhaustion seeped into every limb, every muscle, ligament and sinew and in no time at all, I slipped willingly into darkness. Next thing I knew, the wail of an air raid siren filtered into my sub-conscious, waking me with a start. In the distance came the rumble of aircraft and then the crump of an explosion. I jumped up, dusted myself down and quickly pulled on my clothes before grabbing my cycle and dragging it outside – another crump. I glanced at my watch. Four o'clock in the morning. Twilight. I drank in the early morning wash of cool air as I pushed off and headed towards Saint-Amand.

I had memorised the route Fournier had advised me to take, and I also had a list of safe houses that were scattered along the way. For some annoying reason, the distance flitted through my mind like a red flag, as if to taunt me into defeat. There were many more miles to cover. It was one thing to reach Chateauroux and quite another to make the return trip with minimal stops. I had to focus on the outward-bound journey. Little steps, I told myself. Henri's words whispered in my ear. 'I have never known a woman like you, Nannie. You are incredible, mon amour.' My chest pinched, and I sucked in a deep breath. How many times had I carried out journeys through France, slipping past Germans, on trains and roads? Too many to recall. This was just another trip. The memory of the bounty on my head resurfaced. The Germans had their ways of finding out about people. My feet pushed down on the pedals and I gritted my teeth.

At a small village on the way to Bourges, I was fortunate to find sanctuary at the home of one of my contacts, a young Frenchman who gave me food and coffee. It was a relief to be able to wash and brush my hair.

'Be careful when you reach Bourges,' he said. 'The Germans raided the town yesterday and took many hostages. They shot them this morning.'

'Christ.' I shuddered at the news.

'There is a German checkpoint on the road into the town. I will show you a safer way, Madame Andrée.'

I didn't stay long, just long enough to finish my meal of bread, ham, and cheese. As I bid him farewell, he gave me a fresh bottle of water.

Bourges. I slowed as I passed on through. The streets were desolate, stores closed. The air eerie, oppressive, sad, mourning with the rest of the town for all those lost. It was like a disease that clung to me as I passed through. A column of German soldiers appeared up ahead, marching towards me, the stomping of jackboots growing like a crescendo as they marched by without even a glance. I blew out a breath.

My feet pinched and throbbed as I pedalled, the skin rubbed raw on my toes and heels. Every muscle ached, and my thighs harboured a persistent inner soreness. I was now in the Puy-de-Dome, cycling uphill through the mountainous region. My chest pounded as I sucked in humid air, my legs juddering as I turned the pedals slower and slower until finally, I came to a halt. Well, nothing for it but to walk, so I staggered along on jelly-like pins, pushing my bicycle uphill, taking frequent stops to rest for a minute at a time.

Issoudun lay half-a-mile away. The road in was a moderate incline, and my legs ached as if they were going to slip into a cramp. I stood for a moment, took some deep breaths and steadied myself. 'One foot in front of the other. One more step,' I muttered. Once I reached the village, I found a small bistro and ventured inside. Several couples were dining at small tables, chatting, words cut short as they watched me head over to the counter. I put a hand to my hair, smoothing it down, felt the coating of gritty dust on my palm, aware of my blouse clinging to my back like a wet cloth. The patron nodded in acknowledgement and picked up a pen and paper.

'Bonjour, Madame. What can I get for you?'

I looked at the special's board on the wall behind him. Menus were so limited these days. 'Bonjour. I'll have whatever's going.' I noted his curious glance. 'And throw in a bottle of brandy.' I stepped into the ladies and looked at myself in the small mirror that hung on the cream painted wall. My hair was more than a little windswept, my face scarlet and shimmering with perspiration. I removed my jacket and took out the small face cloth from my inside pocket. I washed first and then brushed my hair, pinning it neatly back into place. Next, I applied a little ruby lipstick and sprayed myself with perfume. I found a table by the window and sat down, my stomach grumbling, nausea swirling, legs shaking.

As I waited, I watched the people in the bistro and kept an eye on the street outside, although I doubted the Germans would come by, given the remote location. Best to be on your guard. I listened to the various conversations which were mainly about mundane things, and as frustrating as it was, not one person spoke of the war. I needed to keep abreast of the news, especially local news. More importantly, I needed to know the Germans movements to avoid them. A young waitress headed across to my table with a plate of steaming food and a carafe of water.

'Merci,' I said, and the girl smiled and walked away. I poked at the food with my fork – rabbit stew. After an hour had passed, and most of the other customers had left, the patron strode over.

'Your brandy, Madame.'

'Ah, merci, Monsieur. Why don't you join me?'

His eyes lit up, and his craggy face broke into a wide grin. 'Why not? Merci, Madame, you are most generous.'

I poured and watched as he drained his glass in one mouthful, so I poured him another as I talked, passing the time as people do.

'The Germans are scum.' He scowled, a bitter look in his eyes. 'They come and expect to have the best food and the best drink for little money. Some don't pay at all. What can I do?' He held up his hands.

'It's the same all over,' I said. 'They demand free food from local farms, leaving families to go hungry.' Within half an hour, we were laughing and joking, and I had discovered the local news, the quickest way to the local markets, and the location of all checkpoints. As I left, I longed to find somewhere to rest, but there wasn't time. I had to reach Chateauroux before curfew. The final leg lay about one and a half hours away. A raw, soreness radiated from my backside, and my weak thighs juddered as I cycled, wincing with every turn of the pedals.

As I neared Chateauroux, the roads became busier, with truck after truck hurtling past, crammed with German soldiers, some of whom waved and called out to me. Thank God they didn't stop. Looking ahead, my heart sank – a dratted checkpoint to clear. I took a deep breath, opened another button on my blouse, hitched my skirt up and carried on pedalling, gritting my teeth against the pain while flashing a smile at the young German soldier. His colleague was busy scrutinising the papers of an old man, and after glancing at me briefly, he waved me through. I could hardly believe my luck.

The town was surprisingly peaceful, and I spotted small groups of German soldiers seated in cafes, laughing, drinking, and I wondered how many French people they'd harmed or killed. After sailing around the town twice, I found the bistro Den had told me about, and I ventured inside and ordered a Pernod. After a short while and a few more drinks, the patron began to talk, and I mustered up the courage to ask if the man with the scar on his left cheek was still around. The patron nodded and told me where I might find him.

As I got up to leave, a familiar face caught my eye. 'Achilles,' I said. We embraced there and then. As it turned out, he was searching for a Free French radio operator as their own had been killed in action.

'I will come with you,' he said.

Armed with the address, we set off, following the directions the patron had given. The address turned out to be an apartment block, and the man's flat was on the first floor. When I knocked, there was no answer, so I tried again and waited. Within a minute I heard the tap of footsteps, and a man opened the door, cautiously, a prominent, long scar on his left cheek, running from the side of his nose towards his ear lobe.

'I am Madame Andrée, with the Maquis of the Auvergne.' The man went to close the door in my face, so I placed my foot in the way and pushed to keep it open. 'Please, Monsieur. It's urgent. We need to send a message to London.'

'What is the password?'

Damn! We didn't have the password. I blew out a breath. 'I don't have it. Please, if you can just …' I said in haste.

'I cannot help. You could be a German spy.' He banged the door shut, and I staggered backwards. 'If I were a spy, I would have arrested you by now.' Strewth it was ridiculous. I heaved out a breath, ran a hand through my hair.

'Come with me,' Achilles said, jogging back downstairs and out into the street. 'My contact is not far from here.'

My entire being ached, but I heaved myself onto my bicycle and tagged along behind him. We went to another bistro where he found his contact, and we learned that the radio operator was hiding in the woods not far from the town, in the department of the Creuse. He too had fled the Germans who were lying in wait at his apartment. 'Just as well you didn't have an address,' I said. The town was thick with the enemy, marching this way and that and the incessant rumble of military trucks, so we rode separately to the woods. We met up at the forest, and before long discovered the Maquis in a small clearing. Achilles spoke for both of us, making his request first. I then asked if the radio operator might send my message to Colonel Buckmaster in London. 'Tell him my group has no radio or codes and need both replacing, urgently.'

'I will ask my radio operator, Madame, and if he agrees to this then the message will be sent,' the maquisard said.

I bid farewell to Achilles and began the journey back. Day turned to night, and a myriad of stars peppered the sky. Exhaustion was an understatement, and I began to doubt I'd ever make it back in one piece. And the Germans could stick their checkpoints as I had greater concerns. I needed to pee, but I didn't dare stop, not for fear of being seen but I was terrified I wouldn't be able to climb back on my cycle and move. The urge became so great as stomach pain gripped me and there was nothing for it but to pee as I rode. I sucked in a breath and exhaled gently as I concentrated on performing such an unnatural act, but, as it transpired, it was simple. The relief was immense, but as warm urine trickled between my thighs, the skin stung and burned, as if rubbed raw. With my bottle of water, I trickled a little over the top of my thighs, the fresh coolness soothing the sting, my cycle wobbling as I continued pedalling.

Before the night was over, I came upon another empty barn, and I stopped to rest. Sitting on straw-filled ground, I took a few sips of water and leaned back against the cold stone wall, keeping my eyes open. I told myself I'd take half an hour's rest; that was all. I had to fight sleep. My eyes were lead-heavy, and I knew I'd fall asleep within seconds, so I slapped my cheeks and sat up. I was too weak to stand, so I clambered onto my knees and dragged myself up. With a heavy heart, I climbed back onto the bicycle and pushed off. Everything ached, burned and trembled as the cycle rolled along the road. My calves were tight and aching, while my bottom was killing me so much I couldn't bear to sit on the seat. I decided to try standing up to cycle, which helped to relieve the pressure, but I didn't have the strength to do this for long. I must have looked a sight too, my cycle wobbling all over the road.

At the first German checkpoint in Issoudun, I took some deep breaths and unbuttoned the top button of my blouse again, having already removed my jacket earlier. I hitched my skirt just a little, to reveal a little more flesh and smiled as I approached. The German was only a little taller than me, his hair white beneath his cap. I looked directly into his light blue eyes. 'Bonjour.'

'Bonjour, Madame.' He paused, his pale lips twitched at the corners and formed a smile as his gaze zipped down my body. 'Papers please.'

A familiar knot in my gut twisted, but not in fear. There was a certain air of adventure about it. But this was no game. I was an agent, and an enemy of Germany and I'd go down fighting if need be, and so I returned the smile and grandly leant forward over my handlebars as I reached into my bag. I passed my papers to the young soldier, my breath paused, but he barely glanced at them, preferring to return his admiring gaze to look me up and down. I played my part as best I could, fluttering my eyelashes, smiling while exchanging pleasantries.

'Have a pleasant day, Madame.' He waved me through.

I mounted my bicycle, momentarily forgetful of how sore my behind was as I sat on the hard seat. Stifling a groan so as not to draw attention to myself, I bit my lip and pedalled away, glancing up for a brief moment to the heavens above. 'Thank you,' I muttered. I had to press on, no matter what, because if I got off my cycle one more time, I doubted I'd ever make it back on. The hours slipped by, the sun burning the top of my head, smothering me in fierce heat, my mouth bone dry. I sipped my water as I rode, and when I needed to pee, although I dreaded the pain, I released it, waiting with gritted teeth for the subsequent sting. Each turn of the pedals chaffed the skin more, and as evening drew closer and the sun dipped down, I drank the last of my water.

After another few hours, my backside felt as though I'd been kicked black and blue, and my inner thighs burned like fire as I pedalled. 'Just keep going, Nance,' I mumbled through gritted teeth. 'For you, Henri.' I pictured his face in my mind, and I pushed on, knowing we'd soon be reunited. As I gazed up ahead, my heart sank at the sight of a figure in the road. Dark clothing. Was he German? As I drew nearer, I realised it was my escort, Pierre. My spirits soared like the swallow's overhead and for the first time in many hours, I smiled.

'C'est un garcon,' he cried out.

'A boy? Oh, congratulations!' I tried to sound pleased, but I was in so much pain I think I failed.

'Madame Andrée, you look rough.'

'Don't I know it.'

'You must rest.'

I shook my head. 'No. If I stop now, I'll never get back on this damn thing. Must. Keep. Going.' I pushed on, wincing. Just one more turn of the pedals, I told myself – just one more turn. A blinding headache was kicking in, and I was glad of the sunset. A little dimmer, a little cooler, and a slight breeze pushed against us as we rode back to Saint Santin.

When at last we returned, friendly faces milled around in the grounds. Pierre sailed on ahead of me while I cycled as slow as a snail up the winding driveway. 'I've only bloody made it,' I whispered. Den was in the front yard, and he glanced up. 'Hey, she's back.'

Fournier and Tardi came outside, eyes wide, huge grins spreading across their bronzed faces. A huge weight lifted, leaving a mix of sadness, joy, and extreme pain to wash over me. Once I reached the lawn, I ceased pedalling, leaving my legs to dangle, my feet skating over grass as the cycle slowed to a halt. I planted my feet on the ground and stood for a few seconds before my legs buckled, and I toppled sideways onto the grass, crying out. I rolled onto my back and lay staring up at the twilight sky. The moon was waxing, almost full, yellow and hundreds of stars blinked back at me, and I wondered if Henri was looking up at the night sky right now. Was he thinking of me? I let out a huge sob, a gut-wrenching heart-breaking cry and the floodgates finally crumbled as I broke into tears and men rushed to my side.

'Gently,' Den said to Fournier as they each took an arm and hoisted me back to my feet.

'I can't stand,' I said, over and over, between crying out in pain and shedding tears.

Gently, firmly, they held me up between them and half-carried me into the house and set me down on the sofa.

'Bring water to drink,' Fournier yelled at a young, bewildered Frenchman. 'And brandy, fetch the brandy.'

Den held my hand, while Fournier stared at me, shaking his head, his large brown eyes soft with concern. 'You did it, Gertie. You're a marvel. Thank God you're back safe and sound.' Den arranged cushions behind me, beating them briefly with a clenched fist. 'Lie back, luvvie.' He lifted my feet and legs up. It was a relief to lie down and take a little weight off my behind. I must have looked a sight. 'I'm going to get a bowl of warm water and a towel, and we'll get you freshened up. Clean clothes too, I think.' He smiled kindly. I still couldn't speak. All I could do was cry, huge sobs that left me gasping for air in intervals. Perhaps it was the stress of the past few years, of leaving Henri behind, of having my perfect life ripped apart because of this damn war. We had all lost so much I told myself, but it didn't make me feel any better.

Den returned with Collette, a young woman who was part of Fournier's group. She carried a pile of fresh towels and clothes in her arms. Den placed a blue and white bowl and a pitcher of water down on a table by the sofa. 'I'll leave you to do the necessary, Collette. See you shortly, luvvie.' Denden retreated and closed the door behind him.

Collette was very kind and gentle. She helped me out of my filthy clothes and covered me with a towel while she washed me. One glance at my thighs and she screwed up her pretty face. 'Mon Dieu.' She marched to the door, opened it slightly. 'Can you bring some clean dressings, please? She has terrible sores on her legs. We must bandage them. And iodine.'

My legs were a mess. No wonder that last day on the cycle had been hell. My thighs were blistered, rubbed raw, bloody, with skin hanging in strips. I spotted the brandy on the table, grabbed it, and took a swig, savouring the sweet warmth that slid down my throat, spreading a little fire. I decided to keep hold of the bottle. I glanced at Collette. Poor thing, she looked a little unsure of what to do. She was from a farming family, so was probably more used to livestock.

'Do not worry, Nancy,' she said in a gentle voice. 'I have seen much worse.' She nodded, tucked a stray brown curl behind her ear and picked up the bottle of iodine.

I laid my head back and closed my eyes, thankful to have made it back in one piece. Five hundred kilometres in seventy-two hours. A momentous journey. Nausea swirled in my gut, my head pounded, and my throat ached. Every inch of me ached and was lead-heavy. At least now I could sleep.

TWO DAYS LATER, as I lay in my bed trying to sleep, a faint droning sailed over from the west. I turned to the window. The moon was full and bright, and the droning grew louder. My heart raced and, despite the pain I was in, I couldn't help but grin from ear to ear. 'They sent the message. You beauties! Woohoo!' Our men were waiting at the drop zone. With a radio and codes on the way, we were back in business.

Chapter 34
BACK TO THE FRAY

A week later, having recuperated, we were on the move again. Tardi had found us a new camp in the department of Allier, not far from his own. Ambushes were his speciality, and he planned his missions meticulously like a general. He was a natural-born leader. If I hadn't been in love already, I could have fallen for him, but as it was, I loved him like a brother.

The drive there was glorious, and I embraced it, having been unable to move for days. I'd had enough of reading and staring at walls, and I disliked being useless. The village doctor had been summoned to tend to me and instructed me not to walk about for a few days. Now I had my freedom, my heart skipped. The sky had never been bluer nor the sun more gold.

And first thing that morning, Den had stood beaming like a Cheshire cat in the doorway. 'I've got a lovely surprise for you.'

'Hmm, let me guess,' I said, musing. 'A radio?'

'Ha! Better than a mere radio, Gertie.' And with that, he propelled a tall, young chap into my room. 'Meet Roger, your new radio op, all the way from Ohio.'

Roger was very young, good-looking with fair hair, a Marine and a radio operator, he said. 'It's an honour, ma'am,' he said with a charming soft drawl, his mouth curving into a smile.

We were set and ready once more, and I looked forward to being close to Tardi, even though it meant camping out in the forest again. If only we could swap the forest for a house.

~

'MADAME ANDRÉE. My men need Bren guns. Can you get them?'

Tardi towered over my position beneath an ancient oak tree, my shade from the fierce midday sun, and I squinted at him, his outline traced in golden light. I considered his request, already aware that they needed fresh supplies. All of the Maquis groups did after our recent battles. My thoughts wandered to our present situation. 'On one condition,' I said, amused by the boyish smirk that flickered on his lips. 'I'm tired of living beneath the stars, Tardi. I need to be indoors. Sleeping on a lumpy, damp, forest floor with a carpet of pine needles has taken its toll, my friend. I need walls, a roof, a mattress.'

He looked away to gaze up into the burning blue. 'I have an idea. My men will see to it,' he said with a wide grin creasing his face. 'And you can get the Bren guns?'

I nodded. 'Oui.' Just what he had in mind, I wasn't certain, but I no longer cared just as long as I didn't have to sleep outdoors again.

Only two days after our move, thirty young Frenchmen wandered into our camp, all evaders of the *releve*, escaping the German compulsory labour force. I welcomed them all, of course.

The next evening when I returned to our little camp, I came face-to-face with a bus, Tardi leaning against it, a huge grin stretched across his face.

'What the heck?'

Tardi laughed. 'Welcome to your new home. We acquired it two hours ago. The passengers were not pleased with having to walk the rest of their journey on foot, but as I said to them, it was a great service they were doing for France.'

I laughed. A whole bus for me. What a hoot. I followed him inside and there, at the back, were two seats facing each other, and a mattress placed on top. Pure luxury all for me.

'Try it.' He patted the mattress. 'A local shopkeeper supplied it.'

I was touched by the kindness of others and wasted no time in scrambling onto my new bed which felt like heaven. Soft, comfy and the complete opposite of that forest floor. 'Oh, Tardi. You're a marvel. Thank you so much.' I threw my arms around him and hugged him tightly.

'You are most welcome.' He cleared his throat. 'Now, Bren guns?'

I smiled. 'I'll get a message to London. You'll have them on the next drop, my friend.' The next thought that claimed my attention was bedding, but I remembered I had an old parachute stowed away. The silk would make perfect sheets. It was such a blessing when a plan came together. I felt so happy, despite our dire situation, the war, and my separation from Henri. You have to make the best of things, and that was all I aimed to do, day by day. 'I take it we can drive this?'

'But of course. And it will be useful when we have to move on. We can put all sorts in here.'

'Hmm, useful indeed.' Nothing dirty, though. This was my sanctuary.

IT WAS REASSURING BEING close to Tardi, and I aimed to stay so. We made a good team, I thought. The night air was cool and fresh, the moon large. Our drop tonight was a little different. I was collecting men for once – two American weapons instructors. One of my maquis-ards offered me his hip flask. I took a mouthful. Brandy. 'Merci.' The silhouettes of aircraft sailed nearer, then there beneath the stars a chute of white silk blossomed in the velvet darkness, followed seconds later by another. I watched as they drifted towards us, descending until they slipped behind trees and hedgerows to land in the adjacent field. Three of my men strode away to retrieve them. We also received a batch of containers even though I hadn't asked for anything. One of the men opened the first one and dragged out a weapon. Bazookas. Wow. The men gathered, joy springing to their faces, although they hadn't the faintest clue how to use them. Thank goodness for the new weapons instructors. Captain Reeve Schley and Captain John Alsop landed without a hitch. We shook hands. 'Great to meet you.'

'Likewise, ma'am. Gee, I'm glad you speak English because neither one of us speaks any French.'

I assured them both it wasn't a problem, while at the same time wondering how they were going to communicate with the men. Leaving the maquisards to deal with the cargo, I drove our new recruits to a barn close to camp, where I'd arranged for them to stay. Earlier, Den had helped me make up beds. and we'd put an old wooden crate between the beds upon which I'd placed a bunch of wildflowers in a jam jar. 'That's more homely,' I'd said, laughing at Den who cast me a puzzled glance. How odd life was, doing such things amidst a brutal war. What would my brother Stanley think of me? He'd probably be horrified if he knew what I was doing, but hopefully proud of his little sis.

∼

THAT EVENING, after we'd eaten, Schley and Alsop joined me for a drink on the bus. The maquisards in this camp had seemed pleased at the thought of weapons training and using bazookas.

'So, have you had any attacks by the Germans here?' Alsop leaned back on his seat, a cigar in one hand and a brandy in the other.

'A few. The latest was just this morning.'

'Do you think they'll be back soon?'

I didn't think they'd be back tomorrow, so I said so. It wasn't their style, although the Germans weren't predictable. I was going on gut instinct.

More drinks flowed as I got to know a little more about our new men. They were both captains in the US Army and had seen active service. They'd been based in England a while now. I pulled a bottle of whisky from my stash, which went down well, and Schley handed me a cigar. 'Thanks,' I said. 'It's been an age since I had one of these.' It had too. I was with Henri then, one of our cosy evenings at home. I poured myself a generous whisky and downed it quickly, the warm glow in my gut smothering the icy sting. I poured another. 'Come on, boys,' I said. 'You're lagging.'

'I hope you're right about those Germans,' Alsop said.

'I'm usually right.' I rested my head against a side window, my mind and body relaxed for the first time in a while. Maybe it was the cigar or the whisky, or both. I'd sounded confident just then, overly confident perhaps, almost smug. Perhaps that was my weakness.

THE NEXT MORNING, I woke with a banging headache, or something was banging. Which was it? I lay dazed for a few moments, straining to listen. No birdsong. Footsteps thudding around outside. I looked up from my bed. Schley and Alsop were dozing on seats near the front of the bus. Strewth that was some drinking session, bleeding into the small hours. My mouth was so dry. The ground beneath the bus shook, the water in my glass sloshed around, and one of the men yelled outside. 'The Germans are coming!'

I sprang out of bed. Luckily, I'd slept in my clothes. I rushed through the bus, shaking the men as I passed and flung open the door. Birds were flying this way, and that and a mortar shell exploded close by, too close for comfort. 'Jesus, hurry up lads. We're under attack.' I had to think quickly. There were roughly two hundred men here, along with Den and us. 'Bloody hell.' I rubbed the sleep from my eyes, straining to focus while I thought. 'Pack up, quick. We're shipping out now. Spread the word.'

Den was at the door waiting. 'Put your stuff in the bus, Den.' I glanced around the camp. Already our two hundred strong army was racing off, weapons in hand to face the enemy.

'You can ride in the bus with me, Den, and whoever else wants to jump in.' Some of our new recruits piled in, while the rest jumped into a spare truck. I stood in the open for a minute listening to birdsong, uncertain chirps see-sawing through the bows of the forest. Up above, the sun peeked into a flawless sky, and a mighty crump erupted in the distance. Mortar shell followed by the rat-a-tat of machine-gun fire. It was then that Den realised we'd left the bicycle behind and he ran out to grab it, releasing a bone-chilling cry. I glanced over to where he stood beneath the trees, leaping around, cycle at his feet, eyes wide, bulging, his face growing rosier by the second and I realised. He'd snagged his shirt on the electric wires. Fortunately, he fell to the ground, freeing himself in the process, and he lay there for a few seconds breathing hard. Poor Den. That must have hurt, but even so, the entire episode was so comedic. I pressed my lips together, stifling a snigger, but it was too much, and I burst out laughing while Schley and Alsop stood watching, their faces a mix of shock and disbelief. 'Come on, Den.' He picked up the cycle and heaved it inside the bus, shooting me a dazed look while I laughed and swiped tears from my eyes.

I jumped into the driving seat and started the engine. 'To pastures new.'

'Every day's an adventure, Ducks.' Den hurled himself on to the seat behind me, dazed, breathing hard.

'We'll drive down near to the men and get stuck in.' That way we'd have the bus close for our retreat, and then we'd move to Tardi's camp.

'Around six thousand Germans are coming this way,' one of our scouts said, a young maquisard, breathless from his sprint back to camp.

Strewth. We were little more than two hundred strong facing an army of thousands. 'Right.' I turned to Schley and Alsop. 'We don't have much manpower. Let's use bazookas.'

'But the men haven't been trained,' Schley said. 'And neither of us speaks French.'

'You instruct, and I'll translate.'

I organised the recruits then led the way to the Front line where the others were fighting. We needed a good position to retaliate. Machine-gun fire ricocheted all around, interspersed with a peppering of grenades. I decided it would be best to use the cover of the thick woods as opposed to the track, as we made our way closer to the front line. Unfortunately, some of the younger boys wandered off and took the track, despite my warning. We lugged the bazookas with us, along with rifles slung over our shoulders, grenades, and ammunition. Then, sustained machine-gun fire, loud, close, and screams. A sickening, sinking feeling set in my gut and instinctively I knew what had happened. The Germans had aimed their fire on the boys heading down the track.

One of the maquisards yelled out. 'Madame Andrée. They've cut them down in the road.'

'There's nothing we can do for them now. We have to press on, or they'll have all of us.' I gritted my teeth and surged forward, occasionally glancing at the men around me. Their eyes stern, jaws set. They were more than ready for the enemy. As we neared the battle, anti-tank fire exploded nearby, and the ground trembled beneath my boots, a dust cloud billowing into the blue.

'We can fire from this range,' Schley said. 'The Germans are just over that ridge there,' he pointed into the distance. Just then, two of our men limped towards us from their front line position, bloodstained, one helping the other who was more badly injured.

I turned to Schley. 'Form a line.'

He organised the men and showed them how to hold the bazookas while I beckoned to the injured men to shelter deeper in the woods. Schley instructed, and I translated, telling the men how to aim and fire. Alsop moved up and down the line, along with Schley to keep a close eye on the exercise, correcting the men's aim where necessary. Now, 'Fire!' For a brief moment, a silent pause ensued before the Germans returned fire. A grenade sailed overhead, and I dived for cover. The ground shook, and for a minute, the scream of the impact filled my head. I sprang up and darted back into action, hurling a grenade back for good measure. Some men brought more of our wounded back from their front line position.

'Den, you're in charge of the wounded.' I grabbed my rucksack and threw it over. 'There are dressings and a gallon of alcohol in there.'

He winced. 'I can't bear the sight of blood, Gertie.' He scooped up the bag.

'You'll manage.' I returned to my bazooka squad, surprised at how quickly the men had mastered the new weapons. There was less return fire from the enemy and from our higher position, I could see many Germans crumpled on the ground. My thoughts flitted to my recruits, dying or wounded in the road. We'd retrieve them later. More bazooka fire. We'd be out of ammo soon. I turned to Schley. 'I need to get a message to Tardivat. There's another camp nearby with Spanish maquisards. If I can reach them, they'll get the word across to Tardi. We need his men to hold off the Germans while we escape.'

Schley nodded, returning his attention to the battle. I saw Jacques, a young maquisard, crouched down by the roadside, aiming his rifle. 'Jacques, come with me. I need to get a message to Tardi.'

We slipped away, into the trees, cutting through to the fields, where we crawled like snakes from one side to the other. German machine-gun fire reigned down all around and targeted us in the middle of the field, but we kept moving. My ears were muffled as crumps from explosions pulsed through my head. Finally, drenched in sweat, we surfaced two fields away from the German position and made our way into the woods. The Spanish sentry looked surprised to see us. I explained what was happening and asked him to send our SOS to Tardivat.

'I will send word.' He nodded graciously.

We returned to the battle. It seemed to me that the Germans were not pressing forward. Perhaps we'd surprised them with our display of aggressive firepower. The men used the last of the ammunition, firing a last barrage from their bazookas, and the resultant lull gave us a chance to retreat to camp. Hopefully, Tardi would come soon and distract the Boches. We had made an impact at least and taken out several German posts. 'Withdraw,' I yelled, maquisards repeating my order towards the front.

We headed back through the woods. My heart yearned to return to those young boys lying on the road. At the very least we needed to get the wounded out, but it was too dangerous to break cover.

'I got a box of quality cigars in my stuff. A gift from my father,' Schley said. 'I'd hate to see the Germans get their hands on them.'

'Go and get them. You'd better grab your stuff from the farm. You can put it all on the bus,' I said. I left Schley and Alsop to it while I glanced around at the men. Some were injured, but not badly. 'We'll need the doctor, Jacques,' I said. 'Let's get ready to go. Get the wounded on board.' Then I saw Den, carbine over his shoulder, ammunition belt bulging with grenades around his waist, dazed eyes and a comical grin etched on his face. He staggered as he went from one patient to the next. He bent down, took a dressing pad and placed it over the shoulder wound of a maquisard, took out the bottle of alcohol and took a mouthful. Lord, he was drinking the stuff. He was bloody drunk. Quickly, I unclipped his ammo belt. 'Bloody idiot. You'll end up blowing yourself and us to smithereens.'

'Sorry, Gertie. Dutch courage.' He grinned impishly.

Another man had a nasty thigh wound. 'Lucky. The bullet missed the artery; otherwise, it would have been far worse.' He wasn't bothered. Hard as nails, most of them. 'Get the wounded into the trucks,' I said. 'Be ready to move out.'

Schley and Alsop dumped their kit in the bus and Schley offered me a cigar. 'Thanks,' I said, taking one. I sat down, pulled out my lighter and lit up, and then the three of us sat and puffed away on cigars, not saying a word. It was casual, pleasant, and complete madness as we all knew that the enemy was probably closing in. Had Tardi received our call for help? Gunfire in the distance. Rifle shots. 'Tardi!' I clenched the cigar between my teeth and yelled to the rest of the men. 'Fall back.' I jumped into the driver's seat and turned over the engine. Tardi had probably come just in time, thankfully.

THE EVENING, having re-grouped, Tardi arrived with his men, all unscathed.

'Aren't you glad you gave me all those Bren guns?' he said, a boyish grin breaking on his lips, his face creasing.

I couldn't help but smile, albeit briefly. I nodded. 'Thanks, Tardi.' I was glad, but before we did anything else, there was a pressing matter that needed my attention – the dead.

Chapter 35

LAST OFFICES

The cloying stench was all-consuming, drifting up to the rafters: the barn, an oven beneath the unyielding morning sun. I took a deep breath as I moved from one body to the next. Seven young, fresh faces I barely knew, but I knew where they'd come from, how old they were, and how they'd spoken of going home once the war ended. How determined they'd been. Some had told me how their fathers had fought in the first war; their words edged with patriotism and determination.

In the past, there'd been no time to bury our dead. So often men were buried where they'd fallen. Sometimes, there was no choice but to leave them behind. They all deserved a decent burial, and that's what these boys would have.

I had water, cloths, and clean clothes, and I set to work, cleaning each man with care. I washed away grime and blood, my old nurse training resurfacing as I dipped the cloth into warm water, a halo of earthy wash slapping around the bowl. Three of the boys had a clean bullet hole in their foreheads, a sign of having been shot afterwards. I hoped they'd been unconscious before such an inhumane act. 'Bastards,' I muttered, hatred boiling up inside me, guilt niggling because we didn't go back to them in the heat of battle. Maybe we could have saved them, some of them. Maybe. I huffed out a breath and carried on, changed dirty shirts for clean ones before combing and smoothing hair. After a few hours, I stood back, took a deep breath and rested on an upturned wooden box, my gut twisting and writhing, a heavy ache crushing my chest. Guilt rooted deep, thorny. Those boys hadn't known any better, and I felt responsible; after all, I was there to train them, lead them. At least I could do this for them, on behalf of their mothers, and I knew their mothers would have wanted this for their sons. Footsteps shuffled behind me, and I turned to find Tardi standing in the doorway. 'I've finished.' I swallowed, the words hollow in my heart, and I knew I'd never be finished hating the Nazis.

He pulled off his beret, nodded, and moved closer, casting a glance over the seven men. 'It is all arranged. The local priest, the church. Three o'clock.'

Funerals. Always sombre. I felt it deeply, weighing me down, and swallowed the lump in my throat. 'Have you asked the men to dress in their finest? It's only right that we make an effort, do things right.' I looked away, unable to stem the tears any longer.

Tardi placed a hand on my shoulder, firm, warmth flowing through my skin. 'You have done them proud. Their mothers will know of this.'

I glanced at him. His eyes flashed with concern and determination. I've done my best. 'I'll go and get cleaned up.'

ARMED GUARDS STOOD at the church gates, and outside the village. The men were clean, wearing their Maquis best, flying their colours, weapons in tow, marching tall and proud into the churchyard. Seven freshly dug graves. The priest read a short sermon. As the last man was lowered into the ground, dirt thrown in after them, I turned my face to the heavens. 'I'm sorry,' I muttered. 'God bless you all. France will soon be free.' I sniffed. After the war, I'd make sure they had tombstones with the words, 'Mort Pour La France' engraved – died for France. The men, sombre, resolute, saluted at each grave. A fitting send-off, just as their mothers would have wished. I slipped on my sunglasses as we headed back to camp, striding off into the glow of the late afternoon sun.

~

LONDON'S INSTRUCTIONS now came thick and fast. Since the Allied landings, operations had changed, and I'd been instructed to visit Maquis groups further south. My area had increased dramatically overnight, which meant lots more travel. It also meant dealing with groups I'd never met before. The leader of one such group was most vexed when I told him we could not arm his men, and I'd left his camp followed by a barrage of abuse. New groups were springing up everywhere, bearing their personal political agendas, something London had no wish to be involved in. Ex-Vichyites, ex-Miliciens, communists and more.

No sooner had I arrived back at my camp, tired, dusty, and desperate for a bath, Jacques marched over to me.

'Madame Andrée. I have heard something which troubles me,' he said, nervously glancing around as if to ensure he could not be heard.

'What is it?'

'A band of Maquis nearby have three women hostages.'

'Why haven't I been told about this?'

'I think that they are using them for, well, you know.' He nodded, raising his eyebrows.

Instinctively I knew what he meant. They were using them for pleasure. Well, not on my watch. 'Merci, Jacques.' I couldn't believe they'd do such a thing. I felt sickened, so I decided to visit the group and interview the women myself that afternoon.

~

'THE GIRLS WERE all working for the Germans, Madame Andrée.' The leader, Cesar, towered over me, his rifle slung over his shoulder, his hand stroking his stubbly chin, wild, bushy hair the colour of coffee beans framing his grimy face.

'Well, that's for me to decide. And you should have informed me that you'd taken them in the first place.' Anger flashed in his eyes.

As it transpired, the first woman, in her thirties, had fallen in love with a member of the Milice and for that, the Maquis had undoubtedly taken their revenge. The second woman was merely seventeen years old. 'I am not a spy,' she said. 'I would never betray my country, Madame.' I confess I believed her completely. She was called Sophie and was very beautiful with a voluptuous figure, and I suspected that was the only reason behind her capture. The third woman, however, was a problem. 'It is my duty to support the Germans, and I will gladly do whatever it takes to help them. They will defeat the British,' she said, defiance flashing in green eyes.

'Not if I've got anything to do with it.' I stared at her, unnerved by the smirk that spread across her thin lips. Her wild eyes and dishevelled state betrayed the defiance in her voice. She wore rags, undoubtedly her own clothes dirty and torn, revealing toned, tanned thighs and a little too much cleavage. I knew that the other two presented no danger, but this one was different. She was a spy and couldn't be trusted. A sinking feeling settled over me. It wasn't right to keep her there in the camp as the men would continue to abuse her or worse. 'We can't let you go.' I looked into her eyes. 'You must have known there would be penalties for being in league with the enemy, for being a spy. You will be executed.' The woman didn't say a word, merely nodded, blankness veiling her face, and I wondered how she felt in that moment. Memories of my incarceration resurfaced. Days of beatings, thinking the worst, that my execution was imminent. I swallowed, surprised by my own resolve, for I didn't feel sorry for her at all. In truth, I felt nothing. She'd made her choice and one that could not be undone. I left her with the Maquis guard while I went to organise the firing squad. Her appearance preyed on my mind too, and I decided to rake out a dress she could wear.

'Madame Andrée,' Cesar said. 'It is a little extreme. We cannot execute a woman.'

'Why not? She's a German spy for Christ's sake.'

'But, a woman?' He looked around at the men gathered behind him, all of whom seemed against this.

'I'm not asking. It's an order. My order. If you don't do it, I will.'

He stared at me, stony-faced, eyes like slits. 'Very well.'

The execution was arranged for the following morning.

~

A HEAVY FEELING hung over the camp the next morning. I arrived soon after dawn, tired and hungry, having been up half the night dealing with another parachutage. A man was making coffee, and I asked for a cup before going over to sit down beneath an old oak tree. I leaned back against the trunk and rested my head for a few minutes. Fingers of sunlight stretched through the trees, streaming beams of light to dance in the forest. The firing squad had been selected. Three maquisards lined up, weapons ready. Another led the girl out beneath the boughs of an oak tree. I took a croissant from my coat pocket, unwrapped it from the napkin and took a bite. Sweet heaven. I loved croissants and coffee for breakfast. I looked on, saw the girl shake her head when offered a blindfold. Brave to the end. She turned her gaze to me, her eyes defiant. She spat on the ground then ripped the dress off, pretty ocean-blue floral fabric slipping from her bronzed skin. Well, that was unexpected and one hell of a way to make a statement, no matter how pointless. She stood tall and proud clad in white under-garments, the early morning breeze cool, then extended her right arm out in front to perform a Nazi salute. It was ugly, just as the crowd had been that night at the Berlin rally, and I felt a mix of anger and sadness. I sucked in a deep breath. Well, it was too bad.

'Ready,' Cesar said. 'Aim.'

'Sieg heil!' she yelled; voice shrill, thin on the last syllable which quivered like a cry.

'Fire!'

The crash of bullets filled the air, birds rose and scattered from woody perches, my gaze followed their black silhouettes flitting into the blue. I had no wish to see her fall, but I glanced to where her body lay, splayed out on the forest floor, three maquisards still, staring, faces blank, rifles dangling from their hands. For a few seconds, all was still. No voices, no gunfire or rustling leaves, then finally a bird chirped sweet notes. I took another bite of my croissant, savoured the taste. They never really filled you up, I thought. I stood up, brushed away stray crumbs from my khaki shirt and swigged the last of the coffee, handing the enamel cup back to the maquisard who'd made it. I nodded to Cesar. 'Merci. I have to get back. I trust you can deal with the body?'

'Oui.' He stood watching me while I jumped in my truck. I knew he wasn't happy, hadn't agreed with my order, but it had to be done. That girl had posed a huge risk. How many men would have fallen because of her? How many families would have suffered as a result? It was one less spy, and possibly many, many French people saved as a result. I felt ruthless, but I knew that if it had been the enemy dealing with one of us, they wouldn't have batted an eyelid at our execution.

'Madame Andrée.' Sophie ran to me. 'Can I stay with you?' she said, pushing a stray golden curl from her eyes.

'I said you could go home.'

'I have no home or family, Madame. I have nowhere to go.'

I sighed. 'Sophie, I move around all the time.'

'But I can look after you at your camp. I can cook and clean, organise things. Please, Madame.'

Her blue eyes were imploring and, as she turned to look over her shoulder at the men in the camp there, I could tell she was uncomfortable. Perhaps she doubted they'd release her. 'Get in,' I said. It had been a long time since I'd had any such help, but I supposed I could find her something to do. She was a sweet young thing.

Chapter 36
SET EUROPE ABLAZE

We struck at lunchtime, as the German officers were settling down to their hearty lunch. It was Tardi's idea. Sabotage was our game, and that's what we gave them – a taste of their own medicine. I ran up the steps of the Town Hall two at a time, now the Gestapo HQ in Montluçon, a grenade in each hand, Sten gun slung over my shoulder, several men along with Tardi, behind me. The rest of the men waited outside, on guard, our drivers ready, waiting in their seats. Outside the door of the officer's mess, I paused. German voices bleated on the other side. Laughter. The chink of glasses. Fat cats' bingeing on France's finest food and wine. Bingo! I pulled the pins, yanked the door open, and hurled in two grenades. A momentary glance and I noted several startled faces, men low to rise from the table, hands instinctively reaching for pistols. I slammed the door. 'Go!' We sprinted down the steps and out into the sun, the sound of an explosion drowning out men's shouts. Tardi and several maquis-ards had targeted other rooms in the building, and more explosions crashed in the air, along with the rat-a-tat of gunfire. I turned to see one of our men firing his Sten before running to the waiting truck. Women ran inside shops to hide. Startled shopkeepers peered out from doorways. My heart, still racing, caused me to catch my breath. I clambered into the truck alongside Tardi as the rest of the men piled in the back. The air shrieked with the shouts of wounded men. As we sped off locals flooded into the road ahead of us. Our driver stamped on the brake as people, grinning and cheering, swamped our small convoy. My ears were muffled from the sound of the explosions. Our driver honked his horn repeatedly while Tardi yelled out at the locals. 'Clear the way. Vite! Vite! Return to your homes.' Our driver revved the engine as he crawled through the slowly receding masses. We were through. The faces of the people had lifted my spirits. Surprise, joy, and hope set them all aglow.

'That will show them,' Tardi said, triumph flashing in his eyes.

'We had the element of surprise. Such a pity we disturbed lunch.'

'The last supper,' Tardi muttered beneath his breath.

He was angry and grieving, as we all were. Grieving for our fallen, for all the suffering and France. His thigh pressed against mine as we sat squashed together, his body warm at my side, and a warm, fuzzy glow spread in my chest. Me and Tardi were the perfect match, the best of friends in no time at all.

'I have an idea.' He glanced at his watch, a wicked grin tugging at his mouth.

'What?'

'We will drive to Cosne-d'Allier and stop the train. If we hurry, we should make it.' He turned to his driver. 'Vite!'

Our truck sped up, kicking up clouds of dust that billowed up around us. 'What do you intend to do? Not blow it up, surely.'

'Non. We will stop the train, to show the people that the Germans are not the only ones who can do such things. We are taking back control.'

I liked the sound of that. 'Let's do it.' I smiled at him, a warm glow filling my heart. He was like a brother to me, and it was as if we'd known each other our whole lives. We were soul mates, so alike, and I admired him greatly. We pulled up alongside the rail tracks on the outskirts of the town.

Tardi checked his watch. 'The train is due.'

We jumped out. The men grabbed their Sten guns and took up positions along the line, while Tardi stood up front. We heard the shriek of the train first, and then the black engine chuffed round the bend. Tardi stood on the tracks, waving his arms. A young maquisard behind waved a flag bearing the French colours and the train slowed to a halt. Tardi and his men opened carriage doors along the train and motioned to the people to step out. They asked for their papers, checking identities and reasons for travel, and making sure no one was working on behalf of the enemy. Fortunately, we identified no such person. I stood with a few of our men, watching the spectacle before me, biting my lip as I tried not to laugh.

The journey back to camp was quiet. The truck lolled and rocked along bumpy, pot-holed tracks, and I leaned against Tardi, my head back against the seat, my eyes heavy as lead. I think the people on that train had received the message Tardi intended. We were gaining in strength. We were fighting back and winning, and France would soon be ours once more.

I GAZED at the dress on the hanger, running my hand over the bodice, the nipped-in waist and full skirt, soft silk brushing my palm, smiling. It was my creation, fashioned from the parachute that had set me down on French soil months ago. Make do and mend and all that. I took the dress from its wooden hanger and slipped it over my head. Perfect. Not that I could see properly. There was no mirror aside from the tiny compact. Still, it was sheer luxury to wear a dress after being stuck in combats, dusty boots and a shirt for months. I'd forgotten how it felt to feel like a woman. I cast an eye over the few cosmetics I possessed, reached for my red Helena Rubenstein lipstick and added a little dot on both cheeks, smoothing it in for a slight rosy glow. I added a dab to my lips and applied a dash of Chanel perfume. My hair was neat, loosely curled, resting on my shoulders, pinned back at each side.

'Madame Andrée.'

Den stood to attention by the door of my bus, dressed in his finest SOE best. He held out his arm, then led the way to our seats. The sight before me was magical. Tardi and his men had transformed our little camp. Tables had been set up, made from logs, draped with tablecloths and parachute silk and the odd borrowed bed sheet. Flowers sat in small vases, and we had real silver cutlery. Den and Hubert had hung lights in the branches of trees overhead and rigged them up to batteries, creating an enchanted, twinkling forest. I took my seat and Tardi, and Den sat either side of me. One of the men, acting as waiter, poured French champagne. A local chef had agreed to do the catering and, for safety, was kidnapped at gunpoint that very morning in case the Germans suspected him of supporting the Maquis. Everyone was dressed in their finest. I don't think I'd ever seen the men looking so clean, or shaven for that matter. The meal was wonderful, champagne flowed, along with much laughter. 'How did you come by the champagne, Tardi?'

'Local farmer supplied it. France's finest. They stashed crates of the stuff away at the beginning of the war, for fear of the Germans taking it. One farmer had crates buried in his field!' Tardi sipped his bubbly and laughed. One of the men rose from the table and returned with a fiddle. As he placed, I sat, mesmerised. He was a tall, burly chap, with long, unruly hair, usually rough-looking, unshaven, a tough fighter when it mattered, and a man of few words. The music was ethereal, haunting, and invisible energy fluttered in my heart and soul. With his bow, he spoke of love, loss, and triumph, scything notes that whispered the names of France's fallen. We all felt it, each man there motionless, listening, watching, remembering. An ache swelled in my throat and tears pricked my eyes to spill across my cheek. Tardi took my hand and squeezed.

I sipped champagne, savoured the bubbles that fizzed on my tongue, warmed my throat, while happy voices murmured all around. It was a surreal moment, a lull amidst war. A reminder that life goes on, no matter what. And I thought of Henri at home in Marseille. Our time was nearing. I felt it more strongly than ever before. We would soon be reunited, and France would be free. Thank goodness there was no parachutage until the next night. I had a feeling I'd sleep soundly after the festivities. The men laughed as they recalled battles, boasting of the number of Germans they'd killed, some disagreeing over that with others teasing them about it. How odd life was. One minute we were in a heated battle, dicing with death, and the next here enjoying a celebratory meal. The world had turned on its heel. Nothing was as it ought to be, and I longed for peace and my husband.

~

August 1944

Chateau de Fragnes was a blessing. Tardi, Hubert, and I decided that it was about time we had bricks and mortar and a solid roof. The Allies were fighting fiercely, beating the Germans back mile by mile and we could take the risk of a permanent camp. I'd claimed my boudoir, one with an adjoining bathroom. Life now came with a touch of luxury. Sophie had her work cut out for her with rooms to clean, although when I said this, she was unfazed. The day after we moved in, I waltzed into the kitchen to find Tardi standing at the head of the table, poring over a map.

'Bonjour, Andrée.' He smiled, his blue eyes sparkling.

'Bonjour. What's this?' I sank on a chair and poured myself some coffee.

'The next target.' Tardi jabbed his finger on a specific point on the map. 'The bridges here at Cosne-d'Allier.'

Operation Dragoon was in full flight, and tens of thousands of Allied soldiers had landed on our southern shores and were now fighting their way north. The Germans were in retreat, headed north through the Rhone Valley. We were tasked with the job of espionage, blowing up bridges, specific factories and depots, to hinder the enemy's efforts. I shifted across to Tardi and leaned in over the map. 'We began in Cosne-d'Allier,' I said. It was one of the first places Hubert and I went when we first arrived. I remembered it well, and I knew the bridges. 'Intelligence reports state the Germans are headed for the Belfort Gap, a direct route through the mountains back to Germany.' I sipped my coffee and grabbed a croissant.

'Exactly,' Tardi said. 'Take out the bridges, halt them in their tracks.'

I nodded. There was no time to wait for nightfall, not now we knew the Germans were retreating swiftly.

He folded the map carefully, tucked it inside his jacket pocket. 'We go now.'

~

COSNE-D'ALLIER WAS a sleepy little town. We drew up by the first bridge and Tardi, Schley, and Alsop grabbed the explosives from the back of the truck. We'd collected our stash from one of the drop zones where we'd buried it some weeks ago. Tardi ordered several of his men to guard the bridge at both sides. There was a knack to blowing up bridges, so we were shown during SOE training. You had to identify the weakest point, and then plant the explosives in such a way to do the most damage. It wasn't easy. We had to move quickly, and we waited as Tardi fetched ropes from the truck.

'Take the explosive devices and strap them around your waists,' I said, taking one and doing just that. 'We'll climb down the struts and plant the devices.' Tardi secured the ropes, and we scaled down the side of the bridge along with Alsop and Schley. Once the explosives were planted, we hauled ourselves back up, and I left Tardi to set the fuse. As I made my way along the bridge, the townsfolk had come out to see what was going on. Men, women, and children streamed towards us, some making their way onto the bridge! I waved my arms at them. 'Get back,' but they stood, smiling, gawping, some cheering.

'Get them off the bridge,' Tardi said.

The men rallied round and helped move the people on. Some moved back willingly; others were too excited by our activities.

'We are free, yes?' one woman said. 'France is free.'

'Non, Madame.' I tried to explain. 'We are here to blow up the bridges. The Germans are on their way as we speak. They are fleeing back to Germany, using these bridges.'

Tardi lit the fuse then sprinted towards us. 'Get down!'

I crouched behind our truck, waiting for the crash, my hands over my ears. It was still a shock when it came, shaking the ground beneath our feet, a thunderous boom inside my head while bits of debris and dust sailed through the air. My heart thumped with the adrenaline and the buzz of excitement. We were buggering up everything we could; a persistent thorn in Germany's side. 'Try crossing that,' I yelled. Tardi laughed.

~

THE NIGHT WAS DARK, the waning moon a crescent, smothered by a veil of cloud.

'Andrée,' Tardi said. 'You and Pierre will take out the sentry at the west gate, and Jean-Paul and Claude the east gate.'

I nodded. There were two guards on duty tonight at the armaments and munitions store in Mont Mouchet. I recalled my training – hand to hand combat, killing a man with my bare hands. I knew what to do. I only hoped I could do it deftly. It was supposed to work. Doubts bubbled, and sweat ran down my neck, tickled my spine. I blew out a breath. We kept to the bushes, out of sight, slithering through the undergrowth on our bellies like snakes. The ground was wet, and I was glad of the last rainfall as the soggy leaves dampened any noise we made. As I glanced up, I spotted both guards meeting together as they marched to and fro, their ramrod silhouettes just visible in the velveteen darkness. After around twenty minutes, we were close enough to strike, but we had to wait for the right moment when the guards were far enough apart. The crunch of jackboots upon gravel echoed in the night's silence. My palms were wet, my mouth dry, heart drumming, booming in my ears. I saw the outline of my guard's helmet, and as he turned, I noted the straight line of his nose and a strong, square chin. A quick glance to my colleagues. Jean-Paul waved his arm pointing forward. I raised my hand, gestured okay. Slowly, I got to my feet and crept forward. The guard was right in front of me, then turned suddenly, his hands poised on his rifle. He'd seen me. Damn! I moved quickly, noting the look of shock on his face, the glint of a steel bayonet as he raised his rifle. With the side of my right hand, I hit his neck hard, just below the ear, and he crumpled to the ground.

Gasping for breath, I gazed at his face, young, some mother's son, lifeless at my feet. I felt a sting cutting deep to the bone in my right arm. Something wet trickled down over my wrist. Wincing, I lifted my arm and noted inky dark lines streaking over my hand, the fabric of my jacket frayed where the bayonet sliced. An odd feeling descended over me, giddiness and nausea, and my legs became heavy, wobbly. I signalled to the others to proceed, and as I turned to Pierre, I staggered, falling into strong arms.

'Andrée, you're hurt.'

'I'll be all right,' I mumbled, half-gasping, barely recognising the sound of my voice. He helped me back to the truck, hitched me up onto the seat. Then, he pulled his scarf from his neck and tied it around my arm. The driver sat, watching.

'Keep your arm up. It will slow the blood.' Pierre glanced back towards the factory. 'They're coming now.' He jumped in the truck beside me, took hold of my arm to keep it elevated. I hadn't the strength.

'Andrée, what's happened?' Tardi's voice. He climbed in beside me.

I tried to speak, but no words came out. A cacophony of male French voices erupted all around, slipping in and out of my head. The truck lurched forward, bouncing over rough ground and I was thrown around. Tardi put his arm around me, pulled me close. I felt so drugged, my eyes heavy and they fluttered like wings, and all became fuzzy and then … nothing.

~

VOICES FLOATED INTO MY HEAD, Tardi's and another I didn't recognise. My eyes were so weighted I couldn't lift them, my body like lead, and nausea swimming right through me. My eyes flickered, lamplight glowed, then I glimpsed the hazy outline of a man with black spectacles and grey hair standing over me.

'Ah, Madame. Welcome back.'

My mind was foggy as I tried to work out what had happened. My arm stung and throbbed, and I squeezed my eyes tight, gritting my teeth. Where was I? It seemed I was lying on a table, the surface hard beneath me, and I tried to sit up.

'Stay there, Andrée.' Tardi stepped forward. 'You have hurt your arm, but the doctor has stitched the wound. You will be all right, but you must rest.' He placed a hand on my shoulder, the pressure gentle, warm, reassuring.

'Madame Andrée, I have bandaged the wound and put your arm in a sling. You must keep it up for a few days. I will call and check on you then, but I think it will heal satisfactorily.' He flashed a warm smile and handed me a glass. 'Brandy. It will help.'

I drank it slowly, and for a moment, the pain dulled as fiery warmth swelled in my stomach. 'I missed the fireworks.'

Tardi laughed. 'You did. And it was a grand display.'

'Thanks, Tardi.' Lady Luck had smiled on me once again. It could have been worse, and I recalled the guard lying dead at my feet. Just a boy, really. Just a boy. But I am just a woman and Henri, just a man. We are all 'just', and so it must be that we fight for what we know in our hearts to be right. Fight on until the end. Never look back. My eyes swam, and Tardi swiped tears away with his finger then took hold of my hand, his fingers warm, wet. I closed my eyes, forced a smile, despite my crumbling resolve. To have so many good friends to take care of you was a blessing, but sometimes there were moments when pain and sadness consumed such blessings, banished them to the background, leaving you to dwell.

Chapter 37

LIBERATION

I'd slept for hours and was still so tired. Tardi had seen to the parachutage for the last two nights, allowing me to rest. My arm was healing nicely, according to the doctor aside from the stinging pain. Anyhow, the sling was off, and the doctor had placed a light dressing over the wound. I'd been fortunate. Thank goodness we had the chateau and I had a real bed. A commotion suddenly erupted downstairs. Men were shouting. What the hell was going on? I slipped down to the kitchen to my rabble of maquisards, to find them laughing, hugging one another, and in their midst, Den, his headset hung around his neck, the radio on the table.

'Gertie. Paris is free.' He flung his arms around me and squeezed me tight. Next, Hubert hugged me, kissing me most unexpectedly on the mouth.

'Liberated, at long last. I can hardly believe the news.' I was surrounded by joyous men all congratulating one another, pouring cognac, brandy, and whatever else they could find. I reached for coffee and a piece of bread left on a plate. Free. It was 25 August 1944 and I'd been there for four months, yet it felt like a lifetime. I drew in a deep breath, soaking up the excitement all around as I thought of Henri. Please be safe, my love.

'The Free French have marched into the capital, along with the

Americans,' Den said excitedly. 'We've got the buggers on the run now.'

'There will be many celebrations there today,' Tardi said, a smile tightly stretched across his face. 'Music, dancing.'

The swastika flags would be torn down, and Paris would be Paris once more, clean, free. I would have loved to have seen that. Henri will be waiting for Marseille's freedom, and waiting for me too, I hoped.

30 August 1944

Tardi held out his arm and led me around to the rear of the chateau, where we stood at the top of the stone steps. He presented me with a beautiful bouquet. 'Happy birthday, Madame Andrée,' he said softly, followed by applause from everyone. Denis, Hubert, Schley, Alsop, everyone who was able to be there was there.

'Merci, Tardi.' The flowers were divine, and I sniffed them, the sweet, subtle scent of pink roses stirring my senses.

'And now, for another surprise.' Tardi gestured with his hand for me to watch. He nodded to one of his maquisards who whistled. There, from around the corner of the great house, came a procession, the sight I never thought or expected to witness. The Maquis, all dressed in their finest, bearing rifles, marching, parading, saluting *me* as they strode past. An endless stream of men. My goodness, just how many of them were there? We had thousands in the Auvergne, but surely, they hadn't all journeyed to be with us today. Tardi was beaming, but more than a kind smile danced upon his handsome tanned face. There was a flash of amusement in his eyes. I turned my gaze back to the men. There, the man at the front. I'd seen him already, hadn't I? I turned to Tardi. 'Are the men marching round and round this house?' Everyone burst into laughter. 'Oui.' Tardi chuckled, signalled to the men to halt.

'I knew it.' How hilarious, and yet so touching. I laughed too, moved by the effort they'd all made, and the splendid performance they'd given.

'The men wanted to give something back.' Tardi touched my arm lightly. 'You have done so much for all of us, Andrée. It seemed only right to thank you.' He cleared his throat, a smile springing back onto his serious face. 'And now, we eat.'

My birthday celebration went on all evening, into the small wee hours. Everyone brought a gift which was so remarkable because honestly, almost everything was in such short supply. Some of them must have spent hours scouring all the shops in various villages. The Spanish maquisards presented me with a beautiful bouquet of wild-flowers plucked from the forest and wrapped snugly in a Spanish flag, along with a poem. I was so touched by the thought and effort they had taken, just for me.

My thoughts turned to Henri. It was my thirty-second birthday and I knew he'd be thinking of me. The pull towards him had grown as the days sailed by, and questions bobbed in my mind constantly. I replayed our parting over and over, and the bad dream preyed on my mind. Each time I thought of him, my chest tightened, and my stomach rolled with unease. I had to get to Marseille soon or I'd go mad.

PEOPLE LINED THE STREETS, joyous, emotional, looking on as we marched through the streets of Vichy, many rushing towards us, speaking swiftly in French, thanking us, over and over. The Germans had fled, and we'd raced here as soon as we'd heard. Hubert had joined forces with Gaspard, and we marched into Vichy together. It was a momentous day, a German-free zone. We scoured German HQ and the Vichy offices. Petain and his government had already fled. Rumour was they'd been taken to Germany. All other collaborators had fled. People engulfed us everywhere we went. They hugged us, grabbed our hands to shake, kissed our cheeks, thanked us profusely, and brought food and drink. The atmosphere was electric. People hugged and kissed and wept and danced beneath the late summer sun as if they'd emerged from a chrysalis, wings slowly unfolding, embracing life. And all around, the leaves on the plane trees were vivid green, shimmering beneath the sun, the buildings more elegant, rid of enemy flags, and children ran, giggling, springing over flowers that swayed and dazzled in the breath of wind. I drank it in for this freedom and victory was all ours. It was such a natural feeling, one so giddy and high.

The next day, we attended a service at the war memorial. The mayor addressed the crowd, and then the various representatives stepped forward to lay a wreath. My group nominated me. Afterwards, as I stood with my men, I glimpsed a familiar face among the crowd. It was the receptionist from L' Hôtel Louvre et Paix, and she weaved her way through the crowd towards me.

'Bonjour,' I said.

'Madame Fiocca.' She embraced me, kissing both cheeks, then stood back and shook her head, a look of surprise flashing in her eyes. 'What are you doing here? We all thought that,' she glanced down at her feet, nervously, 'well, how wonderful to see you.'

'I'm with the British Forces, but I'm hoping to go home and see Henri as soon as I can.'

A cloud of blankness wiped the smile from her face. 'But surely you know?'

What was she talking about? 'Know what?'

'Well, I'm not sure how to say this but, your husband is dead.'

'No.' I shook my head. 'Not Henri.' He couldn't be. He was my rock, my soul mate. My eyes misted and tears slipped down my face, cool, wet, quickly turning tacky beneath the sun. She placed a hand on my arm, but nothing could comfort me now. Nothing. I stepped sideways and bumped against Den, my head fuzzy and light.

'What's wrong, Ducks?'

'Get me out of here, please.'

'I'm so sorry, Madame Fiocca. The Germans arrested him. They held him for five months before …'

I didn't want to hear any more details. My chest ached, a huge lump swelled in my throat, and I released a wail like a banshee. Den placed a protective arm around me and ushered me away from the crowd, to a shaded spot beneath the trees. 'Henri's dead.' As I heard my voice speak the words, it was as if a blade struck my heart. It was surreal. Maybe she was wrong. People made mistakes all the time.

He opened his mouth, but no words came out, and he drew me to him, hugging me tight, stroking my hair now and then while I sobbed like a child. And I remembered the day Dad never came home. The day he abandoned me, and I felt that desolation, that pain all over again. After all we'd gone through. 'I shouldn't have left.'

'Shush, luvvie. You've had a nasty shock.'

'But it's my fault, Den, don't you see?' His eyes were blank, as he flashed a weak smile. He didn't understand. How could he? I'd never told him everything. Careless talk and all that. All this time I'd assumed Henri was safe, alive, simply unable to reach me. All joy had vanished, dragged away on the tide of a retreating enemy. The Nazis had torn my life apart. 'I have to go to Marseille.'

'You can't go now. We'll have to let Hubert know.'

'I must. Don't you see?' It was unbearable and I had to know for sure. I had to go home.

Marseille

The sun beat down on our heads as we strolled along arm in arm. Den was quiet. He was never quiet, but I was glad to be left with my own thoughts. I turned to look one last time at our apartment and stopped in my tracks. Whether it was a trick of the light or not I didn't know, but I saw an outline of a figure standing at our living room window, and for a moment I swore it was Henri.

'Are you all right, Ducks?' Den stopped beside me.

I smiled, eyes misting over. 'I will be.' I took his arm, held my head high, and strolled on, leaving all I'd held dear behind. As we rounded a corner, I froze, almost running into the man before me. My father-in-law. And the look of anger and disgust etched on his face told me that he still despised me.

'You killed my son!' He hissed the words, anger etched into each one.

No, please, I screamed inside my head. I couldn't have done anything differently. I didn't know what to say. Should I protest? Apologise? How could I? I was guilty.

'Murderess,' he spat.

Intense pain gripped me, squeezing my throat, crushing my chest, and my eyes swam with tears. Something snapped inside, and I slapped him across the cheek. It was so quick I shocked myself. He glared at me. Henri's sister gripped his arm, pulling him away.

'Papa, non,' she said, flicking me a hard stare as they strode away.

'I take it that's your father-in-law,' Den said.

'Yes, and sister-in-law. They never liked me.' It dawned on me that it was almost one year since Henri's death. He would be buried, probably here in Marseille. I'd have to find out where and visit his grave.

Hubert, Alsop, and our doctor friend Pierre Vellat had all come along to keep me safe. They were very kind and deeply concerned, and I was glad of the support. Den and I found them sitting outside a small bistro overlooking the harbour. Sunlight danced across the ocean, leaving thousands of diamonds in the wake.

'Did you find what you were looking for?' Hubert said, passing a glass of brandy to me.

I downed it in one gulp, savouring the taste. 'Not really. There wasn't much left.' I glanced at my old book, emotions rising and falling like the yachts bobbing in the harbour. I thought for a moment. What did I need to do now that I was here? I knew I couldn't stay as I was still attached to SOE. The war was over for us, or just about. I wondered about my little dog, Picon. Where was he? Was he still alive? He was my only link to my old life, to Henri, and I was compelled to go and search for him. Scraping my chair back, I got to my feet. 'I need to try and find an old friend of mine. Den, will you come with me?'

'Of course, Ducks, of course.'

I set off to the butchers, to see if the Ficetoles still lived there. When we reached the shop, it was closed, and my heart sank. Fortunately, a neighbour there explained how the Ficetoles had moved to a house just outside of the town after their home was destroyed in an air raid. We returned to the others, explained what had happened, and Hubert offered to drive me out to find them. Eventually, after a few false starts, we found their house a few hours later. I knocked on the door and a dog barked. It was a bark I knew well. 'Picon!' The door swung open, and there stood Monsieur Ficetole, his eyes growing wide as he stared at me. Picon scampered behind him, and I crouched down as my little boy jumped into my arms, yelping and howling, licking my face, his tail wagging vigorously.

'Madame Fiocca.' He smiled. 'It is Madame Fiocca,' he called behind him. 'Please, come in.'

We were shown into the kitchen. Madame Ficetole drew her hand to her mouth as she looked at me. 'It cannot be,' she gasped. 'We thought you were dead!'

I realised that everyone I'd ever known had probably assumed the same. 'Thank you for taking care of Picon,' I managed to say, gritting my teeth, swallowing my sobs, tears soaking my cheeks.

We sat down around the kitchen table, and Monsieur Ficetole made coffee. 'The Germans arrested Henri in May last year. They held him until October, and then.' He shook his head and reached across the table to pat my hand. 'We are so sorry, Madame. It is terrible, but then so many terrible things have happened.'

So, they'd arrested him soon after I'd left. He should have come with me. 'When did he die?' I had to know the date to fit all of the pieces together.

'16 October.'

'How?'

Monsieur Ficetole exchanged an awkward look with his wife, then cleared his throat. 'They shot him.'

I nodded, closed my eyes, unable to stem the tears. I was thankful for the method. It was better than the guillotine, I thought, at least there was that. It was about mid-October last year when I'd had that awful dream. Goosebumps prickled my spine and arms, and I knew that had been Henri's final goodbye. The dream joined the rest of my memories. They would always be mine to treasure, to remind me of what we'd shared. To state proudly that we'd lived, truly lived, together, if only for a short while. And I thought of the woman with the bullet in her head in the woods and I was glad. A spy. I was sorry I hadn't killed more.

'We took Picon as soon as Henri was arrested,' Madame Ficetole said. 'We just wanted to help, to do something, and you had always been so kind.'

I wiped the tears away with the back of my hand. 'Merci.' I snuggled my face against Picon who hadn't stopped wriggling since I'd sat down. He was too excited, working himself into such a state. Our doctor friend decided that perhaps he should administer a small sedative to allow Picon to rest, and I agreed.

'The Germans were looking for you. They hung posters everywhere. They called you the White Mouse. There was a bounty of a million francs,' Monsieur Ficetole said. 'Your husband never told them anything.'

The words sliced through me sharper than any bayonet. It was all my fault. I'd placed Henri and his family in jeopardy. I'd sacrificed my husband to fight, to do my bit for the war and I had to live with that. Madame Ficetole sat down, dabbing her eyes with a corner of her apron. Den put his arm around me, drew me to his side.

'We need to leave,' Hubert said gently.

I nodded. 'I'll take Picon now. Thank you so much for everything. I'll be in touch soon.' I hugged the Ficetoles and bid them farewell before scooping up a drowsy Picon. Hubert drove us back to the chateau at Montluçon. The RAF and the Americans had destroyed the main bridges, and the roads were clogged with burned-out German tanks and vehicles, forcing us to take many detours, making the journey twice as long. We joined the ranks of a steady stream of people heading north, crawling along roads like swarming ants. When we arrived back, I shut myself away in my room, settled Picon down on my bed, and crashed out beside him. I wished I'd had a picture of Henri, but all personal items had been left behind in London, and I visualised his picture that sat in a silver-gilt frame on my bedside table in our small London flat.

It was time to leave. SOE had established a branch in Paris, and we had been summoned. Our American colleagues returned to London, and maquisards said their farewells and returned to their homes. Despite my grief, I felt joy in my heart, the joy of having contributed to our freedom, to ending the suffering. My dear friend, Henri Tardivat, announced he was going to fight with the French, to fight on until Germany capitulated. I understood as I looked into his eyes one final time. 'Knock 'em dead,' I said, grinning fondly as we each prepared to leave the Chateau du Fragnes. There was no awkwardness, and I hugged him tight, my friend, my brother in arms. 'When this is over, I'll return,' I said. 'I'll find you, Tardi and we'll have a drink together.'

'I will expect it, Nancy.' That was the first time he'd used my real name, and it was nice. It was as it should be. Ordinary times would soon be restored from the extraordinary and yet there was a sadness there, waiting in the wings. I felt deflated as we piled into our car and set out on the road for Paris. I was at sea, alone, battling a tormented ocean, the rise and fall of the waves, tossed this way and that – smiles and laughter versus deep gloom and darkness. And I wondered what would become of me now I was a widow. Where would I live? Where would I work? Nothing would be the same nor feel the same ever again. And as fleeting as a swift in flight I thought of Mum, a pang of pain piercing my heart. Like her, I had to begin again, I thought, as I raised my chin and gazed into the burning blue. So much loss, and pain. At that moment I knew I'd visit Mum and my family as soon as I could. There was much to say, and so much had been left unsaid. Life was short.

My thoughts turned to Henri. We'd been so happy together, enjoying many fun times and moments of laughter. He often said I was a breath of fresh air. Perhaps that's why he chose me – after all, he could have had any woman he desired, but I'm glad it was me. A war would have arrived regardless, and I would have acted as I'd done. And so, Henri chose me and saved me, and for that, I would be eternally grateful, despite deep regret. He was the greatest love of my life, but I still had Picon. I scratched his chest, his tail wagging as he sat on my lap. It was just the two of us now, and I turned my gaze to the window, to the flashing countryside and the lines of people walking, cycling, riding in carts and cars, all making their way back to their homes. We were leaving ours behind.

Germany surrendered to Montgomery on 4 May 1945. The war in Europe was finally at an end. Eisenhower accepted Germany's unconditional surrender on 7 May, and Stalin on 8 May. Victory in Europe was declared that day. Apparently, one couldn't move in Paris as thousands of people celebrated in the city centre. People sang "It's a Long Way to Tipperary" from the Place de la Concorde all the way to the Arc de Triomphe.

I was stuck in Marseille, filled with mixed emotion. I'd said my goodbyes to friends, having concluded my business. The money Henri left in a safety deposit box at the bank had gone. Like so many, the Germans plundered our savings and valuable possessions. But I had my memories. They were my gold, my diamonds, my love. Marseille was empty, desolate, and held nothing for me anymore.

I had a visitor recently, a padre who had been arrested by the Gestapo and imprisoned alongside Henri. He sought me out, determined to pass on a message. He told me of the beatings Henri endured. They exchanged words through cell walls whenever they could. He explained that Henri's father visited one day and pleaded with him to give me up, but Henri simply said, 'Leave me in peace, papa.' It was difficult to hear of the final days of his life, but in a way, it brought closure.

Soon afterwards, Étienne, an old friend took me out for dinner. He was a doctor and explained how Henri was suffering from uraemia. That time he'd been ill and hospitalised, his doctors advised him to stop drinking and take better care of himself. I'd had no idea. The condition was incurable and would have shortened his life. I suppose what Étienne was trying to say so indirectly was that even if Henri had not died in 1944, he would not have lived for much longer. But such information doesn't make it any easier to bear.

'He refused most dinner invitations,' Étienne said. 'He preferred to stay at home in the evenings, although sometimes he came to dinner and we would play cards.' So, no dining out with any female companions. He'd lived as a bachelor, and my heart ached as I realised that what we had was rare and exquisite, tears spilling as I hung on his every word, each one adding depth and colour to the story.

So, while I spent weeks fleeing Germans and clambering up mountains in the Pyrenees, Henri sat at home nursing brandy and his thoughts, with Picon by his side. Now I have Picon by my side.

I was still in service and on the cusp of returning to Paris, the city where it all began. The Plane trees would be flowering. Henri told me once that Napoleon ordered the planting of Plane trees along roadsides to provide shade for his marching troops. 'Van Gogh painted beneath them as he sheltered from the sun,' he whispered in my ear. And everything seemed to lead back to the ancient Greeks. 'Did you know, Nannie, that the Trojan Horse was carved from the wood of Plane trees?' Fond anecdotes sailed on a sea of memories, his voice a whisper that kissed my soul. Tears clouded my eyes, but I smiled. We shared so many good times. Henri gave me so much, perhaps more than I deserved, and accepted that I had to follow my conscience despite the risks. 'You died for France, and for me – and I salute you. Adieu, mon amour,' I whispered into the night breeze as the moon pulsed against the velveteen sky flanked by a myriad of stars. 'Forgive me.'

When my time comes, I wish to be cremated and have my ashes cast over the mountains of the Auvergne, where I fought side-by-side with my maquisards. And if there is such a person as Saint Peter, I'll make it easy for him and plead guilty on all counts. I wouldn't have it any other way.

Author's Note

"IT WAS DREADFUL because you've been so busy and then it all just fizzles out." Nancy Wake, The Australian, 25 April 1983.

When I first decided I wanted to write about Nancy Wake, I did not realise just how insurmountable a task lay before me. She was an enigma, a courier who ferried hundreds of evaders including Jews to the foothills of the Pyrenees, the fierce Guerrilla fighter who fought side-by-side with the Maquis. The well-decorated woman of some military fame who claimed to be fearless. Her real story reads like a Hollywood fable, dabbed in beauty, shrouded in mystery, tainted with sadness. So, in search of the truth, I realised Nancy was far more than a warrior with the Resistance, and I longed to uncover the life she led before World War Two.

All that I'd ever read, all that I thought I knew, were facts to be pushed to one side. I scoured the internet, sleuthed Genealogy sites, read newspaper archives, trawled through numerous interviews, dramas, and film productions, and finally, devoured every available biography. I also managed to obtain copies of her military records. All of this information enabled me to sculpt a picture of Nancy Grace Augusta Wake, the young woman who ran away from home, travelled the world, became a journalist, and carved out a new life from a petite apartment in rue Sainte-Anne, Paris.

Before leaving France at the end of the war, Nancy visited O'Leary while he recovered at the Palais Royal Hotel, having survived Dachau. Overjoyed to see a dear friend and saviour, she found him to be in good spirits. But happy reunions were equally tinged with sadness as she also learned the fate of her old friend and Resistance worker, fellow Australian, Bruce Dowding. On the 30 June 1943, the Germans executed him by beheading at Dortmund. On 13 September 1946, Bruce was mentioned in despatches for 'gallant and distinguished services in the field'.

In January 1946, Colonel Buckmaster was asked to present the French Government with a Lysander aircraft, as a gesture from the British Government and SOE. Nancy, still grieving and feeling depressed, refused the invitation to attend the ceremony, but Denis Rake persuaded her otherwise. She returned to Paris where she met up with old friends, including Henri Tardivat.

Back in England, at a crossroads with little money, finding work became a priority. Denis told her of his new role with the Passport Control Office, based in Paris, and encouraged her to apply. In a matter of a few weeks, Nancy learned she would be joining him, working in the same office. Her time there signified a fairly happy period in her life and allowed her to catch up and socialise with old friends. Of course, her darling dog, Picon, accompanied her and even slept beneath her desk at work.

As for Harold Cole, the traitor, or Paul Cole as he was widely known, justice prevailed. In 1946, acting on a tip-off, police surrounded the apartment building where he lived with his partner. Cole, having heard footsteps on the stairs, opened the door and fired, only to be shot in return. He bled to death on the apartment floor in central Paris. When the news reached Nancy, she was able to reassure others equally affected by Coles treachery.

Sadly, she would lose her beloved terrier late in 1947, when he fell ill with dropsy. The vet advised euthanasia. He was a good age – thirteen – not that it made it any easier to bear. Picon, her last link to the good old days. Now Nancy said goodbye to the second love of her life, leaving her truly alone and bereft.

In 1948, she was honoured when Henri Tardivat invited her to attend his daughter's christening and to be godmother. As a touching tribute, the baby would be named Nancy. Tardi, as she so affectionately called him, had been injured during the fighting at Belfort Gap, and had to have his left leg amputated. Like so many, he made the best of his life, established a business in Paris and had a family of his own. His friendship with Nancy continued for life, such was the closeness of their bond.

Many investitures were held at the British Embassy in Paris during those post-war years, and while Nancy waited for her turn to be decorated, she caught up with old friends once again. One, in particular, held the best dinner party of the year, as she said. Hector – the man who she and Hubert had met after parachuting back into France in April 1943. He'd been arrested and had spent the war in Buchenwald.

At the end of 1948, Nancy resigned her position choosing to return to Sydney, a decision she later regretted as she found it challenging to re-settle in Australia. She sailed into Sydney Harbour in January 1949 to a rapturous welcome by the Australian press. The Sunday Sun reported, 'Six Medal Heroine Returns.' People stopped her in the street, shook her hand and wished her well and her family welcomed her. The reunion undoubtedly brought her some peace while she grieved the loss of Henri, and it enabled her to reconcile with her mother. She was also reunited with her beloved elder brother, Stanley, and was so relieved he'd survived his incarceration as a Japanese prisoner of war in Changi.

All too soon, she was looking for new opportunities, eager to have a fulfilling role. A contact in the Liberal Party suggested she try her hand at politics, prompting her to run for the Federal seat of Barton in the forthcoming elections. Politics had never appealed to Nancy before, but she spotted an opportunity to make a difference. Speaking to the press at the time, she explained that she recognised much political unrest in Australia, some of it reminiscent of Germany prior to the war.

Naturally, the press was all too eager to cover her recent decision, and once again, Nancy found herself making headlines. 'Maquis Heroine Tries Politics.' After tireless campaigning, and the Federal elections in 1949, Dr HV Evatt, her Labour opponent, retained his Barton seat. Nancy, however, had managed to shrink his majority and was encouraged to carry on, sailing into the 1951 elections. Once again, she was defeated, with Dr Evatt retaining his seat. However, she'd worked her magic once more, shrinking his majority considerably and he won by a mere two hundred and forty-three votes. Nancy was the first woman to run in the elections, an achievement in itself, but she'd had enough and decided to return to England and her little flat in London.

I must say, having studied those election results, and the proceeding years, I have a strong notion she might have won the next election in 1953 if only she'd stayed.

Back in England, a new role with the Air Ministry beckoned. Nancy was part of a team of four who gave lectures on evasion and escape, an area with which she was well versed. Later, she was nominated to write the Manual of Combat Survival, a classified publication that would be of particular interest to aircrews in the event of them becoming stranded in an unfriendly country.

It was during this period that she first met John Forward, an RAF officer stationed in Malta. They met at a friend's dinner party. Such was the impression Nancy made on the slightly younger pilot, that he turned up at her flat one grey, rainy day and never left. They married in 1957, and Nancy returned to Malta with her new husband. She and John were happy together by all accounts. The next chapter in her life brought more recognition and fame when the biographer, Russel Braddon, wrote a book about Nancy and her wartime exploits. When John's posting ended in 1959, he retired from the RAF, and he and Nancy decided to relocate to Sydney, Australia. Later, they would move to Port Macquarie.

After deciding to write her own biography in the early eighties, The White Mouse was published to huge acclaim in 1985. Soon afterwards, a Sydney production company produced a mini-series, an event in Nancy's life which took her back to France, to find old friends such as Madame Sainson who still lived in the same small flat in Nice.

In 1994, Nancy sold her medals at auction, receiving quite a tidy sum of money. When asked if she would have preferred to keep them, she replied, 'There was no point in keeping them. When I die, I'll probably go to hell and they'd melt anyway.'

Later, in 1997, John passed away in his sleep, leaving Nancy a widow once more. In the years that followed, her own health declined after suffering one or two minor strokes. In 2001, having decided to live out her years in London, Nancy left Australia for the last time. She took up residence at the Stafford Hotel in St James's Place, where the staff came to know and love her immensely. They even had a chair made especially for her, placed by the bar, ready for her arrival at eleven o'clock every morning when she would order the first gin and tonic of the day. When her funds eventually ran dry, the hotel soaked up the costs, gratefully receiving generous donations from particular well-wishers and benefactors. Rumour had it that HRH, The Prince of Wales, was one such benefactor. A spokesman from St James's Palace later confirmed that the prince was indeed contributing to Nancy's hotel bills which reputedly amounted to around eighty-thousand pounds annually.

In 2003, she moved to the Royal Star & Garter Home, having become too frail to remain at the hotel. While there she received visitors over the last years of her life, and mail, often from children who also sent drawings, and I imagine that warmed her heart, planted a smile on her lips and set a twinkle in those blue-grey eyes.

On 7 August 2011, Nancy died in Kingston Hospital, London, having been ill with a chest infection. She was almost ninety-nine years old. In keeping with her express wishes, she was cremated, and her ashes scattered near Montluçon, over the mountains of the Auvergne. Such a fitting tribute to a remarkable lady who once lived and fought with the Maquis.

Appendix

Nancy wake became one of the most highly decorated heroes of World War Two. For her service, she received the George Medal, 1939-45, France and Germany Star, Defence Medal, British War Medal 1939-45, French Officer of the Legion of Honour, French Croix de Guerre with Star and two Palms, US Medal for Freedom with Palm, French Medaille de la Resistance, and the New Zealand Badge in Gold.

George Medal Citation

Presented by Sir Oliver Harvey, British Ambassador in Paris on 21 April 1948.

This officer was parachuted into France on 1st March 1944, as assistant to an organiser who was taking over the direction of an important circuit in Central France. The day after their arrival she and her chief found themselves stranded and without directions through the arrest of their contact, but ultimately reached their rendezvous by their own initiative. She worked for several months helping to train and instruct Maquis groups.

Ensign Wake took part in several engagements with the enemy and showed the utmost bravery under fire. During a German attack due to the arrival by parachute of two American officers to help in the Maquis, she personally took command of a section of ten men whose leader was demoralised. She led them to within point-blank range of the enemy, directed their fire, rescued the two American officers and withdrew in good order. She showed exceptional courage and coolness in the face of enemy fire. When the Maquis group with which she was working was broken up by large-scale German attacks and wireless contact was lost, Ensign Wake went along to find a wireless operator through whom she could contact London. She covered some 200 kilometres on foot and by remarkable steadfastness and perseverance succeeded in getting a message through to London. It was largely due to these efforts that the circuit was able to start work again. Ensign Wake's organising ability, endurance, courage and complete disregard for her own safety earned her the respect and admiration of all. The Maquis troops, most of them rough and difficult to handle, accepted orders from her, and treated her as one of their own male officers. Ensign Wake contributed in a large degree to the success of the groups with which she worked, and it is strongly recommended that she be awarded the George Medal.

About the Author

Suzy Henderson lives with her husband and two sons in Cumbria, England, on the edge of the Lake District, a beautiful and inspiring landscape of mountains, fells, and lakes. She never set out to be a writer, although she has always loved reading and experiencing the joy of being swept away to different times and places.

In a previous life she was a Midwife but now works from home as a freelance writer and novelist. While researching her family history, Suzy became fascinated with both World War periods and developed an obsession with military and aviation history. Following the completion of her Open University Degree in English Literature and Creative Writing, she began to write and write until one day she had a novel.

Other interests include music, old movies, and photography – especially if WW2 aircraft are on the radar. Suzy's debut novel, *The Beauty Shop,* has been awarded the B.R.A.G. Medallion. She writes contemporary and historical fiction and is a member of the Alliance of Independent Authors.

Visit her at: suzyhendersonauthor.com

facebook.com/AuthorSuzyHenderson
twitter.com/Suzy_Henderson
instagram.com/authorsuzyhenderson

Also by SUZY HENDERSON

Book 1 The BEAUTY SHOP: A WW2 NOVEL

Book 2 SPITFIRE

Book 3 Christmas in the Highlands

Made in the USA
Middletown, DE
16 December 2023

45893949R00179